HARRY NAVINSKI

The Last Walk

Contents

Prologue

February 2016

Dense grey cloud clung to the Dumfriesshire hills, blanketing the lush green farmland, and releasing continuous drizzle. Jack Reynolds was oblivious to the dreary February weather. It was part of life as a farmer. His old man had always said, "There's no such thing as bad weather, son, just the wrong clothing." As water dripped from Jack's hat, he unconsciously shook his head, raindrops spiralling away from the rim.

Jack's primary concerns were the soil, the grass and his livestock. Although right now it was the lack of a quad bike that was foremost in his mind. His daughter's trail bike was fine for getting around his lands, but he couldn't carry any feed on the bike. He turned as he heard a vehicle lurching along the rough lane to his farm, splashing water from the numerous puddles, its driver struggling to steer the vehicle through the deep ruts.

The police car drew to a halt by the gate and a uniformed constable emerged, grabbing his rain jacket and donning his hat before closing the car's door. Jack wandered over to the gate to meet the policeman, his boots squelching in the mud. The PC looked like he'd only just started shaving. Most of the police seemed to be kids just out of school nowadays, he thought. What did they know about life?

"Mr Reynolds?" The PC enquired, looking quizzical.

"That's me," Jack replied gruffly.

"I'm PC Bailey, from the Dumfries station. Sorry to hear you've had another quad bike stolen. I believe you had one taken only two months back?" The officer sounded genuinely concerned.

"Aye. Last time, they broke into me barn and took the quad. I couldn't get around to check on me sheep and cattle. When I eventually did me rounds, I found two dozen sheep had gone missing. Bastards!" Jack spat.

PC Bailey's head pulled back sharply in response to Reynolds' forceful remark.

"We lost a dozen sheep just five months back, as well! How am I supposed to make a living when these sods keep stealing me stock?" The anger was evident in Jack's growling tone.

PC Bailey looked sympathetically at the farmer, as the breeze brought the smell of the cowshed to his nostrils. "So, you might have lost more sheep, I guess, as you'll have not been able to check on them yet." He tipped his head to the side, showing his curiosity.

"You're probably right, Constable," Jack mumbled in response. He informed the PC about all the thefts that had been happening in the area. Adjacent farms had also suffered. "What I'd like to know - and my neighbours - is what you lot are going to do about it. It's all very well acting sympathetic and issuing crime numbers but we need these thieves caught."

PC Bailey explained there were too few police in the area to prevent the thefts and too many crimes for them all to be thoroughly investigated. He rested a hand on the rough fence post, immediately withdrawing it, suppressing an 'ouch,' as a splinter jabbed into his palm. "It's a resource issue, sir," Bailey said, embarrassed, looking at the sore red spot on his hand. "We wish we could do more."

"Well, if the police didn't spend so much time doing liaison visits to primary schools, chatting with shop owners, and watching football matches or policing bloody tree-hugging environmentalists' demonstrations, there'd be more time to investigate crimes and catch the criminals, wouldn't there!" Jack grumbled.

Bailey tipped his head to the side. "I understand your frustration, sir. I really do. But the shop-owner liaisons and school visits are carried out by police community support officers, not police officers. The PCSOs are not trained to investigate crimes."

After noting the details of the theft, Bailey passed a crime number to Jack and turned to leave, inwardly agreeing with the farmer's assessment of the situation. Too much police time was taken up by such things. If he were the Prime Minister, he'd ban demonstrations and make football clubs pay for their own security.

"Is that it then?" the farmer barked as PC Bailey walked away. "No bloody investigation at all. No taking fingerprints or boot casts! You'll never catch them. They'll continue to break into our sheds at night and steal our stuff. Mark my words, one of these days someone is going to get hurt."

PC Bailey stopped and turned back, apologising again before adding that the crime scene investigation department charged for its time. They couldn't afford to send them out on minor crimes. Resources again! He turned and stepped away towards his car for the second time.

"Bloody waste of space, you lot," Jack called after the departing policeman. "If I catch them here again, they'll face two barrels of me shotgun, so they will."

PC Bailey spun on his heels and returned to the gate, his face stern. Although he suspected the farmer was just blowing off steam, he couldn't walk away without warning him about taking the law into his own hands. Turning a deaf ear to the statement could be seen as endorsing the action.

"Look Mr Reynolds. If you go around firing off your shotgun

near anyone, even if they are criminals, you could end up in jail on attempted murder charges - or worse!" He stared into the farmer's eyes, a serious expression on his face.

Bailey continued, "I've got the chassis number of the bike and a full description. We'll keep an eye out for it. We might not have the time to do detailed investigative work when these crimes are committed but we have plain-clothed officers at the auctions, looking out for stolen property. They browse eBay, Gumtree, and the likes, as well. We *do* follow up. And occasionally we convict someone for stealing farm machinery." He paused to see if Reynolds had taken in what he'd said, before adding, "I'll let you know if we get anywhere with this one."

Jack Reynolds acknowledged the officer with a nod of the head and a grunt before turning away. Jack understood the resource issue. No one had unlimited resources, and all had to make choices. He had to choose his priorities daily. But he bet if one of the coppers had been burgled, they'd find the resources to investigate properly.

As the police car manoeuvred in the track, Jack's wife, Margaret, called to him from the open farmhouse door. "Jack, love! I've a pot of tea brewing if you'd like one?"

He turned and wandered towards her, sensing from her tone she had something important to say. But he didn't ask her what was wrong. It was probably best said over a cuppa in their cosy kitchen, in front of the warm, glowing log-burning range, rather than outside in the drizzle. He followed her into the house, feeling gloomy.

Margaret poured Jack a mug of tea and handed it to him before speaking, her face neutral. "The insurance company won't be able to get their assessor here until next Tuesday."

"For Christ's sake! Why do they need to send an assessor?" Jack roared, spilling some of his tea. "It's a quad bike that's been stolen. There's nowt to assess. Bloody ridiculous! How the hell am I supposed to do my job without the quad?" His eyebrows formed a single hairy line across his face, the gap between them having disappeared as he scowled.

Margaret rose, collected a cloth from the sink and mopped up her husband's spillage. "Well, love. You might prefer the quad, but you can use the tractor instead," she said, using a mother-son tone. "That will do the job."

Jack bit back, "Might have known you'd take their side-"

"How dare you accuse me of taking their side!" Margaret's face reddened as she blurted the words. She glared into her husband's eyes, her jaw clenched, daring him to answer back. "Of course I'm not on the insurer's side but I can see it from their point of view. It's the second quad bike we've had stolen in as many months. They'll no doubt want to review security. Unless we do something to reduce the risk of further thefts, they'll probably refuse to insure us."

Jack sulked for a minute, mulling over his wife's statement. Margaret was a wise woman. Kept him on the straight and narrow. "S'pose you're right. The tractor will have to do."

He supped his tea, then took a piece of home-baked gingerbread from the plate in the table's centre. As he chewed the gingery cake, the tension left his face. He thought how lucky he was to have such a wonderful wife. Married now for thirty-plus years. They'd been through a lot together. Three wonderful kids, although only Ainslie still living locally. The other two had headed off to Edinburgh and Newcastle for work, wanting no part of farming. They'd seen how difficult it was to earn a living, how many hours had to be worked, the hard graft, and the worries. Jack licked his fingers where the cake had left sticky marks, not wanting to waste any.

Tea drunk and cake eaten, Jack acknowledged to himself he'd have to apologise later for accusing Margaret of not taking his side. He returned to his duties around the farm but felt downcast, tired of the drudgery and lacking hope that things would improve. Life was a daily challenge. Nature was always throwing fresh problems his way. The government kept introducing new, costly requirements, and lazy, benefit-claiming scumbags, who couldn't be bothered to do a proper day's work, stole from him while he slept off his weariness at night.

He would attend the next auction and see if he could pick up another quad, but for the moment, he'd just have to churn up the field with the tractor.

Jack thought about what his wife had said. He guessed the insurers would insist they get CCTV cameras and alarms installed. Extra expenses they couldn't really afford. Damn the parasites who came at night to take what was not theirs. No matter what the officer said, he would have his shotgun ready if they returned.

Chapter One

Monday 25th April

The twisted tree stood atop a grassy Scottish hill. Having lost its fight to reach straight up to the sun, it leaned away from the prevailing wind, tired of the effort. Sheep were sprinkled across the green slope and lambs ran in playful groups, leaping four-footed into the air.

Jack Reynolds opened the field's gate, then rode his recently acquired quad bike through the opening. Having closed the gate, Jack opened the throttle. The quad bike bucked over the ruts as he tore along the track, standing on the footplates, his knees bent, riding the bumps. This was his territory. Knew it like the lines in his wife's face.

He summited the brow and dropped into the next valley. The sheep were huddled into a corner of the field. Something had frightened them, but he could hear nothing and there was no other activity. An unusual mound caught his eye, then a second lump. He stopped the bike on the track and walked towards the unnatural objects. Green rubber protruded from the denim jeans on a motionless body. An olive waxed jacket covered the torso, the clothes soaked in blood. Long, wavy, grey-blonde hair lay strewn around its head, dirty with blood and mud.

Jack's ruddy face turned pale, his heart rate raised by the adrenaline that now flowed. He stepped closer to the body, turned it over and felt for a pulse at the woman's neck, his sleeve and hand now red with her sticky blood. He detected no life. Her skin was cool but not yet cold. The woman couldn't have been dead long.

Jack turned away, but the image was fixed in his mind. Her face, dirty from its contact with the soil, was still made up. Green eyeliner, mascara, and red lipstick. She had the wrinkles of a fifty-year-old, but she had been a good-looking woman. Her abdomen was a bloodied mess. He tightly sealed his lips as bile rose into his throat. Jack had seen enough dead animals to know the damage would have been caused by a shotgun blast.

He soon recovered from the involuntary retching and checked out the second mound. It was a dog. Its long golden fur matted with blood, its jaw open and its tongue lolling through its yellow-tinged teeth. Another shotgun injury. The blast had caught its face and upper abdomen. "Poor lass," he said to himself. "What a beauty you were. Who would have done this? Why would anyone shoot the woman and her dog? And why on this farm?"

His mind sprang back to his conversation with the police constable after his last quad bike had been stolen, and he remembered he'd used his shotgun this morning to shoot rabbits. He'd seen enough TV crime series to know what the police would think. Two add two makes five...

He left his phone in his pocket, returned to his bike and rode up to his sheep. She'd not be going anywhere. Let someone else find her.

* * *

The Brownlows had planned their short holiday two months back and Catherine was glad to have finally come to explore this part of Scotland. She'd seen Dumfriesshire's Criffel mountain so many times from across the Solway Firth at Mawbray and Silloth, when walking along their rather different seafronts. She'd become impatient to see this land and Gavin had seemed enthusiastic, too. They walked a lot.

It was part of their weekly exercise regime.

The weather had not been kind to them, but they were equipped for wet weather and dry, so that wasn't a problem. They both enjoyed the fresh air, exercise, and nature. They could never be city-dwellers. Living in a man-made concrete and tarmac jungle was not for them.

The Brownlows had been walking for two hours and their legs were tiring. Gavin referred to his ordnance survey map, before climbing the stile, happy they were still on the chosen route. Catherine joined him and they trudged up the field towards the next stile, roughly south of where they were.

"What's that, Gavin?" she said, pointing ahead and to her left, curiosity in her voice. Two grass-less alien mounds stood out from the lush green slope.

Gavin studied the two mounds and guessed what they would be. "Stay here, Cat. I'll take a look." He gingerly approached the largest lump, worried by what he would find. He'd lived a sheltered life. Never witnessed violence or even death - apart from his father's cold body in the chapel of rest before he was cremated. The lifeless mound appeared to be a woman with long greying blond hair! She was face up, her open eyes looking to the sky. There wasn't much left of her stomach or chest - just a bloody mess.

Catherine saw her husband retch, his hand rapidly covering his mouth. She shivered as a sense of evil ran through her, having now recognised the mounds for what they were. Fear ran through her veins.

Gavin glanced across to the shaggy heap two paces away, recognising a golden retriever. He pulled his phone from his pocket but found he had no signal. "Damn these hills... Cat, do you have a signal? We need to call the police."

Catherine was frozen to the spot. Unresponsive. Her face had paled; her eyes staring at the two lumps.

He raised his voice. "Catherine!"

Shaking herself from her immobility, she responded. "Sorry, Gavin." She pulled her phone from her pocket and looked at the screen. There were no bars on the signal strength icon, but as she went to give him the bad news one small bar appeared. She passed the phone to Gavin. He dialled 999.

* * *

Detective Sergeant Tosh McIntosh enjoyed his job. Based in the Dumfries Criminal Investigation Department, it was an easy number. They rarely had murders in Dumfriesshire, unlike the cities. Most of the crimes were minor. Robberies and assaults, although the uniform guys mostly dealt with those. Fiona, his wife of ten years, liked him at home every night and most weekends, and he could normally comply with those wishes. But today that routine had been blown out of the water. He'd taken the call just as he was biting into his Scotch Pie, the smell of cooked lamb emanating from its broken pastry. He'd sprayed half the contents of his mouth across his desk when he'd been told a body had been found near a public footpath, and it looked like murder.

As a sergeant, he was the senior detective in Dumfries. There was a Detective Chief Inspector at the Divisional HQ, Scott Aitkin, but he was away on holiday. The Dominican Republic, if he recalled correctly. He grabbed his blue waterproof jacket and rubber boots before heading out into the rainy morning, stopping as he passed Inspector Ferguson's office to let him know where he was headed and why.

"Aye. I know," Ferguson responded, "two of our guys are on the ground. I've just come off the phone to the Crime Scene team and the pathologist. They're also on their way. I'll get more officers out there to help with the cordoning and searches. This'll keep us busy for a while, no doubt."

"Aye, you're right there, Ed. Could you call Carl for me? I'll keep you informed of progress. See ya later." Tosh and Ed had joined the police at the same time. Both ex-soldiers who had served together they got on like a house on fire. Ed had outdone him in the promotion race but that was because he'd stayed in uniform. Easier to shine in front of your bosses. But Tosh was hopeful he'd catch him before long. This murder could be just the case he needed to get recommended.

On the journey to the crime scene, Tosh surreptitiously took bites from his Scotch pie. He'd probably not get to eat anything for a while now. Strictly, it was against the rules of the road to eat while driving a car. But he reckoned no one would notice and the rule was made for idiots, after all. It was entirely possible to eat and drive safely, provided you had your wits about you, especially in rural areas. And Tosh was confident in his abilities.

Chapter Two

Tosh stopped his car on the track nearest to the field where the bodies lay. Other police cars were scattered around in gateways, as well as a vehicle he didn't recognise - a Range Rover. He couldn't see the Crime Scene Investigator's van or the pathologist's car. He donned his wellies, coat, and hat before setting off up the track and through the gate. The grey clouds masked any attempt by the sun to break through and heat the land, adding to the gloom. It was drizzling and a cool breeze blew the moisture into his face. Even on the short walk to the fence, water had formed into droplets that trickled off his chin and down his neck.

He could see uniformed colleagues up the hill ahead, placing cordon tape around the crime scene. A middle-aged couple were huddled together, looking anxious, cold, and damp. He went to his colleagues first.

PC Stevens greeted him as he approached. "Great weather for frogs, eh! What kept you?"

"Watch your cheek, Logan. Don't you go forgetting I'm a sergeant." He paused, as Stevens grinned back at him, showing that he knew full well that, as drinking buddies, his pal wouldn't really pull rank when there was no one else in earshot.

"That the couple who found the bodies?" Tosh said, indicating the man and woman holding each other close.

"Aye. I told them they'd need to hang on until you arrived, so you could have a chat with them."

"Good. I'll do that in a minute. We'll need to get boot prints from them both, to compare with those taken by the CSI guys when they get here. Speak of the devil..." He turned his head to where his eyes had just glimpsed their van arriving. He waved and noticed a hand respond from behind the windscreen. "Right. I'll go talk to the couple, so they can be on their way before they get hypothermia. I take it you already have their details?"

"Of course. What do you take me for? Even verified their identity by taking pictures of their driving licences." He referred to his notebook. "They're Mr Gavin Brownlow and Mrs Catherine Brownlow. Up from Cumbria."

"Very good, Logan. We'll make a good copper out of you yet," Tosh said with a grin.

The woman and her dog were several metres away and Tosh didn't want to contaminate the scene any further than it had been. He looked across at the two bodies. "You'll have been right up to the bodies, I assume?"

"Aye, I have, that. Needed to confirm what they'd told me and check for a pulse, even though it seemed pointless, given the bloody mess of the woman's stomach and her eyes staring into space. Before you ask, I walked back from the scene in reverse, standing in my own prints, so as not to make any more, or cover up anyone else's."

"Good stuff, Logan. Did you avoid all other prints on your approach to the bodies?"

"That I did," he said with a tilt of his head.

Tosh acknowledged PC Steven's professionalism with a nod. "By the way, do you know whose Range Rover that is?" he said, pointing back down the track.

Logan looked at the vehicle as if it was the first time he'd seen it, then shrugged his shoulders.

Tosh noted the registration number before turning away from his friend, speaking as he moved. "I'll let you get on then, Logan. The CSIs will no doubt have work for you. See you later."

He wandered over to the Brownlows. The husband, Gavin, was a wiry fellow. In his forties, Tosh guessed. From what he could see of his head, he looked to be completely bald, but there could have been hair hiding under his olive-green Tilley hat. He hadn't seen one of those for a few years. Australian, he believed. Waterproof and guaranteed for life. His jacket was also green, as were his trousers. They looked good quality. As did his boots. Not short of money then, he surmised. The man's features were squashed into the lower half of his face. His eyes were slits, his lips matchstick thin and his nose a mere pimple.

Catherine Brownlow was slightly shorter than her husband, with mid-brown hair in a pixie cut. Her features were also small but not as minuscule as her husband's and more spread out. Normal! She wasn't what Tosh would call pretty. Plain, perhaps. She had matching green clothing but wore a woolly bobble hat. Tosh could see no blood on their coats or gloved hands.

"Mr and Mrs Brownlow. Thanks for waiting. I'm Detective Sergeant McIntosh, from Dumfries CID. I just need to ask you a few questions, then you can be on your way."

The Brownlows looked relieved as they separated from their hug, then started shuffling from one foot to the other. "Ask away, sergeant. We'd like to get back to our guesthouse and warm up as soon as we can."

"Where is it you're staying?"

"The Farmstead at Rockcliffe," Catherine replied.

"I tell you what. There's nothing I can do here until the Pathologist has done his bit, and the Crime Scene Investigators have recorded all the evidence. Let me give you a lift to Rockcliffe. We can get a cup of tea and have a chat there."

"Oh! I don't think they serve tea during the day. Only at breakfast," Catherine said.

"I'm sure Mrs Beatie will accommodate us, given the circumstances," Tosh countered.

The Brownlows looked surprised that the detective knew their landlady. "Come on; let's get out of this damp weather." He led them to his car, briefly stopping to chat with the CSI team leader, Pete Southergill, a likeable and pragmatic man.

* * *

Detective Carl Penrose listened to Mrs Archer explain about her shed, which had been burgled the night before. They had levered off the shed door's hasp and taken her lawnmower, strimmer, and several of her late husband's toolboxes. She didn't mind too much about the lawnmower, as it was getting old anyway, and she'd be able to claim new for old on the insurance. But the burglary had been distressing, because the thief or thieves had intruded into her property, breaking the impression of safety she'd always had about her own house and garden. And they'd stolen her Fred's tools.

Mrs Archer had been planning to donate them to a charity in Carlisle, *Tools for Self Reliance,* that refurbishes tools. She'd heard they ship them in kits to Africa, where the charity would equip poor people with the skills and tools to set up their own micro-business. Her voice had cracked, and she'd broken down in tears as she concluded the theft would deny some poor African from earning a livelihood.

Carl felt sympathy for the old lady but wished he could just get the details recorded and be on his way. He wasn't a social worker! He hoped she would have relatives with whom she could share her emotions with. When his phone pinged, it came as a relief. He skimmed the message from Inspector Ferguson about a dead body, noticing he also had two missed calls from the inspector. His phone signal icon showed just one bar. Then none.

Carl excused himself, having noted all the details, advised Mrs Archer about how she could make her house and garden safer, then left. He doubted they would ever recover the tools or catch the criminals. It's not that they hadn't tried in the past, but there was rarely enough evidence to convict the criminals, even if they identified them. And that was a big IF! If only she'd had CCTV installed at the rear of her house, they might have captured the thieves on camera. Oh well!

* * *

Once at Rockcliffe, Tosh chatted with the Brownlows before asking the real questions he needed answering. "I understand you're from Wigton. Does the town still smell of rotten eggs?" He had been right; Mrs Beatie *was* happy to provide tea. She also gave them a plate of Rich Tea biscuits before leaving them to talk in the guest lounge.

"Actually, Wigton is our post town. We live in Abbeytown, about eight miles away," Gavin Brownlow responded. "You're right, though, it can be a smelly place, but I wouldn't say the smell is that bad. It's the food-packaging film factory that causes the stench."

"Oh! Is that right? I always wondered. So, what brought you to Rockcliffe?"

"Just a little break, Sergeant," Catherine Brownlow replied. "We see the Scottish mountains from across the Solway Firth. It's a beautiful scene. We've walked extensively in the Lake District National Park, so decided we should explore the other side of the water for a change."

"Very good. How many days have you been in Dumfriesshire?"

"We just arrived yesterday. This was our first walk," Catherine said. "I'm not sure I want to stay any longer. Finding that poor woman and her dog has shaken me." She shivered as she turned to her husband, her face pleading. "Can we go home tomorrow, darling?"

Gavin looked like he understood her feelings and desire to get back to somewhere she'd feel safe but didn't agree with the proposal. "Let's talk about it later, sweetheart. I'm sure the sergeant would prefer to focus on the death and what we can tell him."

"Well, we can't tell him much, can we?" She turned to DS McIntosh. "We were on our walk and as we strode up the field, I saw two lumps. They looked unnatural, so we went closer to find out what they were." She recalled how Gavin had got her to stay back while he investigated. Then they'd dialled 999, and had done nothing else until the police arrived, just hung around getting cold. "It was awful," Catherine concluded, then broke into tears. Gavin cocooned his wife in a reassuring hug as she sobbed into his shoulder.

Tosh waited for her to settle down before speaking again. "How far away from the bodies did you stop, Mrs Brownlow?"

She shook herself. "Sorry. It was a huge shock finding them." She paused, holding back further tears. She wiped her eyes with an embroidered handkerchief that appeared in her hand, then blew her nose before tucking it back up her sleeve. "I must have been... ten paces away from them."

"And you, Mr Brownlow. How close did you get?"

"Not close enough to touch the woman, perhaps five feet. I had thought to check whether she was alive, but it was evident when I got close that she couldn't be, so I backed off, and we called the police." Gavin returned his attention to his wife, who yet again buried her face in his jumper and started sobbing.

"Did you come over the stile at the bottom of the field?"

Gavin responded, "Yes. But we had gloves on, in case you're thinking about fingerprints."

Tosh was surprised at Brownlow's sharp thinking. "We'll need to take your gloves for evidence, then. The CSIs will extract fibres to match with the fence posts by the stile."

Catherine withdrew from her husband's embrace and stood. "I'll get the gloves for you." She dawdled out into the hall, returning a minute later with both pairs of gloves, her eyes still red rimmed. "We will get them back, won't we? Only, they're not cheap gloves." Before waiting for an answer, she turned to her husband. "We'll definitely have to go home, Gavin. I can't go walking without my gloves."

He smiled indulgently at her.

"The gloves will have to be retained until the CSIs have completed their work and forensics services have done their thing," Tosh said. "But we'll get them back to you as soon as we can. No guarantees when, though. I'll leave you to sort yourselves out now. Thanks for your time. We'll be in touch if we need to ask any further questions and to let you know when you can have your gloves back." He rose and left them to their now tepid tea.

Chapter Three

Detective Penrose arrived at the crime scene to find several marked police cars obstructing the lane. He didn't want to get blocked in, so reversed back along the single-track lane until he found a gateway. He parked up, slipped on his wellie boots, then trudged back to the site.

A uniformed policeman stood guard in front of the gate, beyond which white-suited bodies went about their business. Blue and white tape marked off the area where they worked. Carl could see plates had been laid across the field and around the bodies. One of the white-clad people carried a camera and was busy taking pictures from all angles. Carl spoke to the officer on guard. "How're you doing, Logan? Been here long?"

"Long enough to get chilled, now that I'm stood around doing nothin'. Tosh was here earlier. He took the couple who found the bodies back to their guesthouse, to take their statements."

"Aye, I know. Just spoke to him. He wants me to liaise with the CSIs, then visit the local farms to ask questions."

"You'll need to don one of those there boiler suits before I can let you pass," Logan said with a grin.

Carl smirked, his eyebrows reaching for his hairline. "Give us one, then."

Covered head to toe, Carl ambled across the artificial stepping-stones to the stile and gate that controlled the field's entrance. One

CSI was gathering evidence from where people may have touched the posts or clothing might have snagged. The CSI noticed his approach and looked up. "Hi Carl," Pete Southergill said, looking him in the eye.

"Oh! Hi Pete. I didn't recognise you. We all look the same with these snow suits on."

"I know what you mean. When I look around at my team, it sometimes reminds me of a James Bond movie, except they're not chasing anyone down hill on skis, carrying machine guns."

Carl smiled, then asked, "How much longer do you expect to be on site?"

"It's an enormous field, so we'll be here for days. But we should have covered the main areas - the trail and the farm tracks, and the immediate area around the body by the end of the day."

"Can I take a look at the bodies?"

"Aye. You'll need to stick to the stepping plates, of course. And don't go anywhere near them without checking with Doctor Michaels," Pete said, indicating the pathologist who was crouching near to the two mounds.

Carl cautiously tiptoed across the plates, stopping a few times to scan the field's borders for signs of potential entrances and exits. There appeared to be just the two. The one he'd just come through and one at the top right-hand corner of the field. These had already been identified and marked out by the CSI team.

Carl waited for the pathologist to rise from whatever it was he'd been focusing on before speaking. "Hello, Doctor Michaels." He paused, waiting for the doctor's eyes to meet his own, and to look for any sign that the pathologist might recognise him. He saw none. "Detective Constable Carl Penrose. Anything you can tell me yet, doc?"

Michaels' face softened a little, as if a pleasant memory had surfaced when he'd heard Carl's name. "Ah! DC Penrose. It's been a while since we last met, hasn't it?"

The pathologist was right. The last unexplained death that had brought them together must have been two years previously.

"As you'll appreciate, Constable, until I can complete a thorough and detailed examination of the body, I can't be more specific than to say that death appears to be from extreme trauma to the abdomen. Most likely caused by a shotgun. Death would have been quick given the severity of the damage to her organs and the subsequent loss of blood. Time of death probably between 6 a.m. and 10 a.m., today, going by the woman's internal temperature."

"Thought as much, doc. When can we expect your postmortem report?"

"Well, young man, you'll understand that it will take some time to get the body back to the mortuary. I'll get the postmortem done first thing in the morning. I should be able to give your boss a verbal report by mid-day, but my formal report will not be until later, of course."

"Happy days! I'll let DS McIntosh know. If you've nothing else for me, I'll leave you to it?"

The pathologist shook his head, turned, and went back to his work. Carl retraced his steps, checking with nearby CSI officers if they had anything for him, before returning to the lane leading back to his car. He stripped off the boiler suit and overshoes, then said cheerio to Logan before striding away.

On returning to where he'd left his vehicle, Carl found the gate open and his car missing! He looked around, wondering if this was the correct gateway. He was certain it was.

The sound of a tractor caught his attention. It appeared to be coming from up the hill in the field beyond the open gate, but he couldn't see it because of the tree line. He squelched through the muddy patch just inside the field and saw the tractor. It had forks attached to the front and was moving hay bales. Then his car grabbed his attention. It was inside the field near the line of trees. He immediately understood how it had gotten there.

Carl checked the bodywork for damage, finding vertical scuffs on the passenger side, probably about the width of the tractor's forks. "Shit!" This would cause him a load of paperwork. He stomped up the field, waving at the tractor driver, his face red from anger and exertion. When the tractor was about ten metres away, the driver noticed him. Instead of stopping, he spun his vehicle around, circling Carl, and headed back to the gate.

Carl took off down the slope, the descent assisting his speed. One foot skidded out from under him, sliding forward as his other leg went backwards. A comedic looking but painful involuntary splits brought a cry to Carl's lips. He fell sideways to avoid the pain in his groin, landing with his face in a cowpat. Now he *was* angry.

The tractor disappeared through the gate and turned left, speeding away from the crime scene. He hobbled down the field as fast as he could, taking more care this time of where he planted his feet, then splashed through the mud by the gate. Carl saw the tractor just fifty metres along the lane, and beyond the tractor was the familiar gun-metal grey of Sergeant McIntosh's Ford Focus.

The tractor driver was leaning out of his window, gesticulating, and shouting for the driver to reverse back up the lane. Carl saw the Focus reversing, so ran to catch up with the tractor before it escaped, his groin crying out with every step. He pulled his truncheon from his pocket, extended it and hammered on the rear of the tractor. Then he pulled his police warrant card from his pocket and held it up for the driver to see. "Out of the vehicle now!" he shouted. Sergeant McIntosh had stopped reversing and exited his car to find out what was going on.

Hemmed in on both sides and knowing at least one of them was a policeman, Jack Reynolds dismounted.

Carl strode forward, fuming. "What the hell do you think you were doing? How dare you move a police car with your tractor forks, then drive off like it's not your problem! Well, it fucking well is your problem, pal. I'll arrest you for criminal damage and wasting police time."

Tosh stepped up and commanded his constable. "DC Penrose. Calm down." He turned to the tractor driver. "Sir, stay with your vehicle. Don't even think about moving."

Carl's anger was still boiling but he thought better of arguing with his sergeant. He shut his mouth and waited. Tosh took his DC aside.

"Right Carl, what was all that about? You know you can't go swearing at members of the public like that. What's happened to your clothes?" He said, scanning Carl's body.

Carl explained what had occurred, his anger simmering as he recalled the events.

Tosh had to hold back a chuckle when he heard about Carl doing the splits. But soon realised that it would have been extremely painful. He returned to the driver and demanded identification. The name on the driving licence rang a bell. "Jack Reynolds," Tosh said, looking into the eyes of the driver. "Are you the farmer who's had two quad bikes stolen recently?"

"Aye, that'll be me. Lucky bastard, aren't I."

"Look Mr Reynolds, I understand you've had a run of bad luck lately and are frustrated with the perceived lack of police action to catch the thieves. But that doesn't justify you moving a police vehicle with your tractor."

"There's no way of knowing it was a police car. There are no markings on it. The dammed car was blocking my gateway. I have work to do. I can't keep coming back in the hope the idiot might have moved it when I return. Too many of you townies park cars in farm gateways. A bloody menace to us farmers, trying to earn a living." Jack was now redder than Carl had been.

"I take your point, Mr Reynolds. I apologise on behalf of my colleague for blocking your gate."

Carl stared at his sergeant, annoyed that he now seemed to be taking the farmer's side.

"However, you have caused damage to a police vehicle. Here's the deal. We'll not prosecute you for criminal damage, but we'll send you the bill for repairing the car."

Carl cut in. "We'll need my car moved out onto the lane as well. There's no way it will drive across that sodden, muddy field."

Tosh went on, his eyes fixed on Jacks Reynolds, "And you will carefully move the car back onto the track now. Any further damage to the vehicle will be extra on your bill."

Jack's face softened and the redness faded. "Aye. Deal accepted." He climbed back into his tractor and reversed to the gateway, Carl stepping aside to let him pass.

Ten minutes later, Carl's car was back on asphalt and ready to drive. Tosh stepped up onto the tractor's side and indicated the farmer should open his window. "Did you not know there were police down here? There are enough of us! There's a body been found."

Jack looked shocked. "A body? Where?"

Tosh explained where the crime scene was and asked Reynolds whether that was on his land.

"Aye. That's my field. I was planning to head up that way later to check on me sheep. Don't suppose you'll let me in there, now?"

"Afraid not, Mr Reynolds. Not until our crime scene investigators have finished their work. Can't see that happening today, but you'll be able to see them from the gateway as they're all huddled in the bottom corner." Tosh paused, then turned to his DC. "Carl. Have you started visiting houses in the area yet?"

"That was my next job, Sarge. I was planning to go to the Mitchell's farm next. But how could I without my car?"

"Good point. Right, Mr Reynolds, I need to have a chat but before that we need to let DC Penrose get away in his car, to get on with his work. Let's head to your farm."

Jack agreed, although Tosh could see it was reluctant acceptance. They all headed off, leaving the lane clear.

Chapter Four

The Reynolds' sandstone-walled farmhouse and attached barn were ramshackle buildings. Centuries of dirt, dampness and lichen clung to their surfaces like old gravestones.

The farmyard stank of cow muck, and was a mess of mud, concrete, and discarded farm implements. Tosh followed Jack Reynolds into the house. It smelled of eggs and bacon. Tosh knew many farmers got up and out early to do their chores, then returned for a cooked meal. He would never choose this way of life. Too hard graft for his liking. Out in all weathers; long hours; at the mercy of the climate and changing government subsidies. And sheep rustlers, of course!

Jack shouted out to his wife to let her know he was home, then checked the kettle sitting on the range was full and hot enough to make a pot of tea. "Sit yourself down, Sergeant. We may as well take the weight off our feet while we talk." He placed an open glass bottle on the table, half full of milk, a bowl of sugar and a couple of teaspoons. The randomly patterned mugs he dumped beside the spoons were chipped but functional.

"So, Mr Reynolds, did you hear or see anything this morning that might help us with our inquiries?"

At that point Margaret Reynolds entered the kitchen, looking perplexed that her husband was home already, and even more so when she saw a stranger sat at their table. Tosh stood. "Afternoon, Mrs

Reynolds. I'm DS McIntosh."

Jack's wife was as tall as her husband, but not as wide. She mirrored her husband's features. She had a broad nose, large ears, a high forehead, a prominent chin, and a ruddy complexion.

"DS?" she queried.

"Sorry, Detective Sergeant."

"And what brings you here, Sergeant?"

"As I was saying to your husband, a body has been found on your land."

Jack interjected, mentioning the name of the field the sergeant was talking about.

"From what we understand, the person will have died fairly early today. We can't say when yet, as the pathologist has yet to do the postmortem."

"But you suspect foul play, though?" Margaret said, her bushy, dark brown eyebrows raising in question.

"Yes. I can't tell you any more, though. We have to keep these details close to our chests at this stage of an investigation. But what I need to know from both of you - since you live close by, and it was on your land - is your whereabouts this morning. And to learn of anything you might have seen or heard that might be of significance. If you'd be so kind, Mr Reynolds," Tosh said, pulling out his pad and pen.

Jack poured his wife's tea, then a mug for Tosh and himself before putting the teapot onto the edge of the range hot plate to keep warm. Tosh wondered whether the milk he'd just added to his tea was fresh from the cow and unpasteurised. He considered letting it go cold but decided to take the risk.

"Well, I was up at quarter to five and out the door on the hour. Pulled the cows in for milking, then herded them back to their field. That took me 'til about eight, when I came in for me breakfast."

"That would be right. I had his breakfast sizzling in the pan at eight.

He's rarely late in for his scran."

"And after that?"

"I did a round on me quad bike. The third I've owned in the last four months," he said, emphasising the point for Tosh's sake. He was still miffed that he continued to be targeted by thieves, and the police had failed him. "All was quiet and fine. Saw nothing in the field where you found that woman. After that, I attended to the broken fence post up at Marybank, then back here for a cuppa, before taking the hay bales down yonder, where I had the run in with your constable."

"What's this about a run in with a police officer?" Margaret asked, her brow furrowed.

"Och! I'll give ya the details later, hen, but Constable tosser had parked his car in the gateway to Upper Field. I had to move it to get on with me work."

Tosh ignored the jibe at his colleague. He could see from her expression that Mrs Reynolds was puzzled. Tosh guessed she was wondering whether the DC's surname might be Tosser. He continued making notes in his pad as he asked his next question. "Mrs Reynolds. If you could let me know what you were up to this morning, as well..."

"I usually get up as Jack slams the kitchen door on his way out. I do me housework first, then get breakfast ready for eight."

"Is that what you did today?" Tosh asked.

"Aye. Same today as yesterday, and tomorrow, no doubt. After that, I went for me messages."

"Where did you go shopping this morning, Mrs Reynolds?"

"Same as ever. Into Dalbeattie. It's about a quarter of an hour from here. Visited the butchers, the bakers-"

Tosh was expecting her to say candlestick makers next.

"... the newsagents and the Coop. I'd got back here around eleven." She paused. " I had a cuppa, then put the washing out and fed the chickens, before cooking dinner."

"Okay. I'm guessing there will be plenty of people in Dalbeattie who can confirm seeing you?"

"Aye. For sure. I had a wee blether with Iris in the bakers. And Charlie in the butchers."

"Do either of you recall hearing anything early this morning?"

"There were a few bangs, as usual. Shotguns. Rabbit hunting, probably. One of our cows broke its ankle when its foot went down a rabbit hole last year. Had to send it to the abattoir. They're blooming pests, so they are," Margaret stated.

"What time do you think that would have been?"

"About seven, I reckon. Thereabouts, anyway."

"Could you tell where the shots came from?"

"No. The sound bounces around the hills and is muffled by the woods."

"And you Mr Reynolds?"

"Margaret's right. I shot some rabbits meself. Early on, that was. But I also heard shots around seven. Two shots."

"Did either of you see anyone around that time?"

"I was in the house," Margaret stated bluntly.

"Nothing out of the ordinary," Jack reported.

"But did you see anything *ordinary*?"

"Can't say I did. Never saw anyone around at all."

Tosh paused for a minute, thinking about his next questions. "So, Mr Reynolds, you'll no doubt have one or more guns on the farm?"

"Aye. Of course."

"And you fired one of them this morning."

"Aye. As I said, I took me shotgun out with me on the quad. Bagged a couple of rabbits. They're hanging in the boot room."

"I'll need to see your guns and the rabbits, please."

Jack slurped down the last of his tea and stood. "Right. Come this way, Sergeant." He set off across the kitchen and opened a rustic door

29

leading into the rear of the farmhouse, its paint dirty and scratched from wear.

Tosh chucked back the last of his tea and followed the farmer into the dark stone-flagged corridor. Jack took a key from his pocket and unlocked a sturdy wooden cupboard mounted on the wall above a rack of boots and shoes, coats hanging on hooks to its left. With the doors swung wide, Tosh could see three guns attached to the cupboard's back by clips, and a space for a fourth. "I take it you have licences for all these guns?"

"Of course." Jack responded, his tone calm and flat.

Tosh stepped forward and looked closely at the weapons, donning a pair of silicone gloves. He unclipped each of the guns and examined them, ensuring they weren't loaded. He felt for the temperature of each barrel before taking a sniff from the open end. Two were chilly and smelled faintly of sulphur. The third was warmer and the odour of rotten eggs was obvious. "I'll need to take this one in for forensics to check out." He took a large polythene bag from his jacket pocket and placed the gun inside, noting that in the room's corner, two rabbits hung from their rear legs. Jack just tilted his head nonchalantly, indicating acceptance.

"Where's the gun that used to be mounted here?" Tosh asked, indicating the vacant gun holder.

"Haven't had a fourth shotgun in years," Jack responded. "The misses never shoots nowadays, so we got rid of it."

They returned to the kitchen, where Margaret was drying the teacups and saucers.

"You don't shoot anymore, Mrs Reynolds?" Tosh enquired.

"Nae, lad. My shooting days are over. I've arthritis in me shoulder. Hurts too much to go shooting."

"Right, I'll be off now," Tosh said, "but I'll have to send one of the CSI team up here to take impressions of your boots and the quad bike tracks, for elimination." Tosh noticed a flicker of Jack Reynolds' eyelids. "I'll get the shotgun back to you as soon as possible. And we'll be in touch about my DC's car."

Mr Reynolds nodded. His wife looked perplexed again. "Nae bother," Jack said. "Just wish you lot would put as much effort into taking evidence when my sheep are rustled and the quad bikes are stolen!"

Tosh chose not to respond to the dig. "If you think of anything else. Please call me." He dropped his card onto the kitchen table, then left.

Chapter Five

Carl pulled his Vauxhall Astra onto the side of the lane making sure he didn't block any farm gates. He didn't want any repeat of the previous conflict with Jack Reynolds. His nose twitched from the smell of cow muck, and his shoes squelched as they slid on the muddy surface.

He couldn't find a bell-push on the Mitchell's door, so thumped on it. A barking collie dog, stood behind a wooden half-door across the yard, also announced his arrival.

A chubby-faced, short woman responded to his banging a minute later.

"Afternoon. I'm DC Penrose, Dumfries CID. I'd like to ask you a few questions.

"Okay, Constable, fire away."

Carl flipped open his notepad. "First things first. Could I have your name, please?"

"Aileen Mitchell." She responded. "What brings you to my door, young man?"

Aileen's mousy hair had been drawn back harshly into a ponytail, exposing her rather large ears.

"Not sure if you'll have heard yet, but there was a shooting incident this morning just down the valley from here."

"Aye, well, there's plenty of shooting goes on around here. Rabbits mostly. What do you mean, incident?"

"A person has been shot."

Aileen recoiled, her eyes widening. Then she frowned. "You're joking... right?"

"Afraid not Mrs Mitchell. In fact, the shooting led to the death of this person, so it's a murder inquiry. Her dog was also killed. Could you tell me where you were between 6 a.m. and 10 a.m. today, please?"

"So, it was a woman that was killed then. I was home this morning. I've not been out of the house yet."

Carl chastised himself for letting slip that the victim was a woman but quickly continued his questioning. "And did you hear any shots fired this morning?"

"Probably. It's common to hear shotguns going off. I don't really register them anymore."

Carl noted her comments. "Does anyone else live or work here?"

"Aye. My husband, Jim, and my two sons, Archie and Morgan."

"Are they here now for me to have a chat with?"

"Nae, lad. They're all out and about. The boys will be up on Top Field, fixing the gate post. Jim had to go into Dumfries this morning for some equipment."

"Okay. I'll need to speak with all three men, but if you could let me have some details of how their morning will have been filled, that would be helpful."

"The boys were up early to milk the cows. After breakfast, Archie checked out the sheep and Morgan dealt with the slurry." She paused in thought. "Jim was in the office first thing, then went off to the farm suppliers."

Carl got Mrs Mitchell to put some approximate times to these happenings, then bid her goodbye. He left his card and asked her to get the men to contact him so he could speak with them.

* * *

When Tosh parked up near the crime scene, he saw an ambulance loading what he assumed to be the woman's bagged body into the vehicle. A second smaller bag, presumably the dog's body, lay on the ground. The ambulance crew closed the rear doors and walked to the cab.

"Are you not taking the second body?" Tosh asked.

"We're not allowed to take animals in the ambulance, in case of contamination. The CSIs will take the dog with them."

"That's discrimination. We'll have animal lovers complaining that we're treating dogs unfairly if it's left lying there," Tosh quipped.

The ambulance driver smiled. "Aye. Right." He closed the vehicle door, started the engine, and drove off gingerly along the rough track.

Tosh noticed the police cordon tape had been extended down to the gate and the uniformed colleagues stood guard at that point. He should have ordered that himself. Just as well Pete Southergill was on the ball. He could see Pete's white-suited CSI team searching the field, and the pathologist heading towards him. Tosh had had little contact with the doctor, with murders being so rare, but he knew the man by sight, and was aware he liked things to be kept formal. No first names.

"Doctor Michaels. I see you've finished your on-scene work. What can you tell me from your initial findings?"

"DS McIntosh, isn't it?" He continued without waiting for a response. "I've already briefed your constable, DC Penrose, earlier. Hasn't he updated you yet?"

"Yes. He mentioned an approximate time of death and when to expect the postmortem report, but that was all."

"There's nothing more I can add, Sergeant."

"Okay. Thanks Doc. I'll see you tomorrow, then."

Tosh strode over to where Logan still stood, controlling entry to the crime scene. "How's it going, Logan?"

"No idea. But I'm frigging freezing. I hate standing around in bad weather! You'll need to talk to the CSIs. They don't tell me anything."

"That's because you're uniform branch, pal. I keep telling you, if you want to be involved in meaningful investigations, rather than standing on guard, you need to become a DC. Not sure you've the intelligence for the job, though?" Tosh said with a grin and a friendly punch to Logan's shoulder.

Logan responded, "You know full well that I'm better at pub quizzes than you. And crosswords, and maths, and everything, actually!"

"Except the courage to put yourself forward to be a DC..."

"Aye. Well. I mostly prefer the uniform role. It's just times like this that I get pissed off."

"If you ever change your mind and want me to back you up, Logan, just say. Okay?"

"Aye. Sure."

"See you later. I need to know if they've identified the victim," Tosh said, as he stepped past Logan. Rather than suit up, he shouted to the CSI team leader. "Hi Pete." He waited for the man to look up before continuing. "Did you get any ID off the woman? I don't even have her name."

Pete ambled towards him before replying, avoiding shouting a response. "Back again so soon, Tosh. I'm surprised you never asked before. You must be getting forgetful."

"Well, did you get an ID or didn't you?"

"She wasn't carrying a handbag but had a purse and mobile phone in her inner pockets. We'll analyse the phone later. But what I can tell you, from her driving licence, is her name. Isla Grace Muir." Pete showed Tosh the victim's driving licence, her address visible through the polythene bag that contained it.

"Kippford, eh? If I'm right, her home's a mansion, overlooking Urr Water. Probably worth a million."

"I think you're right, Tosh, although I doubt it's worth that much.

I'd say it's a small mansion. Perhaps three quarters of a million?"

"Whatever! It's still a mansion. She's obviously moneyed. I'd best get down there and break it to the family."

Chapter Six

Tosh turned onto a side road and followed the lane to its end where the Muir's substantial home came into view. He'd been informed that Mr Muir had been away for a couple of days on business, but he should have returned by now. A Jaguar XJ sat outside the front door, its boot open. As Tosh parked up, a tall, grey-haired, well-dressed man emerged from the house and marched to the car. He spotted Tosh and turned to towards him, a puzzled expression on his face.

Tosh got out and strode over to where the man stood, his feet crunching on the shingle. "Mr Muir?"

"Yes, that's me. And you are?" He said, his voice indicating curiosity rather than annoyance.

"Detective Sergeant McIntosh, Dumfries CID. May I have a word?"

A frumpy, middle-aged woman appeared at the door, wiping her hands on her apron. Tosh assumed her to be the housekeeper.

"What's this about?"

"It would be better if we spoke inside, sir. Could I give you a hand with your bags?"

Mr Muir pulled a large bag from the car boot. He placed it on the floor, then grabbed a small hold-all and a briefcase, before closing the boot lid and locking the car with his remote. "Thanks for the offer, Sergeant. Follow me." He walked away through the front door, the housekeeper moving aside.

Tosh picked up the large case and followed Muir into the house, the smell of freshly baked bread emanating from the kitchen. The entrance hall had parquet flooring and a sweeping staircase rose to the upper floor, a polished mahogany banister taking Tosh's eye upwards to where a colossal crystal chandelier cast its sparkling light into every corner of the hall and landing.

"Leave the bag there, Sergeant. We can talk through here," Muir said, leading the way into an expansive living room, its rectangular bay window giving views of Urr Water as it snaked its way out to the Solway Firth.

Muir stopped and faced Tosh. "So, how can I help you?"

"Could we sit, please, sir?" Tosh said, moving towards the sofas that framed the fireplace.

Muir followed Tosh's lead, worry lines spreading, as the proposal to take a seat hinted at bad news. As he realised Isla was not around, nor their dog, the furrows in his brow deepened.

They sat facing each other across the cherry-wood coffee table, the plush fabric on the sofa soft against Tosh's touch. "There's been an incident this morning. Your wife and dog were involved."

Muir's face drained of colour. His eyes welled. His voice broke as he spoke. "Is she in hospital? I told her to drive more slowly. She's always nipping around the country lanes. How is she?"

"Sir. It wasn't a car accident, and your wife's not in the hospital. There was a shooting. I'm afraid..."

"No! No! You can't be right. I spoke to her last night. Where is she?" He stared at the officer, as if willing him to retract his words.

"Mr Muir. You wife is dead. And so is your dog... I'm really sorry."

"Where did this accident happen?" Muir asked, the tears now running down his cheeks.

"Sir. We don't believe it to have been an accident. We're treating it as a murder enquiry."

Muir broke down then, sobbing. He turned and stared into the cold, unmade fire.

Tosh sat quietly, observing. He'd never informed anyone that their loved one had been murdered. It would be bad enough hearing about a death, but murder took the grief to another level. He felt for Mr Muir. He wondered how he would feel if someone told him his wife, Fiona, had been killed.

It was two minutes before Muir spoke again. Wiping tears from his eyes, he turned to Tosh and asked, "Where did this happen? Where is Isla now? I want to see her."

"Your wife and the dog were discovered by walkers this morning. It was on farmland over Caulkerbush way. We believe their injuries to have been caused by a shotgun." Tosh watched as Muir absorbed what had been said, the realisation sinking in. He covered his eyes and cried again. The sobbing went on for several minutes.

Tosh waited patiently until the whimpering became sniffing, before speaking again. "Mr Muir. Do you have any idea why your wife would have been walking her dog in the Caulkerbush area?"

Muir shook himself, wiping his eyes before looking up and connecting with Tosh again. "She's been looking at some land around there with a view to purchase, I think. Perhaps she was surveying the land? I don't really get involved in her property development business."

Tosh noticed the present tense in Muir's reply. It had not yet sunk in that his wife was now past. He thought back to when his mother had died, about three years ago. She was only in her early sixties. It had been a tremendous shock and his father had continued to talk about his wife in the present tense for about four months after she'd passed. "Could you give me access to your wife's business documents and accounts? It could be important. We have to find a motive for the murder."

"Yes, yes, of course, but first I need to see Isla." He stood as if to leave. His eyes were red-rimmed and still sodden with tears.

"That won't be possible just yet, sir," Tosh responded as he stood. "Mrs Muir will be at the mortuary, but the pathologist will need to complete his examination before you will be allowed in to see her. I'll ensure you are informed you as soon as the mortuary is ready for you. We'll need you to identify the body. In the meantime, I really need a look into her business dealings."

Acceptance registered on Mr Muir's face. "Right. Yes. I understand... Isla ran the business by herself. She employed specialists and contractors, as she needed them. Her office is upstairs. She took over a bedroom at the front of the house so she could look out over the Urr." He paused, then added, "Why would anyone want to shoot Isla? *And* Sunset?"

"That's what we intend to find out, sir. With your help." Tosh hesitated before continuing. "You mentioned your wife's office?"

"Sorry. Of course. Come this way, officer." He led Tosh out of the room, up the stairs and into his wife's business HQ. "Help yourself, Sergeant."

"Thank you, sir. I'll have a look around now to see if anything stands out. I'll probably get someone else to assist with the removal of the documents for scrutiny.

Muir left the room, his eyes still red and moist, as Tosh started browsing. Isla Muir's mahogany desk had a dark red leather writing surface, although Tosh doubted there had been much writing done on it. Everything was done on computers nowadays. An expensive-looking ergonomic black leather chair sat behind the desk, providing wonderful views through the window for its occupant. A grey metal filing cabinet hunkered in the corner, its key sitting in the lock.

He opened the top drawer, noting the orderly filing system, with each suspension file carrying a clear plastic clip, with an insert identifying its contents. He scanned the titles: Gorsebank, Kirkennan,

Kippford View, Caulkerbush, Douglas Hall...

There must have been at least twenty files in the drawer - an expansive portfolio of properties, or potential developments. He delved into a file. There was farming land for sale at Douglas Hall, next to the golf course. He read the notes and analysis. Mrs Muir had purchased the land and was in the process of applying for planning permission for a small development of executive homes, with views across the golf course and the Solway Firth. He knew the distant fells of Cumbria's Lake District National Park would also be part of the vista for anyone buying one of those houses. If she got permission, she'd likely make a mint from the project.

He opened the next file: Caulkerbush. Tosh's eyes fell immediately on the map with a parcel of land outlined in red. It included the field where the woman had been shot. He closed the file and tucked it under his arm. He would get a team to go through the rest of the files, but for the moment, he wanted to study this one.

Before leaving the room, he scanned it. No computer. He wondered where it would be. There were pictures hanging on the wall on either side of the window. Family, by the looks of them, their body language and ages, suggesting familiarity and bonds. One picture showed Mr and Mrs Muir on their front lawn, with Urr Water as their backdrop and the golden retriever sitting between their legs. A separate photo pictured the dog alone. Its name was on a frame-mounted brass plate: Sunset. An unusual name for a dog, he thought.

Mr Muir stood staring into the distance through the living room window. He didn't notice Tosh's approach and jumped when spoken to. "Mr Muir. I'll be off now. I'll take this file as it's about a potential development at Caulkerbush. A team will call in later or perhaps tomorrow, to delve into your wife's business affairs." Mr Muir stood blank-faced, giving no sign that he was taking in what Tosh was telling him.

"Mr Muir," Tosh said, raising his voice to gain the man's attention before asking his question.

Muir's eyes turned and engaged.

"Do you know where your wife's computer will be?"

Muir was slow to respond. "I don't know Sergeant. If it's not in her office, I guess it will be in her car."

"Thank you, sir." Lastly, "Could you please inform me where you were between 6 a.m. and 10 a.m. this morning?"

Muir looked surprised at the question, then indignant at having been asked for his whereabouts. But as realisation dawned that this was routine questioning, he replied. "In bed, Sergeant, until seven thirty." He paused. "I took breakfast in the hotel about eight. Then on the road from just after nine. I stopped off for a coffee around eleven. Arrived here - well, you know when I arrived. It was just before you turned up."

"And the hotel you stayed in, please?" Tosh asked, tilting his head.

"The Randolph Hotel. It's near the Oxford Playhouse, if that means anything to you?"

Tosh's lips pursed. "Not really. I've never been to Oxford. May I ask why you were in Oxford?"

"Lecturing at Balliol College. I'm a professor of English."

"Thank you, sir. That's all I need for now. An FLO will also visit, to offer support and liaison between you and the police."

"An FLO?"

"Sorry. Family Liaison Officer. It's their job to keep you informed of progress in the investigation and answer your queries." And, to report back on anything of interest to the investigating officers, of course, Tosh kept to himself. "By the way, sir, what car does your wife drive?"

"She has a green Range Rover."

"Would her number plate be SM15 XMN?"

"Yes. That's her number."

"Thank you for confirming. The vehicle will be returned to you once it's been processed by the CSIs. Do you have any questions for me?"

"Just one, officer. Why Isla?"

"That's what we intend to find out, sir..."

Chapter Seven

Suzanna McLeod strode towards the church's exit -having just been told she was needed to lead a murder investigation - leaving her boyfriend James wondering what was going on. No sooner had she put her phone in her bag, it had rung again.

Exiting through the double glass doors into the church's foyer, Suzanna spoke into her mobile. "The mysterious Greg Lansdowne pops up in my life unexpected again."

She'd last encountered Greg in an airport departure lounge, on her premature return from her holiday in the Alps. He'd gone out of his way to meet her face to face, having used his power to gain access to the lounge without a boarding pass.

"It's mystery that puts the M in MI5, Suzanna."

"I didn't expect you to call so soon. I've not even heard officially that a Major Investigation Team is to be formed in the Edinburgh area, and my team might be affected. What's the rush, Greg, and why an evening call?"

"No rush, Suzanna. It's just that we need to firm up our plans for the growing Counter-terrorism teams. Sorry about the out of hours call. I didn't want anyone else knowing about our conversation."

Suzanna said nothing, so he continued. "It's going to need a superintendent in Scotland sooner than later, given the resources being ploughed into this field."

Suzanna remained silent, not wanting to show any interest in the suggested promotion, as Greg carried on. She hoped he would soon exhaust himself, so she could get her journey underway.

"I'm sure you're aware of the ongoing threat from Al Qa'ida and the risk posed by Daesh..."

Suzanna turned as Greg spoke and saw James staring at her. She felt guilty at letting work override her personal life and relationship again. She mouthed 'sorry,' then continued to turn until she faced away from his glare.

"These, and other Islamist groups, are exploiting the Internet to push warped alternative narratives. They're urging extremists within our own communities to subvert our way of life through simple but brutal violence. They're grooming our vulnerable young people to join their movement, and to commit acts of senseless violence. Home-grown terrorists."

He paused for effect, but getting none, continued. "As the Home Secretary recently said - well actually, I drafted the words for her - 'The stark reality is that it will never be possible to stop every terrorist attack.' But the Government has acknowledged we must try harder. And - in line with the recommendations in the recently published National Security and Strategic Defence and Security Review - it has agreed to recruit and train almost 2000 extra staff." Greg paused as if he expected her to respond at once by saying, 'I'm in.'

But again, she remained silent. What Greg had said was important but there was no point giving him hope.

Greg filled the space. "We need you, Suzanna, more than ever. We must recruit the best there is. And you are at the top of my list."

She understood the threat from home-grown terrorists and knew that more effort had to be put in to combatting this menace. She had already given time to thinking about Greg's request that she join counter-terrorism and work alongside MI5. It might be exciting but could be boring. She knew all too well that surveillance operations could go on for hours, days, months, even years. And waiting for something to happen was mind-numbing work. At the other extreme, undercover agents put their lives on the line daily. Two extremes: tedium or tension. She didn't think it was for her.

"Look, Greg. I appreciate your attempts to recruit me and it's rather flattering, but I have a murder investigation to lead right now. I'm sure the number two on your list will do the job as well as I could. Probably better." She ended the call and returned to her table, slipping quietly onto her chair next to James, as the evening's compere welcomed everyone. She whispered into James' ear, "Really sorry, love, but I have to go. I've been appointed SIO of a murder investigation. I have to drive to Dumfries this evening."

The Alpha talk got underway, the speaker repeating the title, "Christianity, boring, irrelevant, and untrue?"

James looked peeved. She'd left him on the French ski slopes earlier in the year, abandoning him to lead an investigation. She didn't seem to know how to say 'No,' when work called. He whispered back, "Can't it wait until the morning?"

"Sorry. I need to be there tonight, so I'm ready to pick up the reins first thing in the morning. The first day's work can be crucial." As she finished speaking, her attention was caught by the speaker, projected on the overhead screen. She wasn't sure if they were playing a video or if it was a live link to another church. She wanted to hear more of what this eloquent speaker was saying, but felt compelled to leave, having already committed to arriving that night.

James noticed Suzanna's attention being grabbed by the speaker and made one last attempt to persuade her to stay. "You could rise early and drive straight to Dumfries in the morning. That way, you'd get to hear the rest of the talk."

Suzanna considered the suggestion but quickly rejected it, whispering back. "I'd not get a good night's sleep if I did, and I need to be sharp in the morning. Besides, I'll not be able to concentrate on the talk, now my mind is elsewhere. I need to get going." She pecked him on the cheek, grabbed her coat and bag and tiptoed out of the building, trying to avoid disturbing others attending the course. As the door swung behind her, she strode out, eager to get underway.

On closing her car door, Suzanna's phone rang again. On the screen 'Alistair Milne'. Her boss. "Good evening, Alistair."

"I take it you had the request to assist Dumfries and Galloway?"

"Yes. Sergeant Miller called me about ten minutes ago. I'm on the way home to pack my bag. ETA Dumfries 10 p.m. I'm told the division's DCI is away in the Dominican Republic. Apparently, he'd only just arrived for a well-deserved two-week break."

Alistair could tell by her tone that she considered the holiday to be a poor excuse. "I know you cut short your skiing holiday to return for the George White case, but you *were* halfway through and much closer to home. Anyway, glad to hear you're on the move. Just don't stay too long down there."

"At least we have a full team in at the moment. Angus and Una will undoubtedly hold the fort commendably."

"Aye. Well, you drive safely. And call me if you need any assistance."

Chapter Eight

Tosh arrived back at the station shortly after Carl, his coat dripping as he hung it behind the CID office door. Carl looked up. "Would you like a cuppa, sarge?"

"Aye, please. I could do with something to warm me up."

Carl returned a minute later with a full mug of white coffee for his colleague. They shared with each other about who they'd spoken to and what information they'd gathered. Carl had called on three of the farms closest to the crime scene and gained nothing of any significance from his questioning of the occupants.

Inspector Ferguson walked into the office. "I've had a chat with district HQ about a senior investigating officer. As you know, we don't have one at the moment. They called Police Scotland to ask for assistance. From what I hear, they're sending a DCI from Edinburgh. She's well respected up there. A bit of a star, they say. Best conviction rate in the country. And not afraid to get stuck into the work instead of just sitting behind a desk, like most DCIs."

Carl asked, "What's the star's name?"

"Suzanna McLeod."

"I've heard of her," Tosh commented. "She's a bit of a looker, apparently. A blonde bombshell! Fit too! Although too old for us. I hear she's middle-aged."

"Just watch yourself, Tosh," the inspector replied, frowning. "You know full well we're not to indulge in sexism or ageism anymore," he said with a wink, his false frown relaxing. "Did you hear about the Indian woman found washed up on the banks of the River Forth earlier this year?"

"Yeah. I hear she'd been trafficked into Scotland from India," Carl said.

"I guess it was DCI McLeod that found her killer, then?" Tosh added.

"Aye, you're right. She took herself off to West Bengal to find out who the victim was and where she was from. I'm told she's a skilled fighter. A judo black belt. Took out a few Bengali criminals while she was there."

Carl and Tosh looked impressed.

"She's due in around ten," the inspector continued. "So, you've three and a half hours to get something to eat and get your act in order before you have to brief her."

"Aye. Sure thing, Ed."

Ferguson looked sternly at Tosh but said nothing. Tosh should know better than to call him by his first name when in the presence of others. He would have to talk with him later about that. "Show me where the body was found, sarge," Ed said, making the point about rank.

Tosh looked quizzically at his friend. Then his expression changed to one of understanding. He pulled out an ordnance survey map of the area, unfolded it, then scanned the terrain, following the roads with his finger until he found the right area. "It was on this slope," he said, pointing to the crime scene's location. "There were just a couple of steps separating the woman from her dog."

Inspector Ferguson bent closer to the map as Tosh's phone rang. "Excuse me a sec," Tosh said, before turning away from the table. He walked out of earshot to take the call. "Hi Fiona. I'm in a meeting at the moment so can't speak for long."

"I hear there's been a body found."

"How did you get to hear that?"

"It was on the local radio. I guess you'll not be home for your dinner tonight, then?"

"Doubt it, love. I'll grab something locally. I'll have to be here when the SIO arrives from Edinburgh. She's due in about ten. You'll likely be asleep by the time I get home."

"Okay, Tosh. Try not to wake me when you climb into bed."

"I can't promise that. If this DCI McLeod is as sexy as they say, I might be in the mood-"

"Don't you go disturbing me if I'm asleep, Tosh McIntosh. I'll not want you touching me if it's another woman that's got you feeling randy."

"But if you're still awake, maybe I'm in with a chance, then?"

"Is it your birthday?" Fiona concluded, then hung up.

Tosh grinned. Inspector Ferguson had gone back to his office by the time Tosh finished his call.

"How'd the missus take it, sarge?"

"Fine. She knows it's rare for me to work late. Have you told your partner yet?"

"Surely you'll not need me here as well, when you brief the DCI?"

"I suppose not," Tosh acknowledged. "Tell you what, let's get things organised, then head off to the pub for a drink and some food."

"Happy days," Carl concurred.

* * *

A short stroll down the road from the station, saw Tosh and Carl at their local pub. It looked dingy on the outside. But inside the building had been opened up, creating a light and airy space. And the welcome was always friendly. "Alright, lads?" the barman said as they approached.

Tosh responded. "Aye. Good. How's things, Jimmy?"

"Good. Good. The usual?" They responded with nods, and Jimmy poured their beers. "I bet you'll have had a busy day - what with the murder?"

Carl's eyebrows rose in surprise, but Tosh already knew the word was out. "Aye. You're right there, Jimmy. Guess we'll be busy for the foreseeable future. Unless we're lucky and the murderer walks into the station to confess what they've done," he said. His eyes looked towards the heavens, indicating his low expectation of that happening.

Pints in hand, the two detectives found a table away from the small crowd around the bar. The old snug area at the back suited them well, as they wanted to talk without being overheard. The snug's original dark wood panelling, chocolate-coloured ceiling beams and oak furniture matched well with the pub's external gloomy look.

They had both ordered stovies, so they wouldn't have to wait long for their food.

Carl took a swig from his pint of Orkney IPA. "So, you say this DCI is a bit long in the tooth?"

"No. In her mid-forties, I heard."

"The inspector said she had a reputation for having the best conviction rate in Scotland. Let's hope they're right. She'll have this wrapped up tomorrow, then we can get back to normal."

"No one could solve the case that quick; even Sherlock Holmes. And it'll be good to work on something other than the mundane minor thefts and burglaries."

"Yeah, you're right. And it could be good for our careers if we help solve a murder. Especially for you. You've been a sergeant for a while now, eh?"

"Aye. True. It would be great to get promoted. I could do with the extra income." As Tosh finished speaking, he noticed Carl's eyes disengage and look beyond him.

"Hey. See that woman on the table in the corner?"

Tosh glanced over his shoulder and peered through the snug's open doorway back into the main bar area. "Aye."

"You heard of the butterfly effect?"

Tosh turned his attention back to Carl. "Sure."

"I reckon with those false eyelashes, if she blinks, it'll cause a tornado on the other side of the world."

Tosh chuckled. "Maybe the DCI will have false eyelashes. If she blinked, she'd blow you across the room."

"The only blowing I'd like from her, if she's as hot as you say, is–" Carl saw the frown on Tosh's face and decided to keep his final words to himself.

Tosh's attention was grabbed by the meaty aroma of their stovies as it preceded the cook, waiter and co-tenant, Agnes Batty, as she shuffled across the room towards them. Agnes placed the plates on the table. "Alright, lads?"

"Aye. Thanks, Agnes. How are you keeping?"

"Nae bad, nae bad. Thought you'd be busy with this murder case, Tosh," she said, stepping back from the table and unsuccessfully attempting to straighten up. Her osteoporosis was taking a toll on her body.

"Aye. I am. Just grabbing some supper before the hard work starts."

"Mind you catch the bugger who did them in. It's not just the woman. She might have made enemies, but he killed her innocent dog, as well. Unforgivable!" She turned and wandered away.

The two men got stuck into their steaming plates of mashed potato with onions and minced meat. The dish was warming and easy to eat. A simple but tasty meal. Their voices fell silent as they stuffed their mouths.

When Carl finished his meal, he checked his watch. "I've just noticed the time. The game started an hour ago," he said, then downed the rest of his pint. As he stood, he grabbed his coat off the back of his chair.

Tosh responded, a disappointed tone to his voice. "You didn't say you'd be rushing off, Carl. I'll look like a sad old man, supping his pint in the snug, with no friends. What will that do for my reputation?"

"Sorry sarge. I forgot to mention it. But I don't want to miss the action," Carl replied, looking guilty.

Tosh grinned. "It's no problem. I'd best be getting back to the station, anyway. See you in the morning, Carl."

Chapter Nine

When Suzanna opened her entrance door, the herb-infused-tomato smell of the pasta dish she'd shared earlier with James hung in the air. The wok with leftovers still sat on the hob. She'd been told it was normal for Alpha courses to put on a light meal. But the one they'd decided to attend, because it was on a day of the week when they were both free, had chosen to only provide hot drinks, biscuits and a dessert. She hoped he wouldn't be too mad with her for abandoning him at the church.

Suzanna loaded the dishwasher and set it running, then packed a small suitcase with what she expected to need over the next week or two.

She exited Edinburgh on the familiar A-road towards Dumfries - the same road she used when travelling to her sister Charlie's house in Cumbria. She settled into cruising and let her mind drift to the call from Greg Lansdowne. The MI5 officer seemed determined to get her into the counter-terrorism team. She'd already considered the idea when he'd first proposed it, and she had rejected it. But things change.

She wondered again whether it would it be the right move for her? It would mean leaving her team, a team she'd invested over three years of her career into developing. Her two DIs, Angus and Una, had both proven themselves to be top class investigators and Angus would make a good chief inspector. Una needed more experience and had to learn risk assessment skills and to control her ambition to make arrests. She could have died when the drug dealer she'd confronted stabbed her to escape. Perhaps Angus could take over the team if she moved on? But she still didn't think it was time to leave them. And if they had another DCI posted in to replace her, similar to Inspector Ferguson - her boss when she was a sergeant - God help them!

As she continued her journey southwest, a black Range Rover passed by in the other direction. It reminded her of the vehicles favoured by secret service operatives in spy thrillers. Counter-Terrorism... Should she, or shouldn't she?

* * *

It was just after 10 p.m. when Suzanna was escorted through to Dumfries' small CID office and introduced to its only occupant. He stood respectfully as she entered and extended his hand. "Thanks for coming down so quickly, ma'am. I'm DS McIntosh."

The sergeant's hand felt dry and rough; his shake firm, hinting at latent power. About six feet tall and in good shape, Suzanna immediately recognised his military deportment.

"Can't say I'm pleased to be here but good to meet you anyway, Sergeant, nonetheless."

"How do you like your coffee? Or tea?"

"Do you have any decaf coffee? I don't want to stay up all night. I think it best if you bring me up to speed now, then take me to the crime scene in the morning."

"Not sure about the decaf, ma'am. I'll check."

Suzanna watched him as he foraged around on the table at the back of the room. His short-cropped, dark brown hair had a few stray grey hairs.

"Aha! Found one of those little hotel sachets of decaf."

Sat with coffees in their hands, Tosh briefed her on what he knew and what he'd done. Suzanna interjected with questions as he went along, ensuring she knew answers to the standard formula: what, why, when, where, how and who. Many of these could not yet be answered.

She added comments to the board to remind them what they'd need to follow up before they retired for the night, drawing three overlapping circles, titled Location, Victim and Offender, with the central, triple overlap marked as Homicide. They knew who the victim was and where the crime had been carried out. Obviously, the drive of the investigation would be to identify the offender. Adding as much detail as they could in the other zones would be helpful.

"Do you have a team, Sarge? Or is it just you here?"

"Just the two of us. DC Penrose has already finished for the day. Hopefully, he'll be bright and breezy in the morning."

"Hopefully?"

"Well, he does enjoy a pint while watching his team play footy on the TV!"

"And which team does he support?"

"Wrexham. He's a *boyo*. From the north coast somewhere."

Suzanna noticed a small CID staff board on the wall over the sergeant's shoulder. It pictured the two officers: DC Carl Penrose and DS Edward McIntosh.

"By the way, Sarge, what do your colleagues call you?"

"Tosh, ma'am."

"So, why Tosh, not Edward or Ed?"

"Goes back to my army days."

"Well. Come on. Don't keep me in suspense!"

"I left school and joined the army. Did a few years' service, before leaving and joining the police. There was another Edward in my troop."

"It gets confusing on the battlefield if two guys have the same name. The leader shouts, 'Ed, do this' and both Eds move. The other Ed was

Ed Ferguson. They tried calling him Fergie, but he objected to that as it sounded too feminine, like Prince Andrew's ex-wife. When they continued to call him Fergie, he got pissed off and punched one of the guys in the face."

Suzanna registered the name Ferguson. There would be thousands of men with that surname but, after her experience of working under the control of one particularly horrible man - the man that had nearly ended her police career - she couldn't help but react whenever she heard the name.

Tosh went on. "Split his lip wide open. So, they thought it best to call me Tosh and him Ed, to avoid conflict. I didn't mind. And it stuck. Even after I left the army, I'd got used to being called Tosh, so I just stuck with it."

"Tosh it is, then."

* * *

Suzanna was unhappy as she dumped her bag on the single bed. The hotel was smart and clean, the public rooms appointed to a high standard. But although she'd booked a double room, the receptionist informed her they only had a twin room available. They would, however, have one vacant tomorrow. She'd just have to put up with this narrow bed for tonight. She didn't bother unpacking.

As she lay in the bed, teeth cleaned and her scarce makeup removed, her silver-blonde hair spread across the pillow, she pondered her situation. Earlier that day, she had abandoned her boyfriend in church as the Alpha Course, that they'd both agreed to go on, started its introduction session. She'd been getting prods from numerous sources over several months about attending one.

She questioned again her need to rush away when the call had come in, requesting she assist Dumfries and Galloway Police as the SIO on this murder case. Could she have delayed her journey until the following morning, or set off an hour or two later? Perhaps.

Suzanna yawned as fatigue caught up with her. Time for sleep. She checked her phone for messages from James before slipping into bed. Nothing. He must be seriously annoyed with her. Although it was now after midnight, she WhatsApped him. 'Hi James. Really sorry about leaving so quickly this evening. I trust the session was good. Did you enjoy two sweets? Will try to attend Alpha when I get this case wrapped up. Sorry again. Hope you can forgive me. Will call tomorrow. Love Suz xxx.'

Suzanna wouldn't be distracted by her relationship worries now. She'd be able to focus on the case. She turned the phone face down to switch on the do-not-disturb feature, snuggled up under the quilt, adjusting it to cover all her body without drafts, then closed her eyes and drifted off, content that she'd apologised.

Chapter Ten

Tuesday 26 April

At eight sharp, Tosh turned into the hotel's broad, tree-lined drive and pulled up outside the entrance. It was a grand-looking red-sandstone country house, with dual pillars framing the Georgian-style door.

Suzanna emerged from the entrance immediately, evidently having been waiting for his arrival.

She opened the passenger door and climbed in, fastening her seat belt as she spoke. "Morning, Tosh. Good to see you're on time. Shows good planning and respect. Did you get a decent sleep? It's likely to be a long day."

"Yes, thanks." Tosh pulled away, breathing in the classy floral scent of his new boss. "Didn't even get a bollocking from the missus for disturbing her! Was the hotel room alright?"

"It was fine." She paused. "When will I get to meet your DC?"

"He'll be at the site, ma'am, to say hello before he heads off to interview more locals."

A breeze had risen while Suzanna was at breakfast and yesterday's showers looked likely to continue today but in between there would be much sunshine. The asphalt was dry as Tosh pulled out onto the road and headed southeast towards Dumfries. They were soon away from the town and out into the farmland. The smell of manure drifted through the car vents, blotting out the more pleasant smell Suzanna emanated. It was fairly flat terrain, but as they headed south, the roads became narrower, and tree-covered hills rose gently from the plain.

They recapped on the previous evening's discussions, revising what had been done so far and their next moves. Half an hour later, Tosh turned into the narrow track leading to the crime scene and parked up, conscious of the need for farm vehicles to get through. DC Penrose's car was parked further up the track and its door opened at the same time as Tosh stepped out of his car. Carl waved but showed no sign of walking towards them. After donning wellies, they trudged along the track to meet with the DC.

"Morning, sarge," Carl called as the two detectives approached. He shifted his gaze to meet the eyes of the woman accompanying his colleague. "Hello, Chief Inspector. I'm DC Carl Penrose. Good to meet you." He held out his hand and lent towards Suzanna.

She took his offered hand, gripped and firmly shook. Penrose stood two inches higher that Suzanna; had a round face, receding hairline and prominent nose that looked like it had been broken at least once. A rugby player, she guessed. "Good to meet you, Carl. Anything new to report?"

"No, ma'am. Just got here. I'll be heading off to talk with more of the farmers next. Just wanted to introduce myself, before getting stuck into the work."

"Have you worked on a murder case before?" Suzanna enquired, studying Carl's reaction.

"No. First one for me. Fortunately, they're rare in this part of the country. I hope I don't have to help investigate many more."

"Too true," said Tosh. "How did Wrexham get on yesterday, by the way?"

"Beat Tranmere 2:1. Brilliant performance." Carl's face brightened. "Last time we played them, it was a two-all draw!"

"I'll let you get on, Carl." Suzanna broke in. "We need to get our heads together later today. What time would you anticipate having completed the interviews?"

Carl's brightness drained as his mind returned to the reality of their task. "Difficult to say, ma'am. Depends on whether they're available when I call. I might have to track them down, although my car will not get me close if any of them are working in fields away from the roads."

"Just don't go blocking any more gates, Carl," Tosh jibed, his mouth breaking into a crooked grin.

Suzanna looked at the sergeant, wondering what the background was for that comment. Carl's face crinkled before he turned and opened his car door, murmuring words Suzanna couldn't make out.

Tosh recognised the DCI's look. "I'll tell you about it later. Let's take a look at the crime scene." He led on before Suzanna had time to respond. They left Carl doing a seven-point turn in the narrow lane.

The CSI team were still working the field, looking for any evidence that had yet to be collected. Tosh and Suzanna donned white coveralls and trudged through the field to the place where the bodies had been found. Tosh pointed out where the Brownlows had walked and their intended path out of the field, as well as the quad bike tracks. "The CSIs have casts of the tracks and the boots. But we've yet to match them."

Suzanna stood quietly, scanning the scene, taking it all in, imagining how it was the morning of the death. Tosh remained silent, giving her the time and space she needed. She tried to place the players in the event, by the marks on the ground. "So, the woman's body was lying face up, there," she said, pointing, as she recalled what Carl and Tosh had told her. "And the dog had lain two paces away, its head facing towards its mistress?"

"Aye. That's right."

"And the pathologist reckons she was shot at close range with a shotgun. The boot patterns suggesting the assailant was uphill from the victim... The force of the shot would have propelled the woman backwards, so that might account for why she was lying in that position. But there's blood on the grass up hill from her body. It looks to me like the body was turned onto its back after falling face down."

"Agreed." Tosh was impressed by his boss's assessment. "The pathologist said similar. His hypothesis was that the shot, having been to the abdomen, resulted in the upper body crumpling forward as the centre of the body was driven rearwards, so they would have fallen forward. Turning the body would have resulted in it coming to rest where it was found." His voice trailed off.

Suzanna could tell the sergeant had more to say. She looked at him and waited, her curious expression inviting more.

"But the man who came across her insisted he'd not touched the woman."

"Then someone else did!" Suzanna declared. Armed with these thoughts, she re-imagined the scene. The person with the gun would have approached from the brow of the hill, walking down towards the victim. The woman probably turned to face her murderer before she was shot. Why would a woman walking her dog in the countryside get shot at close range and left to die? That's what they needed to find out. "Can we tell from the prints whether the killer moved forward and turned the victim before leaving the scene?"

"I don't know. Forensics haven't completed their work on the prints yet."

"Okay. Do the boot prints from the couple who found the body match with their account of where they walked?"

"Aye. From the bottom of the field, heading up towards the exit at the top but diverting towards the bodies, stopping short by about two paces before moving away. Then lots of movement in a small area, no doubt from where they hung around waiting for us to arrive."

"Their story sound believable to you, Tosh?"

"Absolutely. Everything fits. Checked into the B&B the day before, then up and out after an early breakfast for a walk. Stumbled across the bodies." He paused. "It wrecked their little getaway."

Suzanna imagined the shock the couple must have encountered stumbling on the bloodied bodies. "Are they intending to stay on in the area as planned?"

Tosh thought back to his interviewing of the couple, remembering Mr Brownlow's lack of emotion. "Mrs Brownlow definitely wanted to go home, but her husband was less inclined. He didn't seem bothered about finding the woman and her dog. Seemed willing to carry on as if nothing had happened. I asked them not to leave the area before informing me, in case you wanted to talk with them first."

"Thanks. I probably will. Have you checked them out at all? Confirmed their identities, home address, etc?"

"Not yet, ma'am." Tosh made a mental note to follow up on that.

As Suzanna turned to leave, a flash of brown caught her eye, then a cry and rustle of feathers as a sparrowhawk snatched its victim out of the sky and flew away. It seemed that this little vale was Dumfries' death valley.

Chapter Eleven

Carl stepped fully into the open porch of the Mitchell's farm, to shelter from the drizzle, having successfully avoided the cow pats on his way.

A young, rosy-cheeked man opened the door to his knock, a piece of toast clamped between his teeth and a mug of tea in his left hand. He bit off a piece of toast, taking the remains with his other hand, then mumbled, "Are you the constable who called yesterday?"

"Yeah. I'm DC Carl Penrose," his Welsh accent obvious to the Scot.

"Not from round here then, eh?"

"No. I'm sure you don't need any clues about where I'm from. As your mother will have told you, I need a chat about your whereabouts yesterday morning, and your brother's."

"You'd best come in." He stood back, allowing the DC to enter, before pushing the door to with his foot. "Take a seat."

Carl did as invited. Archie Mitchell lifted the teapot and offered Carl a cup, which he gratefully accepted. With the door closed, the smell of tea and toast flushed away the farmyard stench.

"You'll have heard about yesterday's shooting," Carl said, watching the young man for his reaction.

Archie flipped his long fringe out of his eyes before responding. "Aye. Terrible thing. From what I heard, it was no accidental discharge. The woman and her dog killed, eh?"

The response sounded genuine to Carl. "Yeah. It's our job to find out who shot them. So, if you could tell me where you were and what you were doing between 6 a.m. and 10 a.m. yesterday, that would be helpful."

Archie sat opposite Carl, at the chunky kitchen table, his eyes on the officer as he spoke. "As me mam would have told you, Morgan and I were bringing in the cows and milking them before breakfast. Had breakfast around eight thirty, then I did me rounds of the fields to check on the sheep; to make sure they were all accounted for and none of them were poorly."

"And were the sheep all in fine fettle?"

"Aye. No bother."

"Is your brother here?"

"Aye, he's just gone to change." Archie grinned. "Had a run in with a cow earlier and the cow won. Should have seen the state of him. Covered in muck from head to foot. He'll be back in a minute, no doubt."

As he spoke, the door to the hall opened and the brother walked in. Morgan was two inches taller than his younger brother, his hair curled on top of his head, the back and sides cut short by clippers.

"Who's this then, Archie?"

"The detective mam mentioned. DC Penrose." Archie turned to Carl. "That's right, isn't?"

"Yes. You're Morgan, I take it?" Carl said.

"Aye. Mam said you needed to know where we were yesterday morning. Why's that? Are we suspects?" Morgan replied.

"We need to ascertain where you were to eliminate you from our enquiries. And to find out if you saw or heard anything that might help us progress the investigation," Carl said diplomatically.

"I was with Archie 'til the cows were done milking."

"And after breakfast, you sorted out the silage?" Carl continued for him.

"You got it." Morgan sat beside his brother and poured himself a mug of tea, then stole a piece of toast from his brother's plate.

"Hey!" Archie said as he elbowed his brother. "Get your own toast."

"Is your father around?" Carl asked to keep things on track.

"Nae. Da's had to go to Dumfries again. The parts he bought yesterday for the tractor repair did'nae fit.

"What's the name of the supplier he visited yesterday?" Carl asked, opening his notebook and pulling out his pen.

"Johnston's."

"Is that the one on the way to Torthorwald?"

"Aye. That's the one."

"Okay! Thanks. Did either of you hear any shotgun blasts yesterday morning?"

Archie was the first to respond. "Aye a couple."

"Me too," Morgan confirmed. "Just after seven, I'd say."

"That'd be about right," Archie said. "I remember it was after the 7 o'clock news on the radio."

"Was it just the one pair of shots you heard? And were the shots close together or separate?"

Morgan spoke first. "I reckon there was a small gap between the shots. About three or four seconds. What to you think, Archie?"

"Sounds about right. I don't recall hearing any other shots that morning."

"Did you see anyone when you were out and about around the farm?"

"Nothing out of the ordinary," Morgan responded.

"But what about the ordinary?" Carl probed.

The two lads thought before answering, their minds reliving that morning. Archie responded first. "When I crossed the road to West Field, a couple of cars passed by. I think one was a Citroen Picasso but not sure about the other. Couldn't tell you anything else about them. Sorry."

Carl took a swig of his now cool, strong tea. Disgusted by the taste, he had to fight the urge to spit the liquid out. He made a note not to accept the offer of a drink if he visited again.

Morgan took over. "Only thing to mention was I heard a couple of motorbikes down towards the Reynolds' farm. One would likely have been a quad, I reckon."

"You can tell the difference?" Carl queried.

"Aye. The quad's a heavier machine. Has a larger engine."

"And this would have been around what time?"

"About seven. Just a few minutes before the shotgun blasts."

"Happy days!" Carl almost sung, in his Welsh accent. "That's very helpful. I'll leave you to get on with your breakfast. Thanks, lads."

Carl let himself out as the brothers poured themselves another mug of tea. Once the door had closed, Archie nudged his brother. "What's this 'happy days' lark, eh?"

"Ah dinnae ken. There was a Welsh lad at the agricultural college with me, and he never used that phase. Odd guy, that DC!"

Carl climbed into his car, then used his smart-phone to look up the tractor suppliers. The phone was answered on the second ring by a man with a cheerful voice. "Johnston's. Good morning to ya. How can I help?"

"Good morning. I'm Detective Constable Penrose from Dumfries CID. Do you happen to have Mr Mitchell with you at the moment?" He said hopefully.

"Nae, Constable. You've missed him. Just now walked out the door. Do you want me to call him back for you?"

"No, that won't be necessary but thanks for offering. Could you tell me if Mr Mitchell was in yesterday as well?"

"Aye. He was that. I served him meself. I'd only just started work around eight. And he was me first customer. Must have left about twenty past."

"And your name, please?"

"It's Gordon Dunbar." Gordon noticed customers waiting to be served. "Look, I need to go. Work to do."

"Happy days. Thanks for your time, Mr Dunbar." He hung up, pleased that he'd established Mitchell's alibi. Another one off the list.

Chapter Twelve

Tosh took the DCI back to her hotel to collect her car, before stopping off at the CSI offices in divisional HQ as he'd heard they'd found a computer.

"Anything of interest in the victim's car, Pete, other than the laptop, of course?" Tosh asked the Dumfries' CSI team leader.

"Nothing out of the ordinary, Tosh. The car was immaculate, apart from a bit of mud on the tyres and in the wheel arches. Showroom condition, I'd say. There were car park tickets from Carlisle and Glasgow, dated within the last month. We brushed them for prints and will match what we find with the victim for elimination. I'll let you know if we find any other useful prints."

"The thing you may be most interested in, other than the laptop," Pete continued, tucking his wavy ginger hair behind his left ear, "is a leather attaché case containing some personal items and documents."

"Great. Can I take that yet?" Tosh asked. If Pete let his hair grow any longer, he thought, he'd just need to wear a tam-o'shanter to look like he had on one of those daft hats that tourists bought.

"Aye. No Problem. We've already taken prints from it, so you can take it with you, along with the laptop. Good luck with finding something significant. I'll keep you posted on progress from our end."

"Cheers, Pete. Appreciated. Oh! And can you send me images of the tickets, please, so we can start looking into Isla Muir's movements?"

"I sure can, and will, my friend," Pete concluded.

"See ya, Pete," Tosh called as he walked away.

* * *

Back at the station, Tosh emptied the contents of Muir's attaché case onto his desk, then foraged around to ensure nothing was left inside the case. Satisfied everything was now on the desk, he lifted each item in turn and studied it. There were pens and pencils, an eraser and pencil sharpener, and a pink lipstick, all contained within a small cloth zip bag.

He picked up a notebook, then flipped through its pages, stopping occasionally to read its contents. It was a to-do list, with tasks ticked off. Several tasks were outstanding: speak to construction company; reassess quotes for land clearance; chase quotes for ground works. It went on. Nothing shed any light on her murder.

Tosh turned his attention to the laptop. He tried a few passwords without success, becoming frustrated by his failure to get into the computer. He was resigned to sending it off to the Digital Forensics department when Suzanna stepped in, having noticed his whispered curses. "Did Mrs Muir have any children?"

"I don't think so, ma'am."

"Best you find out, Tosh," Suzanna said, surprised at his lack of knowledge. "It's common for people to use children's names in their passwords and their birthdays."

"Right," Tosh acknowledged. He silently questioned himself. Why didn't I know that?

"Have you tried Muir's husband's name and date of birth?"

"Not yet." He checked their records, then tried to access the laptop again. "No luck."

"What was the name of the victim's dog?"

70

"Sunset, I believe," Tosh replied.

"Try sunset123."

Tosh typed it in, shaking his head as it rejected his attempt.

"Try an initial capital."

He typed again. "No, not that either," Tosh said, turning to look up at the DCI. He watched as she stared into space, evidently thinking.

"Okay. The dog's name and husband's date of birth - just the year," Suzanna suggested.

"No. That didn't work. I'll try the other four figures." Tosh checked the DOB again: 23rd May. He typed Sunset2305. "Bloody hell! We're in." He grinned, looking up at Suzanna, impressed with what she'd achieved. Maybe next time, he'd be able to do it without her help?

Tosh navigated around the computer, plugged in a USB memory-stick and copied the folders and files onto it - just in case. As the files copied, Suzanna suggested he examine the Internet browser history. Nothing jumped out at them. She had researched Caribbean cruises, holidays in Athens, city breaks in Rome and Florence, as well as an epic train journey through the Canadian Rockies. Very nice if you can afford it, he thought.

"Take a look at her contacts list."

Tosh switched to Microsoft Outlook and clicked on the Contacts tab. Suzanna bent and looked over his shoulder, frowning as she tried to read the screen. There were hundreds of contacts.

"I'll get them printed out, ma'am."

"Export them into a CSV file as well, so we can manipulate the data in a spreadsheet application. There's too much data to analyse in one sitting."

"CSV?" Tosh questioned.

"Comma Separated Values," Suzanna responded, astounded that Tosh didn't know the term. "Do you know how to export from Outlook?" Suzanna peered at Tosh, her expectations now reduced.

"Can't say I've done it before, ma'am." He looked sheepish, realising the DCI expected him to have these skills. He frowned as he admitted the shortcoming, concerned his lack of technical know-how might adversely affect her post-investigation report on his performance. Perhaps his promotion was further away than he had hoped.

Suzanna indicated he should move aside, so he stood and let her take his seat, then bent down to watch what she did. Instead of just exporting the data, Suzanna demonstrated the process step-by-step. "Got it?" She asked, turning to look up at him. She stopped abruptly when her lips almost collided with Tosh's.

Tosh almost fell over as he pulled back from the near contact. They both laughed.

"Right then. I'll deal with the contacts. Get Carl to analyse the web-browsing history and emails, going back as far as he can. You check the files."

"I was thinking, ma'am. We could do with another pair of hands," Tosh said, looking at Suzanna expectantly.

She had been thinking the same, herself. "Agreed. I'll ask for more manpower. That should speed things up."

"Shouldn't that be person-power, nowadays?"

"I prefer PC to stand for police constable, not politically correct. All this PC stuff is a distraction. Anyway, we're all humans, aren't we? Manpower is just an abbreviated term for human-power, or woman-power, as well as the masculine form. It's generic, like guys has become an accepted term for a group of men and women, even though it was originally used for just men."

Tosh's eyes widened as he listened to his boss's mini-rant. He was surprised at her passion about the subject. Suzanna returned to her desk just as Carl walked into the office carrying a grease-stained paper bag smelling of sausage rolls.

"Late breakfast," Carl mouthed.

Tosh checked the files he'd extracted from Muir's laptop for viruses before opening the folder on his own computer. Satisfied the transfer had safely worked, he passed the USB stick to his boss, then carried the laptop to Carl's desk. He told him what the DCI had instructed them to do and left it with him to check the web-browser history and emails. Perhaps they would find something useful.

* * *

Suzanna scanned the exported victim's contact list, having sorted the data in Excel. Nothing jumped out at her. She frowned, then sorted the data by 'location', instead of surname. Still nothing. She reordered the data by 'telephone numbers', wondering if the same number might show up against two contacts - one a personal contact, the second against a business. Still nothing. Next, she sorted on the 'titles' column, then scanned down, looking for anything interesting. There were several names using Councillor as the title. 'Hmm!' she thought.

The next thing to do would be to check the names against the Police National Computer system. Perhaps that might show something up. There was no one free to do the PNC task at the moment, so she printed the rearranged list and put it aside, highlighting those with Councillor against them.

One final re-sort put the data into 'type of contact' order. The annotations used were intriguing: Enabler, Landowner, Agent, Financier, Supplier. She re-checked the Titles list and noted that all councillors were annotated as Enablers.

Suzanna noticed Tosh return to his desk, so called across to him. "Tosh. Have you found anything significant yet?"

Tosh shrugged his shoulders. "It's difficult to know where to start.

There are masses of files."

Suzanna scooted her chair across to Tosh's desk, its worn wheels squeaking. "Let's forget the electronic files for the moment. Didn't you bring a hard copy file away from Mrs Muir's office?"

Tosh foraged through a pile of documents on his desk and extracted a blue cardboard folder. He opened it and placed it on the desk between them. "This file relates to a field at Caulkerbush. The very field where the murder occurred." He looked into his boss's eyes to ensure she had recognised the relevance of what he'd said. "I had a quick scan of it and found that a number of fields around there are up for sale, as a package. They belong to the Reynolds. I've not figured out yet why they'd interest Mrs Muir."

"Hang on," Suzanna said, spinning back to her own desk. She grabbed her laptop and searched the contacts list for Reynolds. Nothing showed up. Then Caulkerbush. A name, Grant Stonewall, appeared. "Does the file have this name in it?"

"Aye. The land details pages have a header for Stonewall Land Agents. Hang on." He checked the signature block on a covering letter attached to the details. "Aye, it's Grant Stonewall."

"Okay, I think I need a conversation with Mr Stonewall. I just hope he doesn't live up to his name."

Tosh smiled, then returned to scanning through the documents in the folder.

Chapter Thirteen

Suzanna parked her BMW on the road close to the land agent's office in Dumfries. Unlike Edinburgh, where it was always challenging to find a parking space and then buy an extortionately priced ticket, it was free parking on the street for up to two hours, provided drivers displayed a time of arrival disc on their dashboard. One advantage of small towns.

As Suzanna entered the agent's office, the opening door set off an electronic bing-bong sound. A woman appeared through a door in the rear, smiled and asked, "Good morning. How may I help you?"

Suzanna stepped forward and held up her police ID for the woman to read. "I called earlier to request a chat with Mr Stonewall."

"Ah! Yes. Just a minute." The woman's smile disappeared. She returned to the door she'd just emerged from and spoke to its occupant before turning back. "Mr Stonewall will be with you shortly."

"By the way," Suzanna said, "Do you have a parking disk to put on my car?"

The assistant's smile returned. "Yes, of course." She extracted a disc from a small stack and passed it to Suzanna, who immediately returned to her car.

When Suzanna arrived back in Stonewall's outer office, a balding, middle-aged man was waiting for her. "Chief Inspector McLeod. Welcome." He offered his hand, which Suzanna shook.

"Please come through." He stepped back into his office, waited for Suzanna to enter, then sat behind his desk, inviting Suzanna to sit in the client chair opposite. "How can I help you?"

Suzanna quickly assessed Stonewall. He was well dressed, well spoken, confident and professional. Nothing unusual considering his position as managing director of a company offering professional services. He came across as friendly and genuine. But that could just be a front, of course.

"I understand you are acting for the Reynolds in the sale of some of their land near Caulkerbush?"

"Yes, that's right." He paused, waiting for the next question, whilst holding his chubby chin with his right hand.

"I also understand that a Mrs Muir was interested in purchasing that land." Suzanna stared into his eyes as she asked her question. "Had a deal been done?"

Stonewall looked perplexed. "I have to say, I'm curious how you would know of her interest. It's not common knowledge."

"We're investigating the murder of Mrs Muir."

Stonewall's mouth fell open. His eyebrows attempted to leap off his face. "But she was just in here yesterday," he exclaimed.

"It can't have been yesterday, Mr Stonewall," Suzanna corrected. "She was dead before office hours yesterday morning."

Stonewall frowned. Suzanna waited for him to rethink his statement, watching his expression for any give-away signs. Could Stonewall be a suspect? Might he have a motive?

"It must have been Friday then." He paused again. "Of course, I wasn't in the office yesterday. Had to go up to Glasgow to meet a client."

"What can you tell me about Mrs Muir and her land purchases?"

Stonewall's face returned to normal, and he swallowed before responding. "Isla is well known to us. I suppose I should say *was* well known. Over the years, she has put a fair bit of business our way, purchasing land, developing part of it, then selling on the rest. I get commission on both sales. Very useful."

"That's interesting to hear. So, had a deal been done on the Caulkerbush land?"

"No. Isla hadn't put in an offer. She was assessing her options and the potential for profit. There has been no interest in the land from other parties, either."

"Do you have any idea why Mrs Muir may have been interested in this parcel of land?"

"She's quite a canny lady, Isla. Doesn't give much away. But from knowledge of her previous deals, my guess would be she was interested in getting permission for a holiday home park. Caravans or lodges perhaps. Either in a sheltered valley with easy access to public footpaths, or with views of the coast. Perhaps the land that abuts the A710. There are views across the Solway and good transport links. A bus runs along that road several times a day."

"I'd like to hear about past deals she's done, please. Perhaps someone might have been unhappy about the deal?"

"I wouldn't have thought so. Everything is above board. The owner wants rid of the land, and someone makes them an offer. They don't have to accept the offer. No one forces them to sell. How could that cause any issues?"

"I'm not sure at the moment, but it's something we have to consider, so if you could talk me through the deals Mrs Muir has transacted, that would be helpful."

"That could take quite a while and I have a client meeting in twenty minutes."

"Do you wish to see Isla's murderer brought to justice, Mr Stonewall?"

He sat up straight in his chair. "Yes, of course."

77

Suzanna stared at him in silence. Stonewall looked at his watch before walking to a filing cabinet and bringing out a folder. He sat again before speaking. "I've managed four land purchases for Isla in the last five years. They are all in here. If I run out of time, I'll get Jenny to copy the relevant information for you to take away."

Suzanna smiled in acknowledgement. 'That wasn't so difficult, was it?' she said to herself. "Thank you, Mr Stonewall; that would be most helpful." She opened the folder and scanned the documents within; too numerous to take in within the next quarter of an hour. Suzanna looked across at Stonewall, who had relaxed into his chair after handing over the folder. "I think it would be best if I took away copies."

She handed the folder back to Stonewall, who immediately stood and walked out of his office. Suzanna could hear him talking with his assistant but couldn't make out what he was saying. On returning, he remained standing.

"Jenny has made a start on the copying. If you wouldn't mind waiting in the outer office? I need to prepare for my next meeting."

Suzanna stood and shook his hand. "Thank you for your cooperation, Mr Stonewall. You mentioned that Isla Muir was in on Friday. What was the purpose of her visit?"

"She wished to discuss the potential for making an under-asking-price offer."

"Your role is to represent the seller and gain the best price for the land. Am I right?" She said, leading him.

"Yes, of course. The owner of the land is my client. My duty is to them."

"So, what advice did you give Mrs Muir?" Suzanna's eyebrows rose and hovered as she awaited his response.

"Obviously, I couldn't suggest a price that might be acceptable. All I could say was there was no interest from other parties and the

Reynolds would be open to offers."

Suzanna locked eyes with Stonewall. "And your expectation would be that Mrs Muir would subsequently engage your services to sell the remaining land, after she had hived off the piece she wanted to develop?"

"Yes. Just what are you suggesting here?" Stonewall responded irritably.

"I'm suggesting nothing, Mr Stonewall. Just exploring possibilities."

As she exited his office, she turned back. "Just one last thing: where were you between 6 a.m. and 10 a.m. yesterday morning?"

Suzanna could see his eyes looking skyward as he relived yesterday morning. He pulled a ticket out of his wallet and returned his attention to Suzanna before replying. "I left home about 7:30 and drove to Lockerbie. Caught the 8:14 to Glasgow. My client's office is near the train station, so it makes sense to use the train. And I can work while I'm travelling."

"Can anyone confirm you were at home between six and seven thirty?"

"Yes. My wife. She was still at home when I left for the station."

Suzanna leaned towards Stonewall as he offered her the sight of his train ticket, which appeared to confirm his travel arrangements. "Thank you. If you could just let me have your client's name for the records, I'll trouble you no more," Suzanna responded, concealing her thoughts. They may need to check with his wife and do background checks on Stonewall to eliminate him conclusively.

Armed with a name and contact number, she left his office and took a seat in the waiting area, as Jenny fed papers into their copier. Suzanna wondered what the documents might reveal.

Chapter Fourteen

Tosh slapped the local newspaper onto the desk. Its front page had a grainy picture of the crime scene, with white clad people scattered across the field. The bodies of the woman and her dog were visible as the CSIs erected the gazebo to protect the scene from prying eyes. Too late!

The headline read 'Dumfries Dog and Owner Slaughtered.' Its subtitle set the scene for the article: 'Respected local business women and her beloved golden retriever murdered on their morning walk.'

Suzanna and Carl looked down at the picture, amazed that someone from the press had got there so early. "Bloody press photographers! They've no respect for the dead or their family." Tosh boomed. "Disgusting parasites!"

"They'd publish a picture of their own dead granny if it earned them some cash or kudos," Carl added, sneering.

"I doubt that," Suzanna said calmly. "But I know what you mean." She'd seen this sort of journalism many times. "I guess it's the competitive system they operate within that encourages their behaviour. If you're ambitious, you need the scoops; the exclusive pictures. Interesting that they mention the dog first in the headline!"

Suzanna pushed the paper aside and turned it face down, ending the discussion, then briefed Tosh and Carl on the land deals Muir had completed. "I think we need to focus on the most recent deal and work back from there. Before we get started on that, what did you find from reading through Muir's files, Tosh?"

"Not a lot. Just that she'd bought land, got planning permission for a development, then sold off the rest of the land, making a hefty profit each time. Nothing jumped out at me, though. No alarm bells."

"Okay. My thinking is that she may have angered someone by her actions and her killing could be revenge. So, we need to look into those who might have lost out by the deals: the vendor, most likely. But why, I'm not yet sure. We'll need to speak with the sellers face to face. Perhaps we'll pick up on underlying issues that way. Okay?"

"Sure thing. The most recent was Gorsebank. I'll look into that," Tosh volunteered.

"Okay. What's the next most recent project, Tosh?"

"Kirkennan."

"Right. Give me the details. I'll follow up on that one."

Tosh contacted the Scottish Land Information Service to obtain details of current and previous owners for the land that Isla Muir had developed. He dropped off the Kirkennan details with Suzanna, then returned to his own desk.

The previous owners of Gorsebank were Mr and Mrs Allanach. He checked on their current address, then arranged a meeting with them and headed out.

* * *

The pebble-dashed detached bungalow had a handrail bordering the steps and a ramp that lead up to the front door. Tosh pressed the bell button, then stood back while he waited.

A slightly jowled and rotund Mrs Allanach opened the front door.

"Detective Sergeant McIntosh, I take it?" She enquired. Tosh confirmed with his ID.

"Come in, officer." She stepped back and ushered him through to the lounge. An even more overweight, grey-haired man sat in a fireside chair, a Zimmer frame beside it. He stubbed out his cigarette in an overflowing ashtray as Tosh entered. The gloomy room was still thick with swirling grey particles, like a swarm of microscopic insects waiting to attack his lungs. Tosh coughed.

"Sorry about the smoke, officer," Mrs Allanach said, opening a window to let fresh air wash away the tobacco smoke. "He's smoked all his life, and I canna get him to change his ways."

Tosh stepped close to the window to benefit from the inflow, keeping his coat buttoned up.

"Aye. You canna teach an old dog new tricks," Mr Allanach stated, his voice gravelly.

Tosh wondered whether he should mention his sixty-year-old father who had said those same words shortly before nearly dying from an aneurysm caused by smoking. He'd kicked the habit immediately after his by-pass operation.

Tosh coughed again but could tell the open window was thinning out the pollution. "As I mentioned on the phone, I wish to talk to you both about the sale of your land at Gorsebank."

Mrs Allanach spoke. "It was my father's farm. I never wanted it and there were no brothers or sisters to take it on. He hired in help in the early days and a manager when he got too old to run it himself. When he passed away, it came to me. I just wanted rid of it, so we put it up for sale."

As Tosh made notes, his mind diverted again. He'd like to have inherited a farm, or any house. They'd had to take out a maximum mortgage when he and Fiona had bought their first home. They'd had no help from their parents. Not that he blamed them. Neither set of parents had spare cash in the bank, and they both lived in modest homes. Just as well he'd received a gratuity from the Army when he left and had tucked it away in a savings account for a house deposit, instead of spending it as many of his ex-military pals had.

"For months, there were no offers for land, so we were glad when a potential purchaser eventually showed some interest. The woman struck a hard bargain and we had to let it go at much less than we'd been told it was worth."

"Aye, that's right," her husband added. "But we'd just retired, and annuity rates had taken a tumble, so my pension was going to be a lot less than expected. As Davina says, we needed it sold."

Mrs Allanach continued, "I did a bit of digging and found out she was a property developer. I've seen what she's done with past land deals and had an inkling why she was interested in our land. So, I got our agent to get her to agree that we'd get a portion of any uplift in the land's value if she got planning permission to develop it."

Tosh nodded. Very sensible, he thought. "And?"

"Well, about a year after we sold the land," Mrs Allanach continued, "she got planning permission for holiday properties on part of the land. She got that part cut away from the rest and sold the farmland on. I found out she'd got more for the farmland than she paid us for the whole lot. We never got offered a penny for the raised value of the land used for holiday homes."

The husband spoke again. "We took her to court, but the judgement went her way. Her legal team had written the clause about sharing 25% of the uplifted value with us. They had slipped in words that made the clause void. Having split up the land and not sold on the portion affected by the planning permission, we were due nothing." He paused, and when he continued, his voice gave away his disgust. "Our legal adviser evidently wasn't worth his fees because he didn't pick up on any problems with the draft contract. What a waste of space he was."

Their circumstances certainly created a motive for the shooting of

Mrs Muir. Tosh delved into their thoughts with his next question." So, I bet you're angry about that?"

"Wouldn't you be," Mrs Allanach squawked. "That woman knew full well she would be cheating us out of what the land would be worth, and she got away with it. There should have been another hundred thousand coming our way. She denied us our dues."

Motive established, Tosh pushed to uncover whether they had the means for murder. "You came from a farming family, Mrs Allanach. Did your parents teach you to shoot?"

"They tried. Every farm has a shotgun. But it was not my thing. No more than mucking out cow sheds is!"

Tosh could see the distaste written on her features. She seemed genuine in her reply, but she hadn't said she couldn't shoot, only that she didn't like to. "Do you have a shotgun?"

"No. My father had one, of course. Licensed to him. It will have been sold off, along with most of my parents' effects, when he died, or even before that. Mother had passed on just a year before him."

Now for the opportunity, he thought. "For the record, could you tell me where you were between 6 a.m. and 10 a.m. yesterday morning?"

The Allanachs looked at each other before answering in unison. In our bed until about eight o'clock."

The wife continued. "We likely finished breakfast around nine. Why are you asking these questions?"

"Have you not heard the news? Mrs Muir was shot dead yesterday morning."

Chapter Fifteen

Suzanna pulled up outside the Kelly's house, a stone-built, detached dormer bungalow. As she walked up the path, she noted the garden was uncared for. It was overgrown with grass and weeds, the hedges out of control. She tapped on the front door but there was no response. After waiting a minute, she knocked harder. Eventually the door was opened by a wizened old man.

"Sorry to trouble you, Mr Kelly. I'm DCI McLeod. I called earlier." Looking down on the elderly man, she could see his head was almost hairless, and his scalp covered in red blotches and flaking skin.

He looked puzzled, as if his brain clerk was wondering around inside his head looking for that memory. "Ah! Of course. Come on in, lass. Excuse the mess. My cleaner's due in tomorrow."

The garden's neglect was mirrored inside. If he had a weekly cleaner, they weren't doing a great job, or he was extremely messy. Fluff had collected alongside the skirting board. The hall table was covered in dust, and the carpet was dulled by ingrained dirt.

Suzanna closed the door behind her, then followed him along the corridor and into his living room. The room smelled stale. A dark oak, drop-leaf dining table sat in one corner of the room, a sofa opposite a coal fire, and a tall armchair next to the fire. Mr Kelly lowered himself into the chair and indicated Suzanna should sit on the sofa.

She brushed off some muck from the seat cushion before sitting.

Her hand felt dirty. "You're on your own then, Mr Kelly," Suzanna said, observing his response.

"Aye, lass. Lost me wife three years back." He spoke matter-of-factly, having evidently accepted the loss. "Murdina was ten years younger than me. I was a lucky man catching such a prize." But as he thought back, his face dived, sadness taking over. "I did'nae expect she'd die afore me." He sighed deeply. "Telly's me only company nowadays."

When Suzanna responded, her voice was soft, sympathetic, steering the conversation where she needed it to go. "As mentioned, when I phoned, I wanted to have a chat with you about the land you sold off at Kirkennan three years ago. Did you live there before you sold it?"

There was a moment of silence before Kelly spoke. "Aye. Murdina and I had our home there for forty years. She used to keep a few animals: sheep, goats, chickens and guinea fowl. She loved her animals. Cared for them as if they were her own children. And looked after the land like it was her back garden. I suppose it was, really. Her garden, I mean. An enormous garden..."

Kelly continued, "I gave up work fifteen years back. Took me pension early, because I got fed up with working away from home, on tother side of the country. It's a long way from Redcar to Dumfries... I used to help her out with the animals, but it was still *her* thing. I didn't share her love for the creatures." A single tear glistened in the corner of his left eye as he reminisced. He wiped it away before continuing.

"It wasn't long before the arthritis kicked in and I could'nae help her anymore. The Lord took her young. Just sixty-seven. I reckon he did it to punish me. She'd always gone to the kirk, but I never set foot inside it. Couldn't be doing with all that religious stuff and cold, hard, upright pews."

He paused, and Suzanna imagined his mind wandering around, looking for his next point. She waited patiently for him to continue.

"There was no point in me staying out there by meself," he said eventually. "So, I sold up. The house was not in a good state. They found loads of stuff needing doing and offered me much less than the agent had said it would be worth. But with no other interest, I sold it and bought this place. There's more folk around me here and taxis within the town are much cheaper than if I'd stayed out at Kirkennan."

"What do you think about Kirkennan having been developed into a holiday site?"

"She's made better use of it than I could ever have done. Although the woman probably did me out of what the property was really worth, I couldn't get upset about it. We'd bought it for a few thousand pounds. Inflation soon turned our mortgage into a minor outgoing. So, we did well out of it, anyway. We were happy there all those years. And, as they say, a house is only worth what someone is willing to pay for it."

* * *

Suzanna and Tosh had steaming mugs in their hand when they sat down to talk in the incident room. Suzanna took a sip of her black coffee, then wished she'd picked up a real coffee from one of the local cafes down the street from the station. Instant coffee just didn't do it for her.

Tosh slurped his tea, then asked, "So, you reckon there's no chance the previous owner of Kirkennan could have anything to do with Muir's murder?"

"Correct. The old guy, Kelly, had difficulty shuffling to the door. No way would he have been able to track down the victim in the countryside and shoot her and her dog. This looks like a sheep-worrying gone wrong to me," Suzanna concluded.

She watched her colleague drink again from his mug. The only tea she'd ever drunk and enjoyed was black tea, without milk or sugar.

Just the one occasion in her life. At a tea plantation in the foothills of the Himalayas, near Darjeeling. She'd done a plantation tour with a small group and learned that the tea in our tea bags was the dust left over after they had boxed the good stuff. The dregs from the process.

Tosh swallowed, then responded. "Aye, you may be right, but I'd say Mrs Allanach is a possibility. She's still angry about the deal and justice not having been done in court. The husband didn't seem so bothered by it. I reckon he's accepted the loss, but she's still got a chip on her shoulder about it. But they both say they were at home around the time of the murder. Unless we can prove that to be a lie, we've nothing on them."

"Okay. They have motive - revenge. But apparently not the opportunity or means. Get an ANPR check done on any cars they own. I take it there are some ANPR cameras in Dumfries?"

"Aye. A few," Tosh responded.

"And check the gun registration records for Mrs Allanach's father. We need to know if his gun *was* sold off and where it is now. Where's Carl, by the way?"

Just then, the door opened, and Carl walked in carrying a paper bag, the smell of pastry and meat wafting from it. "Hey Carl. Did you get us some snacks as well?" Tosh asked with a grin.

"I didn't know when you'd be back. I've just got a Scotch pie. I don't think that will go far if we share it."

Suzanna turned her nose up at the idea. "Even if you bought a bag full, you'd have them to yourselves. I'm a veggie."

Both men looked at her with shocked expressions. She'd seen it many times. They'd be asking themselves how she could be a veggie, given her muscular body. Meat eaters often had the view that vegetarians were pasty-faced, skinny little things.

"What have you been up to while we were away, Carl?" Tosh asked.

"Having a wonderful time looking at the victim's browser history and emails. Tedious, or what!"

Suzanna turned her chair. "And what have you found, Carl?"

"Can you give me five minutes please, ma'am? I'd like to eat my pie while it's warm, if you don't mind."

"Okay." She turned back to her desk and continued what she'd been doing.

Chapter Sixteen

Carl finished munching on his Scotch pie, swallowed the last mouthful and wiped his lips with the back of his hand. "Ma'am. Sarge. I can brief you now if you like?"

They gathered around Carl's desk, the aroma of pastry and meat still hanging in the air, and waited, hoping something useful would emerge. Tosh leaned in, unable to contain his curiosity. "What did you find in her search history?"

"I trawled through the last twelve months of her browser history. Records prior to that had been wiped clean. She had been fixated on expensive holidays - cruises, long-haul stuff, and some Greek islands - but nothing budget-friendly like Benidorm or the Canary Islands. She had looked at Madeira, though."

"Okay, we get the picture," Tosh jumped in abruptly; impatient. "Posh holidays. No cheap breaks like you and I would take."

Suzanna glanced sideways at the sergeant. She'd not seen this side of the man. Carl nodded, then continued. "Apart from the lavish holidays, she had browsed loads of women's clothing websites. High-end brands mostly. But the bulk of the browsing had been related to her business. So, building suppliers, caravan and lodge manufacturers, marketing consultants, and land sale searches. She had restricted her browsing to the Dumfries and Galloway area, although there were some companies just over the border in Cumbria as well. But she'd also searched for kinky stuff."

"What, precisely?" Suzanna enquired, her head tilting to the side in curiosity.

Carl's face turned beet red as he responded, his voice faltering. "You know... sex toys, sexy underwear, that sort of thing. And she had a thing for erotic literature."

Suzanna's eyebrows raised momentarily. Could this interest in sex be a hint at something relevant? Had she wanted to enrich her marital relationship, or could she have been looking elsewhere for excitement? She encouraged Carl to continue. "Okay. Anything else of note in the search history?"

"No. That about covers it. I've made a list of all the firms related to her business but didn't bother recording the holiday and sexy stuff."

"Why not?" Tosh asked. "If nothing else, it might have been interesting." Carl and Suzanna looked at Tosh, surprise written on their faces.

Tosh noted their reaction, so quickly changed the subject. "And the emails?" he prompted.

Carl paused for a moment before responding. "As you can imagine, there are thousands of emails on the computer. Fortunately, she was well organised and had Outlook folders for multiple topics. I concentrated on the business related folders and printed out a list of them. I've not looked at any of her personal stuff yet."

Carl slid the list across the desk. "She had generic folders for accounts, marketing, land, planning and buildings. There were also project-specific folders, such as Gorsebank, Kirkennan, etc. I concentrated on the project folders first. There were multiple emails between her, the agents, and the solicitors. Nothing jumped out at me, but when I delved into the planning folder, I came across correspondence between Mrs Muir and numerous other people. All members of the planning committee."

Suzanna's eyes lit up in expectation of a useful lead.

"From what I can see," Carl went on, "she had taken them all to lunch or dinner. And she took some of them to events. I can't confirm her company funded all these jaunts, yet, but checking the accounts might reveal something."

Suzanna nodded, impressed. She responded enthusiastically. "Okay. Well, *that* is interesting. It seems she was buying favours from the planners, then; greasing the wheels for her projects."

Suzanna pondered for a minute, then - before announcing what *she* thought they should do - asked Tosh and Carl, "What do you two believe we should do with this information?"

Tosh responded. "Whether what's been going on is relevant to the murder, we don't know, but it could certainly point towards illegal goings on. Perhaps fraud or corruption. I think we should investigate further."

"Yeah, and it's possible that one of these planners had a falling out with Mrs Muir." Carl suggested. "Maybe she pushed them too far to support an application?"

"Good points, guys." She could see they were thinking along the right lines, but maybe needed direction on the actions to take next. "First thing we need to establish is whether any of these planners have formally declared an interest in an application, prior to the decision being discussed or decided. Given their association with the applicant, they should all have done so."

"I'll contact the council then," Carl said, "and get copies of the planning meeting minutes. It should be a standard agenda item for members to declare their interests."

Impressed by Carl's knowledge, she continued. "Good idea, Carl. We'll need that information prior to interviewing them. As well as that, we should seek sight of the council's gifts register. If any official accepts a gift from someone outside the council, they are required to register this gift. That includes gifts in kind like hospitality, as well as actual items."

Carl interjected, "I may as well request that at the same time as the declaration of interests."

"Tosh, run background checks on all of them. Once we have that information, we'll confront them. Put them on the spot and see if any crack."

"Oh, by the way," Carl added, before they broke up to get on with their new tasks, "the pathologist is ready to brief you any time you like, ma'am."

* * *

The clonking of their shoes on the hard floor echoed off the walls as they walked over to where the victim lay on a stainless-steel table. Typically, the room reeked of disinfectant and blood. She had been in too many mortuaries, viewing cold naked bodies. It was the nature of her role. She'd learned to cut off her emotions, and to look objectively at the evidence. But she still had to brace herself before each viewing.

Muir's abdomen was a mess, although no longer bloody. The Pathologist, Richard Michaels, led her through his report. There was little new to be learned. A close quarters shotgun blast that had ripped her open, tattering both breasts and fragmenting most of her organs. He hadn't been able to tighten up on the time of death. The shotgun pellets had been sent off for forensics analysis. And blood samples had been sent to the hospital lab to be tested for anything out of the ordinary.

Suzanna thanked Richard for his report. She remained with the body as he returned to his office. How would her assailant have gotten so close before firing the weapon? A shotgun is not easily hidden. Perhaps she knew the person who had committed this crime and didn't see the danger. Otherwise, she would have run away from the threat and been shot in the back. She returned to her earlier theory. If it was a sheep-worrying gone bad, who would have been the person pulling the trigger? Jack Reynolds? Surely it *had* to be the person who owned the sheep!

Chapter Seventeen

Suzanna dumped her bag and coat on her desk, then went for a coffee. She'd stopped off at the supermarket to pick up some better-quality instant. It would have to do for now, because there was no cafetiere or filter machine. Returning to the incident room with her hot mug, she called to Carl and Tosh to gather around the incident board.

She addressed her new and rather small team. "Right. I just want to review where we are. Carl, what progress have you made?"

"I've been in touch with the council about their declarations of interest and their gifts register. They said they'd photocopy the relevant pages but wouldn't let the register leave the building without an official request. I'll head there now and pick up the copies."

"Check the copies against the registers while you're there, in case they accidentally or purposely miss copying a page."

"Will do." Carl nodded and made a note in his book.

"Tosh?"

"I've initiated background checks on the planning officials, including bank statements going back five years. It will take the banks a day or two to get those to us." Tosh glanced down at his notes. "None of the officials have criminal records. A couple have traffic offences logged against them but that's all." He looked up, signifying he'd finished speaking, wondering whether his new boss would be satisfied.

Suzanna thanked them both, then briefed them about the pathologist's report.

"Well, we knew that already," Tosh commented disdainfully, rolling his eyes.

"Right. What's next?" Suzanna asked, then pondered in silence. With no ideas coming from the men, she answered her own question. "We can't interview the planning officials until we have those council documents, so you'd best get away now, Carl."

"Happy days!" He responded, then grabbed his coat and left.

Suzanna looked perplexed by Carl's reply, noting the unusual acknowledgement of the tasking. "Tosh, did we get ANPR results for the Allanach's cars?"

"Ah! No. I'll chase them." Tosh went to his desk and picked up the phone.

That was a quick meeting, Suzanna thought. She stared at the board, going through the what, why, when, where, how and who list.

They knew *what* had happened, but still didn't know *why*. They knew *where* the murder had occurred, *when* and *how*, but the *who* was also unknown? And they still didn't know how the murder came about. Yes, she'd been shot with a shotgun but how did the murder occur? The angry landowner theory remained a strong possibility.

Any other scenario required the murderer to have known she walked her dog early in the morning. And they would have had to follow her to Caulkerbush in another vehicle. Most owners walk their dog first thing in the morning, of course, but often just a quick walk around the block, to let the pet do its business. Taking long walks in the countryside early in the morning was less common. And shooting someone with a noisy shotgun out in the open was a risky way of killing. It just didn't seem right.

Suzanna left Tosh at his desk in the station and went for a walk to free her mind from the building's confines. Her brain worked better when she was reclined in a comfortable chair or outside and walking.

She marched to the road's end, the air cool, her mind as blank as the overcast sky, then turned right. She passed the long, red sandstone Academy building. As she wandered the streets, she tried to focus on the case, but there were too many distractions: the noise of car and truck engines, tyres rolling over the asphalt, pedestrian crossings beeping, people talking. She couldn't shut them out.

When she reached Nunholm Road, the traffic quietened and the River Nith's bank met with the road, clear of the trees that had masked it along the main road. The houses opposite all seemed to have their own little riverside gardens. Sadly, no park benches to rest on and watch the water stream by. She sat on a garden wall, and swung her legs over to face the river, the stone abrading her hands as she swivelled.

She brushed off the dirt and moss on her palms, then looked out across the countryside beyond. It was flat terrain by the river, a floodplain. But beyond, the land rose gently to distant hills.

She settled her mind and let it wander... We haven't run the victim's contact list through the criminal records database yet. Perhaps she might have an association with an undesirable?

What about the husband? Have we checked his alibi? Could he have killed his wife? Does he have a motive? We'll need to verify his whereabouts and do a background check.

Her mind continued to drift. Who would have known Isla Muir was walking in that location that morning? Someone who knew her well and knew of her plans. Statistically, it's usually someone close to the victim who commits the murder.

Are there any other relatives who might gain from her death? Does she have a will? That might provide clues.

Satisfied that she had identified fresh lines of inquiry, Suzanna headed back to the station, striding along the road for efficiency and exercise. She realised that, so far, they'd not been properly documenting their theories and findings other than on the incident board. It's too easy to miss something if it's not logged and monitored.

On return to the station, Suzanna went straight to the board and wrote up the questions she'd just raised while on her walk.

Tosh joined her and read the extra notes. "Good questions, ma'am. I'll get on to Mr Muir's hotel, and initiate background checks."

"We'll also need to talk with family and friends. Might they have noticed any tension between Mr and Mrs Muir?"

"That might take a while, ma'am. Not enough boots on the ground."

"Yes. I'm aware we're short staffed. I'll get on to the top brass at your HQ in the morning. They'll have gone home, or be on the golf course by now," she said after looking at her watch.

Tosh nodded agreement. "By the way, we've had feedback from the ANPR system about the movement of the Allanachs' cars."

Chapter Eighteen

Suzanna's phone pinged. There was a message from James. 'Are you free to talk?'

She had just settled down in the compact armchair that was squashed into the hotel room's bay window. A cup of instant coffee sat on the side table, ready to drink. She adjusted her position in the chair. There was barely enough width to fit her neat body, let alone anyone carrying a bit of weight. She took a sip of her drink, then picked up the phone and called James on WhatsApp.

He answered on the second ring. "Hi Suzanna. How are you?"

He seemed happy to see her, his tone gentle and loving.

"Okay, thanks, James. Have you forgiven me for abandoning you at the church?" she asked, hoping the answer would be positive.

"You make it sound like you left me at the altar, with a ring in my pocket, as you ran away dressed in flowing white." He smiled.

Suzanna was reassured by his words and smile. "Not pissed off at *all*?" She finger-brushed her hair back behind her ears.

"A little. You put work first again. Just as well I had cash for a taxi home." James looked serious.

Suzanna tried to justify her leaving him. "Sorry, James. When the call to duty comes, I can't refuse."

"Well, maybe you should learn to say no. They could have found someone else, if you had."

"I guess you're right. I just can't help myself," Suzanna admitted. " Anyway, how did The Alpha Course go? Did you enjoy the session?" She said, diverting James' questioning.

"It was an excellent talk. That fella, Nicky Gumbel, was impressive. Had an amazing testimony. He'd been training to become a barrister, and sharing accommodation with another legal student. Apparently, the other guy, who'd become his close friend, had started going to a Christian group and was embarking on a course. Nicky was an atheist at the time and was afraid his friend might get brain-washed. So, he went along with him to make sure that didn't happen. Being a good, legally minded chap, he thought he had best arm himself with the evidence to fight his case. He read the four Gospels. Incredibly, he became convinced of the truth that Jesus was the son of God and he had given his life, so those who repent of their sins would be forgiven."

James paused, then exclaimed, "He ended up becoming an Anglican vicar! And he now leads the world's biggest Christianity teaching pro-gramme. I'll definitely be going to the next session." His enthusiasm level rose another notch. "Oh! And there was one thing he said that grabbed me. 'Church is not an organisation you join; it is a family where you belong, a home where you are loved and a hospital where you find healing.' I think that's brilliant."

Suzanna was silent as she absorbed what James had said. It fitted with what her mother had told her several years back. She recalled all the nudges about going on the Alpha Course that she'd been getting from various sources. Her parents and sister, of course, and James. But also, the leaflet Mairi had brought back from her trip to Iona, when she'd gone to interview a person of interest and a potential victim in their last case.

"Sounds like it was an excellent session. I wish I hadn't cut and run so quickly, now. If it's not too late to join in when I get back to Edinburgh, I'll definitely give it another try."

"Great." James' face brightened as he enthused at her response, then changed the subject. "Anyway. How's the investigation going?"

"Fine. We're making progress. You know I can't tell you anything about the case."

"Sure. Of course. I understand. Didn't expect you to. Just wanted to know how you were getting on. How's the hotel?"

"Okay, as far as hotels go. As usual, nowhere to sit for more than half an hour without getting backache. I guess they want to encourage guests to go to the bar and spend their money, rather than sit in their rooms. And the room only has single beds. They said they'd move me to a double room after the first night but took a booking for a couple to stay and couldn't move me after all. I'll move out tomorrow. I've found a place that seems ideal. Out of the town, so a bit further to travel to the station, but it should provide me with the space and privacy I need."

"Great. Any idea when I might get to see you next?"

"Too early to say at the moment. We have to progress things quickly as trails can be washed away."

James jumped in. "A bit like tracking outlaws in the deserts of North America, in the western movies. Are you the Native Indian, bending down to examine marks in the dust, or the marshal leading his team of deputised townsfolk?"

Suzanna smiled at James' simile. "A bit of both, I suppose. But certainly not townsfolk. The local detectives, although not experienced in murder cases, had already got things going in the right direction before I arrived, and they're doing a good job. We are a bit short staffed, though."

"So, when are you going to call in support?"

"Actually, I'll be making requests tomorrow."

"Good to hear it, Suzanna. The sooner you get the case wrapped up, the sooner I'll have you back in Edinburgh."

"Look. If the case drags on, I could take a Sunday off. Perhaps you could drive down and we could have time together here?"

"Sounds great. I'd love that."

They said their goodbyes and Suzanna dug into her bag. She'd stuffed the Alpha booklet there when she'd hurried away from the church. She started reading the first section. *Christianity. Boring, Irrelevant and Untrue?*

Chapter Nineteen

Wednesday 27th April

Suzanna approached the hotel reception. Its mahogany counter was decades old but well maintained, shiny from a recent polish and smooth to her touch. She looked around as she waited for the receptionist to finish his phone conversation.

"Good morning, madam. What can I do for you?" His voice was cold and business-like, not friendly. He didn't offer an apology for keeping her waiting!

"Please prepare my bill. I will check out after breakfast."

"But you're booked in for the whole week," he exclaimed. "There will be cancellation charges."

"There will be no such charges," Suzanna stated. "I booked a double room, but the hotel has failed to provide one. Therefore, I'm within my rights to leave."

The receptionist gawped at her. She turned and strode into the dining room.

The night before, she had researched other options and found a log cabin overlooking the Solway Firth that was available, so she'd booked it.

Suzanna was excited by the idea of having a temporary place of her own on the coast. No one could complain about the move, as the new accommodation was cheaper than staying in a hotel or B&B. And the money spent on paying for breakfast was a waste. She never ate fried breakfasts. Just a cup of coffee and a bowl of muesli was all she needed or wanted.

* * *

Suzanna called Dumfries and Galloway Police HQ and discussed the allocation of additional resources with Divisional Chief Superintendent Gillian White. As a rural force, they had few trained detectives to draft in, so Suzanna agreed to speak with Edinburgh to see if they could spare one. It would suit her to do so, anyway, as it would be someone she already knew well and could rely on.

As Suzanna was about to hang up, the Chief Superintendent asked, "You're obviously not a Scot, Suzanna. Hope you don't mind me asking, where *are* you from?"

It was a question she'd had difficulty with many times in the past, but the answer still didn't immediately come to her. She thought about her past again. As the daughter of a Royal Air Force officer, she'd had no single, stable home, a place to say she was *from*. She had attended schools in different countries before heading off to boarding school. 'Where *am* I from?' she silently asked herself. 'A nomad. One base or another around the UK and overseas. No town to which I can return to when my work years are over, and I want to settle down with old friends and family around me. No familiar stomping grounds. My old school chums are scattered around the world, as far as Australia.'

'So, where am I from? What was it Paul Young sung? Wherever I lay my hat, that's my home! I guess I'm like that. Of no fixed abode... No, that's not true. I have a lovely apartment in Edinburgh. I have great work colleagues. And many lovely friends there. I might be English, but Edinburgh *is* my home. I've lived there longer than any other place.'

Gillian White spoke again. "Suzanna? Are you still there?"

"Yes. Sorry. Still here. I'm from everywhere and nowhere, ma'am. My father was in the Armed Forces," she responded. "But now Edinburgh is my home." She ended the call, promising to phone her Edinburgh boss, Superintendent Alistair Milne, immediately.

He answered on the second ring. "Hi Alistair. How's Edinburgh?"

"Fine between the showers. How's it in Dumfries?"

"The same. But I'm sure you'll know I didn't call to chat about the weather. How's the team fairing up with me absent?"

"Exceptionally well, of course. You've trained them well, Suzanna. Fortunately, we don't have any murders right now, so it's just the routine burglaries, muggings, etc. How's the investigation going?"

"We're making good progress but hampered by lack of manpower."

"So, you're thinking of stealing one of your team away, then?" Alistair responded with foresight.

"Yes, I had Mairi in mind. I know it's my team, but I wanted to check that you're okay with it?" Suzanna respected and liked Alistair. He was probably the best boss she'd ever worked for.

"It should be fine. I'll leave it with you to talk it through with Una Wallace. The sooner you get the case wrapped up, the sooner we'll have you back," Alistair replied, his smile evident in his tone.

"Thanks Alistair. I'll get onto her straight away."

Suzanna ended the call and immediately dialled Una's number.

* * *

Una answered her phone at the first ring. "Edinburgh CID. DI Wallace speaking?"

"Hello Una, it's the boss."

"Oh! Hi boss. How's it going down in Dumfries?"

"Good, but we're short staffed. There's only me, one DS and one DC, and a lot of ground to cover. That's why I was calling."

"I could jump in my car and shoot down straight away, if you like. It's fairly quiet here."

"Thanks for the offer. It would be great to have you with me on the case. But I don't want to bring in another officer above the locals. DS McIntosh is doing a fine job, and I don't want to undermine him. I was thinking Mairi would make a good addition to the team. She's got the skills and experience I need right now."

Suzanna waited as Una considered the idea. "Should be fine, boss. I'll have a chat with her. I've no problem releasing her. As I said, it's quiet, but I don't know what personal commitments she might have. I'll call you back in a few minutes if that's okay?"

"Sure thing. Glad to know you're thinking about her welfare. It's all too easy to treat people as assets instead of humans, isn't it?" Suzanna said, in coaching mode. It came naturally to her. Developing her team and getting them to perform at their best was her prime responsibility.

Una hung up but good to her word, called back a few minutes later.

"Hi boss. Mairi's good to go. She'll have to go home to pack a bag but should be with you by mid-afternoon." Una sounded cheery. Happy.

"Great. Thanks, Una." Suzanna paused. "How are you doing?"

"Fine, thanks. I was lucky the knife didn't do any lasting damage, although my fitness isn't back to where I'd like it to be. It's good to be back in the thick of things." Una went quiet, as her mind thought back. "The period stuck at home convalescing was boring and not good for my mental health. Better to be busy and involved, I believe."

"Totally agree, Una." Suzanna was glad Una was back at work. "Look, I'll let you go. I need to get back to the case."

Suzanna pressed the red button on her phone. Next job was to speak with Tosh's boss, the station's inspector.

* * *

She reached the office door of Tosh's boss and noticed his name plate; Inspector Ferguson. She froze. Could he be related? Surely not. Just then a uniformed inspector came round the corner.

"Looking for me?"

"If you are Tosh's boss, then yes. I'm DCI McLeod." She extended her hand.

"Ed Ferguson. Pleased to meet you, finally. I was out of the station yesterday. A big gathering at the HQ. Come on in."

He went into his office and pulled a couple of chairs out, then sat in one next to the spare, rather than sit behind his own desk. A good sign, Suzanna thought.

"Inspector... Ed... Ferguson," she said. Ferguson looked puzzled.

"You're not the same Ed Ferguson who served in the Army with Tosh, are you?"

"One and the same. We're old muckers. Same troop. Amazing that we've ended up serving together here."

"You didn't have a father or uncle in the police, did you?"

"Na! I'm the first from my family to have joined the force."

Suzanna was very pleased to hear there was no connection to her old nemesis.

Ed continued. "My father and brothers were normally on the wrong side of the law. Have to admit, I had a run in with the red caps a few times while I was in the Army, as well. But nothing criminal, just contrary to army regulations. Sorry, if you don't know what red caps are; they're the Royal Military Police."

"I'm familiar with the term. The RAF police have white caps. My father was an RAF officer."

Ed's eyebrows rose. "A scaly brat, then."

"Yes." Suzanna resisted the urge to roll her eyes.

"How's the Isla Muir case going?" Ed asked.

"We're making progress but hampered by lack of resources. I've just called in one of my DCs from Edinburgh, but we need more assistance." She looked at the inspector in expectation and wasn't disappointed when he responded.

"Okay, I get your drift. You're looking for one of my guys to join your team. I tell you what, I have a PC who's quite sharp. Perhaps he'll make a detective one day. It would do him good to have exposure to a case like this. I'll pull him off his response duties tomorrow and get him to report to you."

Suzanna smiled. "Great. What's his name?"

"PC Logan Stevens."

Chapter Twenty

Davina Allanach sat on the other side of the interview room table. She stared directly and unwaveringly into Suzanna's eyes, as if trying to see her soul. Her crossed arms and pursed lips suggested a belligerent response would result from Suzanna's questions. But she had come across far more formidable people than this. Her short wavy white hair was held away from her face by sunglasses swung up and resting on her crown.

"The thing is, Mrs Allanach, you lied to my sergeant about your whereabouts on the morning of April 25th. You said you and your husband were in bed until eight that morning and finished breakfast about nine."

Allanach's lips remained squeezed together.

"Well, your car was seen passing north along the New Abbey Road at 7:50 a.m. that day. How do you explain this anomaly in your story?" Suzanna stared at the suspect, demanding a response.

But an explanation was not forthcoming.

"If there is an innocent reason, I suggest you explain why you were driving your car when you said you were in bed!"

Suzanna let the question hang, glaring at the woman, whose eyes had now diverted to look at the ceiling.

The silent pressure took its toll. "I must have been confused over the days. It was the day before we had both lain in until eight."

"Right. So, where was it you were coming back from at 7:50 on the 25th? The day of Isla Muir's murder."

Mrs Allanach faded, her arms unfolding, her lips relaxing "I'd taken a drive to the coast, to look out across the sea."

"What time did you leave home?" Suzanna asked, her tone now more mollifying.

"About seven, I guess. Martin was still in bed. In fact, I was home before he was up. That's why he will have said we rose at eight. He didn't know I'd been out."

"Did anyone see you down by the coast?"

"There was dog walker, but he never came close enough to speak to." Mrs Allanach's voice gave away her realisation that this sounded unconvincing; didn't support her story.

"My problem is that your supposedly mistaken lay-in day is not the only untruth. You said your father's shotgun had been disposed of. But we find it's still registered in his name. We assume, then, that you have kept the weapon and lied to us. My officers are currently on the way to your home to conduct a search, and if they find the shotgun, it will be checked by our forensics department. If it's found to have been fired recently, that will give us reason to believe that you used it to kill Mrs Muir. You had motive, opportunity and means."

"No, no, no, no! You'll not pin that on me!" Allanach screamed. "Yes, I was angry at Mrs Muir. She's a crook, and she deserved to be taken down a peg or two. She probably deserved what she got, given how many people she must have swindled! But there's no way I killed that woman."

"Thank you for confirming your belief that Isla Muir deserved to die. All we need now is the shotgun. When we check the weapon, will we find it's been fired recently?" Suzanna asked.

"I very much doubt it because, as I said before, I don't have the shotgun," Allanach responded pugnaciously.

Suzanna noted the challenge in the suspect's voice. "So you say! But you haven't explained yet why you rose early on the 25th, left your husband asleep, and drove out to the coast?"

Mrs Allanach looked up and met Suzanna's eyes. "My husband isn't a well man," she replied softly. "I've been worrying about him, and about my future. I tossed and turned that night and eventually gave in to the insomnia and got up, around 6:30." She paused. "You see, he's... he's got stage four prostrate cancer." She paused, her eyes breaking contact and moistening, before returning to look at Suzanna. "Despite catching the cancer late, they say there's a good chance he'll survive it. The treatment's quite effective nowadays, but there's a fifty-fifty chance he'll be gone within five years, and perhaps much sooner."

Suzanna connected with the woman, her eyes gently holding those of the suspect, her face released of its tension. Empathetically, she spoke. "I'm sorry to hear that, Davina," she said, purposely using the woman's first name. "I know how hard that must be for you."

Mrs Allanach nodded in appreciation of Suzanna's understanding words, then continued. "I never earned much of a pension, you see, and we're reliant on Martin's income. When he goes, the pension goes with him!"

"That must compound the worry." Suzanna paused, thinking. "It does, however, make your motive for revenge even stronger."

The woman seemed to age several years in front of Suzanna's eyes.

"Given your admitted motive for killing Mrs Muir, I must ask you to remain here until the search has been conducted of your home."

Suzanna left the interview room, asking the uniformed PC to make Mrs Allanach a hot drink. She had other work to do now.

* * *

Martin Allanach waddled his way to the front door, his wrap-over slippers dragging on the carpet as he shouted, "You've not forgotten your key again, have you, Davina?" He rarely needed to answer the door nowadays, as his wife always did that, and it took him an age to get there with the support of his Zimmer. Having not shaven that morning, his jaw was covered in steel-grey whiskers. He manoeuvred himself into position to reach the lock, then opened the door. Allanach's jaw dropped at the unexpected sight of two police officers.

"Mr Allanach?" The officer spoke business-like but politely. He continued before Mr Allanach responded. "Your wife is currently being interviewed at the police station and we have a warrant to search your house."

Martin Allanach's eyes widened with the shock, his mind befuddled by the news. "What do you mean, she's at the police station?" He became flustered, his eyes taking on a life of their own, randomly seeking understanding for Davina being questioned at the station. "You want to search our house? Why?" His eyes settled on the policeman who had made the announcement, his eyebrows furrowed. His lips hanging open after he spoke.

"I've not been given the details, sir. Just been instructed to search your property."

Still flustered, he replied. "Right... Well... You'd best come in." He didn't wait for an acknowledgement, instead turned away to head slowly back into his home.

Both officers removed their hats as they stepped over the threshold to follow Allanach into his living room, moving at the man's snail-like pace. Mr Allanach dropped back into his chair, the padded seat absorbing the man's weight, with a sigh. He indicated they could sit, if they wished. The officers stayed standing.

"Before you get started with the search," Allanach asked, "could one of you put the kettle on for a cuppa? I'm exhausted now." The shock, worry and exertion had sapped him of what little energy he'd had. PC Payne went straight to the kitchen. They could all do with a drink.

An hour later, having searched the house, including the loft space, the two officers moved to the garage. They lifted the up-and-over door, revealing a jungle of objects. They looked at each other, eyebrows lifting in unison. There was no clear floor space. Every inch was covered with junk, boxes, a lawn mower that looked like it hadn't been used since 1940, bicycles of a similar vintage, garden tools, ladders and other items they couldn't imagine what they were for. The place was a treasure trove for collectors. "This will take a while, then!" Payne said to his partner.

They started extracting items, moving them out onto the driveway, to give them further access into the garage. Fortunately, the rain had stopped, and the sky suggested it would stay dry for a while. As they progressed, a large item came into view near the rear of the garage, covered by a tarpaulin. They pulled it off, creating a cloud of dust. Both officers sneezed. When the dust had settled, a deep red, vintage Triumph motorbike was revealed, an aluminium boat-shaped sidecar attached. The sidecar's cab matched the motorbike's paintwork, its roof made of black canvas. Both officers exclaimed, "Wow!" The bike would be worth a fortune.

An hour and a half later, they'd gone through the entire garage and not found what they were looking for. As they went about the restocking of the garage, they realised one box had not been opened. They found a screwdriver and released the wooden crate's lid. As they slid off the cover, and unpeeled a crumpled waxy canvas, their expectations rose. Their eyes widened at the sight of the object. They looked at each other knowingly. Their report to CID would be welcomed.

Chapter Twenty-One

"Mr Allanach," PC Payne said as he entered the living room. "We'll be leaving soon. Would you like another cup of tea before we go?"

"That's very kind but Davina will be home soon, won't she?" He stared at the police officers, wishing them to agree with his presumption.

"I'm sorry to say, sir, that's not looking likely. We found a shotgun in the garage."

Mr Allanach sat bolt upright, his eyes trying to escape their sockets. "That canna be!"

"The gun will have to be tested. And we've been instructed to bag up your wife's clothes and boots for forensic testing."

Realising they were serious, Mr Allanach slouched into his chair again. His brow furrowed, and his jaw dropped open. Then he recovered and spoke. "But surely you canna suspect Davina killed that woman? She's a gentle person. I know she was angry about being ripped off by Mrs Muir, but she'd never harm her - or anyone. She does nae even kill wasps!"

PC Payne wasn't convinced that wasp-killing was relevant, but he could understand how the man must feel. He looked at Mr Allanach sympathetically. Mr Allanach sat staring into space. Worried that his wife appeared to be a murder suspect. Worried about what would happen to her, and worried about how he would cope without her.

"We'll let ourselves out once we've bagged the clothes and boots," PC Payne concluded as they left the room.

Mr Allanach called out. "I'll take that cup of tea, if it's still on offer..."

* * *

As Davina Allanach entered the blandly decorated interview room for the second time that day, she saw a large polythene bag sat on the table. Inside it was a shotgun. Her brow furrowed. She was worried and perplexed.

"Mrs Allanach, please sit." Tosh paused while she settled herself onto the hard chair.

"Officers have now completed their search of your home and uncovered this weapon. Does this look like your father's shotgun?" Tosh asked.

"Aye, it does. A Rizzini. I know that was the make of his gun, but I couldn't say for sure whether this one was his. Especially inside that bag." She leant forward, the legs of her chair squealing as it slipped backwards. She looked closer, peering at the weapon intently. "I think it probably is. There's a chunk out of the stock's side that looks familiar. It would have been from when I dropped it. That was the last time my father let me handle it. Just as well, anyway, as I never wanted to fire the gun. Where did they find it?"

"It was in your garage. The officers had to empty it to get at anything. It was stored in a screwed-down wooden crate."

The creases left Davina's brow as she relaxed. "No wonder I never saw it. Most of the junk in the garage was my fathers. We'd meant to get it to the auction rooms but never got around to it." She paused. "I thought the gun had been sold off before his death."

"Earlier today, you said all your parents' effects had been auctioned off. So, how come you're now saying you have a garage full of their stuff?"

"I should have said most of their stuff went to auction. That's true of the household effects. But the stuff in our garage had been in the barn and they missed taking it."

Tosh thought the explanation to be feasible. "At first sight, it appears the weapon hasn't been fired for many years. It was cold, devoid of oil, and lacked gunpowder smells in the barrel. However, the fact is you *were* in possession of a weapon for which you have no licence, having told us you did not have the gun."

"It may have been in my property but as your officers know, it was hardly in my possession." Davina looked defiant. "Anyways, your lot should have routinely checked the weapon was properly locked up. I remember the licensing people calling around once in a while for routine checks when I was a child. You canna blame me, when I did nae even know I had it."

Even though technically she was wrong, Tosh couldn't argue with that. He suspected she was innocent of having knowingly possessed an unlicensed firearm. He stood. "Just a minute, Mrs Allanach." He left the room and went in search of his boss. Mrs Allanach folded her arms and crossed her legs, looking both impatient and hopeful.

Tosh returned five minutes later. He sat again and looked Mrs Allanach in the eye. "I've explained the situation to my boss, and she has agreed to release you. But only after the CSI officer arrives and checks the clothes you're wearing for blood."

"That's wonderful." Her face brightened from relief. "Martin will be worried. How long will it be before I can go? I need to get Martin his dinner. I don't know how he'll cope if I'm not around."

"I can't be certain, but I'm told they're on their way here, now. Perhaps an hour? You need to know that we have taken all your clothes and boots for testing, so you won't find any outer clothes in your wardrobe when you get home. These will be returned to you just as soon as they have been checked for blood. We will, of course, retain the shotgun for forensics testing."

Mrs Allanach clasped her hands together, worry showing itself again. "What am I supposed to wear, then? If you're going to be testing these clothes as well? Will you be sending me home in one of those prison jumpsuits?

Tosh ensured he had Mrs Allanach's full attention before continuing. It was important that she understood the terms of her release. "The CSI officer will test your clothes for blood and return them to you, provided they're clear." He let his words sink in before continuing. "Letting you return home does not mean you are no longer a suspect."

Mrs Allanach's brightness faded.

"Please do not leave the area without first informing us, in case we need to speak with you again. This is a murder case." Tosh said, emphasising the seriousness of the situation. "Also, it remains possible you will be charged under the Firearms Act of 1968, for illegal possession of a firearm."

Davina pursed her lips and frowned as Tosh completed his statement. She folded her arms and rested back into the chair as the sergeant left the room.

Chapter Twenty-Two

Carl sat at his desk in the incident room, head down, trawling through the council records. It was not Carl's favoured type of work. He much preferred to be outside, visiting people and conducting interviews. His task was to scan all the planning committee meeting minutes to check the Declarations of Interest section for entries relating to Isla Muir. With meetings held monthly, there were sixty documents to trawl through.

Fortunately, the relevant section was close to the top of the first page and usually there were few entries. Those entries he found were all related to applications for a location close to the committee member's home or because they had a close personal or business relationship with the applicant. It took him only thirty minutes to skip through all sixty records, systematically moving documents from the unread pile to the read pile. Isla Muir's applications didn't show up on *any* of the declarations.

Carl moved on to checking the registration of gifts and hospitality for the same five years. He was surprised there were few entries. He wrote up his analysis on a single sheet of paper, before standing with a smile of satisfaction on his face - pleased with his efficiency at completing the work - and took his findings to the DCI's desk.

Suzanna looked up, as Carl held out his summary sheet. "Thanks, Carl." She took the sheet of paper and placed it on the desk, then scanned the contents. She immediately noted one name was absent.

"As you can see," Carl continued, "none of the committee members have ever declared any interest in applications made by Mrs Muir. There are a few logs in the register, noting where members have received gifts or hospitality from a relevant person or business. But none of those entries reference Isla Muir."

"Okay!" She was happy to hear Carl confirm her assessment of the list he'd provided. "Now we have this evidence – as well as the emails and WhatsApp messages – we can start questioning the councillors."

Suzanna paused, thinking, then turned to her sergeant. "I know we don't yet have the committee members' bank statements, Tosh, but we have Isla Muir's business account statements. Have you looked to see whether any payments were made to these people?"

Tosh placed his pen on his desk and swallowed his mouthful of coffee before answering. "Unfortunately," he splattered, having spoken too soon, "there are no references on the statements that give names against the suspect entries." He wiped his mouth with the back of his hand. "We'll need the recipients' banks statements to tie the payments together."

Suzanna ignored Tosh's coffee accident, but noticed Carl suppress a snigger. "Right, let's make a start on speaking with the suspect officials."

* * *

Suzanna's first stop was at the council offices, where the Planning Officer worked. She was shown through to his office, his face giving away his surprise at having a police detective call. "Mr Forbes, thank you for agreeing to answer some questions."

"Please sit, Chief Inspector. Would you like a tea or coffee?"

"Black coffee, no sugar, please."

Forbes left the office to arrange for drinks. Suzanna scanned the room while she waited. Blank beige walls. No window to the outside world, but obscured glass windows connecting his office to the planning office, which was flooded with light from an entire wall. No pictures of family. Nothing to give her a feel for the man.

"So, how can I help you, officer?" Forbes sat in his chair, the desk a barrier between them.

"I need to check on some details about planning procedures. Specifically, the requirements for planning committee members to declare interests in any applications."

"That's fairly straightforward, really. Before the meeting starts, committee members need to sign in and make a declaration. He dug in his filing cabinet for a declaration form. Then read out the statements on it.

"I declare and affirm that prior to this meeting, I have not been given any instruction by any person, body or political group about how to vote on the matters that are to be determined."

He continued reading, his face blank. "I also declare that I have no interests in the outcomes of these decisions that prevent me from considering them solely in the public interest, and in accordance with planning policy and the law. I intend to listen to representations and deliberate the planning merits before deciding how to vote."

Forbes passed Suzanna a copy. "Does everyone attending the meeting have to sign this document?" she asked.

"Yes." Forbes paused, then added, "well, everyone with voting rights."

"Does that include yourself, Mr Forbes?" Suzanna pried.

"No, of course not." He sat up straighter as he responded. "I'm not a voting member. I'm an adviser to the committee on planning matters but have no say in the decision."

Suzanna nodded, then asked her next question. "Am I correct

in thinking you write a report on each of the applications detailing any issues with it? And you make recommendations on whether the application should be approved, along with conditions that should be applied, if any?"

"That's correct." Forbes looked worried about the line of questioning.

"I'm not making any accusations, Mr Forbes. Just trying to understand the procedures and processes. I was surprised to hear there is no requirement for you to sign a declaration, given your significant influence on the outcome of the applications."

Forbes looked flustered. Clearly, he didn't like his integrity being questioned. "As I said, I don't have voting rights, so there's no need to declare an interest. That's just how the system works. I didn't make the rules, Chief Inspector."

"I see. So, it would be fine for you to be wined and dined by applicants and not declare this?"

"Nobody wines and dines me. That would be wholly inappropriate."

"How about coffee and cake or lunch? Would that also be inappropriate?"

Forbes' fluster turned into anger. "Exactly where are you going with this questioning? Should I call a solicitor?"

"I'm just trying to discern what's acceptable when it comes to receiving hospitality."

He slurped down the last of his tea and stood as Suzanna sipped at her coffee. "I think my time has run out, Chief Inspector. I must ask you to leave."

Suzanna looked up at him calmly. "Sit down, Mr Forbes. I am here about a serious matter. Perhaps you would like me to call in on the Chief Executive?"

Forbes sat again, a look of resignation on his face.

"I think I now understand, so let me be more specific." She took another sip of her drink, letting him hang. "On Tuesday April 12th, Mrs Isla Muir called into this office and asked to speak to you. She was told you were unavailable. At 12:20 p.m., she phoned you and spoke for two minutes. Five minutes later, you met her in the hotel just up the road, where you took lunch with her, and she paid the bill. Do you recall this event, Mr Forbes?" Suzanna said, speculating that he had met with Mrs Muir. She took another drink of her coffee, her eyes never leaving him.

His flustered face was back. He paused before replying. "Look. I can't deny that I had lunch with Mrs Muir, but it was not for her to persuade me to recommend an application. She was just seeking advice. Advice that anyone thinking of submitting an application may request. As you say, she had asked to see me, but I was committed to other appointments and all my staff could offer her was an appointment the following week. She offered to take me to lunch to ask her questions. I accepted the offer, giving up my lunch break to help her. I don't see that her paying the bill for fish and chips, and a diet coke is anything of concern. It certainly wouldn't influence me in my duties to the council." His face had transformed yet again; now indignant.

"Fair enough, Mr Forbes. I'm glad to hear that you are a man of integrity. What advice was it that Mrs Muir was seeking?"

"She wanted my opinion on whether a further holiday lodge park would likely be granted. It wasn't so long ago that the council had approved her last project at Gorsebank. I guess she didn't want to waste her energy and money on an application that wasn't likely to succeed."

"Thank you, Mr Forbes. We will be in touch," Suzanna said, as she rose to leave.

Chapter Twenty-Three

Suzanna thought Forbes had been telling the truth, although he would remain on the suspects board until the bank statements arrived. There were six councillors yet to be interviewed. All had been treated to a meal on more than one occasion over the last five years, and all events had been in the month leading up to the planning committee meeting at which her applications were to be considered. One such councillor was the Chair of the Planning Committee. She would take that one next.

Suzanna parked in one of the visitor slots outside the J Bryce Haulage Ltd's offices. The large yard, mostly devoid of trucks, was surrounded by a six-foot-high fence. The office building was in good condition. All the windows and doors looked to have been recently double glazed. A two-year-old Bentley Continental was parked in the Managing Director's slot. She entered the reception, adorned with framed pictures of large trucks illustrating the company's history, and was shown to Bryce's office by his personal assistant.

"Councillor Bryce, thank you for agreeing to meet with me," Suzanna said, as she shook his podgy hand. It reflected his chubby face and swollen abdomen. The man's wavy hair was almost black but streaked with grey, and bushy sideburns reached to the bottom of his ears.

"Happy to oblige, Chief Inspector. I take it you're not from around here?"

"No. I'm down from Edinburgh to help out for a while."

Going by his face, it was not the answer he was expecting. They sat in soft brown leather easy chairs opposite each other in the spacious office. The leather of the chair felt gorgeously soft to Suzanna's touch. A cafetiere rested on the table between them, freshly delivered by Bryce's PA.

"I'm sure you're a busy man, so I won't waste your time skirting around the peripheries of the questions I've come to ask."

"Happy for you to get straight to the point, young lady."

Suzanna crinkled at the term used to address her. She kept her cool, even though she was annoyed by his condescending vocabulary. It was likely another way of demonstrating his superiority, like the car he drove. "Do you know Mrs Isla Muir?"

"Yes. I've met her from time to time." He looked curious. He evidently had not yet heard about her murder, or he would have been more concerned by the question.

"How would you describe your relationship with Mrs Muir?" Suzanna asked.

"Acquaintances. Not friends. We have overlapping business interests." Bryce remained calm as he responded. "She uses my trucks to bring in the caravans and lodges for her holiday parks."

"Do you recall when you last met with Mrs Muir?"

He looked puzzled by the question. The aroma of quality coffee exuded from the pot as Bryce plunged, then poured the dark brown liquid into both cups, using this action to fill the gap as he pondered his answer. "I don't recall. A couple of months ago, I suppose. Look, where are these questions leading? You said you would get straight to the point."

"Indeed, I did." Suzanna took a sip of her coffee. It tasted good. "As you don't recall, let me remind you. You had dinner with her at the

Auldgirth Inn on January 21st. Mrs Muir picked up the tab."

Bryce's brow furrowed as his eyebrows rose. "And your point is?" he responded brusquely.

"On the 28th of January you chaired the Planning Committee Meeting, at which an application of Mrs Muir's was under consideration, but you did not declare an interest and you went on to vote for its approval."

"I must have omitted to sign the declaration. Mr Forbes was busy getting all that admin stuff done before we got underway, and he must have missed me out."

"So, when we get sight of the declarations from that meeting, there won't be one signed by you?"

"I shouldn't think so. If I'd had to read and sign the declaration, it would have prompted me to declare an interest, and Forbes would have minuted it."

Suzanna stared into his eyes, seeking the truth. "Come now Mr Bryce, as chair of the committee you must have known you could not contribute to the decision on an application submitted by an associate of yours, and one with whom you had dined at her expense just a few days before the meeting? Even if you didn't sign the declaration, I find it hard to believe that your memory could be that short!"

Suzanna took a gulp of her coffee, suspecting that she wouldn't have much time left to drink it.

"I see you are effectively accusing me of fraud. I think you had better leave." He stood. "Next time you wish to speak with me, you will need to give me sufficient notice so I can call in my solicitor. Now please leave." He opened the door and called to his PA to escort Suzanna out of the building.

Suzanna finished her coffee and stood. She looked him in the eye as she replied to his assertion. "The next time I interview you, Mr Bryce, will be in the police station under caution and you will, of course, need to have your solicitor present."

She knew full well that he *had* signed a declaration but not mentioned any interests in matters to be considered at the planning meeting. Her focus for the moment, however, had to be on the murder. And until they had the bank statements, there was no obvious motive for Bryce to have killed her.

She walked past Bryce, then out of the building, having purposely ruffled his feathers. It would be interesting to see what he would do next.

* * *

Back at the police station, Suzanna's phone rang. It was Chief Superintendent White. Her tone suggested she was most unhappy about something. Without any pleasantries, White launched into what she wanted to say. "DCI McLeod, I've just received a call from Councillor Bryce accusing you of harassment and trying to trick him into admitting guilt without first having cautioned him."

'Good afternoon to you too,' Suzanna spoke silently.

"The councillor is a powerful man in this neck of the woods and well respected. But I'd like to hear your side of the story."

Suzanna frowned. Despite the offer for her side of the story, it sounded to her as if the Chief Super had already made up her mind.

"Interesting," Suzanna responded. "I wondered what he might do following my visit. He's clearly afraid of the consequences of his behaviour. And by the sound of it hoping a little pressure from the top will get me to lay off." She paused.

"The thing is, ma'am, I already have evidence that Bryce has accepted hospitality in breach of the code that, as a councillor, he is required to follow. This can lead to disqualification from holding any public office for a period of up to five years. That's probably the first reason he's scared. He won't want to lose his influence in the council and see his status trashed. But it's going to happen."

"And the second thing?" White still sounded officious.

"Once we have hands on the bank statements we've requested, we may have evidence of bribery, which, of course, is a criminal offence that could see him doing jail time. Corrupt acceptance of a gift or hospitality can lead to a heavy fine or up to seven years' imprisonment."

"What's going on here, McLeod?" the Chief Super said reprovingly. "You were attached to us to investigate a murder. How come you're investigating corruption?"

Suzanna kept calm, despite the Chief Super's accusatory tone. "We have yet to identify a motive for the killing. One line of inquiry, given that Muir is a property developer with multiple controversial projects, is that she may have made someone angry, either through cheating someone out of what their property was worth or because she has threatened someone. All her projects have slipped through planning with little objection from the committee members, even though there had been much public objection to them. Hence our delve into the planning committee."

"I see!" the officer's tone remained challenging. "Go on."

"Well, it turns out that six of the committee members have received undeclared hospitality from the victim shortly before her applications were considered and all of those councillors voted to approve the applications. Again, we have yet to ascertain whether any of them actually took any money from Mrs Muir, a bribe, or whether she has influenced them merely by paying for a meal in an expensive restaurant. Either way, those individuals should not be entrusted with decision making on behalf of the communities they serve."

"Whoa!" White bellowed. "You're suggesting that six of the councillors could be disbarred from service, not just from the planning committee, but as county councillors. There would have to be by-elections. It would be chaos in the county. I think we need to tread carefully here. Don't go arresting any of them without absolute proof and without gaining my authority. Do you understand?"

"Yes ma'am. I understand," Suzanna replied. But understanding the direction didn't mean she would be certain to obey.

Suzanna ended the call after concluding, "We must bear in mind, ma'am, any of those six councillors could have been in conflict with Isla Muir about their ongoing support of her projects, and perhaps had a motive to kill her. I will certainly keep you informed of developments."

Chapter Twenty-Four

Long-standing colleagues, Suzanna and Mairi, were chatting freely as they entered the incident room.

Tosh and Carl looked up, their eyebrows raised in unison, expressing their surprise. The DCI was a looker but Mairi was young and stunning. Curvy, tall, and gorgeous. Green eyes peered out below bleached blonde hair, framing her high cheekbones, full lips and dimpled chin. Even though Suzanna had told Carl and Tosh that Mairi was engaged, she would still be a source of distraction for the two men.

Carl stepped forward, holding out his hand, looking into her eyes; transfixed. "DC Carl Penrose. Good to have you on the team, Mairi. Welcome." He shook her hand for a little too long, before pulling back and allowing Tosh to welcome her as well. Tosh winced as Mairi squeezed his hand harder than necessary.

Mairi had seen the men eyeing her up and exchanging glances and winks. There was no way she'd allow them to think she was just a pretty face. She had proven herself over the years in uniform and the CID that she was a highly capable officer, both in combat and in detective work.

"Would you like a cuppa, Mairi?" Carl asked. "I'll see if I can find a spare mug."

"Thanks, Carl." She dug into her shoulder bag and retrieved her own mug. "I brought one with me." She smiled. "Coffee, white, no sugar. Cheers!" She passed him her mug and he headed out of the room, leaving the DCI to continue her introduction to the case.

Suzanna tasked Mairi with the office manager role, correlating all the material and entering it into HOLMES, the Home Office Large Major Enquiry System. She found it amusing that they had added in a redundant word, *large*, so the system's acronym would be HOLMES, after Sherlock Holmes.

Mairi's face fell when she heard the news. She wasn't pleased at having this role thrust upon her.

"Mairi. I can see you'd prefer to be out and about involved in the investigative work, but this is Tosh and Carl's home patch." Suzanna continued, showing sympathy in her tone and expressions. "They know it better than we ever will, and they know the people. The Office Manager's role is crucial to the efficiency and effectiveness of an investigation."

"Very true, ma'am. I understand," she said, accepting there could be no argument.

"It's the documentation of all the evidence and data that's holding us back. If you get it organised for us - and I know you're good at that - we can get on with driving the case forward. Once you get on top of it, I'll see if I can get you involved in other aspects of the investigation; okay?"

"Sure. That's a deal." She smiled at the woman who had been her boss for the last three years. The DCI had coached her to where she was now. Perhaps the rank of sergeant was within her grasp. "Once I've been briefed on the case, I'll crack on and get us organised."

"Great." Suzanna turned away but spun back when Mairi spoke again. "By the way, ma'am. Did you hear our team is to be broken up..."

* * *

Suzanna's heart was thumping in her chest as the anger-created adrenaline flowed through her body. Mairi had shocked her with the announcement about the dismantling of her team. How could Mairi have known before they had officially informed or consulted the team's leader?

She called her boss, Alistair Milne. Before he had a chance to say hello, Suzanna blasted out. "What's this Mairi tells me about my team being broken up? We spoke earlier today and you didn't mention anything. Now Mairi arrives and drops that bombshell."

"Hold on, Suzanna!" Alistair interrupted authoritatively. "I've just got back into my office. Been tied up in meetings all day, and not had an opportunity to call you. I don't know where Mairi got that from. I've not told any of your team yet."

Suzanna calmed a little. Her breathing slowed, but her face was still red.

"I'm sorry to say, though that she's right. The announcement was made official just after lunch." He paused. "As expected, a new Major Investigation Team is to be formed at the Tulliallan headquarters with half your team moving there to be part of it. It's a credit to you and the team that they want them in this new team. The MIT will take over the juicy stuff: murders and organised crime. The remnant of your team will deal with burglaries, muggings, assaults, car thefts, and drug dealing on the streets of the city."

Suzanna knew this change was coming but had not foreseen being blindsided like this. She expected to have time to decide where she wanted her career to go. She hadn't even been asked if she wanted to apply for the head of MIT, although the Chief Super had said she was a front-runner for the job, if she wanted it. Surely they would have called her first to discuss the options, before announcing the changes!

If she didn't get that job, her other option would be to take up Greg Lansdowne's offer to lead Scotland's Counter Terrorism unit. It would mean a certain promotion to superintendent. If she didn't accept the counter-terrorism job, though, it wouldn't automatically result in her getting the MIT job.

"Did they also announce who would be leading this new MIT?" Suzanna asked, her voice now less strained. She was worried that she may have missed the boat.

Alistair responded. "They've not named any individuals yet, just that it's happening in three months' time. A project manager has been appointed to lead on the setting up the new team."

Suzanna's mind was whirring as she listened to Alistair. If she rejected the counter-terrorism role *and* didn't get the MIT job, what then? She'd undoubtedly have to move. James' position as a partner in his business was not transferable. Might they have to live apart, meeting up for weekends? Would their relationship survive? Her heart skipped a beat as the thought flitted through her mind.

Alistair continued. "They said the project manager will contact you to discuss names and seek your help in planning the change."

Suzanna wondered who she would choose from her team to make that move? Who were the most talented and best suited to the role? Of the two DIs, it would definitely be Angus. More experienced, better skilled at interviewing and directing investigative strategy. Una was a good DI but needed more time to reach her peak, and of course she may not be fit to return to active duties - ever!

"I should hope so, too," she replied. "But what about the Head of MIT role?"

"They're working on the shortlist now, and I know your name is on it. They haven't said when the decision will be made but I suspect within the next two weeks. They'll need the new team head closely involved with the set-up project."

Which sergeant should it be? Suzanna wondered. Caitlin or Rab? They were both excellent at their job. Both had similar experience.

Rab had proven himself as an acting SIO, though. Caitlin had not yet stepped up to that level, even for a short period. It would be Rab.

Two out of the four DCs. That choice was much easier to make. The comic duo of Murray and Owen were sound, steady constables but may have already reached their peak. They lacked the dynamism of Mairi and Zahir, both of whom had shown outstanding courage and combat skills when faced with violent criminals. And they had proven their investigative abilities, suggesting lines of enquiry, not just carrying them out. Initiative, rather than mere obedience.

It would be those four officers she would recommend for the MIT team, and to continue working with her if she got the job. She reiterated the names in her head: Angus, Rab, Mairi and Zahir. What a team!

Suzanna's mind switched back to her conversation with her boss. "But, Alistair, I haven't yet officially put my name forward for the role!"

"Even so, I know you're on the list. If they offer you the job, you don't have to take it, of course."

Suzanna's mind returned to her dilemma. MIT or CT, what was it to be? She knew in her heart it was detective work that she loved. Tracking down criminals and having them convicted for their crimes. Terrorism was an ongoing threat. But she would not enjoy the routine of overseeing covert agents and conducting surveillance on potential terrorists. Occasional periods of wild panic - when a threat looked like becoming a reality and it would be their job to prevent the resultant carnage - would certainly be exciting. But short-term excitement, interspersed with long periods of tedium? No! That wasn't for her. They would find someone else for the role. She would take her chance at winning the MIT head position. Decision made.

"So, Alistair. How should I make it official that I want the job?" Suzanna asked, feeling less stressed, her heart now back to its resting rate. Her face's red glow had been washed away by the calm she now felt for having chosen what she wanted her future to look like.

Chapter Twenty-Five

To help Mairi get up to speed and recap on where they were, and should head next, Suzanna called the enlarged team together. Tosh had spoken with Councillor Ferrier. The outcome was like Suzanna had encountered when interviewing Councillor Bryce. Ferrier had clammed up when confronted with having met Mrs Muir and not declared this interest. They decided to leave any further interviews until after they had bank statements in their hands.

As the recap was ending, Mairi asked, "Has anyone checked the husband's alibi? I noticed that line of inquiry on the board but it wasn't mentioned."

Suzanna looked to Tosh, expecting an answer.

"Not yet. Haven't found time to follow up that line."

"I'd be happy to do that. You never know what we might find. Could surprise us," she replied.

Suzanna smiled. "Thanks, Mairi. Good to have you on the case."

"What about the couple who found the body? Have they been background checked yet?" Mairi added.

Tosh responded. "I don't believe it's worth the effort. They just stumbled upon the body. The wife, in particular, was upset by the experience and wanted to go home."

Mairi parked the idea but thought she might have a look at that when time permitted. What if the husband had committed the crime, then returned later with his wife? It would have covered up for him having been there earlier - would justify his boot prints being found at the scene!

Might he have a motive? Maybe there would be a connection. Before serving with DCI McLeod, she had just done as she was told, not taken much initiative. In fact, when she had suggested possible lines of inquiry to her previous boss, she'd been put down and told to leave the direction of the investigation to the SIO. Suzanna McLeod, however, was a different breed of detective. One she much admired.

* * *

It was incredible how quiet the roads were around here, Suzanna thought as she drove from Dumfries towards the coast. In Edinburgh, she would pass more cars in the first two hundred yards than she'd seen in the last ten miles.

She pulled off the main highway onto a minor road, the views on either side masked by hedges. As the houses were left behind, the road narrowed to become a single track with passing places. Lush green fields spread out on both sides of the lane. Trees huddled together in spinneys.

She turned onto a gravel track and followed it away from traffic, unwanted human interactions, and unwelcome smells, until a log cabin blocked her path. Stopping her car, she stepped out, breathed in the fresh sea air and looked out across the Firth towards Cumbria's Allonby Bay.

With the drive now over, the tension left her face. A sense of calmness came with the gentle wind that swished Suzanna's hair against her jaw.

She automatically locked the car - even though the risk of theft was minuscule - and left it, walking towards the water, eager to check out the beach. Pebbles crunched beneath her feet as she strolled along the water's edge. Washed-out broken branches lay discarded by the ocean, seaweed dangling like Christmas tree trimmings, adorning the wood's paleness. She lifted a small piece of the driftwood, its structure enticing her, telling her to own it, to take it home and display its rustic beauty. She gave in to the temptation, tucking it under her arm.

Suzanna looked out across the Firth, the tide on its way out. The sun headed towards the horizon on which sat a distant fishing boat. Her eyes remained locked on the scene as peace settled over her. The only noise was that of small waves rolling onto the beach, shifting pebbles, and the cry of gulls riding the winds above. The smell was that of salt and sea life. No diesel fumes or other man-made aromas.

She stood for several minutes enjoying the sensations, then shook herself as a cool breeze wrapped itself around her exposed neck. The chill motivated her into action. It was time to move into the cabin, then cook. She returned to her car, looking forward to more solitude and time to think. She grabbed her bags, turned the key in the door's lock and stepped inside.

The log cabin was spacious but cosy and smelled of seasoned wood and old smoke. It had a single living area, with bedrooms off. A log-burning stove sat in the middle of the wall, a centrepiece for sofa occupants to stare at when not head down in their books. A large, worn Moroccan rug lay between the sofas. Eclectic cushions decorated the seats. Pictures adorned the walls, with scenes of boats and seas. One frame held words, rather than an image. She stepped close and read its message.

'People are often unreasonable and self-centred. Forgive them anyway.

If you are kind, people may accuse you of ulterior motives. Be kind anyway.

If you are honest, people may cheat you. Be honest anyway.

If you find happiness, people may be jealous. Be happy anyway.

The good you do today may be forgotten tomorrow. Do good anyway.

Give the world the best you have and it may never be enough. Give your best anyway.

For you see, in the end, it is between you and God.

It was never between you and them, anyway.'

Mother Teresa.

It wasn't the first time Suzanna had seen quotes from this amazing woman, famous for having dedicated her life to helping the poor in Kolkata or Calcutta as it was known in her day. Kolkata's Park Street metro station still had pictures and quotes honouring her. Suzanna had seen them on her recent visit to the country, when she had returned to the city to track down traffickers who had subsequently murdered a young woman from West Bengal's rural Murshidabad District.

It brought back more memories. One in particular. An outreach worker with the social enterprise Suzanna had worked with in her year out from the police, had shared her testimony with a group of foreign men and women, of which Suzanna was part. The story was of how, as a Hindu teenager fleeing Bangladesh, she had been tricked by a trafficker who *kindly* offered her a bottle of Coca Cola.

The drink had been drugged and when she'd come around she was locked in a room, naked. She was in Sonagachi, one of the largest red-light districts in the world. Beaten, humiliated, raped multiple times, and her tears exhausted, the woman had eventually given in to her fate. It had been over twenty years of hell before she'd exited the sex trade with the help of the social enterprise DigniTees.

A tear trickled from the corner of Suzanna's eye. She could still see the woman. Knew her name. Had held her hand. Had seen the sadness in her soul. It had touched Suzanna. A woman and a story she would never forget. And a crime she would always passionately tackle. Many crimes had little effect on the victims, but not that of rape and forced prostitution. The women, and sometimes men, were victims every day they were enslaved. An ongoing living nightmare.

She roused herself from her recollections. It was time for food.

After a dinner of couscous with stir-fried vegetables in a chipotle sauce, Suzanna sat in an easy chair by the unlit log burner, her hands wrapped around a warming mug of coffee. She crossed her legs and snuggled into the plush cushions.

Earlier, Suzanna had found a Bible in a bedside drawer, and remembering what James had said yesterday about Nicky Gumbel's testimony, decided she too would read the Gospels. Tonight, Matthew.

Chapter Twenty-Six

Davie stood on the bleak shore, the sea having receded, exposing wooden stumps and leaving salty pools. Atop a tall post, a gull sat gazing out across the estuary to the far coast. A tree-covered promontory jutted out, stabbing the otherwise blank seabed.

Overhead, the heavy charcoal sky threatened rain, but a glimmer of light from the low sun up-lit the clouds, defying the heavenly threat, and lifting the gloom. Davie pulled his coat tighter around him, eyes fixated on where the sea met the sky; to where a fishing boat had just appeared, its silhouette hinting at work to be done by the hardy men who manned her.

The boat chugged closer, the diesel engine's thudding note carrying faintly across the still water. This channel, separating the two countries' coasts, had witnessed many a battle in years past. Two thousand years ago, the Romans had built fortlets along the Cumbrian seaboard, with lookout towers a mile apart. Evidence of these ancient fortifications remained, Davie knew.

Despite the Roman fortifications, Scottish raiders had crossed the Firth, raping, pillaging homes and stealing sheep. And later, when taxes stole the profits of importers, entrepreneurs had turned to smuggling their produce, landing their commodities at other locations along the coast. In small bays and creeks, where the Revenue men couldn't see.

Davie watched through binoculars as the fishermen paused on their journey to lift pots and cast them back into the sea. He knew lobster fishing didn't normally extend this far into the Firth. But the crew had reason to travel further today.

As the sun set into the watery horizon, Davie smiled as he saw the boat deploy its final pot and turn back towards Maryport harbour, along the Cumbrian coast. A harbour that in the eighteenth and nineteenth centuries had been a hub of shipbuilding and trade between England and the Americas. But Davie wasn't there to admire the scene or reminisce about its history. He was expecting a delivery. He was an importer and distributor of a product that was in high demand. A product that would make him a rich man.

Davie hadn't done well at school, and the work he found when he left education – as early as he was allowed – was unskilled and low paid. Subsequent jobs were similarly poorly paid and hard graft. Life hadn't been good to him in those years. He had to share basic accommodation with other young men who shared his lack of income. The flats and terraced houses were always tips. No one could be bothered to clean.

Moving from one job to another, Davie had never learned a trade; hadn't gained useful skills. He'd been stuck in a rut. A rut leading to just another crap job. Until he'd become a courier for a secretive trader. That's when the money had started to roll in. He'd become more streetwise. A dodger, like the young guy in Dickens' Oliver Twist story. He had moved up the rankings as he gained experience, proved himself, became successful in his role. And now he was his own boss.

Davie sighted the buoy with a compass and noted the bearing from his current position before getting into his car. He kept the buoy in his sights as he moved up the coast to another waypoint from where he plotted the buoy again. He had to be certain of its location. It would be dark by the time he emptied the lobster pot of its valuable contents into his small black inflatable boat.

Now his sponsor was out of the picture, he was fully in charge. He was the one taking all the risks, handling the merchandise and at risk of arrest. It was his business. And now the profit would be all his!

* * *

It was gone midnight when Davie pulled up in the car park at Carsethorn. The lights were off in all the houses. Even the Steamboat Inn was silent and dark. He would need to be quiet when closing car doors, so as not to be spotted by curious residents. He didn't want anyone noticing his little sea trip.

Davie pulled the inflatable dinghy from the back of his Land Rover and carried it quietly to the beach, breathing in the salty sea air, then returned for the oars and the outboard motor before easing the tailgate closed. He'd already donned his black wetsuit. He zipped it up and had to suppress a cry as he caught chest hairs in the teeth.

Returning to the beach, he went to work with the hand-pump, the dry neoprene of his wet-suit sticking to his skin. The little dinghy soon inflated and he stuffed the floorboards in place to give it some rigidity, before mounting the outboard.

Davie dragged the boat off the beach and pulled it into the shallows, the gentle sound of lapping water of no concern. The tide had come back in now. It would have been impractical to launch the boat if it had been out. Fortunately, the skies had settled and the sea had calmed since he'd observed the fishing boat dropping its last pot. He reckoned he'd reach the buoy around slack tide.

Boarding his boat, he took up the oars and rowed down Carse Gut toward the Solway Firth, hoping for the calm conditions to remain when he rounded the point. As he reached the Firth, Davie turned right along the coast, then headed away from the land and started the outboard motor, confident he was now away from sensitive ears.

He smiled. The drop had been planned well, the weather perfect. Calm conditions, a moonless cloudy sky and no running tide to combat. His GPS would be the only way to find the buoy in these conditions and without a torch.

When the GPS indicated he was close, Davie cut the engine back to an idle and scanned the surrounding sea. Nothing. He opened the throttle a little and spiralled out from the point he'd expected it to be at. He knew the buoy could drift. It shouldn't take long to find it. But his concern grew with every minute.

After ten minutes of motoring around, Davie frowned; worried. His suit was damp inside from a cold sweat. Had he not plotted the position correctly? He thought he was pretty good at that sort of thing. If he'd cocked up, he might be out at sea too long. Conditions could change and the tide would start running back out at a pace. He'd need more engine power to fight the current and the noise could attract attention. "Damn! Damn! Damn!" he said to himself. "Where's that fucking buoy?"

As the expletive left his mouth, Davie's mind raced as he considered the options. There was really no choice. He would have to use the torch, even though he knew that risked him being seen from the shore. There was a faint light from a cabin near the coast. He'd have to hope they were tucked up by the fire, not peering out across the Firth.

He switched on the torch and scanned the sea. Something caught his attention. He focused on it and turned the boat in that direction. *There* it was!

He pulled up alongside, the water lapping noisily against the boat's rubber hull. It wasn't easy heaving the pot up from the seabed. He'd done it in his days as a fisherman. But that was on a sturdy boat, where he could stand and haul unrestricted and stable. In a floppy dinghy, he could only sit and pull. The rope slid over the tube of the rubber hull, screeching as it did. He stopped, wondering whether anyone could hear the squeaking rubber. This wasn't working out to be as easy as he'd expected.

He returned to hauling the pot out of the sea. By the time it surfaced, sweat was running into his eyes and dripping off his chin. He dragged it over the boat's side, then took a breather, his heart pounding in his chest.

As the beating slowed, he glanced at the pot. The package was there alright. A watertight bag holding four kilos of cocaine. And a bonus for him - a lobster!

He'd paid £30,000 for the drugs but it should be worth over £100,000 when sold. A tidy profit, and he didn't have to pay back the seed funding for the purchase. An even bigger bonus! With the profit from this one deal, he could upgrade his car, and splash out on a holiday. He smiled at the thought, then fished the package and the lobster out from the pot.

Davie tossed the pot over the side with a splash, then powered up the motor and headed back the way he'd come. Glowing from his optimistic assessment of the future, it never occurred to Davie that he might have been seen.

* * *

Suzanna closed the Bible, having read the whole of Matthew's Gospel. She pondered on what she had read, reaching no conclusion, then glanced at her watch and was shocked to find it was well past midnight. Suzanna rose from the comfy chair and toured the room, closing curtains to prepare for bed. Something caught her eye as she drew the last pair. A flicker somewhere out across the sea. Momentary. Now gone. It was probably nothing, she thought. Bed called.

Chapter Twenty-Seven

Thursday 28th April

Suzanna's running shoes crunched on the stone chippings covering the car park as she strode towards the track leading away from her lodge onto the beach.

She had woken at 6 a.m. to the sound of her favourite musician, Croatian Stjepan Hauser, striking his cello with a bow, more percussion than a gentle melody. She'd set this incredible piece as her iPad wake-up alarm. It's urgency ensuring she would not sleep through it. Drawing the curtains aside, she had stared out at the glorious scene of the Solway Firth, in its unusual calmness almost mirroring the Cumbrian coast. Its beauty, on this bright spring morning, grabbed her, first holding her, then calling. Calling her to become part of the scene.

Her pace picked up into a slow jog as she eased her tired muscles into ready-for-anything mode. She stopped as she joined the track leading to the beach, to take in the view yet again before it was gone.

Off to her left, along the coast, a stream ran into the sea, the current disturbing the still waters of the Solway. The river Nith joined the Firth a little further up the coast. A lone grey seal slipped from a boulder into the dark waters, rings emanating from where its streamlined body had disappeared. White, fluffy clouds drifted across the sky, the wind so light she felt not even a breath against her cheek. Skiddaw stood in the distance high above the lower fells surrounding what she knew would be Bassenthwaite lake.

The dominating Cumbrian fell, pulled at her heart. It had been too long since she'd ascended the challenging slopes of England's third highest mountain. She felt the desire to return to the Lakes soon and visit her sister and niece in the market town of Cockermouth.

Suzanna smiled as she recalled Athena's cheeky grin. She knew she would never have children now - had left it too late. At forty-five, the risk of birth defects was magnified. She'd read somewhere that the risk was one in two thousand at age twenty, but one in thirty at her age. It was a risk she was not willing to take, even if she could be persuaded to take time off from work. Suzanna felt sad. If she couldn't have her own children, she would try to make the most of having a niece to love.

She set off running again. Her feet fell into a rhythm as the track met the beach and her heart settled into a steady beat. On reaching the firm damp sand, she upped her pace, striding at speed, pushing her body, her heart thumping in her chest, her lungs sucking in the cool, fresh, salty, coastal air. She felt alive! This was her escape and her daily preparation for the challenges she might face.

Life as a police detective was a continuing game of chess with the minds of criminals and physical battles with the evil men and women who took from others. Money, belongings, time, mental health. Inflicting pain along the way, they stole it all and more. She was the major, leading her troops in that daily battle and felt it her duty to lead from the front, to set examples for the team to emulate, to coach and encourage them. And knowing she might occasionally have to engage in combat with villains, she was determined to remain fighting fit.

It was 7 a.m. when she sat for breakfast; her face glowing pink, her upper body damp with perspiration, a drop formed and trickled between her breasts. Although she'd just showered, her body still smouldered from the exertion of pushing herself. She ate a bowl of muesli, topped with granola, extra nuts and grapes and drowned in skimmed milk.

* * *

A uniformed officer ambled into the near-empty incident room, looking uncomfortable, his eyes scanning the space for a familiar face. Mairi looked up from her computer screen, offering a warm smile. "Hiya! Looking for someone?" She asked cheerily.

The officer turned towards Mairi, but before speaking froze as he took in the sight of the best-looking police officer he'd ever clamped eyes on. "I've been attached to the investigation," he said, trying not to act like a rabbit caught in headlights. "PC Logan Stevens," he continued, a touch of apprehension in his voice.

"Oh! Yes. I'd heard you'd be joining us." She stood up, stepped around the desk and extended her hand, noticing they stood about the same height. Logan must have been of a similar age to her as well. Mid-late twenties, probably. But that was where the commonalty ended. Logan was stocky, had a broad face but a narrow nose, a weak chin and pinned-back ears. And a moustache! Who had hairy upper lips nowadays? They went out of fashion when Freddie Mercury died in the early nineties, Mairi thought.

"Welcome to the team, Logan. I'm DC Mairi Gordon." They shook hands, Mairi liking that his palm was dry, his skin smooth and his grip firm. "You'll mostly be working with me. Desk-bound stuff, I'm afraid. The others get to do the interesting work: visiting places and interviewing people."

"Aye. I know. Wouldn't mind joining if it was to do the real detective work, but admin is not my thing."

Mairi chuckled. "Have to say, as much as I don't like it, the admin is very much part of real detective work. But I know what you mean.

Better to be out somewhere with your magnifying glass!" Mairi smiled.

"Surely, no one uses a magnifying glass anymore." Logan stated, sounding sceptical. "Never even seen a CSI with one."

"The DCI has one, but I'm not sure she's ever used it on an investigation." Mairi grinned mischievously. "Inherited it from her great-great-uncle, she tells us. They say he was the man that our computer system was named after."

Logan's brow furrowed. "The PNC?"

Mairi just smiled and left him to ponder on it. "Grab a seat at that computer, Logan. We've got a pile of data to record."

* * *

Suzanna arrived shortly after Mairi and Logan had introduced themselves. "Morning, Mairi." She walked across to the newcomer. "Hello. I assume you're PC Logan Stevens." Suzanna held out her hand. "DCI McLeod."

Logan stood to shake it. "Hi, ma'am. Good to meet you. I've heard a lot about you." Immediately after speaking, his expression changed, showing his embarrassment at having mentioned the senior officer's reputation, and worried what she might say to him in response.

"Oh, really!" Suzanna replied. "And what *have* you heard?" She glared into his eyes, like a child on a staring dare.

Logan shuffled his feet. "Your reputation goes ahead of you, ma'am." He faltered, his cheeks reddening. "Best conviction rate in Scotland, they say."

Mairi watched on, amused at Logan's embarrassment.

Suzanna pulled back to take the pressure off. She had just been testing his strength of character. "Well, Logan. It takes a team to achieve that."

Suzanna's voice softened, became more friendly, praising. "From what I hear, you'll be an asset to *this* team. DS McIntosh tells me you have an inquisitive mind, and the inspector reckons you have it in you to become a detective. Which is why you were selected. So, take it as a compliment that you've joined the investigation team. Your time with us is a great opportunity for you to demonstrate your potential."

Logan couldn't quite make out whether Suzanna's tone was that of a schoolteacher or an older sister. Either way, he could tell she was the boss, but she had his best interests at heart. He wouldn't waste the opportunity.

Carl and Tosh walked in together, and in unison, said, "Morning, all." Then, "Hi Logan."

"Anyone would think you two are fellow choristers," Mairi commented. The men looked puzzled. "Singing from the same hymn sheet!" She grinned.

They simultaneously rolled their eyes.

"See. You're doing it again."

Carl and Tosh ignored her, hung up their coats and took their seats, immediately switching on their computers to start work.

* * *

Carl's phone rang. He picked up, introduced himself, then listened. He thanked the caller, put the phone down and called across the room. "Ma'am. We've had feedback from forensics on Reynolds' shotgun."

Suzanna looked up, connected eyes with Carl and waited for him to continue. Tosh paused his bank statement scrutiny, to listen in.

Noticing he had gained their attention, Carl continued. "The weapon had definitely been fired the morning of the murder. Both barrels. Mr Reynolds' fingerprints are on the stock. It was definitely him who last fired it. They've also identified the make and batch of the shot taken from the victims' bodies. If Reynolds has cartridges from that same batch, it could be a good lead."

Suzanna considered Carl's suggested link between the ammunition and gun owner before responding. "Thanks, Carl. Best you get out to the Reynolds' farm and check what ammunition they use. But even if he has the same brand, bore and batch of cartridges, that doesn't prove his shotgun was the murder weapon. You can't match shot to a specific barrel."

"Okay, ma'am. I'll shoot out there now (excuse the pun) and check on that. But what should I do if I find his cartridges are a match to those identified by forensics?"

"If you find his ammunition is a match, bring a cartridge in as evidence. Jack Reynolds has already told us he was out rabbiting that morning, so we still can't tie him to the killing by just that." Suzanna paused. "But find out who supplies his ammunition. Then get onto the distributor and ask whether they sold that batch of cartridges to anyone else. If the Reynolds were the only customers, we'd have reason to bring Jack in. Otherwise, it's just circumstantial."

"Okay, ma'am." Carl grabbed his coat, shrugged himself into it and headed towards the door.

"Just a minute, Carl." Suzanna called. He paused and turned around. "Has forensics made any progress on matching tyre or boot tracks?" she asked, hope written on her face.

"They didn't say. And I didn't ask. Sorry!"

"Fair enough. I'll chase them," Suzanna concluded.

* * *

Carl was just leaving the Reynolds' farm, a cartridge tucked away in a clear polythene bag, when his phone rang. It was the DCI. "Hello, ma'am."

"Carl. I've just been on to forensics. They reckon the tyre tracks found near the bodies are a match with the Reynolds' quad bike tyres. And the wellie boot prints are also a match. Bring Mr Reynolds in for questioning under caution."

Carl grinned. "Yes, ma'am." He ended the call and marched back to the house.

Chapter Twenty-Eight

Jack sat in the police station interview room, intimidated by his surroundings, feeling vulnerable and worried. He'd been a fool for not having reported the bodies earlier, concerned the police would pin it on him. But looking back, he realised they'd be more suspicious now.

Suzanna entered the room, with Carl in tow. They both sat opposite Jack and Carl switched on the recorder. After the formalities, Suzanna opened the questioning. "Mr Reynolds. You know why we've brought you in for questioning. We know you fired your shotgun around the time of the murder. Your quad bike tyre tracks and wellie boot prints prove you were at the scene of the shooting. Yet you failed to mention this before. Why don't you tell us what happened?"

Jack bit his lip, then looked up, meeting Suzanna's eyes. His tone was belligerent as he responded. "There's bound to be prints from my quad bike in that field. I run across it every day, when I check on the sheep or take them extra food. And those wellie boots are common as muck. Half the farmers in Dumfries have the same ones. They're the most popular brand sold at the farmer's shop. So, I don't see how that proves anything."

Suzanna had hoped he'd cooperate; instead, he was continuing to avoid admitting his presence at the scene. She pressed again, but in a more friendly tone, as if she had his best interests at heart. "Look, Jack. The quad bike tyres near the body are the most recently made tracks in the field, and from the impressions near the bodies, the bike will have been stood there a while. Clearly, the quad had been used on the day of the shooting and it's too much of a coincidence that it stood at the very spot the bodies lay on that same morning. Wouldn't you agree?"

Jack broke eye contact and stared at the plain surface of the table. Evidently, he wasn't sure how to respond. Suzanna let time take its toll. Eventually, Jack spoke. "I think I'd better have a solicitor."

"Okay, Jack," Suzanna responded, hiding her frustration. She maintained her friendly tone as she continued, hoping he might still cooperate. "That's your right. But if you're innocent, you shouldn't need one. My job is to find the killer, not to get someone put away for a crime they didn't commit, while the culprit goes free. What would be the point in that?"

Jack couldn't disagree with the logic of what the chief inspector had said. But he was still cautious and remained silent.

Suzanna allowed her exasperation to surface. "Jack. If you're not guilty of this crime, help us out by not wasting our time waiting hours for a solicitor to arrive. Every minute we delay on following the right trail is another minute that the perpetrator is getting away from us. Surely, you want the murderer to be found and brought to justice?"

Reynolds pondered, as Suzanna sat quietly, patiently waiting for his response. This time she thought he might crack. His eyelids flickered before he spoke.

"Aye, you're right. It was'nae me that killed the woman and the dog. But I found them right enough, and did'nae report it, like I should have." Jack explained what had happened and his worry about two and two making five.

Suzanna understood his worry. He'd likely seen too many old crime series on TV, where the police were portrayed as looking for results at any cost, and willing to fit people up. In many of these series, they even planted evidence if they thought it necessary to convict the person who their gut told them was the perpetrator of the crime. She'd never met a police officer who did that.

"Well Jack. I'm pretty good with maths and rarely make such basic mistakes. But your actions have resulted in minus one from the five you thought we'd get from two plus two. It's looking much more like a solid four now!"

Jack sat up straight, surprised by the detective's change of tone. She was no longer the friendly older sister, leading him to do the right thing.

Suzanna continued. "Given the evidence of your presence at the murder scene and the means to have committed the crime, you will remain a suspect and held in custody under the suspicion of murdering Isla Muir while we carry our further checks and tests. Your story could just be to cover up your crime." She stood up and, before leaving the room, stared down at Jack. "You will certainly need a solicitor now."

* * *

Suzanna strode into the incident room, followed by Carl, and called out. "Carl. Tosh." She indicated they should gather round the incident board. "So far, the evidence we have points to Jack Reynolds having shot the woman and the dog, but we don't have a *solid* motive." She paused, allowing the detectives time to offer opinions, hoping to draw out their thoughts.

"Supposing," Tosh said, rubbing his chin, "Jack Reynolds went out rabbiting as he'd said, but saw the woman's dog worrying his sheep. Maybe he shot the dog and the woman raged at him and she got a barrel as well?"

Exactly the scenario Suzanna had been thinking. She was glad she'd waited for a response instead of just spoon-feeding the detectives.

Carl swallowed a mouthful of coffee before speaking. "Yeah, sheep worrying is all too common around here. I've heard numerous complaints from farmers, but there's not been any cases of a farmer actually seeing it going on and taking action. And," Carl continued, his voice tinged with frustration, "then there's the sheep rustling. We've had little luck at catching the thieves. They must have back-street slaughterhouses lined up, over county lines, taking the sheep in at night and disposing of the fleeces."

Suzanna pondered on what Carl had said. He might have hit on something there. One problem with county-based police forces is they don't work closely enough with colleagues in the next county. She'd have to look into the idea of having systems in place for neighbouring counties to stake out or raid slaughterhouses immediately after the report of thefts. She dragged her mind back to the case in hand. "Good point, Carl. But let's focus on the murder for now."

Suzanna continued. "The forensics report states that, going by the spread of the shot, the weapon would have been fired at close quarters. The person who fired that weapon may have had blood splatter on their clothes." She turned her eyes to her sergeant. "Tosh, get a warrant to search the Reynolds' farm and get the CSI guys out to there to bring in all of Jack Reynolds' clothes. And have him change out of the clothes he's wearing now. We need all of them checked for blood splatter." She paused.

"Carl. We need evidence of sheep worrying. I want the sheep that were in that field examined by a vet for signs a dog might have had a go at them. Reynolds had the opportunity, means and perhaps motive to have shot the woman and her dog. But we need evidence of the motive."

"Happy days," Carl responded, then walked away.

Suzanna turned to the board and its overlapping circles. Jack Reynolds was their only suspect so far. She wrote his name in the suspect circle. Perhaps this would all be over quicker than she'd hoped.

Carl was already on the phone, presumably calling the local vets. Tosh lifted the receiver on his phone. "Tosh. Just a minute," Suzanna called.

He put the phone down and returned to the board.

"A thought just occurred to me about the rabbits you said you saw hanging inside the Reynolds' farm. Their presence supports his story that he'd been out rabbiting, which is why his gun had been fired that morning."

"Aye. True."

"Did you check the temperature of the rabbits?"

"No, ma'am. Never thought to," Tosh replied, shaking his head.

"The thing is the rabbits could have been shot the day before and still be hanging in the rear lobby. If you'd checked, we'd have more evidence, either to corroborate his story or to show him up as a liar and support our assertion that he killed Mrs Muir."

Tosh pursed his lips and tilted his head. "I suppose so."

Suzanna spoke quietly, not wanting Carl to hear. "Would you like to make DI, Tosh?"

"Yes, ma'am, if only to catch up with Ed Ferguson."

That wasn't the answer she'd been hoping for. Promotion wasn't about competing with others, it was about having the rank and responsibility that matched one's competence, knowledge and capability. And of course, receiving the earned income that went with that responsibility. But she kept these thoughts to herself as she went on.

"At the end of this case, I will be asked to write an assessment of your performance, to feed into your overall annual appraisal. I won't lie. I won't gloss over any shortcomings but I will note where praise is due. If you want to be a DI, it would be best if you started thinking more broadly when investigating crimes. To look for motives, to pick up on all evidence that could help the case, whether clearing a suspect or providing evidence for conviction."

Tosh frowned as he listened. He obviously wasn't enjoying having his performance critiqued. Suzanna continued, "Look, Tosh. I've been impressed with your performance so far. This little pep talk isn't aimed at bringing you down. I just want you to have the opportunity to shine even more, so I can write a glowing report when I leave. I thought some early feedback would be helpful, to provide that opportunity."

Tosh's face relaxed, a slight smile on his lips. "Thanks, ma'am. I appreciate your concern and advice. I'll try to up my game. Talking of which, I'd better get that warrant sorted out." He turned and went back to make the phone call.

* * *

Another day done, Suzanna returned to her log cabin, glad that she had chosen to leave the hotel, with its cramped, overpriced facilities. Before settling in for the night, she changed her shoes and went for a walk along the shore. The pebbles on the beach crunched under the feet, the sea air salty on her tongue as she breathed it in.

The sun was heading towards the horizon further along the Dumfries coast. The gentle breeze ruffled her hair, sending strands across her eyes. She turned to look out across the Solway Firth. The amber rays illuminated the Cumbrian coast and the Lake District fells, just visible in the distance, making them glow like the embers of a fire.

It was good to be out of the city, and the busyness of its slow-moving traffic. Although she liked her Edinburgh flat and the easy access to city facilities, it would be great to live in the countryside with fresh air and space, surrounded by nature. Maybe one day her job would be based in the countryside. She hoped so.

The Police Scotland Tulliallan HQ where the Major Investigation

Team was to be based was out of the city, as was the Counter-terrorism unit. Perhaps she would get her countryside move sooner that she'd expected. Maybe she and James could buy a house together?

She pondered further as she walked. Were they ready to commit to joint ownership of a property? It was like committing to marriage! They'd both had their fingers burnt by spouses and neither wished to take the risk of being hurt again. But they spent most of their time under the same roof, sharing the same bed. Making love regularly. She smiled at the thought and wished James were with her now. Holding her hand as she walked. Maybe they *were* ready.

Suzanna wandered further along the beach, enjoying the freshness of the coast, watching the sun disappearing behind the horizon. Thinking about the complex solar system and the universe in which it sat, millions of light years away from the other stars. All just an accident?

Her stomach rumbled, and a chill breeze raised goosebumps on her neck. It was time for dinner.

After eating, Suzanna relaxed on the comfy sofa with a mug of decaf coffee and the Bible. The smell of chickpea curry still lingered in the open-plan kitchen-living room. Soothing classical music played in the background. She felt at peace with the world.

Mark was her reading for the evening. The Gospels were not entirely new to her, of course. She had been brought up in the Anglican Church. When she was young, Suzanna just accepted that God existed and Jesus was his son. Until her hormones had kicked in! Then she began questioning everything she'd been told. She rebelled against her parents and their religion. Decided she didn't believe in God. Declared herself an atheist. But twenty years had passed since her youthful rebellion. She had matured and become more open-minded to spiritual matters. By the time she'd finished reading Mark, Suzanna was more convinced of its authenticity. Her naturally questioning, analytical, challenging mind, more accepting. Why? She couldn't say. It had been easy to reject the Bible as a book of fairy tales. But tonight, something had settled in her soul.

Over the years, she had learned to judge when someone was lying to her. She had developed that discernment from multiple interviews and interactions with people. If the Apostle Mark had been across the table in the police interview room, Suzanna felt she would have believed him.

Chapter Twenty-Nine

Friday 29th April

Suzanna was in early the next day. She was keen to get the case wrapped up if the additional evidence they needed was found. She called the forensics department, hoping they might have started work already. They informed her that blood had been found on Jack's clothing and sent off for analysis. But they couldn't say more than that yet.

The phone on her desk rang shortly after she'd replaced the receiver. It was Chief Superintendent White.

"Good morning, DCI McLeod. I understand there have been significant developments in the murder case?"

Suzanna wondered how HQ had already got wind of it. "Yes, ma'am. We arrested the farmer, Jack Reynolds, yesterday. We believe he may have shot the woman's dog for sheep worrying, then the woman when she attacked him, although he denies that. There is evidence of him being at the scene of the shooting. And his shotgun had been fired by him that morning. There's also a connection between the shot he uses in his gun and that removed from the bodies. What we don't have yet is firm evidence to support the motive, or that he actually shot the woman."

"Hmm!" White responded. "We've got press hassling us. Asking why we have charged no one yet. From what you've told me, we have strong circumstantial evidence. I think that's enough to charge the man with the murder. Send over what you have so far and I'll talk with the Procurator Fiscal." The Chief Superintendent hung up.

Suzanna slammed the phone down. Bloody meddling senior officers. It should be her decision as SIO to decide when to take it to the Procurator Fiscal's office.

She made a cup of coffee and sat breathing in the aroma, with her hands wrapped around the hot mug, as she calmed down. Thinking things through was the best course of action. Time to let her heart rate return to normal. The anger to subside.

Although they had arrested Jack Reynolds, she didn't believe they had enough evidence to be certain of a conviction. And it was convictions they needed, not charges laid. Carl would be out with the vet this morning, checking the sheep for any evidence of worrying. Tosh would be on the Reynolds' house search. Once the two detectives reported, she might have the evidence required. In the meantime, though, she gathered together what she had, and sent a report to the Chief Super to comply with her direction. After hitting send, she checked her watch: 8:30 a.m. As she looked up, Mairi entered the office.

"Morning, ma'am," she said cheerily.

Suzanna smiled, trying to hide her frustration. "Morning, Mairi." She joined Mairi at her desk. "I've just sent off a report to the force HQ. It's possible they might direct us to charge Jack Reynolds. But I'm not yet convinced he murdered Isla Muir. Although he lied to us initially, Reynolds' story is feasible."

Mairi watched her boss intently, eagerly awaiting her next line of thought.

"We've been looking at the disgruntled landowners and planners. But what else might we have missed? Now that you've got the data together, have any other lines of enquiry come to light?"

Mairi was pleased to have been asked her opinion. She felt valued. "Only the Brownlows, ma'am. I know it's a bit far-fetched, but it's still possible one of them could have killed Muir, then returned to find the body. What better way to cover your tracks?"

"As you say, Mairi, rather tenuous but possible." Suzanna pursed her lips and looked away as she thought through what Mairi had suggested. It was possible, although unlikely, that one of the Brownlows had murdered her. But it just didn't feel right. She re-engaged with Mairi. "There have been cases of criminals returning to the crime scene to cover their tracks. But what connection could there be between this couple from Cumbria on a walking holiday in Dumfriesshire, and Mrs Isla Muir? If you can answer that, it might be worth more resource being given to following that line."

Now *there* was a challenge, Mairi thought.

* * *

It was another dreich day in Dumfriesshire. As Carl pulled up on the lane where he'd previously had his car moved by Jack Reynolds' tractor, he spotted a Land Rover Discovery parked further up the lane. A man in green overalls stood at the rear of the vehicle with its door wide open as he donned his wellies. He looked to be in his fifties, taller than Carl and broader, with a pot belly. Carl slipped his own wellies on and marched along the track to meet up with the man he assumed was the vet. "Morning Mr Dickson," he said as he approached along the muddy track.

The vet responded as he fastened his overalls. Not looking up from his task. "No need for formalities, officer. Call me Charles."

"Happy days. I'm Carl." He smiled and held out his hand, which the vet ignored, turning to walk away.

Carl frowned, perplexed at the vet's verbalised friendliness but contradictory body language. He caught up with Charles and wandered along the lane with him. "I don't suppose you get many requests for this type of check?"

"No. First time, actually," Charles responded, continuing to look straight ahead. "Farmers will check over their own sheep if they suspect they've been worried. They'd only call me if they found injuries that needed treatment they couldn't administer themselves. Have to keep their costs down. Farming's a high-risk business. Most of them barely eke out a living, from long hours and few holidays."

Carl looked ahead to where a woman was sitting on a quad bike further up the lane. Mrs Reynolds, he assumed. He could tell from her demeanour that she was not a happy lady. But what wife would be cheerful when her husband had been arrested for murder and her house was currently being searched?

As they got closer to the field, he could see the woman's face was sternly set. She wore the farmer's uniform: a green wax jacket, green wellies and a tweed flat cap.

"I take it you'll want the sheep brought down to the pen, Mr Dickson," she said, evidently already knowing the vet, and blanking Carl.

"Good day to you Mrs Reynolds. Please call me Charles."

"Mr Dickson sounds right to me. We're not friends." She stared at the vet, no emotion in her features, her eyes showing no peripheral recognition of Carl's presence.

Charles' face showed his surprise at her attitude but after a moment's hesitation, he recovered his composure. "Aye. That'd be grand if you could get the sheep into the pen, Mrs Reynolds."

Stony faced, she responded. "As you say." She drove off up the field, manoeuvring slowly over and around the humps and ruts. Her dog stood on the bike's rear platform, adjusting its stance as the quad swayed with the motion. The dog jumped down immediately that the bike stopped and ran around the sheep to cut them off. A few minutes later, after numerous shouts and whistles, with the dog running then laying at command, the sheep were safely in the pen.

Carl wondered whether he was invisible today. Neither Dickson nor Reynolds had deemed to look at him.

The vet wasted no time getting on with his task, with Carl staying outside the pen.

Mr Dickson separated each sheep, checking it for signs of bites or abrasions to the legs or rump, before releasing it from the pen. The sheep complained loudly about the disruption and manhandling, with baaing and grumbling.

Carl watched as each animal was released. Initially, they bounded away but soon stopped and gathered with the other free sheep. Within a minute, they started nibbling the grass - trauma soon forgotten.

After his examination, the vet sauntered over to where Carl stood. For the first time, Dickson looked Carl in the eye. "I could find no evidence of these animals having been attacked by a dog. No cuts, bite wounds or grazes. They're all physically sound animals. Sorry if that's not what you wanted to hear."

"Thanks, Charles. Your findings don't support our theory about the sheep being worried, but that doesn't mean it never happened."

"Correct. Often dogs chase the flock but never actually make contact. It's not normally a vicious attack. The dog sees it as a bit of fun, but the sheep don't see it that way. I've known sheep miscarry because dogs have chased them around a field, or even keel over and die from the stress. They're sensitive, anxious creatures."

* * *

With Logan Stevens now on the team and inputting data into HOLMES, Mairi was free to move into the more important role of researcher and analyst. It would be her job to put together charts, spreadsheets and other products to help the SIO and the team see things more clearly. As a refresher, Mairi ran through the list she'd been provided with in training to see which techniques might be helpful in this case.

Timelines – the chronology of events, suspects and victims' placement. Definitely. They already had a basic timeline on the board. But it could do with more detail to flesh out the skeleton, to help them spot issues.

Mapping – Plotting the scene, features, routes, search zones, road checks requirements and poster campaign zones. Road checks weren't appropriate and she doubted posters would be worthwhile, given the rural situation. And a map of the area was on the board, with pins showing the locations of the crime scene and the farms that had been visited. She would add to it the locations of other players.

Flow charts – the movement of money and communication flows between suspects and the victim. Certainly, she thought. Mairi knew the team had already followed up on disgruntled business connections, such as the Allanachs and the planning officials. But they'd not yet plotted all the flow of money and communications. She decided to do that next.

Network analysis – examining links between people and places. The Brownlows had yet to be followed through.

Next was subject profile analysis – background checks on the victim's family, witnesses and suspects. Of course; they already had much of that in hand.

Crime pattern analysis. Looking for patterns or trends and finding links. That wasn't appropriate. This was a one-off crime, not a series, like with burglaries.

Risk analysis came next. What risks might there be to the individuals, such as witnesses, offenders or groups, including the police? Mairi pondered this one. As a shotgun had been used to kill the woman and her dog, the killer may well be willing to kill again. If it wasn't Jack Reynolds, they would need to be careful when approaching other suspects. Perhaps employ armed officers to make arrests and initiate searches. But there was no point in raising this, given the current situation.

Demographic or social trend analysis. Certainly not!

Criminal business profile. It appeared that Isla Muir's corrupt business dealings may generate a motive for murder but they'd yet to find an individual who would have taken their grievances that far.

At the end of her list checking, Mairi had a number of actions to take. The DCI interrupted her thoughts. "The duty solicitor is ready now, Mairi. I need you for the interview of Jack Reynolds."

Mairi smiled at the prospect of interview work; glad to put aside the essential but somewhat tedious analysis work, and keen to see what came out of the interview. With luck, Reynolds would admit to the killing.

Chapter Thirty

Jack Reynolds entered the interview room forlornly, followed by the duty solicitor, a smartly dressed young man, probably not long graduated. Jack had never spent a night in police cells, and it didn't look like he had enjoyed the experience. He was a little dishevelled. His hair was a mess, his clothes crumpled, and he hadn't shaved.

Suzanna questioned him again about the shooting, his solicitor arguing that the evidence only proved his presence at that spot, not that he'd shot the woman and her dog.

Suzanna couldn't disagree, although she didn't verbalise her thoughts. She informed them that the Procurator Fiscal had authorised Jack Reynolds to be charged with murder.

"But I never did it." Jack protested, sweat breaking out on his brow, his hands trembling. "I never murdered that woman. You have to believe me," he blurted out desperately, his eyes moist and his face flushed.

Suzanna felt sorry for the man. She wasn't entirely convinced that he had murdered Isla Muir, having yet to see sufficient evidence, but was under instruction to charge him. There was a knock on the door and Tosh stepped in.

"Ma'am. I have something you'll want to see." He passed two pieces of paper to Suzanna and left the room. She took her time to study the sheets, ensuring she fully understood their contents. PC Bailey had reported on his engagement with Jack Reynolds shortly after the farmer's last quad bike theft, in February. And there was a forensics report on blood splatter. She looked up and fixed Reynolds with a cold stare before speaking again.

"Well, Mr Reynolds, given your stated intention to use your shotgun against people threatening to affect your livelihood, evidence placing you at the scene and your fired shotgun, along with this latest evidence from forensics, I'm more firmly of the opinion that you did kill Isla Muir." She paused for effect. Reynolds' moist eyes now flowed with tears. His nose ran, and he reached for a handkerchief.

Suzanna continued. "We now have results from forensics tests of your clothing. On one jacket, they found blood splatter across the front and some on the sleeve. And the blood on the sleeve is confirmed to be from the victim." She paused again. "I am now charging you with the murder of Mrs Isla Muir. You will be held in custody while we investigate further. Take him to the cells." She stood and strode out of the room, leaving the uniformed PC to play escort again, as Jack Reynolds collapsed onto the table, blubbing.

The duty solicitor slouched into his chair, looking defeated. He couldn't argue for Jack's release, given the latest evidence.

* * *

The team gathered in the incident room, tidying their desks, writing up reports, and rearranging the incident board when the phone rang on Tosh's desk. He took the call, making notes, his face changing to one of concern. "Ma'am. Some interesting news from forensics."

Everyone paused what they were doing and looked up, anticipating something that might reinforce their case against Reynolds. But as Suzanna read Tosh's expression, she knew it would not be positive news. Her jaw clenched in response.

"That was the lab," Tosh continued. "The splatter on the front of Reynolds' jacket is not in a pattern that would support the theory it was blood-spray caused by a shotgun hitting a large close target. *And...* it was found to be *rabbit* blood."

All their faces dropped. Carl slumped back into his chair, rolling his eyes.

"Okay. Let's recap," Suzanna said, also disappointed but not despondent. "There is no evidence that a dog had worried the sheep. And the blood found on Reynolds' jacket is mostly from rabbits. The blood found on the sleeve supports Reynolds' story that when he found the body, he checked her carotid artery for a pulse. I can't see any jury agreeing to a guilty verdict, given that evidence."

Mairi's disappointment grew with this assessment. She'd been hoping it would bring the evidence they needed to support a conviction. That hope had been cast aside. But she quickly recovered and offered a suggestion. "Shall I follow up the Brownlow angle now, ma'am?"

"Yes. Please do. We need to think about other lines of enquiry... By the way, Mairi, you said you'd check out Mr Muir's alibi. What did you find?"

"Ah! Yes... I called the hotel in Oxford where he'd stayed. They confirmed he checked out about 9 a.m. So, there's no way he could have killed his wife."

"True." Suzanna replied. "Unless he had access to a Harrier jump jet, he'd never have been able to get the three hundred miles to Dumfries, kill his wife and be at breakfast in Oxford at 8 a.m. In fact, even if he had a Harrier, he'd not be able to, unless they had a hover pad within the hotel grounds."

"I doubt that would have gone unnoticed by the staff," Tosh said, grinning at the idea of Muir using an RAF fighter jet.

Suzanna was silent for a moment. "I'll get onto HQ and give the Chief Super the news. I think we'll have to release Jack Reynolds. It won't go down well."

Tosh spoke again. "We haven't followed through on the corrupt planning officials yet. I'll chase the background checks on them." He paused. "Oh! And forensics found car park tickets for Carlisle and Glasgow in Mrs Muir's car. We haven't looked into that yet, either."

"Good points, Tosh," Suzanna responded. "What might she have been doing in those cities? Who had she been meeting with?"

"Mairi, if you're heading off to Cumbria to follow the Brownlow line, you could stop off in Carlisle. But you'll need to do some homework before you leave. Do any of Muir's contacts live in or near Carlisle, for a start?"

Mairi's earlier gloomy look was replaced by one of determination. She had two lines to investigate. "Okay, ma'am; on it." She now had a renewed sense of purpose.

"We don't have the manpower to send someone to Glasgow," Tosh said. "But I'll identify Muir's contacts in the city and run background checks on them. Then we can decide what to do next once we have that info."

"We've not had feedback from the lab on the victim's fluids, either," Carl added. "I'll get onto them."

"Great. Let's get to work," Suzanna concluded.

* * *

Carl replaced the phone, his brow furrowed as he considered what he'd been told. Just then the DCI entered the room. "Ma'am," Carl called out, to catch her attention. "I've had feedback from the lab about the victim's bodily fluids."

Suzanna paused her journey to listen. "And?"

Carl responded to the prompt. "The only thing of note was the presence of cocaine in her blood!" His lifting eyebrows gave away his surprise at this revelation. As a middle-aged, respected business-woman, it was that last thing he'd expected to be told.

Suzanna's eyebrows shot up, her eyes popping out of her head. This disclosure opened up other lines of enquiry. Her mind whirled as she considered the implication of Carl's announcement. She shared her thoughts, her forehead still wrinkled. "If she was a frequent user, she will have been in regular contact with a drug dealer. Maybe she crossed the dealer?" She paused. "Carl, compare Mrs Muir's contacts list with any known drug dealers in the area."

Suzanna also knew that, as a cocaine user, Muir's decisions and actions may have been both unpredictable and irrational. And that could create difficult situations and relationship conflicts.

"Okay, ma'am," Carl replied. "If nothing turns up, I'll have a word with the dealers I know. Those who have previous convictions or we suspect of dealing."

"We'll need to search her home for cocaine and see if the lab can match it to any confiscations that have been made. It could help point us towards the right dealer," Suzanna added, her brow now deeply furrowed in concentration. This case was getting more complex by the day. Where else might it lead them?

* * *

Dark clouds rushed overhead with the strong wind as Tosh pulled up on the gravel driveway, the surface crunching under the tyres. Mr Muir's Jaguar hadn't moved since Tosh had last visited. A marked police car pulled up behind him and three officers emerged. Tosh felt a few spits of rain as he strode to the house and knocked on the door. It was answered within a minute by the housekeeper. "Yes?"

"Is Mr Muir at home?" Tosh asked.

"Aye. I'll get him for you, officer." She turned and wandered away, obviously in no rush to do his bidding, despite the rain now falling steadily.

The four officers were getting wet by the time Mr Muir arrived at the door. He hadn't shaved and was scruffily dressed. Such a contrast from his attire and demeanour when they'd met before the bad news had been broken. He'd evidently not taken the news well, Tosh thought. But who would?

"Sorry to trouble you, Mr Muir," Tosh said, "but we need to conduct a search to look for anything that might link to your wife's killer."

Muir's face reddened. "Can't you leave me alone?" He hollered. "It's bad enough losing my wife, but now you want to tear my home apart!"

Tosh kept a passive face and showed sympathy in his tone when he responded. "I'm sorry, Mr Muir but this is important. You *do* want us to find out who murdered your wife?" Tosh's eyebrows raised to add emphasis to the questioning tone in his voice. He waited patiently as his words penetrated the barrier erected by the man's grief.

It took a full minute before Muir's face softened and the colour subsided as his blood pressure dropped. "Yes. Of course. I'm sorry. It's just..."

"I understand, sir. No need to apologise. Can we come in now?" Tosh said hopefully, as the rain trickled down his neck.

Muir stood back, his sad eyes looking to the floor, as Tosh and the search team ambled past, after removing and shaking their coats in the vestibule.

Tosh directed the PCs to their duties, instructing them where to look and what to look for. Tosh returned to Mrs Muir's office to take a more detailed look. He opened drawers and peered within, shuffling their contents to ensure he missed nothing. He extracted books from the bookcase, turning each downward as he thumbed the pages and watched for anything that might fall out. Tosh frowned as he replaced the last book onto the shelf. Having drawn a blank, he stepped across to the window and lifted each of the full-length curtains. All he uncovered was thick fluff where the cleaner had failed to vacuum. He reached up and checked on the curtain rail tops. Nothing!

Tosh lifted every item on Isla Muir's desk, turning it upside down to check for hidden writing or objects taped to the underside, to no avail. He removed the seat cushion from the armchair and felt down the sides, his fingers extracting nothing of significance - just more fluff and sweet papers.

Thirty minutes into the search, Tosh peered out of the bay window across the sea, as the rain stopped and the sun came out. One of the search team entered the room, holding aloft a small container of white powder. He'd bagged it to preserve any evidence.

Tosh smiled and nodded, as he took the package from the officer. He held it up to the light and rotated it, looking for any reflections from prints. He thought he could see something but knew he'd have to wait until forensics did their thing.

Chapter Thirty-One

Mairi would have preferred to be at home in Edinburgh with Brodie. But as she couldn't have that cosy weekend lie-in with her man and perhaps a cuddle, she'd chosen to rise early. So, she was first to arrive at the silent office that Saturday morning.

She had grabbed herself a take-away coffee from a nearby cafe before entering the station. She wrapped her hands around the hot cardboard cup as she pondered on the possibility of Mr or Mrs Brownlow having shot Isla Muir and her dog, then having returned to the scene to cover their tracks. Or perhaps, like an arsonist returning to watch the fire they'd set, gloating at what they'd achieved. Maybe Muir's murderer had done similarly.

Mairi knew the Brownlows were from Cumbria. Somewhere near Wigton. A thought occurred to her. She grabbed the list of Muir's contacts, that now had names and addresses appended. She trawled through the list, looking for a link between the victim and the couple that had discovered her body.

The list was ordered by first name, so it was a while before Mairi reached the one connection. A Mrs Ruth Ingleton of Wigton. She logged into the Police National Computer system and entered Ingleton's details.

As she waited for the formal background checks to come back, Mairi

Googled Ingleton. Her Facebook page was open to be read by the public, so she scanned the woman's posts and details of her family. Nothing jumped out at her.

She noted an interest in amateur dramatics and a local group. Mairi searched for the Wigton Players, found their website and viewed their shows over the last two years. One picture showed the cast on stage after a play they had put on and a second photo showed the whole team, including backstage staff. The piece beneath the photo, named the team members. Her eyes widened. One name stood out. He was the lighting man for the production.

The formal background search didn't show up anything on Ruth Ingleton, so Mairi turned her attention to the gun licensing system data on the PNC. She searched for the name she'd seen on the Wigton Players website. There it was. The link she'd been hoping for!

* * *

"Ma'am," Mairi called as Suzanna entered the incident room, carrying a steaming coffee. "I've found something I think warrants further investigation."

Suzanna smiled; pleased Mairi sounded enthusiastic. She placed the hot mug on her desk, then turned to Mairi, curious. "What is it?"

Mairi explained the research she had carried out and the name that stood out: Gavin Brownlow. "I know the link is tenuous, but, as you've said many times, ma'am, we don't believe in coincidences."

Suzanna nodded in agreement.

Mairi continued. "Gavin Brownlow knows Ruth Ingleton, who also knew Isla Muir. And Brownlow has a shotgun."

There were definite links between Brownlow and Muir. Interesting! "Okay. What next, Mairi?" Suzanna responded, encouraging Mairi to think for herself.

"We need to know whether Brownlow's shotgun has been fired recently, and what ammunition he uses. And whether he's met Isla Muir. That would mean questioning him and Ruth Ingleton. Obviously, we also need to know how Ingleton knew Muir."

"Agreed. What about motive?"

Mairi's mind spun, hoping a reason would be thrown out. She looked into the distance, through the office's one window. Saw clouds rushing across the sky, colliding and merging. An answer came to her. "What if Ingleton had a reason to hate Muir and want revenge? Could she have colluded with Brownlow to kill her?" Mairi wasn't confident about her suggestion, but it was one possibility.

"Perhaps." Suzanna replied. It didn't seem likely to her, but she didn't want to be negative. "It's worth pursuing further. I'll get Carl to trawl through Muir's emails and phone messages for correspondence that might shed some light." She paused. "You get yourself over to Cumbria and interview these players. See what you can come up with."

"Yes, ma'am." Mairi stood and grabbed her coat.

"But update the board first, please," Suzanna concluded.

Mairi put her coat back on the cloak rack, then stepped up to the incident board and added her findings to the Intelligence network chart. It showed the victim's family tree and associate's network. She added in Gavin Brownlow connected to Ruth Ingleton, then highlighted that he was also the person who found the body. Next job: call the Wigton police and let them know she needed to interview people in their district. She didn't want to tread on anyone's toes, especially as she might need their help if arrests had to be made.

* * *

Mairi parked her car on Park Road, Wigton. She looked around her as she ambled along the pavement to the Ingleton home. To the south, just a few trees scattered across the field's edge broke the otherwise uninterrupted view of the distant fells. But to the northeast, the Ingleton's view was dominated by the smelly clingfilm factory.

A concrete path took Mairi through a small recently mowed lawn and past a weed-free rockery - spring flowers blooming colourfully - to Ingleton's front door. Mrs Ingleton opened the door before Mairi pressed the bell button and ushered her inside quickly. A pot of tea and some Custard Cream biscuits were placed on the low table in front of Mairi. "Please help yourself."

The china teapot, cups, saucers and plates were of the same set, adorned with a pretty, tiny flower pattern, in reds, blues and greens. She carefully poured herself a tea, handling the china delicately. Scared of chipping anything.

"So, what brings you to Wigton from Dumfries, Constable? I can't think why you would want to talk to me."

Mairi took a sip of the insipid tea before responding. "I understand you know Mrs Isla Muir?"

Ruth Ingleton's face went from curious to concerned. "Yes. I've met her a couple of times. She's a fellow thespian."

"What's the connection, though? It's an hour's drive from Dumfries to Wigton, so I don't suppose she was a member of the Wigton Players."

"No, no. She came to watch one of our productions a couple of years back, and she stayed on afterwards for drinks. Isla was very complimentary about our play, and I got on well with her. She returned a few months later to watch our next production, Blue Stockings. She loved it."

"Blue Stockings? I've never heard of that play."

"Oh! It's a lovely, moving but comical story set in the late nineteenth century about four young females who fight for the rights of women. They're suffragettes."

Mairi nodded, her curiosity satisfied. "So, Isla Muir returned for that production. Have you seen or heard from her since?"

"I don't understand why you're asking me these questions."

"Mrs Ingleton. Isla Muir has been shot. We're just following up on any connections she had before her death to build a picture and network."

Ruth's eyes widened. "Shot!" She said, surprise in her tone. "An accident? Murder?"

"Yes. Murder." Mairi responded, her eyes fixed on Ingleton, noting her reaction. "Mrs Muir was killed, whilst out walking her dog, a few days ago. I'm surprised you haven't seen it on the news."

Ruth's reply showed her shock at the revelation. "I rarely watch the news on TV or listen to it on the radio. Too much doom and gloom. You never hear good news. Only bad. I try to avoid it."

"Very true. I'd not switch it on myself, but I have to be aware of the doom and gloom, as you call it, because it's my job to know what's happening in that gloomy world."

Mrs Ingleton nodded. Understanding.

"Other than attending two shows in Wigton, what other contact have you had with Mrs Muir?"

"Not much, really." Ruth's eyes danced around the ceiling as she thought. "We swapped numbers and she agreed to let me know when there was a show being staged in Dumfries. I've hardly had any contact with her. Can't think why anyone would want to murder the lady. She seemed so nice."

"You've never visited her in Dumfries or met with her since the last show?"

Ruth shook her head. "No. Actually, our next production is nearly ready for the public, so I was going to inform her. But I haven't got around to that yet."

"Have you not had any conversations with her at all, since she was last here?"

CHAPTER THIRTY-ONE

"None at all, Constable. Is that everything? Only I need to get on."

Mairi was inclined to believe her. She seemed so genuine. But then she remembered that Ruth Ingleton was an actor. She could be acting innocent. "No communication at all?"

"Not that I can think of, officer."

"Emails? Messages?"

Ruth shook her head.

Conscious that Mrs Ingleton wished to be somewhere else, Mairi jumped straight into her next main question. "How would you describe your relationship with Gavin Brownlow?"

Ruth sat up straight, her eyes wide. Evidently concerned at Mairi's line of questioning.

"What do you mean by that question?" Her voice had risen a pitch, indignation now written across her face. "How could that have anything to do with Isla Muir's death?"

"Answer the question, please, Mrs Ingleton."

"Gavin is our props and lighting man. That's all."

"Do you have any contact with him outside of the theatre club?" Mairi's face reflected the seriousness of the question.

"No, no. Of course not. I'm a married woman. That wouldn't be appropriate." She was flustered.

Mairi stared into Ingleton's eyes as she responded. "I note your denial but there is clearly a connection that you don't wish to reveal. This is a murder enquiry, Mrs Ingleton. I'm not here to judge your behaviour. But I need you to answer my questions."

Ruth's lips were squeezed shut, as if trying to hold in the secret she felt was trying to escape. Her face was set stern. Her forehead creased. Mairi repeated the question, then waited patiently for an answer.

"If you must know... Gavin and I meet in the club occasionally, to discuss stage matters."

"And these meetings are *entirely* business-related?"

Ruth looked sheepish, battling with her conscience. "Gavin and I have a close relationship." Ruth replied, reluctantly. "I have to admit that there has been more than stage work discussed."

"Is this a loving or sexual relationship?" Mairi probed, watching Ingleton closely.

Ruth's face reddened at the mention of sex. "Look. My husband doesn't show any interest in that sort of thing anymore. Seems to love his train set more than me. And Gavin's wife, Catherine, can't satisfy his needs. He says she's already gone through the menopause and has lost interest. We were drawn to each other like moths to a flame. A rather fiery flame, I have to say," she said, her face turning to a grin as she thought about it. "But I still don't see what this has got to do with Isla's murder."

Mairi ignored the statement as her mind whizzed around, processing the verbal and non-spoken information. "Did Isla know about your relationship with Gavin? Did she ever threaten you?"

"Good heavens! No." Ruth said, apparently astounded at the suggestion. "Why on earth are you suggesting such a thing?"

Chapter Thirty-Two

Mairi pulled up on Main Street in Abbeytown, having thanked Ruth Ingleton for her time and left her worrying about whether her extra-marital affair might now be exposed. The Brownlow's house was a red-sandstone, semi-detached, extended to the side and with a large parking area leading to a double garage.

She knocked on the front door, her eyes scanning the area as she waited. Horses grazed in the adjacent field and, like in Wigton, Skiddaw was easily visible in the distance. She knocked again. This time the door cracked open. "Yes?"

Mairi smiled. "Detective Constable Gordon." She said in a friendly tone, then showed her police ID. "I've come to return your gloves, Mrs Brownlow. The forensics lab has finished with them."

Catherine Brownlow looked surprised. "Oh! I never expected someone would make a trip over here to bring them back."

"Well, actually I need to have a chat while I'm here. Just to clarify a couple of things."

"Please come in." Mrs Brownlow stepped back and swung the door wide. She waited for Mairi to enter, then closed the door.

"Come this way." She led Mairi into the kitchen at the back of the house and offered her a seat at the rustic pine table, before putting a kettle onto the range to heat.

Mrs Brownlow joined Mairi at the table. "What was it you wanted to ask, officer?"

"Nothing much. We just wondered why you chose to holiday in Dumfriesshire?"

Mrs Brownlow looked perplexed. "I told the other officer. We regularly walk the coast between Silloth and Skinburness, where we see the Dumfries coastline across the water. We wanted to see it up close."

"Whose idea was it?" Mairi asked casually.

"I don't know. I think we both talked about visiting one day."

"And on the morning you found the bodies, who chose the route for the walk?"

"Gavin. He's the one who's good at map reading." Mrs Brownlow's brow furrowed. "Why are you asking?"

Mairi ignored the question, needing to stay in control, and continued. "Was your husband familiar with the area?"

"I don't think so. He studied the map intently before we set off that morning."

"Who was the first to rise that morning?"

"Gavin, as usual. He's normally out of bed before me." The lines on Catherine's forehead had become deep troughs as her concern rose about the questioning.

"Is it possible Gavin could have gone out for a walk while you were still in bed? Would you have known?"

"I suppose so. I sleep soundly." Mrs Brownlow replied, then continued in a schoolteacher tone. "But I think it's time you told me why you're asking such probing questions. You seem to be suggesting something."

"We're just trying to piece together all the details, to gain an accurate picture of what occurred that day. And to examine all possibilities. It's just routine. Nothing to be worried about. I notice you keep chickens," Mairi quickly threw in, to distract Mrs Brownlow.

"Yes. They're good layers, as well. Would you like some eggs?" She rose from her seat. "They produce more than we can use."

"That's very kind of you, Mrs Brownlow but I'm staying in a hotel and not sure when I'll be getting home to Edinburgh." Catherine poured steaming water from the kettle into a teapot, returning the kettle to a warm spot on the range.

"Edinburgh, you say. It's been a while since I visited. Lovely city. I remember going there to see the Military Tattoo when I was a child. But it's become so expensive now, hasn't it? Not sure I could justify spending nearly £200 each to watch a load of bands and a few motorbikes whizzing around."

"Does Gavin have a shotgun?"

Mrs Brownlow was disturbed by the new question. "Err, yes. He keeps it in the outhouse."

"I'd like to see it, please."

Catherine stood and opened a drawer in the dresser. "I don't know what Gavin's done with the key to the box. I never use the gun. Hate guns. Another reason not to go to the Tattoo. But it is useful Gavin having one, because we've had foxes around after the chickens. He's seen them off with his gun. Managed to kill one a few years back."

Mrs Brownlow continued. "But only after it had decimated our chickens. Killed every last one, it did." She moved on to another drawer, foraging around. "Pointless murder. It's not as if the fox could have eaten them all. Seems the dammed animals just kill for the fun of it. All these townies get fired up about the poor little cute foxes being chased by hounds. They deserve all they get, as far as I'm concerned. I blame that Basil Brush character on kiddies TV all those years back. Made a generation of children think foxes are cuddly creatures. But that's a lie. They're vicious killers."

Mairi let Mrs Brownlow have her rant uninterrupted, before asking her the next question. "Has your husband ever taken the gun out of the house? Does he belong to a shooting club, perhaps?"

Catherine poured tea into two mugs and slid one across the table to Mairi. "Help yourself to milk and sugar... No. Gavin has never been into shooting as a sport. He learned to shoot when he was a teenager. His father was a farmer. Still is, actually."

Mairi let Mrs Brownlow talk, knowing that useful information sometimes slipped out when people got carried away.

"His shotgun is one he owned when he lived on the farm. He left it behind at his father's house when he left home, but after our first encounter with foxes, he retrieved it from the family farm and brought it home. It's all properly licensed. The licensing people called round to check on his storage facilities, just after he brought the gun here." Mrs Brownlow gave up on her hunt for the key and returned to the kitchen table.

Mairi switched her line of questioning. "I hear Gavin is keen on amateur dramatics?"

Mrs Brownlow looked up, wondering how the officer knew that. "Yes. But he's not into acting. Just the behind-the-scenes stuff. Making props and operating the lights. That sort of thing."

"My father fancied himself as an actor," Mairi responded. "It kept him busy when he wasn't working. Does it take up much of Gavin's time?" Mairi asked, adding in the personal revelation to show empathy.

"Good heavens. Yes. Once they decide on their next production, he's away building things a couple of evenings a week. And almost every evening leading up to opening night, as well as the production nights, of course."

Mairi tilted her head. "Have you become a theatre widow, like my mam was?" She added a splash of milk to her tea and took a sip - it was much tastier than the cup Mrs Ingleton had poured for her earlier.

"I suppose I am left on my own a lot," Mrs Brownlow responded with sadness in her voice, before perking up. "But that suits me fine. I have my hobbies. Sewing, crafts. And I enjoy a bit of telly."

Mairi had enough information from Catherine Brownlow. Gavin Brownlow was in a secret sexual relationship with Ruth Ingleton. He owned and regularly used a shotgun. The walk route on which they discovered Isla Muir's body was Gavin's choice. And he could have gone out early on the morning of her murder, while his wife slept. Now Mairi was keen to speak with Mr Brownlow. "I'll be calling on your husband next. At his work. He knows I'm coming. But I will need to see his shotgun. Please call him and find out where he keeps the key."

Mrs Brownlow moved into the hall. Mairi could hear her using the landline phone to speak with her husband. She didn't just ask about the key.

* * *

"I hear you've been asking my wife some rather prying questions. Why are you so interested in us? We're not the criminals. We just found the bodies. I don't see why you're delving into our lives. And I'm not happy about it," Brownlow said gruffly, anger in his eyes.

Mairi had just been shown into a small conference room with florescent lighting and blank walls in the building where Gavin Brownlow worked. The metal-legged conference table had a cold Formica top. The chairs were equally cold, Mairi found, as she sat in one.

"Let me get straight to the point, Mr Brownlow," Mairi stated, as she sat beside the table. "We know you found the bodies. We also know that there was a connection between you and the woman who had been shot. Mrs Muir."

Gavin pulled a chair out from the conference table, its feet squeaking across the floor, then sat. His brow was deeply furrowed. "A connection between me and the dead woman. No! How could that be?"

"Mrs Muir was a friend of Mrs Ingleton, who in turn is a close friend of yours." Mairi stared at Brownlow as he took in what she had said, watching for his reaction.

"I wouldn't say Ruth and I are close friends," Brownlow said defensively.

"How would you describe a long-term ongoing sexual relationship, if it's not close, Mr Brownlow?" Mairi asked teasingly.

Gavin stood and paced around the room. "What's going on here, officer? My wife and I find a body in a field in Scotland and you come here probing into our personal life. We'd have been better off not reporting it. Are you going to hound us and fit us up for murder? Can't you find the killer? Is that it?" He said, his voice rising. "You're desperate to solve the case, so you try to pin it on us. I shall make a formal complaint. This is harassment."

"Calm down, Mr Brownlow," Mairi said soothingly. "We have to look at all possibilities; leave no stone unturned. Wouldn't you want us to do that if your wife had been murdered?"

Brownlow sat again. His shoulders slumped, the redness and tension in his face subsided. "Of course, I would. I just don't understand why you think we might have had something to do with the murder."

"Okay. So, this is what might have happened. You're having an affair with Ruth Ingleton. Isla Muir finds out and attempts to blackmail you both, saying she'll inform your spouses. Your marriages would both get wrecked. So, you arrange a little holiday in Dumfries."

Mairi paused. She had his full attention. "On the day of Isla Muir's murder, you rise early, leaving your wife in bed, as you normally do, and take your shotgun with you. You follow Isla Muir and when she's out of sight of the roads, you confront her."

"This is ridiculous!" Brownlow blasted, the blood in his face now trying to burst out under the pressure.

Mairi ignored his outburst. "She's obviously not going to withdraw her threat, so you kill her. The Labrador leaps at you and you kill the dog as well. You return to the guesthouse and shower before rousing your sleepy wife. Your next step is to take your wife to the spot where you killed Mrs Muir, to cover the tracks you made earlier. Problem solved. How does that sound?"

"Absurd!" Brownlow bellowed, glaring angrily into Mairi's eyes. "Firstly, I've never met this Muir woman. Secondly, if it came out that Ruth and I had been seeing each other and my marriage ended in divorce, I'd be happy, as long as Ruth also divorced her husband. It's not just a sexual relationship; I love her." Brownlow paused, his eyes wandering before returning to fix on Mairi with another stare. "Catherine has become a boring, cold fish. I don't know how I've stayed with her for so long. Thirdly, I didn't take my shotgun to Scotland. Fourthly, it's not been fired in weeks. Fifthly, I could never shoot a dog."

"But you could shoot a woman!" Mairi suggested.

"I think it's time you left, Constable," Brownlow blustered. "And next time you want to speak to me, I'll ensure I have a solicitor present. Good day to you!" He opened the door, his arm-gesture inviting Mairi to leave.

Mairi exited the room but paused and turned to address Brownlow one last time. "Don't you think it's time you came clean with your wife, Mr Brownlow? You can't deceive her forever. The truth *will* come out, eventually."

As Mairi meandered along the corridor, heading for the building's exit, Brownlow swung the door closed with such fury that the glass panel cracked. He might not be guilty of murder, but he was certainly guilty of betrayal. She pitied his wife.

Chapter Thirty-Three

Gloomy dark clouds had swarmed across the sky, threatening to drown anyone not hiding away indoors. Carl was one of those people. He stood at the corner of a row of shops, the damp cool air making him shiver, as he shuffled his feet. He hoped the rain would hold off, as he wasn't dressed appropriately for a downpour.

As the first few drops landed around him, he pulled his hood over his head. It would keep his hair and neck from getting soaked for a while. He dug his hands deep into his coat pocket, praying for the activity he'd been waiting for, for over ten minutes now.

His prayers were answered as the door he'd been watching swung open. A man Carl didn't recognise strode away, not caring to close the door behind him, as the return spring did its work.

Carl sprinted light-footed to the door and caught it before it closed. He slipped in and tip-toed up the stairs to Jimmy Price's flat. He tapped on the door, hearing a voice calling out, "Whaddya want now?" The door opened and Carl walked into the flat, gently pushing Jimmy backwards to make space inside.

Price swore. "Ya canna just walk in here without a warrant. I've got rights."

"Shut up, Jimmy. I don't need a warrant to have a chat with a friend." Carl's reputation relied on him gaining Price's cooperation. "Look, Jimmy, I'm after some information about one of your customers."

"What do you mean, customers?" Price said, his eyebrows crunching together. "You know I don't deal anymore."

"If I search your flat, then Jimmy, I won't find any drugs?"

"No. I told you. I don't do that stuff anymore. Hated being in jail last time. I've no inclination to spend more time there. I'm going straight now."

Carl believed that Jimmy had hated prison but wasn't inclined to believe his going straight declaration. "Perhaps I might believe you, Jimmy. Maybe I won't perform a search. But I'd be more inclined to walk away and let you get about your business if you can help me with my enquiries."

"Whaddya want to know?"

"There's a woman lives around here. Bit of a big shot. We know she's a cocaine user. I just want to know who's most likely to be her supplier. If you can steer me in the right direction, I'll leave you be."

Carl knew Price had not been into supplying cocaine in the past and he evidently wasn't now, because he'd be driving something like a six series BMW if he was into big money drugs, rather than the rusting old banger parked around the back of the flats. Jimmy's products had been cannabis, barbiturates and ecstasy.

"Listen. I've never sold that shit. And I don't know who does. The supply chain for that stuff is serious crime. Scary people."

"Don't give me that, Jimmy," Carl said condescendingly. "You might not have dealt in cocaine yourself, but you know who does. If you don't help me out here. I'll be forced to conduct a search."

"Listen. You never heard it from me," Price responded nervously. "But if I was looking for harder drugs, I'd head over to Locharbriggs. There's a disused factory near Quarry Road."

Carl knew where Price meant.

"I hear they use the old office around the back."

"Happy days! That was easy, wasn't it Jimmy? I'll check it out and leave you be. I hope I won't have to trouble you again soon." Carl closed Price's door on his way out and skipped down the stairs, pleased he had the information he needed to follow through. But he knew that his next confrontation might not be so easy.

* * *

The ticket in Isla Muir's bag had been for the Viaduct car park, close to the main shopping area. Mairi had searched through Muir's contacts and identified the only person located in the Cumbrian city's capital. She parked in the same car park that Isla Muir had used three weeks before and set off for Devonshire Street.

Crossing Victoria Viaduct, the smell and growl of a diesel train caught her attention as it passed underneath the street. She strained to look over the barriers to the tracks below. Mairi enjoyed travelling by train and would have used one for her journey into Carlisle had it been practicable. She loved relaxing with a book and glancing out at the passing scenes as she travelled.

The estate agent's office was perched on a corner with display windows on two streets, its entrance door framed by a curved sandstone facade. She entered the agent's office, and was quickly greeted by a dark suited man, his greying fair hair smartly cut and his shoes shining. His pink tie clashed with a blue shirt. He stepped forward. "How can I help you?"

Mairi met his eyes as she introduced herself. "Detective Constable Gordon, to see Mr Michael."

"That's me, detective." He smiled and offered his hand, which Mairi shook.

"You're very punctual. Come this way, please." He led her through a door in the room's corner and into a small office. It was basic. Just two fabric-covered chairs and a beech-effect desk. Framed certificates were the only items breaking the blandness of the white walls.

They sat, Mairi retrieving her notebook before speaking. "I understand Mrs Isla Muir visited you on the 8th of April?"

The agent referred to his diary before responding. "That's correct. She was interested in purchasing a former bank building on Lowther Street. It needed a complete refurbishment and alterations to the layout to be of any use. Mrs Muir thought it might be a sound investment, but after visiting the property, along with her builder, she decided not to make an offer."

"Do you know the builder's name?" Mairi asked, curious whether this additional player might be a useful contact.

"I'm afraid not," the agent said, shaking his head. "She never said... I think she referred to him as Rick, but other than that, I couldn't say."

"And that's the last time you saw Mrs Muir?"

"Yes. She emailed me a couple of days later to let me know she wasn't interested in the property but asked to be informed if another property came on the market."

Mairi absorbed what she'd heard and considered it before continuing. "And did you inform her about any other properties?"

Michael's eyes looked over Mairi's shoulder towards the sound of the outer door opening. "No. Nothing new has come to the market recently. Is that all? Only I have clients to deal with," he concluded.

"Yes. Thanks, Mr Michael. I appreciate your time."

Mairi left the office. She'd never been to Carlisle before and, having over an hour left on her parking ticket, decided to take a look around the city centre before heading back to Dumfries. The charity shops might have some retro clothing to add to her wardrobe. A cup of coffee would also be welcome. And if she still had time after that, she would have a quick look around the Cathedral. She'd heard it was worth a visit.

* * *

Carl drove into the disused truck park by the old factory. Weeds grew through every crack and seam of the crumbling concrete base. He locked his car and meandered around the back of the building, looking for signs of life, his shoe heels clacking on the hard surface.

Almost every pane of glass in the windows above the tall blank walls had been smashed - probably bored kids seeking a thrill. The doors were locked or blocked off by timber fixed over them. He could see no way into the main section of the building, but it was the offices that Jimmy had said were in use.

He heard a car pull up somewhere behind him. Near where he'd parked his car. It would be his uniformed pals coming to back him up. He continued to the single-story office block that was attached to the rear of the hangar-like factory. There appeared to be only one entrance to the office complex. He approached the door, peering into the windows for signs of life.

A shout from behind him took his attention. It wasn't a friendly shout. "What the fuck do you want?"

Two men were striding towards him, both with aggressive expressions on their faces. The man who spoke had short-cropped hair and spiderweb tattoos on both hands. He put his right hand into his pocket and pulled out something small, but Carl couldn't see what it was.

"I asked you a question, pal," the man snarled. "Has the cat got your tongue?"

Carl was concerned. Two probably armed thugs and just him. He should have held back until his colleagues arrived. It was too late now. "Is this your place, then?" he asked, trying not to let his voice sound nervous. "I thought it was derelict."

The men slowed but they were close now. "What's it to you?" the leader sneered.

CHAPTER THIRTY-THREE

"I heard I could pick up some supplies here."

"Who told you to come here? What do you want?"

"I was looking for some C. Do you have any?"

The leader turned to his pal. "Doesn't look like a customer to me. What do you think?"

"Na. I reckon he's a copper." The smaller man was skinny. By himself, he wouldn't give Carl much trouble in a fight, although little whippets like him could be fast with a knife.

"I'm not looking for trouble, guys. Just some C. If you don' have any, I'll just be on my way." Carl made as if to walk off, now scared that he was alone with two drug dealers, both probably armed with knives. They posed a significant threat. He slipped a hand around his telescopic baton, just in case.

"Definitely a copper, I reckon," the leader concurred. "You're not going anywhere, pal." He stepped forward, the object in his hand clicking as its four-inch blade sprung from its handle, the steel glinting in the light.

"Hang on, guys. There's no need for that." Carl said, stress in his voice as he extended his weapon.

The two men noticed Carl's baton. "We were right," the leader said to his pal. "He *is* a copper." He nodded towards Carl, then stepped towards him, laughing. "You think that thing's going to stop me sticking you? Not a chance."

Carl heard a vehicle pull into the car park and caught a glint of blue light reflect off another building. The cavalry had arrived. Thank God! But he knew the danger hadn't passed yet. "Let's not make things more difficult. I only came here for information." He was stalling, trying to delay the conflict, but keyed up to use his baton if he had to.

The skinny man, noticed the running feet approaching and grabbed his friend's arm. "We need to get out of here," he said, indicating with his head the direction of the oncoming danger.

The leader turned and saw two uniformed policemen. "Shit." He turned towards Carl and spat. "Bastard." He made a lunge at him with the knife. Carl jumped back but the knife caught his left arm, slicing through his coat and into his forearm. "Fuck you, copper," the man screamed, then turned and ran after his pal, away from the factory, out into the countryside.

Despite the injury to his arm, Carl leapt forward and swung his baton. It thwacked into the shoulder of his attacker, causing him to cry out in pain and to stumble, but he recovered and continued his escape.

One officer turned and went in pursuit of the two offenders. The other, PC Will Kennedy, paused and shouted, "You alright, Carl?"

"Yeah. I'll be fine, Will." Carl winced. "Get the sods."

Will followed his partner, accelerating, and soon caught up with the other officer. The two drug dealers jumped a low fence at the edge of the plot and turned left, heading towards some woodland. The skinny guy was ahead and widening the gap, but his pal was less agile. He staggered on the uneven surface and fell forward, thumping onto the ground. The two offices pounced on him, holding him down, disarming him and cuffing him in a flash.

They looked up as the other thug disappeared into the woods. Will spoke to his partner. "It's too late to chase him down now. Did you get a good look at him?"

"Not really. Just his back. But Carl certainly will have."

"Aye. Good point," Will agreed.

They led their prisoner back to the car, dragging him roughly over the fence.

Carl joined his colleagues at the cars, holding his injured arm. When they reached the vehicles, Will looked concerned as he asked Carl, "Can you drive with that injured arm? Here. Let me have a look."

As the other officer read the man his rights and placed the criminal into the back of the police car, Will examined Carl's injury, carefully lifting the coat and shirt fabric above the wound.

"It's not a deep cut," Carl said. "I'll be fine. Just need a change of clothes." His shirt, jumper and coat sleeves were all bloodied.

"You'd best get down to A&E and get that attended to," Will advised. "The least it will need is some butterfly strips to hold the wound together. And they'll need to make sure it doesn't get infected."

"Aye. You're right." Carl agreed with a sharp draw of breath as he accidentally moved his hand, opening the wound. "Just hope they can patch it up without too much delay. Can't afford to hang around in the hospital all day waiting for five minutes' treatment."

Will concluded, "We'll get this guy down to the station and booked in, ready for your return."

Chapter Thirty-Four

Tosh liked his coffee strong, milky and sweet. Standard NATO, they used to call it in the Army. He walked back to his desk with the steaming drink, then trawled Isla Muir's contacts for any Glaswegian connections. There was just one. He searched Muir's calendar for appointments that included the words Glasgow or the contact's name. The result correlated perfectly with the car parking ticket date. He called the number on her contacts list.

"Glasgow Land Rover. How can I help you?"

"Hi. This is Detective Sergeant McIntosh, Dumfries CID. I'd like to talk with Mr Christie, please."

"Just a second. I'll check if he's available." The phone went quiet. Half a minute later, the receptionist reconnected to Tosh. "Mr Christie is in today but he's with a client at the moment. Can I get him to call you back when he's free?"

"Aye. Please do." Tosh gave her his contact details and hung up.

Five minutes later, his phone rang. "DS McIntosh."

"Sergeant McIntosh. Gus Christie, here. You wanted to speak to me?"

"Aye. Thanks for calling back so promptly, Mr Christie. I just wanted to check with you about an appointment you had with a Mrs Muir on April 19th."

"Mrs Muir. Aye, I remember the lady. She traded in her Range

Rover for a newer one. Just a year old with only 8,000 miles on the clock. Silver. £82,000. Three-litre, V6 diesel, Sport model. High specification. Full leather seats, built-in satnav-"

"I get the picture, Mr Christie. No need to go into the vehicle's detail for me. What time would you say she left you?"

"She was here prompt at eleven. After inspecting the vehicle, doing the paperwork and paying for the vehicle, she'd have left around 12:45. Paid for the car with her debit card. Most people take out our finance deals and pay over 3-4 years."

"That's very helpful. Thanks for your time, Mr Christie." He hung up. *Eighty-two thousand pounds for a car!* Tosh could never imagine spending that amount of money. His eight-year-old Ford Mondeo had cost him six thousand pounds. Muir's spending demonstrated how much money she must have been making from her property development deals. Perhaps he was in the wrong career? But then he realised that Muir's career may have led to her early demise.

His mind switched back to the business in hand. He checked the car parking ticket. It had been for two hours in a city centre car park around twenty minutes after she'd left the car dealers. He guessed she had taken the opportunity for a shopping trip.

* * *

A second police car arrived at the old warehouse, its lights flashing. Its two officers got out and sauntered across to their colleagues. Clearly, the action was already over. "Alright Will? Carl? How's it going?" PC Lindsey Morrison asked.

Will responded. "Two fellas attacked Carl, then ran off when we arrived. Tom and I caught one of them." He turned his head and looked towards his car, indicating the man's location. "But the other skinny runt got away. Ran off into the woods over there."

"Ah!" Lindsey said. "There are loads of tracks through those woods and many exits. He could be anywhere by now. What did he look like?"

"About five foot six, I'd say," Carl offered. "As Will said, a skinny sod. Had a face like a whippet. Black hoodie, blue jeans, Black Nike cap."

Lindsey frowned. "I think I know who you're talking about," she exclaimed as she sauntered over to the other car. She peered into the rear window and got a sneer from its occupant, along with a single finger thrust upwards.

Lindsey opened the door, crouched down, looked disdainfully at the handcuffed man, then punched him in the side of his abdomen, her colleagues ignoring her action. He yelped, then shouted at Lindsey. "Hey, that's assault. Police brutality." His face contorted with the pain from his ribs.

"If you think that's police brutality," Lindsey sneered, "just give me more lip or another disrespectful gesture, and I'll show you what real brutality is." She looked challengingly at the man. "The police force is like NATO, pal. You attack one officer, you attack us all. Shut your trap, or you'll get a nuclear response." She glared at him, daring him to bite back. Hoping he would give her an excuse.

Knowing he was at the police officer's mercy, the man went silent and turned his head away, containing his anger to avoid further confrontation.

'That'll teach him not to dis me,' Lindsey thought to herself as she slammed the car door and turned back to the others, talking casually as if nothing had happened. "In case you didn't know, the thug in the car is Stuart Ingram. The whippet guy who hangs out with him is Daniel Preston. Reckon I know where he lives."

"Great. Can you drop Carl off at A&E - he shouldn't be driving with that cut on his arm - then call around the skinny fella's house?"

"Aye, sure," Lindsey agreed. "Come on Carl. Let's get you to the hospital."

"Give me your car keys, Carl." Will said. "I'll hang on here and search the car and the offices if I can get in. If you call me when you're finished, I'll come and get you."

Carl handed over his keys, then climbed into the rear of Lindsey's police car. She drove off, chatting to her partner, Gordon, leaving Carl to contemplate his near miss with serious injury. Perhaps death!

Will put on his gloves and searched the suspect's car, shuffling items around and examining each.

"Now look what I have here," Will said as he extracted a small polythene bag from the car's boot wheel well. He carried it over to the police car and laid it on the bonnet before extracting its contents. Bags of pills and two bags of a white powder. He opened the car door. "What's this, then, talcum powder?"

"Na. Icing sugar, ya dumb bastard," came the vehement response.

Will closed the door again, replacing the contents in its original bag, then dropped the entire thing into an evidence bag. His colleague, PC Tom Kerr, had finished searching the car's cabin. He turned to Will, holding up a pistol in his gloved hand. He removed the magazine, noting it contained bullets, then made the gun safe by clearing it, doing his best not to smudge any fingerprints that might exist. Tom dropped it into an evidence bag. "Just as well this had been left in the car," he said, his raised eyebrows suggesting a worse outcome.

Will concurred with his partner's statement, "Aye, you're right. Carl might have had more than a cut arm."

Tom headed off with the bagged evidence safely in the police car's boot, to book the suspected drug dealer into the station.

Now alone, Will walked back to the derelict office. There were several keys on the bunch they had confiscated from the thug, Ingram. He tried the office door lock and was successful on the third attempt.

The place was a tip. When the factory had closed, they must have walked away, leaving behind old chairs and tables, full wastepaper bins, which now laid on their side, with their contents scattered across the floor. The roof seemed to have been leaking. It smelled musty and there was a dark, mouldy patch on the ceiling.

Will wandered around, opening an old filing cabinet and desk drawers. The drawers contained various items of litter but nothing interesting or incriminating. Disappointed, he scanned the room, noticing an old bookcase that was not flush with the wall. Will shifted it and looked behind, discovering the reason for the bookcase having sat at an angle. A black handle protruded from the wall. His curiosity raised, Will shuffled the furniture out of the way, exposing the hidden object.

The key Will was searching for was easily spotted amid the confiscated bunch: it was large, black, and worn with age. Inserting it into the lock, he turned it with ease, then gripped the handle and pulled open the heavy door of the safe, its hinges protesting with a creak. Revealed within was a trove of illicit substances: a hoard of drugs and stacks of money.

Will smiled, happy to have discovered the significant evidence. He reached for his radio to summon assistance from Carl's colleagues and crime scene investigators.

Barely half an hour elapsed before the CSIs arrived, accompanied by DS McIntosh, a seasoned figure in Dumfries. A man for whom Will had great respect.

"Good find, Will," Tosh said. "We'll need to get the drugs to forensics as soon as we can. They could be a critical link with the murder victim. Did you find anything else of interest in there?"

"The safe contents were the only things of interest. The place is a shit heap; litter strewn all over the floor. There's also an old kettle, a camping stove and a couple of filthy mugs. Looks like they've been making themselves a brew."

"Thanks, Will," Tosh responded, his tone formal but friendly. "I'll make sure the CSIs check the litter for prints to link with the two suspected drug dealers."

As if on cue, Will's phone rang, causing his attention to shift. He listened before responding. "Aye. Sure thing. That was quick, Carl. I'll come right away." He turned to Tosh. "That was Carl."

"Aye, I guessed that much when you used his name," Tosh quipped wryly.

"He's been patched up in A&E." Will explained, brushing off Tosh's sarcasm. "I promised to pick him up. If you don't need me any further, I'll head over to get him."

"Aye. Sure." Tosh assented. "You do that. But stop off here with him, please, unless he's been ordered to his bed. I'd appreciate a word with him."

With a nod, Will handed Tosh the keys to the suspect's car and the offices before heading off in Carl's car.

* * *

Tosh was on the verge of getting into his Focus to head back to the station when he spotted the arrival of Will and Carl. He closed the door again and strolled over to Carl's car, signalling for Carl to join him. Will remained in the vehicle, waiting for a lift back to the station.

The two officers ambled towards the rear of the factory, where the CSI van was stationed. Blue and white crime scene tape prohibited the entry of all, except those invited. Tosh initiated the conversation. "Did Constable Kennedy tell you about the safe he found containing a stash of drugs?"

"Yeah, he did. Good news, eh?" Carl replied with a hint of relief in his voice.

"Good news indeed," Tosh agreed, then paused before proceeding more seriously. "Look Carl, although it turned out well, I have to say you took an unnecessary risk investigating this before back-up arrived. Had Will and Tom not turned up when they did, you could have found yourself injured and bleeding out from a knife wound to the gut, in that grimy corner," he remarked, gesturing toward a pile of debris and leaves gathering at the intersection of the office building and the factory.

"Yeah. I realise that, but it did all work out okay in the end," he responded, seeming unconcerned.

"Just as long as you understand how close you came to being dead meat," Tosh said seriously, a deep frown on his forehead.

Carl shrugged his shoulders.

"I'm serious, Constable," Tosh said, emphasising the formality of the chat by using Carl's rank. "When your report about this incident, resulting in your hospital visit, reaches the force HQ, you'll likely be hauled up in front of the Chief Super. Just make sure you have the right attitude to the dressing down you'll undoubtedly get. If you brush it off when being chastised, you'll be in even deeper trouble."

"Okay, sarge. I get it." Carl reluctantly accepted what his boss was saying. "I realise things could have gone much worse. This time I was lucky. I'll hold back in the future." He turned away and wandered back to his car, head down, like a dog with its tail between its legs. Tosh watched him for a moment, then headed back to his own car, his thoughts mingling with a sense of relief and concern over his colleague's well-being.

Chapter Thirty-Five

On return to the station, Tosh ran a check on Isla Muir's contacts list, comparing it against the PNC criminal database. It flagged up one name, a man with a record for violence and suspected of drug dealing. The man they had just arrested at Locharbriggs, Stuart Ingram.

Tosh marched into the interview room, determined to get Ingram talking. He sat opposite the suspect and unwaveringly stared at him. "Right then. Let's get straight to the point. You've been arrested for carrying a concealed weapon, assaulting a police officer, and causing actual bodily harm. We'll be adding to that possession of an unlicensed firearm and Class A drugs with the intent to supply."

Ingram sat opposite Tosh, staring at his fingers, as he dug out dirt from under his nails. He said nothing.

"What do you have to say for yourself, Ingram?"

He didn't look up and nonchalantly replied, "No comment."

"Well, it makes no difference whether you say anything. The evidence is overwhelming. You have only one choice to make. Do you keep your mouth shut, and plead not guilty in court, then go to prison for a very long time? Or do you cooperate, tell us who your supplier is and plead guilty? The second option gets you a more lenient sentence."

Ingram's head remained down, refusing to make eye contact, as he flicked fingernail dirt onto the floor. "No comment."

"Have it your own way. We'll find out who your supplier is, anyway.

I'm happy with that. You'll go away longer. Keeps you off the street and out of my hair."

Tosh passed a picture of Isla Muir across the desk, spinning it to the correct orientation for Ingram to see. "Do you know this woman?"

He glanced up at the picture before returning his eyes to his fingernails. "No comment."

"Thanks for confirming you know the woman," Tosh said, his eyes remaining fixed on the man. "If you didn't know her, you'd have just said no."

Ingram shrugged his shoulders, then rubbed his hand through his spiky hair, before scratching his scalp.

Tosh continued. "Another reason we're confident you knew the woman and we'll prove a connection is we found a bag of white powder in her home. Undoubtedly, it is cocaine that will match with the stash we found in your car and the safe. Furthermore, your phone number is on the dead woman's phone," Tosh concluded.

Ingram sat up suddenly, looking directly at Tosh, his eyes wide. "What do you mean, dead woman? If Isla's been found dead, it's nothin' to do wi' me. You canna pin that on me. Get me a solicitor. I know my rights."

"Thanks for confirming your association with the dead woman, Mr Ingram." Tosh stood. "Put him back in the cells. We'll charge him later when the duty solicitor arrives."

* * *

PC Lindsey Morrison stood outside the drab, pebble-dashed, mid-terraced house, in a housing estate to the south of the town. It was an area she was familiar with, because they had more call outs to this small estate than any other in or around Dumfries. She gave her patrol partner, PC Gordon Falconer, time to get into position around the back of the house, where he would cover any rearward escape attempt, then knocked loudly on the tatty yellow door.

She looked around, noticing wheel-less, rusting bicycles, old sofas and uncut, weed-infested grass in the neighbouring front gardens. The only exception to this group of uncared-for houses was one garden totally covered in concrete paving slabs; not a plant or object could claim this barren patch of land to be home. Impatient for an answer, she thumped the door again a few seconds later.

A voice came from inside the house. "Alright, alright. Keep ya hair on. I'm coming." A moment later, the door opened, and the smell of tobacco smoke and dog wafted out. As if on cue, a dog barked behind a closed door.

The woman's eyes rolled, and she let out an exasperated sigh when she spotted Lindsey. "Might have known," she declared, through nicotine-stained teeth. "Other folk would'nae have bashed the door so loud. What is it ya want? Has that toerag of a son been up to no good again?"

"Mrs Aileen Preston?" Lindsey asked as she scanned the woman's face. She was probably in her forties but looked much older. Her skin was heavily wrinkled and pallid. Her salt and pepper hair hung like straw from her scalp. She wore unpressed grey slacks and an ancient beige Shetland jumper.

"Aye that's me." She made no offer for Lindsey to enter the house, and for the moment she was happy to stay where she was - in the fresh air.

"Is Daniel home?"

"Not likely. Dan does'nae live here anymore. Won't have him in me hoose."

"Do you mind if we come in and look around?"

"Yes, I *do* mind. It's my hoose. He does'nae live here. I've telt ya. So, you've no reason to come in." She crossed her arms and stared at the officer.

Lindsey frowned at the uncooperative response but kept her cool. "It's important that we speak with him. Do you know where he lives?"

Mrs Preston pondered the question, then replied. "Don't you go telling him you heard it from me, but I think he's got digs somewhere near the Dumfries Academy. And that's all I know," she replied with finality, before stepping back and closing the door.

Lindsey spoke into her shoulder mic, recalling Gordon. It was time to leave. Her forehead furrowed as she considered what she'd just heard. A drug dealer living near a secondary school!

* * *

The two officers parked near the Academy, an area of mixed housing, shops and businesses. They wandered the streets away from the shopping zone, lined by traditional stone terraces and modern blocks of flats. Lindsey knocked on doors on one side of the street and Gordon, the other side, asking if anyone recognised their description of Daniel Preston or knew him by name. After half an hour of blank faces and 'never heard of him' responses, Lindsey phoned the CID office, frustrated.

DC Penrose answered their call.

"Hi Carl," Lindsey said, with a hint of surprise. "I didn't know you were back at work already. Can't have been much of a war wound if they let you out that quickly and not sent you home," she jibed.

Carl didn't rise to the bait. "Yeah. As I said to Will, it was just a scratch. Although I have been advised not to tackle any criminals for a while," he replied, smiling.

"Listen. We've heard that Stuart Ingram's pal, Daniel Preston, is living somewhere near the Academy. We've knocked on a load of doors but without a picture of him, we're getting nowhere."

"Okay. I'll see what I can do. Haven't checked the PNC yet to see if he's got a record. I'll call you back in five." Carl hung up, then opened the criminal database application on his computer.

Lindsey and Gordon continued to knock on doors and ask passers-by if they knew Preston. Twenty minutes later, Lindsey's phone rang. It was Carl.

"That was a long five minutes!"

"Yeah. Sorry about that. Preston isn't on the PNC. I'm in the CCTV room now and Ben, here," he said, glancing at the CCTV monitoring operative, "has found Preston. I'll get a still of him to your phone ASAP. He was heading along Church Crescent towards the Academy."

"Ah! We've been knocking on doors at the other end of the school. We'll head down that way now. Thanks Carl."

By the time they reached the place where Preston had been seen, Lindsey had the image. She shared it with Gordon, and they started knocking on doors and going into local shops. They came up trumps at the Turkish barbers. Preston, it seemed, liked a number one cut all over. They said he lived above a tattoo parlour just up the road. He often showed them his latest tat.

The two constables joined up and strode along the road to the tattoo parlour. The ugly, rendered building was squeezed in between two 19th century stone-built character properties, opposite an equally attractive church. They walked around the block, looking for potential escape routes before deciding on the same tactics they employed at Mrs Preston's home. They discussed the potential of him being armed with a knife but decided their stab vests and Tasers would more than even up the score. Going by the last encounter colleagues had with Preston, he was likely to make a run for it out the back.

"Lindsey went to the door beside the tattoo parlour and rang the bell. There was no answer. She looked up and saw the blinds move. Clearly, there was someone in the flat. She pressed the bell push and held it there. Then radioed Gordon to warn him.

The fire escape clanged as Preston charged down the spiral stairs. He'd seen the police officer out front and wasn't planning on giving himself up. Hitting the ground at a run, he sped along the narrow lane at full pelt but as he emerged onto the road, something connected with his legs. He felt pain in both shins, then flew forwards, falling onto his front.

His arms stretched out to break his fall, the skin torn off his palms and shredded at his wrists, his chin grazed, as the concrete surface ground into him. He yelled as his senses reacted to the searing pain.

Before he could rise, a heavy weight fell on him. He shrieked as PC Falconer grasped one of his abraded wrists and wrenched it down his side, then up his back. "Get the fuck off me!" he yelled. Then the next arm went the same way. Another squeal, his face screwing up with the sharp pain.

"Shut your filthy mouth. You're under arrest."

Preston heard feet pounding fast down the road. Another copper on the way.

"Got the little runt, then!" Lindsey declared, catching her breath, as she watched Gordon cuff Preston. They pulled him to his feet, read him his rights, and paraded him to the police car.

Chapter Thirty-Six

It had been a while since the CID interview room had been so well used. It was institutionally bland by design, offering no comfort. This time it was Daniel Preston sitting behind the desk. Tosh opposite.

He seemed to Tosh to be one of those guys who were mouthy and brave in their own environment, but now that his power had been taken from him, he'd shrivelled up.

Tosh leaned forward, studying Preston intently. He looked more like the victim of bullying than a dangerous drug dealer with a knife. This assessment was crucial for identifying the correct interview tactics to prompt the response they wanted. They already had evidence of his involvement in drug dealing. Today's aim would be to identify the supplier.

"So, you're the little sod who knifed my colleague, then ran off into the woods," Tosh opened, glaring at the suspect.

Preston's gaze shot up, a flicker of defiance in his eyes. "I never stabbed that copper. It was Stu. He did it. I never did nothin'. You're not pinning that on me."

Tosh was pleased Preston had so easily confirmed Ingram had stabbed Carl, but he kept his feelings to himself as he continued the questioning. "So you say! Well, when DC Penrose gets released from the hospital, we'll see what he has to say." Tosh replied, knowing full well that Carl was no longer in hospital and had already told him who had attacked him. He needed to build the pressure. "And I'll believe my colleague over you, any day."

Preston stayed silent. His eyes dropped to the table.

"Whether you go to jail for assaulting a police officer or not. You'll definitely end up there on the other charges."

"What charges?" Preston snapped.

Tosh responded calmly. "Carrying a concealed weapon... The knife found in your possession when you were arrested, to start with."

Preston faltered before responding. "I only carry that for protection. I've never used it."

Tosh leaned in, his voice dripping with scepticism. "And we can take your word for that, can we?" Tosh paused. "It doesn't matter what motive you have for carrying the knife, anyway. It's the same offence. But the biggest thing that's going to get you put away is drug dealing."

Preston shifted uncomfortably. "I never had no drugs on me. You canna do me for possession."

"You arrived at the old factory in the same car as Stuart Ingram." Tosh pointed out. "A car that was searched after his arrest and a quantity of Class A drugs found. You'll both be done for possession."

Tosh paused as he watched Preston, looking for signs he might give up more information. "But possession is a minor crime. It's dealing that the judges deplore. It's dealing that gets you put away for many years. And you know what they do with fragile little things like you in jail, don't you?" Tosh hinted.

Preston fidgeted nervously. "I'm no dealer. It's Stu. I just hang around with him."

"Well, by hanging around with Stuart Ingram, that makes you his accomplice. It will be seen as a joint enterprise... You're as guilty as him."

Tosh let his words sink in. The lengthy prison sentence. The potential abuse by other prisoners. He watched as realisation dawned and Preston's expression shifted.

"As I said, there's no doubt you'll be going to prison. You've no control over that. But what you can influence is how long you stay in that hellhole."

Preston looked up again, interest showing in his piggy eyes.

"If you help us out with some information, we won't press charges on some of your crimes. That will lessen your sentence."

"What do ya wanna know?" Preston asked, all the fight extinguished by fear of jail.

Tosh smiled inwardly, leaned back, his gaze unyielding. "Who supplies you and Stu with the drugs?"

Preston hesitated, then sighed. "I told you, I'm no drug dealer. I've never met the guy. Stu deals with that stuff. I just hang around and help him out."

Tosh sat quietly for a minute before speaking again. "Oh! Well. If you've got nothing to offer us, we may as well wrap this up and charge you with all the offences." He stood slowly, straightening his thin stack of papers, by tapping them on the table. He turned and walked towards the door, glancing at Preston as he did, and noting the tension in his face.

As Tosh turned the door handle, he smiled as Preston spoke.

"Hang on a minute." Preston blurted out. "I think I know who it might be..."

* * *

The caravan site warden, Nigel, and his wife, Jill, sat at their dining table, the aroma of freshly poured coffee steaming from their mugs.

"I wish we'd never sold the van to that Westwood chap," Jill said to her husband, her brows furrowed as she gazed down the site. "There are people coming and going at all hours. I'm sure he's up to no good."

"Aye, you're probably right, hen," Nigel replied, with a thoughtful nod, as he stared out the window, watching the rain bounce off the pink and beige paving slabs that made up his patio.

Nestled on the edge of Dumfries town, the site was normally a tranquil place, with owners staying for weekends in their holiday home or sometimes for a couple of weeks. Certainly not a busy place. It was supposed to be a holiday site, open eleven months of the year, with no sub-letting. For owners and families only. Exclusive, respectable and refined. But that had changed last month when Westwood had moved in.

"Unless he breaks the rules of his licence though, there's not much we can do," Nigel went on, now returning his attention to his wife. "The licence doesn't restrict the number of times owners can come and go, or how many visitors they're allowed."

Jill's lips pursed with annoyance. "There ought to be rules on that sort of thing. And that Land Rover of his makes a racket. He needs to get the exhaust fixed."

Nigel nodded in agreement. "I ken what you mean, hen. The license conditions mention occupiers should not make excessive noise, especially after 11 p.m. So, I guess we can push him on that one. If it'll make you happy, I'll have a word with him?"

"Aye, that'd be good; I'd appreciate it," Jill responded, her expression softening and her face brightening now her hubby had agreed to act.

"Right-o, then. I will," Nigel said in a tone that suggested that was the end of the matter for now. He returned his attention to drinking his coffee, wondering how Westwood would react?

* * *

Davie Westwood stared out of his caravan's bay window, noticing the rain had stopped and the sun had broken through the clouds. He peered past the more expensive vans with their large decking areas and outside dining tables to the motion that had caught his attention. The warden had emerged from his caravan and was headed directly towards him, along the recently asphalted driveway, as it snaked through the well-tended lawns.

'I wonder what the old bugger wants?' Davie said to himself, his brow furrowed. He didn't like being disturbed, questioned or challenged.

He had bought the second-hand caravan - one of the cheaper vans on the site - with the profits from his last deal. In the short time he'd been on the site, he'd settled in. It was out of the way. No CCTV systems around. He had no rent to pay. Just annual site fees and the first year's fees had been included when he bought the van.

It was a bit noisy when it rained as the drops hammered against the metal roof. And the outer wall panels rattled in high winds. But otherwise, it was a peaceful place to live. Most of his neighbours only used their caravans for short periods and were empty in between. It suited him. Less prying eyes. Except the warden's wife, Jill. She was a nosy cow. A curtain-twitcher.

The warden knocked on Davie's door. For an old fella, Nigel had a good pace, Davie thought. He opened it and spoke. "Alright?"

"Alright," Nigel responded. "How're you settling in, Davie?"

"Fine, thanks. It's a lovely site you have here. Very quiet." He could smell the mist lifting off the warming tarmac.

"Aye, we like it that way, too. Talking of which, we wondered when you might be getting the exhaust on you Land Rover fixed?" His voice pleaded with Davie. "Only it does spoil the peace a bit."

Davie recognised the "we," to mean the wife. Nigel was just Jill's proxy voice. "Aye. Good point, Nige. It blew a hole the other day, and

I've been meaning to get it sorted. It annoys me as well. Been a bit busy, though. I'll get it seen to tomorrow."

"That'd be grand, Davie. Keep the missus happy too," he said with a wink, confirming Davie's assumption. "I'll let you get on then." He turned and strode away, his jaunty gait suggesting contentment at the outcome of their discussion.

Davie made a note to get the exhaust fixed. It *was* annoying him as well. The V8 engine was loud enough as it was, burbling away in tick-over, but with the hole in the pipe it was a low grumble and on acceleration a loud growl. He didn't want to draw attention to himself in the elderly vehicle as he drove around town. And he certainly could not use it for any night excursions until it was sorted.

Davie was a businessman now. A buyer and seller of commodities. This caravan was just a stepping stone to greater things. After the next deal, he'd replace the old Land Rover with a new one. Well, maybe not new, but newer.

And he would move up to a lodge next. Davie's ambitions shifted up a gear, as he thought ahead. One day he'd have one of those grand houses with a six-foot wall around it, a swimming pool, a bar for when he threw parties, Dobermans guarding the grounds at night, and electric operated gates. He would know he'd made it *then*.

* * *

Suzanna called the team together to catch up on where they were. The bright fluorescent light reflected off the incident board that had changed significantly since they first started the investigation. It was peppered with images of multiple suspects, notes, and threads connecting people and places, thanks to Mairi's earlier meticulous work.

The team exchanged glances as they discussed the various lines of enquiry. Drug dealing was just one of many options. It would be their current focus, but they mustn't lose sight of the other possibilities. They needed to keep an open mind, not be funnelled into a single option. Too many detective teams failed by following blinkered paths.

They recapped on Ingram's and Preston's interviews. They now had a lead to the supplier. A man known to Preston only by his first name. He'd heard Ingram talk about it. And he'd heard the guy was now living in a caravan on the edge of town. Following up on that would be their next job.

Suzanna called in Inspector Ferguson to seek his support.

"Ed, we need to raid a caravan we believe is the home of a drug smuggler with a connection to the murdered woman. He could be the killer and may possess a firearm. Can you arrange for an armed team to attend?"

"Of course. Taking out a drug distributor would be a feather in our caps," Ed responded with a nod, pleased to have been asked. "I'll get on to the armed-response guys. But given the drugs angle, we'd best inform the serious crime boys, as well."

Suzanna's jaw tightened. "It's your team, Tosh and Carl, who uncovered the drug dealing which led us to the distributor. I don't want the serious crime division taking the credit. Let's execute the raid first, then hand it over to them if the man isn't our murderer."

Ed mulled over her words briefly, his hands firmly in his pockets, his eyes scanning the ceiling. "Okay. That's fine with me, but you may get some hassle from them when you make the call," he replied, staring into the DCI's eyes, to ensure she understood his assessment.

"I can live with that, Ed." Suzanna acknowledged with a nod. "Get onto the armed response team and let me know when they could be ready to move in on the location. We have the site location, just not the specific caravan yet. We'll talk with the site warden and call in for backup once we know."

Ed strode out of the room, his footsteps echoing down the corridor. As the door closed with a click, Suzanna's eyes met those of her team members. Determination blazed in her gaze, mirrored by the resolute expressions around her. Eager anticipation grabbed them as they prepared for action.

Chapter Thirty-Seven

Tosh drove into the caravan site and parked up in a visitor's slot. He and Suzanna ambled over to the charcoal-grey-clad warden's office, acting as if husband and wife enquiring about caravans. Jill looked up from behind her desk. "Afternoon folks. How can I help you?"

"We were looking for the warden, Nigel Gibson," Tosh said.

"That's my husband. I'm Jill Gibson. Nigel does the practical work and I do the admin and sales. Can I help you, or do you need Nigel?"

Suzanna took over. "Hello, Jill. I'm Detective Chief Inspector McLeod, from Edinburgh, currently attached to Dumfries CID. We believe a site resident may be involved in a serious crime."

Jill's eyebrows rose.

"You and your husband will know whether anyone on the site is a bit different to the usual owners. We understand the man's first name is Davie."

Reality dawned on Jill's face. "I was just saying to Nigel last night that he doesn't fit here. Most of our owners just visit for short breaks but he lives here all the time and has lots of visitors. Nigel was going to ask the site owners if we could install an automatic barrier that needs a key fob to gain entry. At least that way the visitors would have to park outside instead of driving in past our caravan."

"Which caravan does this Davie live in? And what's his surname?"

"He's in number thirteen. Unlucky for us, I reckon. His name's

David Westwood."

Tosh called the station and asked for a PNC check on the man's name.

"Do you know if Mr Westwood is on site at the moment?"

"Aye. I saw him go in a while back. Not seen him come out yet. He's got a Silver Land Rover. In fact, you can see it from outside." Jill got up and headed towards the door.

"I'd prefer not to let Mr Westwood know we're interested in him," Suzanna said.

Tosh put his phone away. "Westwood has a record for certain activities related to our interest in him," he said, avoiding giving away confidential details in front of the site's administrator.

"Are there many people on site at the moment, Mrs Gibson?" Suzanna asked, conscious of the need to minimise risk to the public.

"Only a couple. Most went home yesterday. I think the Silvesters are in. They're in number eighteen. And I'm sure I saw the Mackays return about half an hour ago. They'll be in number twenty-three."

"Right, Tosh. I think it's time to call in the big boys. Get them on standby somewhere close but not visible from the site. We need to make sure the risk to the other residents is minimised first. Mrs Gibson, do you have any caravans for sale at the moment?"

"Aye. There are two lodges for sale. Number three and number nineteen."

"Okay. What I want you to do is walk us down the site, as if we're prospective buyers. We'll look into the first lodge. Spend a few minutes inside, then we'll walk down to the other one.

"While we're looking around it, I want you to knock on the doors of eighteen and twenty-three and ask them politely to leave. They must leave calmly. We don't want to spook Westwood. Once they're off site, we can make our call on Westwood. Clear?" Suzanna stared into Jill's eyes, stressing the importance of following her instructions.

"Yes, Chief Inspector. I think I can manage that. I'll get the keys for the empty lodges.

The party of three ambled down the site's only road, chatting naturally. After stopping in at number three, they continued their journey, passing Westwood's caravan. They glanced sideways at the van as they ambled by but didn't turn their heads. Inside number nineteen, Suzanna and Tosh sat near the window that had a view of number thirteen. Jill called into the other caravans as planned, then returned. They watched as the occupants of both lodges drove off the site.

"Right, Tosh. Get the team in."

He extracted his radio and made the call. As he did, Suzanna noticed a man exit thirteen and head towards his Land Rover. "Damn! He's on his way out," she blurted out.

Suzanna left the caravan and marched up the site towards Westwood, Tosh on her heels. Westwood looked up, the movement catching his attention. He moved faster, opening the door to his Land Rover and stepping in.

Suzanna sprinted, her heart rate accelerating with the effort and anticipated conflict, driven by the determination to contain the risk within the site.

Westwood closed his door and reversed out of his parking slot. Suzanna reached the Rover as he stopped. She wrenched open the door and yelled, "Police! Stop!"

Westwood moved the gear into drive, and the car moved forward. He grabbed the door handle and tried to close it. But Suzanna had hold of his shoulder. She pulled him with all the strength she could muster. The car moved forward, with Westward hanging half out of the open door, and collided with his caravan.

Tosh ran to the other door, wrenched it open, then reached in and moved the gear leaver into park.

Suzanna dragged Westwood onto the ground, his shoulder thumping hard as he landed. He yelled in pain but quickly recovered, rolled over and got to his knees, ready to fight.

Blue lights on three vehicles flashed as they sped down the site's road towards them. Westwood stood, his hand reaching into his pocket. But before it emerged, Suzanna closed the gap. She trapped his right foot with her shoe and pulled him sideways.

He toppled over, and she drove into him, knocking him backwards. With his right hand unavailable, he couldn't break his fall and crashed onto his side, his head smacking into the car sill. Another yelp left his mouth involuntarily, his face contorted with the pain.

Suzanna leapt on him, grabbed his free arm and pulled him over onto his front, then whisked it up his back. Tosh joined her and knelt on Westwood's back while his boss cuffed one hand, then the next.

The police cars skidded to a halt and ten armed officers jumped out, their weapons trained on the scene. "DS McIntosh," Tosh declared, flashing his ID. "Stand down. It's all over."

The sergeant stepped forward, covered by his team, and checked Tosh's ID. "Okay. Stand down guys."

A search team had been waiting just outside the site. As the armed squad convoy left, they drove in and parked up near the caravan. Westwood was loaded into the back of a police car and taken away to the station, leaving Suzanna and Tosh to speak with the search team. She briefed them to look out for weapons (particularly a shotgun), ammunition and drugs and to look for any evidence that Isla Muir had visited the caravan.

"Right, let's get back to the station. We'll need to do some paperwork before we can knock off for the day. We'll interview Westwood in the morning."

* * *

Suzanna and Tosh had recently returned to the station after arresting Westwood, when Mairi arrived back from Cumbria, having spent most of the day away. Mairi settled into a chair, then briefed them on her findings. Although she'd brought Brownlow's shotgun to Dumfries for testing, she suspected that line of enquiry would be a dead end.

Suzanna's expression during the briefing revealed a mix of relief and intrigue. She nodded as Mairi shared about her actions and thoughts, showing agreement with her DC.

Tosh, on the other hand, leaned forward, his brow furrowed, surprised by what he'd heard. "This stuff about no love lost between the Brownlows just doesn't fit with what I saw when I talked to them in the field near the crime scene. Mr Brownlow had been protective and caring towards his wife, hugging her and reassuring her. I don't get it."

Suzanna leaned back in her chair, her eyes reflecting a hidden depth. "It's amazing what couples can hide from each other," Suzanna said, her mind recalling her ex-husband's behaviour. "How they can act like they care, when actually they no longer love their partner, and are betraying them behind their back."

Tosh noticed the tone of Suzanna's voice. He could tell it was personal. She was speaking from experience, rather than observationally. He felt sorry for her. He hadn't experienced betrayal in his relationship and hoped he never would.

Interrupting the unspoken tension, Tosh redirected the conversation. "What about the shotgun, Mairi?"

"I logged it into the evidence store. I'll get it over to forensics in the morning. There's no one there now."

Suzanna straightened up, her focus shifting to team management. "Okay. Great. Let's call it a day," she said, relieved they had done as much as they could. It had been a long but productive day, and despite the next day being a Sunday, there would be no time off for the team.

She left work with her mind, yet again, revisiting that damaged place and time when she'd been shocked to find her husband engaged in sex with another woman. In their bed! God, it had hurt. There had been anger and tears for days afterwards. She tried to shut it out of her thoughts by asking herself something practical. What would she cook for dinner when she got to her lodge?

The gravel crunched as Suzanna's soft-top BMW came to a halt outside her temporary home. The weather hadn't been great today and her roof had stayed firmly closed for the journey. As she looked out across the Solway Firth, she was glad she'd moved into the log cabin.

The sea was rougher today, white horses on the wave tops as the wind whisked off the spray from the breakers. She could only just make out Cumbria's coast through the murk. The sun had already set, and dusk was relinquishing its fight with the dark of night as she entered the cabin.

She changed out of her formal clothes, slipping on jogging bottoms and a sweatshirt. It was too late to cook a full meal, so she just filled a bowl with muesli. After lifting the last spoonful of breakfast-dinner into her mouth - brinner, she supposed it would be called - she placed her bowl on the side table and picked up her phone, searching for a number she had last dialled three weeks ago. "Hi Charlie," she said when her sister answered. "How's it going?"

"Suzanna! Great to hear from you. It's been too long. About time we had a catch-up. Where are you? What are you up to?"

"Actually, I'm not that far from Cockermouth. As the crow flies that is!"

"Oh, really! And where's that?"

"Dumfries. Well, actually on the coast of the Solway Firth. If it weren't dark and raining, I'd be able to see Silloth and Allonby."

"Wow. Just a short hop away."

"If I was Jesus, I could run across the Firth and meet you for a drink in Silloth, but it's a fair drive around via Carlisle."

"I hope you're not being facetious?"

"Oh! You mean about Jesus walking on water? Sorry. I never meant to be irreverent."

"How's the Alpha Course going?"

"It isn't."

"What do you mean? Did you not go?"

"James and I went to the introductory session, but I had to leave before it even got started, because of this murder investigation."

"Suzie!" Charlie said in a scolding tone. "Surely you could have stayed another hour?"

"Perhaps?" She paused. "On reflection, I could have left after the session. An extra hour wouldn't have made much difference - except to the sergeant who waited around for my arrival."

"Was your call to duty an excuse for you to get out of it?" Charlie gently challenged.

Suzanna's brow furrowed. "No, I don't think so. I just responded, unquestioningly to the call to duty." She paused. "James told me what was said in the first session. He was quite impressed by Nicky Gumbel. But it would seem I've not missed any important content. The next session will be 'Who is Jesus?' I think I know that already, having spent much of my childhood having the Bible force fed. So, even if I don't get back to Edinburgh for that one, I'll still go on the next session."

Charlie's tone softened. "Glad to hear it, Suzie."

Suzanna changed the subject. "How's Athena? Lost any more front teeth?"

"Yeah, she's even gappier now. Her adult teeth are breaking through, but it will be a few months before she can sing without a lisp."

"I was thinking, when this case is wrapped up, perhaps we could get together."

"Yes, please," Charlie said with enthusiasm.

"I won't know until it's all finished whether I'll be able to take time off to stay with you. But if not, perhaps we could meet up in Carlisle for lunch or a coffee."

"Okay. I'm up for that, but it would depend on which day that would be. I can't afford to take a day off work to meet up for a coffee. Need to keep my leave for when Athena's on her holidays."

"Yeah! Understood."

They chatted for another hour about all the things that had been going on over the last few weeks. Suzanna noticed the time. "Look, I'd best go. It's getting late, and I need to be fresh for tomorrow. I'll call or message you when I know I'll be free. Night, sis."

"Night, Suzie."

Chapter Thirty-Eight

Sunday 1st May

When Suzanna arrived at the station the following morning, still glowing from her morning run, she found Tosh and Carl chatting and drinking from steaming mugs.

Tosh was the first to speak. "Morning ma'am."

"Good morning, guys." Suzanna said. "Any word from the search team yet?"

Carl responded. "That's what we were just discussing. They found a small quantity of cocaine. But only enough to charge Westwood with possession; not dealing. There were no firearms discovered in the caravan."

"But..." Tosh interjected. "There was a loaded pistol in the Land Rover's glove box."

"He is not licensed for any weapons," Carl continued, "and the pistol's serial number has been ground off."

Suzanna's eyes widened. "Thank God I caught Westwood off guard, and he didn't have time to use the weapon." She frowned as she considered her previous actions. She hadn't thought before charging out of the lodge towards Westwood. It had been instinctive. Maybe she had been irresponsible in tackling Westwood?

"Westwood is in the cells." Tosh said. "We can bring him up whenever you're ready to interview him."

"I take it the pistol has been sent for ballistics testing?" Suzanna replied.

"Yes," Tosh responded. "But there are no facilities in Dumfries, so it will join the queue at the Glasgow ballistics unit. Might be a while before we get feedback."

"Okay. Tosh. You lead the interview. Brief me when you've finished."

* * *

Suzanna had just sat down at her desk with her second coffee of the day when her phone rang. It was Chief Superintendent White.

"DCI McLeod. I hear congratulations are in order. You now have the killer in custody. And you made the arrest yourself."

"Well, actually-"

"Although I'm pleased that the man has been arrested, I am not happy that you tackled him instead of waiting for the armed response team," the Chief Superintendent said chidingly. "If you'd got yourself or DS McIntosh shot, there would have been hell to pay. The paperwork and inquiry would have kept us busy for months."

"Ma'am-"

"I will, of course, mention this to your superiors at Edinburgh," White continued, without pausing for breath. "And I shall expect to hear from you later today confirming that Westwood has been charged with the murder-"

"Ma'am!" Suzanna exclaimed loudly, to force the senior officer to listen. "Firstly, my action yesterday probably saved a messy shootout, with the possibility that one of the armed squad may have been injured and Westwood killed. Secondly, we do not know whether he murdered Isla Muir. Although we believe he has a motive to do so, we cannot yet place him at the scene, and we have not connected him to a murder weapon. We will charge him with possession of class A drugs and illegal possession of a deadly weapon - not a shotgun, though!"

Suzanna was incensed by the Chief Super's attitude. "I am the SIO. I cannot, and *I will not*, charge him with the murder unless I can be certain he is Isla Muir's killer, *and* the evidence would support a conviction. If you want Westwood charged quickly, the best thing you can do is authorise additional expenditure on forensics analysis."

The Chief Superintendent was slow to respond. "Well! I'll see what I can do." Her voice faltered. She paused again. "If he's not our killer, you're to hand him over to the regional drugs squad without delay. I want this murder case wrapped up quickly." White put the phone down before Suzanna could respond.

"Bloody woman!" Suzanna said, her face angry red.

* * *

Davie Westwood looked up as Tosh entered the room, followed by Carl. He stared at the sergeant, recognising him as one of the two officers that arrested him, his features set and unyielding.

Tosh sat opposite him and returned his stare. Minutes passed, the two men's eyes challenging the other to break the combat.

Tosh spoke, his voice steady, his eyes unwavering. As he delved into the preliminaries, though, his eyes reluctantly shifted to the prepared statement before him. Westwood's lips curled into a smirk, a momentary satisfaction coursing through him as Tosh's focus wavered.

"Right, Mr Westwood," Tosh's tone remained measured. "As you know, you have been arrested on suspicion of the possession of class A drugs and an illegal firearm."

Westwood just glared at him, as if to say, 'So what? Big deal.'

Tosh continued. "Also... the murder of Isla Muir."

Westwood jumped at the announcement, sitting to attention, his blasé slouch brushed away by the words. "Murder!" he barked. "I've never murdered anyone!" He paused. "Who's this Muir woman, anyway?"

"Oh, so you don't know Isla Muir, then?" Tosh said with a knowing nod. "That's odd, because we have Mrs Muir's phone, and your number is in her contacts list."

"That doesn't prove anything. Doesn't mean I spoke with her or met her."

"But her phone records do," Carl interjected, dragging Westwood's attention to himself. "In fact, you've spoken numerous times over the last few months. Many of these calls were for several minutes each time. So, don't bother trying to deny you knew Isla Muir."

"Doesn't mean I met her. Just because we might have chatted," Westwood sneered.

"Oh, so you admit to having spoken with Isla Muir many times," Tosh took over again; Westwood's head swivelling back and forth between the two detectives, like he was at a tennis game. "And what did you talk about on these occasions, given that you didn't know the woman and have never met her?"

"None of your business." Westwood slouched again.

Carl spoke again. "Perhaps you were having an affair with her?"

Westwood sat up straight again; challenging. "You've got to be joking! She's ten years older than me, fat and ugly."

"Interesting that you know what she looks like," Tosh said. "Bearing in mind you've never seen her."

"I said I'd never met her, not I hadn't seen her." Westwood looked flustered. The detectives kept catching him out.

"Funny you should mention never having met Mrs Muir, because we have a picture of the two of you together." Tosh passed a photo across the desk, showing them side by side.

"Ah! Now I remember," Westwood responded, looking pleased with himself. "I did meet her once or perhaps twice. Yeah! We'd met through a dating site, but her picture was a lie. She'd put on ten years and two stone."

"You met for pleasure, then, not business?" Carl said.

Westwood did not reply.

"These WhatsApp messages don't appear to be pleasure conversations." Tosh showed him printed transcripts of the messages. "They prove you have met with Isla Muir on numerous occasions, not just two. At least monthly, in fact. Over the last six months."

Carl took over. "Bank statements also show that Isla Muir withdrew significant sums from her bank on at least two of the days you had met. Indeed, the photo showing the two of you together was taken by an ATM camera, as she withdrew one of those large sums."

Davie shrugged his shoulders and said, "no comment."

"We have now established," Tosh said, staring into Westwood's eyes, "that despite you denying knowing the dead woman, you, in fact, had been meeting with her regularly. And she had been withdrawing money to give to you. Where were you between 6 a.m. and 10 a.m. on 26th April, Mr Westwood?"

"Now let me think... I'd have been in bed, of course," he replied, smugly. "I don't get out of bed until at least eight o'clock or nine. What's the point?"

"So, you don't have an alibi for when the murder was committed?" Tosh stated.

"Nor would half the population of Dumfries, if you asked them," Westwood replied belligerently.

"Perhaps," Carl countered. "But that half of the population of Dumfries has no connection with Isla Muir. Neither do they have a motive for murdering her."

Tosh revealed more WhatsApp messages. They showed Isla pestering Westwood about getting a return on her investment. "These messages confirm she had been giving you money. Investing in your drugs business and expecting a return on her investment."

"They say nothing about drugs."

"I reckon, Davie," Carl said, his brow furrowed, as he stared at Westwood, "that you murdered Isla Muir to write off your debt to her, so you wouldn't have to repay her and could keep it all to yourself."

"You're trying to pin her murder on me. I didn't do it, and I want a solicitor." He lolled back into the chair again and folded his arms.

* * *

Tosh and Carl entered the incident room, chatting. Suzanna looked up and asked with her eyes, how did it go?

"Westwood's admitted to knowing Isla Muir and meeting her a couple of times, but he denies murdering her, and he's asked for a solicitor," Tosh replied. "He has a motive and has no alibi, but we don't have any strong evidence against him for the murder yet."

"No. We don't have any evidence that the money she withdrew was actually given to Westwood. And even if we did, we couldn't prove he spent it on drugs. We haven't even found any, except for the small quantity that would be allowed as for personal use. I still believe he is the dealer who's been supplying the likes of Stuart Ingram. We need to dig deeper. Look for evidence of associates, other locations he might have access to, where he could stash his drugs. Any connections he might have with foreigners. Any trips he's taken to places where we know cocaine can be bought?"

"On it," Tosh responded, looking at Carl, as if to say, 'you and me.'

"But we can't spend too long on this element of the case, because, unless it's directly linked to the murder, we should hand it over to the organised crime team." The two men nodded to acknowledge what she'd said.

Suzanna left them to get on with their research and went for a stroll out of the station to a nearby cafe.

Chapter Thirty-Nine

The cafe's walls were coloured with nut brown paint and the chairs beech. Plasticised brown and beige gingham check cloths covered the tables. Sitting in a corner of the cafe, Suzanna's mind danced around, quietly holding a conversation with herself.

'Was Westwood the murderer? I don't doubt he could have killed Isla Muir. He carries a gun and deals in drugs. But I just don't see him getting out of bed early and following the woman into the countryside to kill her and the dog with a shotgun. Drug dealers are notoriously creatures of the night. And probably, as stated, he was still in his bed at 6 a.m. I'll let the guys follow through with investigations into Westwood, but I think we should also look for evidence that he is telling the truth. CCTV, perhaps showing him going to his caravan and not leaving until after the murder had been committed. I'll get Logan onto the CCTV. He'll probably prefer that to data entry.

She continued her inner conversation. 'Where else should they be looking? What connections had they not yet followed up on or yet identified?' She let her mind drift until she was interrupted by a commotion.

Thumping and clattering sounds came from the ceiling above. Foul words were shouted. Two male voices. A man with a shaved head and scars showing on his scalp tumbled down the cafe stairs, followed by his assailant.

The attacker's nose had been broken and healed with a twist to it. His 3-day beard made him look scruffy. He grabbed a heavy fire extinguisher from its wall mounting. Suzanna instinctively reacted to the threat, rising from her chair. The man on the floor attempted to get up as his assailant swung the extinguisher towards him. Adrenalin coursed through Suzanna's veins as violence raised its ugly head. She leapt to her feet to protect the victim and shouted, "Stop! Police!" But the swing of the make-shift weapon had already begun. The long, red metal tube was arcing towards the other man's head.

Suzanna instantly plotted the extinguisher's trajectory and recognised the danger. Agile as a cat, she bounded across the small gap and her leg kicked out, her shoe's sole contacting the extinguisher, knocking it off its route. It struck a glancing blow to the victim's head and continued its rotary journey, contacting the wall with a resounding clang. As it smacked into the concrete, the vibration shocked the attacker's arm, and he yelled as he released his grip.

Suzanna swiftly grasped the man's arm and yanked it, throwing him off balance, dragging him down face-first to the floor. Within a second, she had his arm stretched out, up and away from his head, using the Aikido technique she'd learned. All her weight pressed through her knee onto his shoulder, pinning him to the floor.

The victim had narrowly avoided a smashed skull, but the blow had knocked him to the floor where he lay motionless and unresponsive. A middle-aged, chubby woman with dyed black hair looked at her, white faced and jaw wide, frozen by the violence. "Ma'am," Suzanna spoke to the woman, her tone commanding. "Pass me my phone from the table. I need to call for support for this man's arrest."

The woman shook her head like a wet dog after emerging from a lake, astounded by what she'd just witnessed, then did as she was asked.

"Now, please call 999 and ask for an ambulance," Suzanna instructed the woman, before calling the station to request police assistance.

She returned her attention to the man beneath her. He was still emitting expletives, telling her impolitely to get off. She had ignored his swearing so far, but now she needed to talk with him.

She shifted his arm up his back and applied some pressure, causing pain in his shoulder. He cried out. Suzanna told him to keep quiet and stop struggling. She read him his rights and explained that he would be taken into custody and charged with assault leading to actual bodily harm. He went quiet but she could see his face was still tense and red with stress and she noticed a dagger tattoo on his left forearm. Rightly or wrongly, she assumed he was a soldier or ex-military, as a dagger tattoo was common amongst combative servicemen.

"Which regiment did you serve with?" she asked. But there came no response.

Suzanna couldn't release her hold on the attacker, so looked around for anyone else who could check the victim's condition. She was relieved when the victim stirred and slowly sat up, holding his head, obviously dazed by the blow.

The cafe manager turned up with a glass of water and handed it to the victim. He drank half the glass, then tried to stand.

Suzanna spoke authoritatively, "Stay where you are. You've been concussed and will need to be checked out by the paramedics. Besides, you'll have to make a statement about what just happened here."

The victim's back slithered down the wall until he was again sitting on the floor, dazed. Silent. The man under Suzanna's knee spoke, his voice strained. "I was in the Paras."

She turned her attention back to the attacker. "Did the Parachute Regiment teach you to use fire extinguishers to attack people?"

The man couldn't breathe easily, with Suzanna pinning him to the floor but he responded, anyway, his words forced. "They taught us to use anything we could get our hands on when our life was at stake.

* * *

Being so close to the police station, uniformed officers arrived quickly. Suzanna explained who she was and what had happened, before leaving them to follow through with medical care, arrests and charges.

Although she had handed over to the uniformed guys, she'd need to make a statement later. And she was curious about what the ex-Para had said about life being threatened. Maybe there was a good reason for his violent response. Assault was against the law, and it was her job to gain justice. But she understood that, like it or not, sometimes people had little choice but to take matters into their own hands.

Suzanna left her desk and walked through the station to find out what had happened to the two men from the cafe. One man had been taken to the hospital to be checked out. The other man was in custody.

"I'd like a chat with the man I arrested earlier," she said to the custody sergeant.

"Sure thing, ma'am. He's in Cell 3. I'll let you in."

As she entered the cell, the man looked up and, seeing her, rose. "You've got to let me out of here," he hollered. "That bastard will be out of the hospital by now. These idiots," he looked beyond Suzanna to the custody sergeant, "won't listen to me. My wife and daughter are at risk." His face reddened as he vocalised his worry.

"Sit down, Mr Jones. I need more detail before I can intervene."

He remained standing. "Don't you understand? He'll beat them both to death if you don't do something now. There's no time for chatting."

"Are your wife and daughter at home?"

"Aye, they should be."

"Right. Give me a minute." She turned to the uniformed officer stood in the doorway. "We can't ignore this, Sergeant. You must have Mr Jones' home address. Get officers round there immediately, as protection, then find out whether the other man is still at the hospital or been discharged. I expect you back here within five minutes to update me on the situation. Got it?"

"Yes. Ma'am." He turned and strode away.

"Right, Mr Jones. Sit down. Tell me what this is all about."

Chapter Forty

Will Kennedy and his partner, PC Ryan Dickson, ran to their car, jumped in and sped out of the station car park, blue lights flashing and sirens screaming. Will threw the car around bends and passed through red lights, watching out for any driver who may not be paying attention to the road. He killed the sirens and lights as they pulled up outside Boyd Jones' home. The Jones' front door opened to a male caller as they stepped out of the car. The man pushed his way into the home and slammed the door behind him.

The officers ran to the door and attempted to open it, without success. Ryan knelt and shouted through the narrow opening of the letterbox, his voice reverberating urgently off the hall's bare walls. "Police. Open the door."

They could hear shouting and the sound of furniture being thrown around. The thump of flesh on flesh. Screams from a woman and echoed by a girl. Will instinctively rushed around the back to attempt entry.

Ryan stood back and slammed his body into the door. It shook but held firm, the officer rebounding. He tried again with a similar effect; his shoulder now hurting. Worry was written all over his face. His thoughts raced around his mind; his heart pounded. If they didn't get into the house soon, there could be two dead females. He tried barging through the door again, suppressing his own cries as his shoulder crashed into the immovable door, then called for backup.

Will sprinted along the house's back lane, ran up the garden path to the kitchen door. He wrenched down on the handle and pushed the door. it swung open, crashing against the wall, to reveal the man as he kicked out at the woman curled up on the floor.

A young girl looked on, fear and anger written across her face, shrieking, "Get off her! Leave her alone!"

Will commanded the girl to open the front door. She froze and stopped screaming; immobile. Then she turned and ran up the hall.

On seeing the officer, the attacker put in one more kick before running out of the kitchen after the girl. Will pulled out his extendable baton and chased after him. The front door was now open, and Ryan stood in the doorway as Will entered the hall.

The man grabbed the girl round the neck, dragged her back from the open door and pulled out a knife, holding it to her throat; trapped by policemen at either end of the room. No escape route.

Nothing was said or done as they assessed the situation. Ryan's eyes connected with Will's and an unspoken message passed between them. They'd been partners for three years, and understood each other's thoughts better than they did their own wives. They knew what to do.

"Put the knife down," Ryan hollered at him as he moved forward, taking his Taser from its pouch and lifting it to point at the man.

The attacker bellowed at the man blocking his escape, his voice laden with hatred. "I'll do her. I swear. Back off or I'll slice her." The knife was against the girl's windpipe. It drew blood as the girl struggled.

Worried the girl might be injured, Ryan pulled back a step, then raised his free hand as if to stop traffic. "Hold on there, pal. Don't go cutting that wee girl. She's not done you any harm. Let her go."

The man's full attention was on the officer and his Taser. "I'm not letting you take me in. Back off, NOW!" He stepped towards the front door, determination and hatred carved into his features, dragging the girl with him.

Ryan stepped back again, his forehead creased in concern for the girl. "You're not leaving this house, except in handcuffs, pal. Just put the knife down and come with me quietly. You cut that girl and you'll be going away for double time."

Tension filled the air, the attacker's face red, his knife arm shaking. "I'm no goin' to prison. I'll go to hell first and I'll take this little runt with me. BACK OFF." He pressed the knife to the girl's neck harder, blood trickling from the deeper cut, then stepped forward again. His head spun back to see where the second officer was, quickly returning to what appeared to be the main threat, when he realised the other officer was in the kitchen attending to the woman. Soothing words being spoken.

"What's the matter with you, pal? What has this wee thing done to you? She doesn't deserve to be killed. You don't want to spend the rest of your life in jail."

"I telt ya. I'm no goin' to jail." He took another step towards the front door, the girl crying in pain as the knife's blade cut still wider.

Will had returned to the hall. As the attacker moved, he strode closer and swung his baton, striking the top of the man's knife-wielding arm with all his might, the man's flesh yielding to the force of the strike. Shock and pain ran down the man's arm, his hand involuntarily releasing its grip. The knife dropped and he yelled in pain.

Seeing an opportunity for escape, the girl stamped her heel onto her attacker's foot and broke away. Ryan grabbed her with his left hand and pulled her to safety, then holstered his Taser, as Will jumped forward, grabbing the attacker by his injured shoulder. He dragged him back and downwards, smashing his body into the rock-hard floor. The man cried out again in agony.

He spun the man onto his front, then smashed his knee into his face. It crunched under the impact. Blood gushed from the man's nose.

"Whoops!" Will said, grinning, having taken some rough justice out on the cowardly attacker. He swung the man's arms behind his back, inflicting more suffering, and cuffed him.

Ryan held the girl close to him, shielding her eyes from the punishment meted out by his colleague. Not legal but satisfying, nonetheless.

* * *

Suzanna sat next to the ex-Parachute Regiment soldier in the cold cell, its padded seat doing little to soften the hardness of the bench beneath. "So, what's this all about, Boyd?" she said, sympathetically, using his first name to put him at ease. "What made you attack the other man? Why was he threatening your family?"

Boyd Jones slumped back against the cell's hard wall, his eyes focused on nothing but staring towards the floor. Suzanna gave him time to answer. She watched as his body relaxed; the tension melting away, relieved that the detective had taken action to protect his family. She could tell he was wrestling with his thoughts. No doubt he wanted to speak out but was worried about the consequences.

"It's all my fault," he said eventually, his voice laced with self-condemnation. "I should never have got mixed up with that bastard."

Suzanna waited for him to expand on his statement, not wanting to distract his chain of thought; his self-pity; his repentance. She understood military men, having been the child of one, and had dealings with others during her career.

"When I left the Paras, I got myself a job as a delivery driver. But the pay was crap and the hours long. And I missed the excitement of army life. The combat, the hard training, the adrenaline rush, the teamwork. I met Tormod in the pub. He said his friend needed someone to make deliveries for them. Ask no questions... The pay would be good, so I knew it must have been a bit shady, but I said yes anyway." He stopped talking.

Suzanna gave him time to gather his thoughts. But Boyd's expression changed, and his body stiffened as he realised he might be giving the police ammunition to charge him.

"Look, I'm not stupid. I'll not say any more without a solicitor."

"But you want us to protect your wife and daughter... From what? Why?" She let her questions hang.

He didn't respond immediately, but when he did, he remained guarded. "I found out what it was I was delivering for them." He paused, and Suzanna could tell he was tossing around the pros and cons of telling her more.

"I told Tormod I wanted out of the arrangement. But he said there was no way I could drop out and leave them in the lurch. I said I was done with it. They'd have to find someone else. Tormod said he'd take it out on my family. He knew he couldn't take me on. The bastard said he'd wait until I wasn't around and beat the crap out of them. Rape my wife. Knew their names and my daughter's age." His voice rose as he finished speaking. "He said he'd have fun taking my daughter's virginity! She's only twelve, for Christ's sake!"

As he relived those moments, Suzanna could see the tension rising again, like it must have done in the cafe. "I lost it. I couldn't bear to hear him say another word about hurting my girls."

Suzanna watched his face and saw the emotions change. His anger transformed into moist eyes as he thought about them. Obviously worried.

"And that's when the fight broke out in the cafe?"

He choked back tears before responding. "Aye. That's right."

"What's Tormod's surname?"

"It's Patterson, I think. Not something that comes up in conversation, but I heard someone call him that."

"Have you any idea where he lives?"

"It's in the Dock Park area. Brodie Avenue, I think. He's got a council flat there."

"Do you know which number Brodie Avenue?"

"No. But it was about halfway down the street."

"Look, Boyd. If Patterson hasn't already attacked your family - and I hope he hasn't - we'll have no reason to arrest him. And we won't be able to stand guard over your wife and daughter indefinitely. You'll have to make a statement and open up about what he had been getting you to courier for him. We'll need to know where you picked up the packages, what was in them and where you delivered them to. Armed with that knowledge, we can pick him up and keep your family safe."

Suzanna let the statement sink in, patiently waiting for him to respond, when the custody sergeant returned to report on the task she had given him. But when he spoke, she was astounded.

"Excuse me, ma'am. The boys who attended that address have got a man in custody. They're bringing him in on assault charges. The woman and girl are on their way to the hospital."

Boyd jumped to his feet, tension written across his features, his blood rising. "It's your fault, copper. If you'd not interfered, my wife and daughter would be safe. You'll get nothing from me now. I want to see my family."

Suzanna went red. If her eyes had been laser beams, they'd have burnt right through the sergeant's head. Idiot! "You," she said to Boyd Jones, "stay there." She marched out of the cell and clanged the door shut behind her. Jones immediately thumped on the door, demanding to be released. Screaming that he'd kill Tormod Patterson if he got his hands on him.

Suzanna's nails dug into her palms as her hands clenched. She wanted to hit something. She had fire in her eyes. "You," she said to the sergeant, pointing at his chest as she released the tension in her fist, "back to your office, NOW!"

Suzanna stomped along the corridors, following the sergeant, and when they reached his office, she exploded. "Have you got no sense? What the hell do you think you were doing blurting out that information in front of the husband and father of those two victims? Totally insensitive! And worse still, you just shut his mouth. He was about to give evidence about drug distribution around the county and perhaps across county lines. We'll never get him to admit it now. You've blown the whole thing apart."

He stood, open-mouthed, realising how thoughtless he'd been, as the DCI stormed out of the office, evidently still extremely angry.

Suzanna strode along the corridor, her flushed face tense. An officer emerged from a side room and stepped quickly back, nearly bowled over as she forged ahead. She ignored her team, as she grabbed her bag and coat, then marched out of the station. She had to escape, to let off steam, to cool down. Carl and Tosh's mouths still hung open as she left the station. She'd been that close to getting Jones to open up and perhaps put a number of criminals behind bars for drug dealing. Now that opportunity was lost.

Chapter Forty-One

Suzanna turned left out of the station and strode away, her feet pounding the pavement. She marched along the street, not noticing the offices, schools, guesthouses and businesses that lined the road, walking on in autopilot, not seeing anyone around her. Her rage faded gradually with each step she took away from its source. When she reached the end of the road, her pace slowed. An Anglican Church, with its slate roof and red sandstone walls, dominated the junction. A grey stone war memorial marked the corner's peak. The statue of a Scottish soldier stood atop the plinth, his rifle inverted as he rested both hands on its butt. She sat on a park bench and stared ahead, not seeing anything. Eventually, her heartbeat settled to its normal rate and the redness in her face subsided.

She couldn't believe the stupidity of the sergeant, his unprofessionalism. She would have to speak with his boss. If he hadn't already learned from his mistake, she would ensure the lesson was reinforced.

What now? Boyd Jones had been about to cooperate. Could she manipulate him again? Doubtful. They had lost the advantage; swept away by the sergeant's words. She would have to hand over the intelligence to the serious crime squad to follow up. Perhaps they might get some success.

Suzanna stood and turned back towards the station. Seeing the church entrance, she was drawn towards it, her feet leading her to the heavy hardwood doors. Her hand turned the knob and pushed. The door creaked as it allowed her through into the dim interior, the coloured glass of leaded-light windows filtering the meagre sunlight. It smelled of old wood, musty stone and incense.

Suzanna closed the door behind her and as its squeaking faded, the silence returned. She wandered down the central aisle, then sat on a pew near the front. After closing her eyes and lowering her head, Suzanna prayed that her calmness would return, that she would think clearly and direct the enquiry where it needed to go, to catch the murderer. A peace came over her as she prayed. She sat, enjoying the calmness for a few minutes, then quietly left.

As she strolled along the street towards the station, her mobile rang. The name on the display showed it was one of her DIs in Edinburgh. She brightened. Happy to talk with a colleague she knew well and trusted.

"Hello, Angus. How's it going?"

"Well, actually, boss, not that well!" he replied, his voice monotone; serious.

Her smile faded at his words. "What's up?"

"Una is back in hospital."

Suzanna frowned. Stopped walking and waited for the explanation that was to come. Concerned about what Angus might say.

"She took a punch to her gut during an arrest, and she fell ill shortly after. She went very pale and fainted. From what I've heard, she's got internal bleeding. They suspect the punch may have opened up the old stab wound. She's in A&E at the moment, but they're planning to open her up and take whatever action they find is necessary once they can see what's going on inside her."

Suzanna's eyes welled up, worried by the news. Una was an excellent DI and a lovely person. She was dedicated to her job, caring and kind, but sometimes too passionate about her work, putting herself at risk. If only she'd asked Una to join her Dumfries team instead of Mairi! She'd not be in hospital, her life in danger again... Suzanna thought back to the previous day, when she had tackled the drug dealer, Westwood. She had to admit that she shared Una Wallace's passion and risk-taking for the sake of justice.

She cast aside her self-blaming thoughts and tried to sound positive and confident when she responded, "At least she's in good hands. The hospital looked after her well last time. I'm sure she'll get the right care and treatment. There's nothing we can do but wait and pray she'll be alright."

"Agreed. I'll keep you posted when I get feedback from the hospital."

"Thanks, Angus. Other than Una being in hospital, how are things going?"

"The usual stuff. Inter-gang stabbings, street robberies, drunken punch-ups and burglaries. No murders, thankfully. Do you expect to be in Dumfries for much longer?"

"Hard to say. We've made arrests but have yet to find sufficient evidence for me to charge anyone with the murder and have confidence in a conviction."

"I thought a man *had* been charged?"

"We arrested the farmer who worked the land where the shooting took place, assuming he'd shot the dog and the woman because of sheep worrying. There was significant circumstantial evidence but once the forensics analysis had been completed, we had to release him because the evidence supported his story, rather than our theory.

"We have another man in custody now. He has a motive but we've yet to tie him to the woman's murder. I don't know whether he's our man. We have some other lines of enquiry, and we'll see where they lead."

"Not a straightforward murder, then. Just as well most murders are carried out without planning, and the evidence quickly links the murderer and victim."

"You're right, Angus. There is no CCTV within miles of the crime scene here. It's making my job more difficult not having the coverage we're used to in Edinburgh. And shotguns, the weapon used, are not so readily matched to the crime, unlike bullets. Anyway, I'd best let you go. I hope to hear good news from you when you next call. I'm heading back to my accommodation now. Please call when you hear something, no matter what the time."

"Aye. Will do. I hope it will be good news as well," he concluded on a lighter note.

Although now calm, Suzanna didn't want to return to the station. She called Tosh and informed him she'd had enough for the day. Told him to charge Boyd Jones with assault and release him.

By the time Suzanna had driven to the log cabin, she had completely settled. Had accepted that what will be will be. Her focus would return to the murder inquiry, undistracted by the drugs trading. It was time to return to the planning officials' motives. She stepped out of the car, grabbed her bag and turned towards the cabin. The air was still and cool, the sky overcast, but the strengthening sun was still high in the sky, bringing brightness to the landscape. She glanced across the firth towards Cumbria, but its coast was hazy and undefined, its mountains hidden in the low clouds.

* * *

Before dinner, Suzanna changed into her running gear for the second time that day and headed out. She ran to the beach and along the coast, jumping over driftwood, pounding through the sand and pebbles, letting the challenge of the exercise distract her mind and let it rest. There would be plenty of time for analysis. Now it was *her* time. Time to push her heart and lungs into overdrive, to challenge her legs, to stride out, to sprint before returning to a steady pace, then sprint again. Fartlek training, as it was known in the running world.

Suzanna had read the word came from the Swedish Fartlek, meaning speed play. She pushed, relaxed, pushed gain, relaxed again, eventually slowing to a steady pace as she returned to the cabin. She felt wonderful but fatigued. Alive! Satisfied that she'd pushed her body, delayed ageing and remained ready for any situation life might throw at her. But right now, she needed a shower and something to eat.

Later, as Suzanna finished loading the dirty dishes into the dishwasher, her phone rang. She smiled when she saw the name of the display. "You beat me to it, James. How are you?"

"Good, thanks, gorgeous. How was your day?"

"I won't go into the detail but rather mixed. How about you?"

"I went to church this morning. It was lovely."

"I'd forgotten it was a Sunday."

"I thought I'd try out the church that's running the Alpha Course."

"What was it like?"

"As relaxed as the Alpha session. Not like any Anglican service I'd ever been to. It was similar to the church your sister goes to in Cockermouth. Guitars, drums and keyboards, rather than an organ. The worship leader has a beautiful voice. It was a real pleasure to listen to and join in with. And the vicar's sermon was actually interesting; not boring. He related the texts to modern-day scenarios, with some humour to hold our attention. Made it relevant." James sounded genuinely enthusiastic about the experience. "Did you read any more of the Gospels?"

"Yes. I've read the first three, now," Suzanna responded, glad that James had enjoyed church, but a little sad that she'd not been there with him.

"That's great, Suzanna. You'll be able to join in with the course when you return." He paused. "Listen. I was thinking, if you're still in Dumfries next weekend, perhaps I could come down there and we'd have some time together."

"Yeah. Sounds great." She replied eagerly. "I'm hoping I'll have it wrapped up by Friday, but you never can tell with murder investigations. We still don't have anyone in custody who has means, motive and opportunity, with the evidence to support our suspicions. That's for your ears only, by the way. I don't want the press picking up on that and headlining 'Cops Floundering on Muir Murder Case.' You know what they're like. Anyway, I'd best say goodnight. Let's chat tomorrow."

As she ended the call, Suzanna's mind returned to what she'd said about journalists. Floundering... Fishermen... Maybe that was the source of light she'd seen out to sea on her first night in the cabin. She'd seen a fishing boat on the horizon earlier that evening. That was most likely it.

Chapter Forty-Two

Monday 2nd May

Suzanna rose from the cabin's comfortable bed after a good night's sleep, despite the worries about Una that had initially kept her awake. Feeling a little weary, she freshened her face, then slipped on her running gear for an early morning jog. Just a light training run, to ease out the stiffness after yesterday's intense training. It had been clear overnight, the air chilly, but clouds were drifting in again from the southwest, and the forecast was for light rain most of the day.

Suzanna felt refreshed after her run, her muscles now free of lactic acid. She was just finishing her breakfast when her phone rang. It was Angus. "Morning, Angus. What news?"

"Morning, boss. Una's out of surgery and resting. Still sedated but stable. They'd been correct in their assumption that the old wound had ruptured. She's been stitched up again, and they're confident she will fully recover."

Suzanna smiled, relieved by the good news.

"But they'll be formally recommending she be placed on light duties once she's fit to return to work. The surgeon is worried that if it happens again, she might not be so lucky. He said Una ought to be given a non-combat role, for her own safety."

Suzanna could hear Angus' concern in his voice. The news worried her too. "I bet she won't want to hear that. Stuck in the office if we can hold on to her. Or she might get transferred into a backroom headquarters role. That would be a great shame because her detective skills would go to waste. She'll be devastated if she can't follow her passion." Suzanna welled up as she thought about the effect this could have on Una.

"Aye. You're right, boss. But surely that would be better than her bleeding to death, if she takes another punch to the stomach. It was fortunate Zahir was with her when it happened and called an ambulance." Angus paused. "Look, I'll let you know how she's doing when I get another update. I'd best get off to the station now."

"Thanks, Angus. Appreciated."

* * *

Suzanna felt refreshed and ready to do business when she got to the station. The custody sergeant intercepted her as she arrived and apologised for his mistake the day before. He had seen the error of his ways and would be more careful in the future. She decided to leave it as it was. Wouldn't raise it with his boss, Inspector Ferguson, content with his positive response to having been chastised the day before.

She greeted the team as she entered the incident room, and they responded as normal, all busy in their work. She felt self-conscious about her actions the previous day, but none of them mentioned her storming out of the office without a word.

Suzanna called the team together for a recap. "So, the guy that attacked Boyd Jones' wife and daughter is in custody?"

"Aye. Tormod Patterson. Nasty piece of work. Evil guy," Tosh responded. "He beat up the wife and threatened to kill the daughter. Just as well we got some guys round there when we did. Will and Ryan did a great job of bringing him in. Might have saved their lives."

"Any update from the hospital on wife and daughter's condition?"

Suzanna looked to Tosh for the answer.

"I hear the woman was badly battered and bruised, and she has some cracked ribs. But she should be alright. Probably be in the hospital for a few days more, though. The girl had a superficial cut to her throat and some bruising, but otherwise was unscathed."

"Physically," Mairi added, hinting at the other aspect of harm she would have encountered.

"Yes. She'll have been traumatised by seeing her mother beaten and her life threatened," Suzanna responded, understanding Mairi's thoughts. "Get social services onto it. She'll need counselling."

Tosh swivelled his eyes to look at Carl, who nodded in acknowledgement of the task, before returning his attention to the DCI. "As you know, ma'am, we've got three men in custody on supply of drugs charges: Westwood, Ingram and Preston. Patterson has been charged with actual bodily harm, but he didn't have any drugs on him. If we get a warrant to search his flat, perhaps we'll strike lucky. As instructed, I charged Jones with assault and released him so he could go see his family."

"You may have noticed my impromptu departure yesterday," Suzanna said. "Jones was ready to share details of his involvement with drugs distribution, and to name places and people, when the interview was interrupted by an update on his family's hospital admission. He clammed up straight away and I doubt will again be persuaded to cooperate."

"Which idiot was that?" Carl responded, sneering.

"I've dealt with him, and I won't be taking the matter further," Suzanna responded. "So, I'll not name him now. We need to move on."

Tosh, Carl and Logan exchanged glances, their eyes agreeing they all could guess who'd messed up.

"How did you get on with the CCTV trawl, Logan?"

"Westwood appears to have been in his caravan at the time of the murder. There's not much CCTV in Dumfries but I found some footage that showed him travelling towards the caravan site on the evening before the murder. And the next time his Land Rover showed up was mid-morning the next day. I also spoke with the site warden, and he reckoned Westwood's Land Rover had been parked outside his caravan that morning."

"Good work," Suzanna said, looking him in the eye, indicating her praise was genuine. "We'll not let him off the hook just yet, though. I'm sure he's our drug supplier. But we don't have the evidence yet. We can use the threat of a murder charge to influence him during the interview once his solicitor gets here. I hear he's coming down from Edinburgh."

"Perhaps you'll have already met him then, ma'am," Tosh said.

"Maybe I will. Have you got a name?"

Tosh grabbed a piece of paper off his desk. "It's a woman, not a man. Arabel McGregor."

"Ah! Yes. I've heard the name. I think she's in the same chambers as Martin Sweetman. He's made life difficult for my team a number of times. You'd better watch out for her." Suzanna paused, then spoke again. "Get that warrant for Patterson's flat. We need to get him put away for a long time." She returned to her desk, leaving the team to get on with their duties.

A clerk entered the incident room and dropped a pile of documents into the in-tray. "Hey, Alpin, I'll take those. I'm waiting for something to arrive."

"Are you too lazy to walk from your desk to the in-tray, DS McIntosh," Alpin jibed. "No wonder you're putting on weight."

Tosh looked down at his belly and wondered whether Alpin was right. Probably. "Ah! Well, at least I have some meat on me. I'm not a walking skeleton, like you."

Alpin grinned back. "If you keep going the way you are, pal, the pallbearers at your funeral will be needing extra payment for the risk of back injury."

Tosh took the mail from Alpin, who turned and walked out of the office smiling. "See ya, Tosh."

There were numerous thick envelopes and he opened them all in anticipation. As expected, they contained bank statements for the planning officials he'd requested a few days back. He immediately got stuck into their scrutiny.

* * *

Boyd Jones sat beside his wife's hospital bed, holding her hand, concern written across his face, his eyes still moist. He'd rushed to the hospital when the police had released him. The anger he'd felt when he found the parking fine on his car windscreen having over-run his allowed two hours of free parking had faded away now. He would just have to put it down to experience. His mind had been on other things while he was locked up in the police station.

Boyd's daughter was across the bed from him, gently grasping her mother's other hand. She had settled again after the initial conflict when he arrived, but her eyes were still red.

Laura Jones was pallid, silent, and motionless, her hair a mess, her face bruised, and her nose swollen. She was connected to drips and bleeping monitors. Their LED displays indicated his wife's condition and the drug-administration dosage rates. He'd seen plenty of these devices on board Chinook helicopters evacuating his pals from the battlefield. And inside field hospitals, where they continued to fight for their lives after shattered limbs had been removed. He found their presence somehow comforting, an overt sign that she was getting medical intervention, surrounded by professionals who cared about her.

Boyd caught his daughter's attention and briefly smiled before speaking. "I'll nip down to the cafe and get a coffee. Would you like a Coke?"

"Yes, please, dad. Can I get a bag of crisps as well?"

"Aye, Skye, anything you want."

"I'll have a Snicker bar as well, then," she said with a cheeky grin.

Boyd held his tongue, biting back his first thought: 'don't push it.' His daughter's initial shock at the attack, and her anger toward him, had faded now, and he wanted it to stay that way.

Skye's injuries had been minor, thank God. She had a few butterfly plasters holding together the superficial cut in her throat. And the bruising where Patterson had gripped her was tender but would soon heal. His biggest worry, however, was what the experience might have done to her.

He smiled backed at Skye before walking away. "I'll just be a few minutes."

Boyd knew his daughter had worried about him every time he'd been overseas on operations. When Skye was younger, Laura had had major problems trying to get Skye to sleep. And she'd frequently been disobedient at home and disruptive at school. This recent event must surely compound her worries.

Would she now live in fear of further attacks - perhaps shy away from contact with men? Would her anger towards him return? He was to blame for what had happened to her and her mam, after all. It was understandable. He walked on in silence, not looking at the nurses, orderlies, and patients that he passed. Not seeing the bland walls or registering the disinfectant smells.

Before going to the cafe, he stepped outside for some fresh air, then moved away from the door and lit up a cigarette. As he inhaled, he felt the rush of the smoke into his lungs and the pleasure of the nicotine.

Despite his 'dirty habit,' as his wife called it, he'd always passed his army combat fitness tests and played football, so it couldn't be doing him much harm. Boyd had heard of people getting lung cancer and bronchitis, but he was convinced it wouldn't happen to him. He was fit and healthy.

As that thought crossed his mind, he coughed violently. Maybe he was wrong about the harm. Perhaps he should listen to his wife. She meant the world to him. He stamped the cigarette into the tarmac and there and then decided it would be his last.

Boyd re-entered the hospital, through the automatic sliding doors, striding out towards the cafe. He wanted to be back beside Laura. But first he needed a coffee.

He was relieved that Skye smiled when he returned to his vigil.

After she had munched her chocolate bar and potato crisps, she asked her dad about the day before. "Why did that man want to hurt us? Why did he do this to mam?"

Boyd pondered on how much to tell his daughter before explaining quietly. "I'd been delivering packages for him and his boss. It was extra cash, with just a little extra work. But I had my suspicions about what was in the packs. I checked one and found what seemed to be drugs, so I refused to take any more deliveries. Patterson told me I couldn't drop out. I was part of it now. He threatened to harm you and your mam. He become our enemy." Boyd's face was set firm as he continued. "The Army taught me to take out the enemy. To kill or be killed. He threatened my family, so I tried to remove that threat. That's when the copper stepped in. She was amazing. Fast. Agile. Skilled. Not like most of those over-weight unfit fu-" He suppressed the swearword, and Skye looked at him disapprovingly. "Just my bad luck she was in the cafe at that time."

"Would you have killed the man, dad?" she asked, her face tense. Worry showing.

"No, lass, just given him a good beating to warn him off. But because I was banged up in the police station, he got to your mam before I could do anything about it. I tried telling them, but they wouldn't listen. Well, the woman who arrested me listened but by then it was too late. Patterson got to the house before the coppers."

"Yeah. I know, dad. I'm still scared." Her eyes welled up as she spoke the words. "Will he come for us again when he's released?" A tear trickled from her eye and down her right cheek. Skye wiped it away with her sleeve and waited for her dad's reassurance.

"He'll be away for a long time, I reckon. Don't you worry." As he said the words, he thought about how long that might be. A couple of years, probably. Then what? He'd go away longer if he were done for drug dealing. Maybe he could find a way to help the police without going away for his part in it?

Chapter Forty-Three

Tosh's head was down, his eyes focused on the statements spread out across his desk. He had Isla Muir's bank statements for each of the months when there had been a planning meeting at which one of her applications was to be considered. And he had statements from each of the planning officials whose phone numbers had showed up in Isla's contacts list.

They had already established that some officials had met with her and been treated to a meal prior to the planning meeting but had failed to declare that interest at the meeting. But that was not a criminal offence. If he could find payments being made between Muir and the officials, that might indicate bribery. And, with illegal activities of any kind, perhaps a motive for murder.

He lined up the six council members' bank statements side by side with Muir's and scanned back and forth across them. Each time there was a considerable sum transferred, he checked to see whether it had reached any of the other bank accounts. He came across the first match halfway down the page and marked the payments with a highlighter pen. He'd nearly given up hope when another match showed its head, just before he reached the last payments on Muir's statement.

Now there were two possible bribery cases to follow up. It would be interesting to hear how these men justified having received money from Isla Muir just before they had supported her planning application.

He still had other time periods to scrutinise before his work was done. Perhaps there would be more payments to the same officials or even other officials receiving backhanders?

* * *

The grey-haired, jowled man lowered himself onto an equally bloated, cracked leather sofa, its colour matching his hair. It creaked under his weight and exuded a whiff of stale, sweaty air. He shifted its blue scatter cushions to the side before settling in.

A boy with cropped hair and sticky-out ears left his Lego plane on the floor, surrounded by random bricks of coloured plastic, and joined the man. His arms wrapped around the old man's arm, drawing himself closer, smiling at the comfort of being snuggled up.

There came a rap on the door.

"Can you get the door for me, please? Save me having to haul myself off this sofa again."

The boy jumped up and ran out of the living room and along the corridor, his feet pounding on the wooden floor. He wrenched open the door, then froze. "Grandpa," he shouted over his shoulder. "There are some policemen here."

Aled ran back to his grandfather and found him struggling to get off the sofa. He grabbed an arm and pulled but his meagre strength was little help for the elderly man.

"Don't worry lad. I can manage," he said, his voice strained by the effort.

Aled stepped back, then turned and ran to the front door. "Grandpa's just coming."

"Okay lad," the officer said patiently.

The old man waddled along the hall, his hips hurting. He'd been promised hip replacements two years back, but still hadn't had an appointment for the first operation.

"Mr Black?" The uniformed police officer asked, his voice giving nothing away.

"Aye. That's me. How can I help you, officer?" Black was puzzled, his mind racing. He couldn't think of any reason the officers were at his door. Then it came to him. "Has there been an accident? Is the lad's mother okay?"

"No accident, sir. No need to worry. But you'll need to come with us. You're required at the station by our CID colleagues."

Black's face dropped, his eyes widened. "Are you arresting me? What's this about?"

"Not at this time. You are being invited to voluntarily answer questions, under caution."

"But you haven't told me why," Black responded, the pitch of his voice rising, his eyebrows arched. "And I have my young grandson to look after." As he spoke, Aled grabbed his grandpa's hand, his face pale, his hands shaking.

"Grandpa. Why do they want you to go to the police station? You're not going to jail, are you?" Aled looked up to the nearest policeman. "My grandpa wouldn't do anything naughty."

Black squeezed Aled's hand gently to reassure him. "There must be some mistake, Aled. Don't you go worrying. Everything will be fine. You'll see." But his weak smile gave away his uncertainty.

The officer looked sympathetically at the boy but didn't respond to the child's statement. Nor did he acknowledge what his grandfather had said. Still business-like, he spoke again. "It might be better not to expose your grandson to the details. Is there anyone you can call to look after him while you help us with our enquiries?" he asked. "If not, he can come to the station with us. We'll find someone to look after him."

Aled looked worried by the prospect of going with the police. He looked up at his grandpa's face, seeking reassurance.

"Hang on," Black said, accepting the need to comply. "I'll call his mam. She should be home from work by now."

* * *

"Mr Black. I'm Detective Constable Carl Penrose. We've requested you attend the station to answer questions on a serious matter." Black sat quietly, his hands clasped together, waiting for the officer to continue. He was still unaware of the reason he'd been taken in by the police. Although, having wracked his brain since leaving home, his suspicions were growing. It could be only one thing. Surely!

"We understand you are a county councillor and have a seat on the planning committee. Is that correct?" Carl wanted to get him responding yes to questions.

"Aye, that's true." The question had confirmed his reasoning. He tried to mask his worry by being challenging. "But why would you want me to confirm something you already know and of what relevance is that?"

Carl ignored the question. He'd been a detective for five years now and had come across many techniques used by guilty men and women to divert the line of questioning. "We also have it on record that you attended the latest planning committee meeting on the 28th of April 2016. Is that correct?"

"Yes. You must know it is. Stop wasting my time, Constable." With every question the detective asked, Black became more certain where it was leading. Out of sight, his hands fidgeted.

"And did you cast a vote on the application made by one Mrs Isla Muir?"

Damn that woman, he thought. "I did that. But, again, you'll know that, if you have the meeting records, which, given your line of questioning, you will have."

"And did you not meet with the said Mrs Muir for dinner just five days before that meeting?" Black didn't answer. He sat still, his face set sternly, frowning.

"I have here a copy of the meeting minutes." He passed the copy across the table to Black. "At the top of those minutes there is an entry titled Members Declarations of Interest. Can you see your name listed there, Mr Black?"

Black shook his head from side to side, his lips puckered. Carl mentioned his action for the tape.

"I also have here the declarations signed by each committee member. Declarations that state that prior to the meeting, you have not been given any instruction by anyone about how to vote on the matters to be determined at the meeting. And that you have no interests in the outcomes of these decisions." He passed a copy of a signed declaration across the table. "Please confirm that is your name and signature."

"It is." Black's resistance was crumbling, his worst fear being realised.

"So, we have established that you attended that meeting, and from the minutes we know you voted in favour of Mrs Muir's application, despite having recently received hospitality from her and having declared no interest in the decision!"

Black shrugged his shoulders.

Carl passed more papers across the table. "Further, these bank statements prove you received a sum of £5,000 from Mrs Muir the day following that very meeting. What do you have to say to that, Mr Black?"

Internally, Black was worried, his future tumbling away, out of control. Below the table, both fists were clenched. Outwardly, he remained calm. His many years as a county councillor had prepared him for awkward, unwelcome questions. "Nothing, Constable. Until

I have a solicitor to advise me." He folded his arms, sat back in the chair, and stared at the detective, his jaw clenched.

Chapter Forty-Four

"Ah! Councillor Bryce. Thank you for coming in to talk with us," Suzanna said, looking down on the two men sat behind the interview room's table. Bryce's body language gave away his anxiety, his hands in his lap, his thumbs whirling around each other. She could virtually smell the fear. Her eyes shifted to the suited man sitting next to Bryce. "DCI McLeod... And *you* are?"

"I'm Mr Bryce's solicitor, Craig Mitchell," he responded, his voice polite and unchallenging. "Firstly, we'd like to thank you for requesting Mr Bryce attend the police station voluntarily, rather than sending the uniformed chaps to bring him in."

A conciliatory tone, Suzanna noted, keeping the surprise from her face. She hadn't been expecting that. Perhaps just a ploy to seek a softer approach to her questioning. It wouldn't work, though. She had only done it that way to placate the Chief Superintendent.

"Right." Suzanna turned her attention back to the suspect, her eyes sharply focused on the accused's face. "Mr Bryce, when we last spoke, you refused to answer my questions about you accepting hospitality from a woman whose planning application you considered and voted on a few days later. There is no doubt this took place, and the matter will be referred to the appropriate authorities. I assume you understand the implications of this serious breach of regulations?"

"My client is well aware that his oversight may see him having to resign from the council. But this is not a criminal matter, so why have you requested this interview?"

"As you say, Mr Mitchell, corruption at that level," Suzanna noticed Bryce's face crinkle at the use of the word corruption, "is not a matter for the police, but *bribery* is."

Suzanna anticipated Bryce's face would turn red with indignation at such a suggestion, and he would rant about being insulted. Instead, his brow furrowed, and cracks formed between his eyebrows. He fidgeted in his seat. He was worried, rather than angry.

The solicitor came to his defence, booming his response. "On what grounds do you accuse my client of bribery? That is a serious charge. A slur on his good name. I demand to see the evidence on which you base this allegation."

"As we know, Mrs Muir met with you on the 21st of January," Suzanna said directly to Bryce, ignoring the solicitor's demand. "And on the 28th of January, you chaired the Planning Committee Meeting, at which Mrs Muir's application was under consideration. We know you did not declare an interest and you went on to vote for its approval. What we haven't yet covered is that on the 30th of the same month, you received a payment of £10,000 into your personal bank account from Mrs Muir." She let the statement hang, waiting to see what excuse he could have for that payment, then handed two redacted bank statements across the table, the correlating payments highlighted in yellow.

Bryce had shrivelled since their last encounter, and he appeared to have no fight left in him. The uncovering of his bribe-taking must have sapped him; broken his spirit. He must have known he couldn't escape the consequences of his illegal practices. He looked up at his solicitor, asking with his eyes what to say.

"There will be a perfectly reasonable explanation for Mrs Muir having made that transfer," the solicitor said. "I will need time with my client to ascertain this. A break in the questioning would now be appropriate."

"I don't think so, Mr Mitchell. Given time, you may come up with some flimsy concocted excuse. No one should need time to recall why such a significant payment had been made just three months ago. I need to know why you received £10,000 from Mrs Muir, Mr Bryce, *now!*"

"No comment."

"You admit it was a bribe, then. There can be no other reason to refuse to respond to that question."

"No comment."

Suzanna stood and paced the room before returning to the table and resting her hands on its surface as her eyes bore into Bryce's mind. "You met Isla Muir again just a few days ago, didn't you? What was the reason for this last meeting, at which there were no pleasantries, no fancy dinners and expensive wine? A meeting called at *your* request."

Suzanna retook her seat opposite Bryce, her eyes not leaving his face, waiting for a crack to show. "I've seen the WhatsApp messages, Mr Bryce. The ones before and the ones after that latest meeting. It's clear that you wanted to end your business relationship with the woman. Was it because you suspected, rightly, that you couldn't continue to take bribes indefinitely without being found out?"

Suzanna paused again, letting him absorb her words, watching his face, guessing his thoughts. "And when she refused to back off, what went through your mind?" Another pause. "You were scared that one day you'd receive a knock on the door by men in uniform, and your wonderful, rich, privileged life would collapse." Suzanna's voice rose as she delivered the challenge. "Is that why you decided to end the relationship in the only way you could think of: *by murdering her?*"

Bryce's face changed from sheepish to wolfish in an instant. He sat upright. His hands, previously holding each other beneath the table, emerged and thumped down on its surface. "Murder! There's no way I would have murdered that woman. Yes, she was like a snake, wrapping itself around my leg, her fangs poised to bite," he growled. "Yes, she threatened me. But I would never stoop to murder."

His voice trailed off and he relaxed back into his chair, but his anger at being accused of the murder still simmered.

"That's enough," the solicitor said angrily. "If you're going to charge my client with any offence, I suggest you do it now, or we are leaving."

"Happy to oblige, Mr Mitchell. But one last question, where were you between the hours of six and ten a.m. on the 25th of April?"

Bryce responded, stating that he'd been at home until 8:30 and in the office by nine.

For now, the charge would be bribery, not murder. Not yet!

* * *

"Tosh, Mairi, Carl, Logan." Suzanna called across the office, her face tense. She felt the need to make progress in the case. It wasn't moving along fast enough for her. She was impatient for success.

Mairi immediately rose from her chair, its feet screeching across the hard floor, and stepped out from behind her desk. The three men followed her lead and joined the DCI at the incident board, which was filled with pieces of paper, pictures, and arrows.

It was time for their collective minds to feed off each other; to magnify their deductive powers. Once they had gathered, Suzanna spoke again. "We know Bryce received bribes from Muir in exchange for supporting her planning applications. We also know he wanted out before he was caught. It would seem Muir didn't want to let him go and lose a valuable asset on the planning committee."

Suzanna scanned the faces of her small team, looking for signs they were listening intently and processing what she was sharing. She was pleased to see every eye was on her, connecting, the communication channels fully open.

"Bryce mentioned Muir having fangs ready to strike. To me, that means she had a way of hurting him, perhaps exposing him. Something that gave her power over Bryce. We need to know what she had. What enabled her to maintain a hold on him? Thoughts?"

As the rest of the team pondered, Mairi spoke. "I was going through Muir's contacts again earlier, matching phone numbers to people, where we hadn't already identified them. One number stood out. It was a burner phone. Not registered to anyone. I called it, and discovered the man who answered it claimed to be a private investigator."

Suzanna raised an intrigued eyebrow, her eyes seeming to swell in line with her mind's curiosity. "Interesting... And?"

"What's the guy's name, Mairi?" Tosh asked, before she could respond to the DCI's open question.

Mairi tapped a pen against her notepad, then flipped to the relevant page. "Alexander Moore," she read, then looked up again.

Tosh's face gave away his recognition of the name. "I know him. Used to be in the force. A sound fella. Been a private eye for a couple of years now. Mostly earns his living by gathering evidence for divorces, investigating insurance claims, and tracking down long-lost family members when someone dies. I sometimes catch up with him in the bar."

"I reckon a catch-up is overdue, Tosh," Suzanna said, ensuring he understood her words were direction, not merely a suggestion.

"Couldn't agree more. I'll call him and set something up," Tosh said, acknowledging the tasking. He'd have done it anyway, without being told.

"If he doesn't cooperate, I'm happy to make it more official and have him brought in."

Tosh shook his head. "It shouldn't come to that, ma'am. If I know Alex, he'll help us out. Leave it with me."

Chapter Forty-Five

"Well. Here we are again, Mr Black," Carl said, having joined the man in the interview room. Sitting beside him was the duty solicitor. The slender young woman had tied her shoulder-length, shiny auburn hair into a tight bun. She wore a two-piece dark business suit and a white blouse. Her youth didn't make him any less cautious though, as he'd often found these fresh inexperienced lawyers to be extremely quick thinking, knowledgeable and fiery, especially the women. Something to prove, he reckoned.

"Let's recap before moving on." He reminded Black of the previous conversation. "So, we know you received a payment shortly after the last planning meeting and there is a pattern of payments to you from Mrs Muir shortly after each meeting, where one of her applications was up for consideration." Carl looked up from his notes, meeting eyes with the suspect. "How would you explain that, Mr Black?"

Black sat with arms folded, a determined look on his face. "No comment."

"Oh! We're back to the no comments, are we? A sure sign of a guilty man. You realise that if you offer no explanation for these payments, the court will assume they were bribes. If there are other reasons for these money transfers, best you inform us."

"No comment."

Carl glanced at the solicitor, expecting her to speak up. Although, there wasn't much anyone could say about the irrefutable evidence of bribery. She showed no sign of being concerned about the accusation.

"Okay. I'm now certain that these payments were indeed bribes from Mrs Muir to influence the decision of the planning committee. You will subsequently be charged with misconduct in a public office and taking bribes, contrary to the Bribery Act 2010."

Black offered no response. Just sat still, his face expressionless. Carl assumed the man already knew that this would be the outcome and there was nothing he could do about it. "You may have heard that Mrs Isla Muir was found murdered seven days ago. Where were you between the hours of 6 a.m. and 10 a.m. on the 25th of April, Mr Black?"

Carl glanced at the solicitor and noticed her calm, unemotional face cracked with the surprise of the implied accusation.

Black sat up, his forehead furrowed. "Sorry!" He blurted, then paused. "You think I killed Isla Muir? Why would I kill the goose that lays the golden egg?"

Carl didn't let his pleasure show as he responded seriously. "Thank you for confirming your part in the bribery. But I still need you to answer the question."

Black looked at the solicitor. She spoke. "I think you should answer that question, Mr Black. If you have an alibi, the police need to know about it."

"Aye. Of course. Let me think." Black frowned. "The 25th. That was Anzac Day. I've a friend in New Zealand. That's how I know." He paused, more relaxed now that he was certain of his alibi. "Last Monday. Same as most Mondays, I will have been getting young Aled, my grandson, ready for school. He stays over Sunday nights, and I get him to school. Gives his mam a night off."

Carl noted what had been said. "What time did your grandson get up? And what time do you drop him at school?"

"I wake him about 7:30 and have him out the door and into school by ten to nine. It's only just up the road."

"We'll need to confirm that, with Aled and his mother. Is there anyone else who could corroborate what you've told me?"

"Only the other parents and grandparents at the school gates, who will have seen me drop him off. Or the teaching assistant in the playground, I suppose."

* * *

While Carl was interviewing Black, a report arrived from forensics. The cocaine found in Davie Westwood's car was a match to that found at the Muir house. But they hadn't found a large stash of the drug so couldn't charge him with dealing, merely possession. It was time for Suzanna to re-visit Westwood's caravan.

She parked up by the warden's office. No one was at home, so she walked into the site looking for the man, a fresh breeze blowing from the southwest. Halfway down the site, Nigel Gibson emerged from a caravan. She waved to him, and he waved back, then ambled in her direction. Suzanna strode to meet with him, the wind flicking her hair into her eyes.

"Good afternoon, Mr Gibson. I'm looking for some help," she said, the brushing fly-away hair behind her ear.

"Fire away, lass," he responded, keen to be of assistance; attentive.

"You'll know Mr Westwood better than most, as he's a neighbour. What can you tell me about him?" she asked.

"I take it I'll not be seeing him living here again, after the other day?"

"We certainly have no intention of releasing him, and I expect him to spend some time in prison, if only for possession of an illegal firearm. But if we get nothing else on him, he may be back on site again within 2-3 years. The maximum sentence is five years but with good behaviour...

"

"Hmm. Maybe we can evict him while he's away?" Nigel mumbled to himself. He responded to Suzanna's question. "What was it you wanted to know about him?"

"Just tell me anything you've noticed. Comings and goings, visitors, hours kept, behaviour, anything that is out of the ordinary."

"Okay. Let's go to the office. We can have a cuppa, while I have a think."

As they sipped their drinks, Nigel told Suzanna all he knew about Westwood, including his wife's view of the man. Not favourable!

As she rose to leave, only a little better informed, Nigel suddenly looked up and spoke again, "Oh! By the way, I noticed those chaps who searched Davie's caravan didn't have a proper look underneath. There's skirting all around it and a hatch. I saw one of them take the hatch off and poke his head in, but he never went under the van. Just thought I'd mention it."

Suzanna's eyes widened. "Thanks, Mr Gibson. Very interesting. I'll take a look, myself."

Suzanna marched down the park to Westwood's caravan and removed the skirting hatch before peering inside the void. She couldn't see anything other than pipes, cables, and mud. About to replace the hatch, something caught her eye. She moved it aside again, knelt and stared into the space. A piece of cord hung from the caravan's frame and when she looked up saw that it was securing a pair of oars.

She took her phone from her pocket, switched on its torch, then crawled under the caravan, glad that she was wearing trousers. A cobweb brushed her face, causing her to flinch, and a large spider dropped to the ground, scurrying away. She wiped the web from her face and continued her search.

A black rubber object was strapped up to the underside and beside it what looked like a small outboard motor, and further in, she saw an ammo tin also tied to the frame. She backed out, turned off the torch and called the office.

It was thirty minutes before the search team arrived at the caravan site. Time enough for Suzanna to think through her next actions. She briefed the search team on what she had found and instructed the team to retrieve them and treat them as evidence. She waited around as the team unfastened and dragged out the objects. The rubber item turned out to be, as expected, an inflatable dinghy, and the other objects were made to be used with it. Smuggler's tools.

It was the ammo tin that made her smile the most. As the lid was opened by the gloved search team officer, it revealed a polythene bagged package. The bag appeared to contain a substance that, from Suzanna's assessment, would be around four kilos of cocaine. Her eyes lit up and she shouted a silent, "Yes. Got him!"

* * *

The pub Alex Moore had chosen was a dingy affair. Small windows, dirty net curtains filtering the light and low wattage light bulbs in dull shades. The dark swirly patterned carpet was as sticky as flypaper, and the place smelled of old ale.

Alex sat on a rickety chair behind a dark oak table. He placed his pint on the single beer mat that was close to being condemned to the bin. Whoever had wiped the table had done a lousy job with a wet, dirty cloth. Alex decided to keep his arms on his lap instead of resting them on the wet surface.

The door opened, then swung shut as Tosh walked in. He smiled before speaking. "Hi Alex. Just beat me to it by the looks of your full glass." They shook hands. "Can I get you another one?" Tosh had been expecting Alex to say no, so was surprised when he accepted the offer.

He went to the bar and bought two pints before returning to the table. Alex had already downed half his glass. "Thirsty tonight?" Tosh said with a grin, indicating the speedy consumption.

"Aye, well. It's been a shitty day," Alex responded, in a tone that matched the pub's gloominess.

"Oh! What's up?" Tosh asked as he sat in another loose-jointed chair. It squeaked as his weight settled on its seat.

"I've just found out my client has gone and died before paying her bill. Owes me fifteen hundred pounds."

"That's a bummer," Tosh said sympathetically. "Her name wouldn't be Muir, would it?"

Alex's eyebrows leapt up. "How did you know?"

"It's the murder case I'm working on."

"Murder!" Alex's surprise turned to shock. "Her husband said nothing about murder. Just said she was dead, and I was to leave him in peace... Is that the shooting I heard about a few days back?"

"Aye. It is."

"You have anyone in the frame for it?" Alex asked with a frown.

"A few... In fact, it's one of the reasons I wanted to have a chat tonight."

"Not just a social, then," Alex replied, before taking another gulp of his beer.

"It's always good to have a catch up over a couple of pints, Alex. But I think you can help me with something. Your client had you do some digging into one or two people for her, I understand?"

"Aye. She liked to know about the people she was dealing with, to give her a 'negotiating advantage'." Alex used his fingers to make quote marks as he mentioned Isla Muir's reason for employing him.

"Who did she have you look into lately?"

"I canna tell you that, pal. Client confidentiality!" Alex replied, uncooperatively, his face stern.

"Come on, Alex. She's dead! And the information is relevant to her murder."

"Good point... Point well made." He scanned the bar to ensure no one was in earshot before continuing. "My last job was background stuff on that Bryce fella. The owner of Bryce Haulage. He's a councillor as well."

"Go on."

"Well, it turns out the man's been playing away from home. He's been meeting regularly with his accounts manager, Mrs Rosalind McCubbin. She's a widow. Not just dinners in restaurants. He's been spending evenings at her place. Got photos of him kissing her goodnight on the doorstep. No bedroom shots, though."

"Anything else?"

"I found an ex-employee. Said he'd been wrongly sacked by Bryce. I asked him why he hadn't sued for unfair dismissal, and he said there was no one willing to back him up. Anyway, he said Bryce has been bending the rules. Overloading trucks, only paying for tyre changes when they blew out on the road, paying people to sign them off as safe, when they would have failed their Heavy Goods Vehicle test."

"Perhaps enough dirt for Muir to have pressurised Bryce into continue supporting her planning applications? Hmm! But enough for him to kill her? I'm not sure," Tosh thought out loud, doubt in his voice.

"Put yourself in his shoes, pal. If you had a huge house, with acres of gardens, the status of being MD or CEO or whatever they call themselves nowadays, of a large local employer, and a county councillor, and the money to fly business class everywhere you go, would you want to risk losing all that. Would you kill the person threatening to wreck everything?"

"I take your point, Alex. They say we're all capable of killing given the right circumstances."

The chat with Alex had proven to be extremely useful. Tosh felt the desire to down the remains of his pint and leave Alex to his second beer, as he hadn't yet checked Bryce's alibi for the time of the murder, but he needed to keep the ex-copper on his side. "How's that missus of yours?" Tosh asked, switching away from police business...

Chapter Forty-Six

Suzanna was relaxing on the sofa in her cosy, rented log cabin, with a good book. Classical music played on her Bluetooth speaker. Her mobile phone rang, suppressing the cello's haunting melody. She picked up the phone. James was calling.

"Hi Gorgeous," James said as the video call connected. His face lit up as Suzanna appeared on his phone screen.

Suzanna smiled as she responded. "Hi James. Good to see you. How did the evening go?"

"As good as the first session," James replied buoyantly. "In fact, better, I'd say."

"How do you mean?"

"The first session was about catching our interest and having a social evening. But tonight, after the talk, we had discussions about what we'd heard. It was interesting hearing the diverse views of the group. They're all lovely people, by the way. Well, there is one rather strange man, Paul, who's a bit eccentric and cranky. He declared himself a full-blooded atheist. He was only attending because his wife was on the course, and she'd insisted he come along." James' eyebrows arched.

"That could lead to some fiery conversations, then."

"Yes. Even though the talk made a solid case for Jesus having been the son of God, Paul said that neither of the other two Abrahamic faiths, Islam and Judaism, believe Jesus is the son of God. He seemed to revel in his undeniable argument that, in the Quran, Jesus is merely a prophet."

James went on. "The argument put forward in the talk was that Jesus was either the son of God, a complete fraudster, or a madman. He couldn't have been just a prophet because he claimed he was God's son."

James foraged around for something off screen before holding up a booklet. "There's a quote in here from C. S. Lewis." He found the right page, then read the quote. *"A man who was merely a man, and said, the sort of things Jesus said, would not be a great moral teacher; He'd either be insane, or else he'd be the devil of hell. You must make your choice. Either this man was and is the Son of God, or else insane, or something worse. But let's not come up with any patronising nonsense about his being a great teacher. He's not left that option open to us. He did not intend to."*

"Interesting," Suzanna said, as she drew her legs up under her on the sofa. The quote had surprised her. She knew C. S. Lewis as the author of the Chronicles of Narnia, of course. But she hadn't known he'd also written books on Christianity. "As you know, James, I was brought up in the church. I never considered that Jesus was anything other than the son of God. But when I was a teenager, I turned totally away from the faith. Even now, having heard what you just said, I'm not sure I believe it... I've seen so many things in my life that suggest there is no god in control of things, as Christianity promotes. All the wars, disease, cruelty, evil..."

"I know what you mean, Suzanna. Can't say I understand that either." James concluded. "Anyway, how was your day? How's the case going? Do you have any idea when you might make an arrest?"

Suzanna welcomed James' change in the topic. "Oh! We've made plenty of arrests and charged several people, but we don't yet have our murderer."

"Didn't I hear a farmer had been charged with the murder, then later released?"

"For your ears only, the forensic evidence didn't support our theory so we released him."

"Anyone else in the frame, as you guys put it?"

"We have some other lines to follow." Suzanna paused as she thought. "But obviously I can't say what they are."

"No, no. Never expected you to." James smiled. "Just wondering when you might be coming home. I'm missing you, and virtual hugs just don't do it for me."

Suzanna returned her lover's warm smile. "Nor me. I'm missing you too... But until we actually have someone in custody and the evidence required to gain a conviction, the job's not done." Suzanna turned the focus onto James. "What have you been up to today?"

"The usual boring stuff that earns me a crust. Nothing exciting like your work. Talking of exciting, I was wondering if you fancied a sailing holiday in the Med, later this year?"

Suzanna's face illuminated at the suggestion, and she replied enthusiastically. "Absolutely! I haven't sailed for ages. Let me know what you have in mind and when, so I can book it in."

James' head tilted down and he looked up as he asked Suzanna his next question. "But will you fly home at the first call you have from your bosses?" He asked.

Suzanna's features squashed together, and her jaw clenched as she absorbed the dig. He was right, of course.

James continued. "Can you not ask them to find another SIO if there's a murder, as Dumfries did when their DCI was away on holiday?"

"I suppose so," she replied, deflated by admitting her tendency to respond without question to the call to duty - putting work above all else. She ought to balance her work and personal life better. She could have allocated one of her DIs, Angus or Una, instead of rushing off to Dumfries, herself. "Anyway, I'd best say goodnight," Suzanna concluded, to avoid further awkward conversation. "Another day calls..."

The two lovers blew kisses and waved before terminating the call. Suzanna recognised James' sadness, as his picture dematerialised. Yet again, she had avoided responding to his proposal about how to handle future duty calls when she was on leave. She recognised her evasion as a weakness that she needed to work on. She couldn't keep dodging such questions. It wouldn't do their relationship much good.

Her mind slipped back from the contemplative to the realities of the trial she still faced. Suzanna still had a murderer to catch, and she wouldn't rest until the culprit was behind bars. Until justice was done. But for now, she needed to sleep, to be fresh for the next day's challenges.

* * *

Suzanna picked her book off the table, marked the page, then closed it. As she stood, the uncurtained window drew her to it. The sun had long ago sunk behind the horizon, and darkness now dominated; it was a foreboding scene. The salty smell of the sea filtered through the window frame gaps, mingling with the old pine of the cabin.

She thought back to the other night when she'd gazed out to sea and momentarily spotted a flash of light out in the Firth. Instead of the fishing boat she'd assumed was the light's source, she wondered if it could have been Westwood picking up his cocaine.

If he had been using his dinghy to collect the drugs, perhaps there had been an earlier drop, with the spot marked by a buoy, like the lobster fishermen use. And if he had been picking up off this coast, he would have had to launch from somewhere nearby. She knew floppy rubber-dinghies like the one she'd found stashed under Westwood's caravan were not suitable for long range trips.

Suzanna's heartbeat quickened as she opened her iPad, her fingers first scrolling, then selecting the mapping app, anticipation pushing her despite her tiredness. The coast sprawled before her, a virtual terrain waiting to reveal its secrets. Suzanna zoomed in, seeking potential launch sites. Her eyes darted around each head and cove seeking possibilities. Only one location seemed viable.

She tapped out a few notes on the device, capturing her thoughts before they could escape, for follow up tomorrow. These hastily typed words may just lead to uncovering the missing threads in the drug smuggling web.

Finally, she headed to her bed, her eyes weary, her heart settling to its normal pace, but her mind still whirring.

Chapter Forty-Seven

Tuesday 3rd May

First thing the next morning Suzanna pulled Tosh aside and briefed him on her theory about the boat launch site, as well as her thoughts on how best to handle the Westwood interview.

Davie was sullen as he was brought out of the cells for further questioning, his mood matching the gloomy weather; grey skies releasing drizzle that coated the police station windows with a fine spray.

Tosh opened the interview, his brow furrowed, by asking Westwood about the boat found beneath his caravan. "What I don't understand, Mr Westwood, is why you needed to strap the boat, its oars and outboard motor to the underside of the caravan. Were you trying to hide it?"

"Of course I was. If it had been easy to see, some toerag would have stolen it," Davie responded angrily.

Tosh kept his cool. "When was the last time you used the boat, Mr Westwood?"

Davie frowned, evidently unhappy with being addressed formally. It gave Tosh a tool to wind up the tension.

"Ah dinnae ken. Perhaps a week or two back."

Tosh glared at the suspect as he asked the next question. "What is it you use the boat for, Mr Westwood?"

There was that formality again. "Just a bit of fishing." Davie looked down at the bland Formica table top, avoiding eye contact.

Tosh pressed further. "What time of day do you normally go fishing, then?"

"Any angler will tell you, dawn's the best time." Westwood's eyes appeared to have sunk back into his face.

He pushed again. "So, Mr Westwood, the last time you used the boat would have been for a dawn trip?"

"Probably," Davie replied noncommittally, trying to hide his irritation.

"Yet, when last questioned you said you never get up early." Tosh could see Westwood's annoyance growing. He smiled internally, happy that his questioning was generating the right responses. "I take it you may have used the boat for some other purpose at another time of day or night?"

Westwood's solicitor broke in, sneering. "Get to the point, Sergeant. We'll be here all day if you continue this snail-like journey."

Arabel McGregor was as arrogant as Tosh expected. One of those solicitors who put winning ahead of morality - their client being a higher priority than seeing justice done. This type had no concern for the victims, only their own victory!

The woman must have been mid-thirties. Attractive but not sexy. Hair tied back tightly into a bun, exposing her face, its petite nose, and thin lips. Her slim body was clothed in a dark suit and a white blouse. Officiousness was written all over her face. He turned his attention back to Westwood.

"Right, Mr Westwood, on the 27th of April, did you launch your boat from Carsethorn, proceed out of Carse Gut to a location just off Powillimount Beach, and retrieve an object from a lobster pot?"

Tosh could see Westwood was astounded they could know that. The boss had been right. His face had just confirmed her speculation.

"And was that package this ammo box containing four kilos of cocaine?" Angus showed him a photo of the ammo box. An olive-green tin, measuring approximately 15 x 6 x 4 inches, with large clips at each end.

Westwood did not deny what Tosh had said, so he went on. "Thank you for not denying it, Mr Westwood. There would have been little point, anyway, as your fingerprints are all over the ammo box. And your car was captured on a house security camera in the Carsethorn car park."

Westwood remained silent. His solicitor said nothing, either. The evidence seemed to be unchallengeable.

"So, we know that Isla Muir funded your little venture. You spent the money on your trip to Spain and the drugs were transferred to Scotland by various boats, the last being one out of Maryport harbour." Tosh had slipped in some speculation again, along with some facts, but Westwood was not refuting his accusation. The man appeared to be stunned into silence and had given up trying to bluff his way out by lies or denials.

"Now. Two days before taking delivery of the goods, Mrs Muir was shot dead, meaning you now no longer need to repay her the money she invested in your venture. A powerful motive for murder, don't you agree?"

The last accusation had evidently been a step too far for Westwood. He leapt up; the table jumping as his knees contacted the underside. "I can't deny the drug smuggling, but I've told you before, there's no way I killed Isla Muir," he shouted. "She deserved her money back with interest. I was grateful she helped me step up a rung."

The solicitor had also stood and was trying to get Westwood to stop talking. But his anger had taken over. "You're not pinning that murder on me. I'm not going down for something I never did. I told you; I was in my caravan that morning. I couldn't have killed her."

Tosh looked up calmly, no emotion on his face. "Sit down, Mr Westwood." He waited until Davie had settled before continuing. "Thank you for admitting the drug smuggling charges. We will, or course, investigate further your claim to have been in your caravan at the time of the murder. Once we have further evidence, we will decide whether the murder charges will be dropped or proceeded with."

At that moment, Logan tapped on the door and entered. "Sarge, I have something you'll want to see." Tosh left the room, returning two minutes later. "Mr Westwood, you will be pleased to know that my colleague has just found CCTV evidence that proves you drove your Land Rover back to the caravan site on the night of 24th April and it was next seen at 11:30 a.m., heading away from the caravan site. This supports your claim to have been in your bed that morning. My colleague will now take your written statement regarding drug smuggling and drug supplying."

Tosh left the room, closed the door behind him and punched the air. He'd already known about the CCTV evidence that placed Westwood in his caravan that morning. But the murder accusation had gained the confession for drug smuggling. It would make things a lot easier all round, and the organised crime squad could pick up on the previous parts of the smuggling route. Having followed the DCI's direction on the interview strategy, Tosh's admiration for Suzanna doubled in an instant. She was certainly living up to her reputation.

* * *

Suzanna leaned back in her chair, studying the whiteboard covered in photographs and notes. Clearing her throat, she called the team together for a strategy discussion. "Alright, team, let's catch up on where we stand with the investigation," she began, her eyes scanning the faces around the room. "We've got Westwood in custody for drug smuggling, but that doesn't make him our killer. So, we need other lines to follow."

Suzanna continued. "There doesn't appear to be a motive for Black to have killed Muir. She hadn't tasked the private eye with investigating him. And it doesn't appear that he had been trying to get out of the arrangement he had with her. The Private Investigator had dug up dirt on Bryce, though, which supports our assumption he may have killed Isla Muir."

Tosh's brow furrowed; he interjected. "But the snag is Bryce has a solid alibi for the time of her murder. His wife confirmed he left home about 8:30 a.m. and their home CCTV backed that up. And Bryce was behind his desk by 9 a.m."

"Did the CCTV show movement in and out of the Bryce home from 6 a.m. through to 8:30 a.m.?" Suzanna asked.

Carl shook his head. "No. None. If he'd left the house early, then returned for breakfast, we'd have seen him leave and return."

Mairi shared her thoughts, her brow furrowing. "Maybe he paid someone else to kill Mrs Muir? People with pots of money don't need to get their hands dirty. He's not driving the trucks himself, is he?"

Suzanna nodded appreciatively. "Good point, Mairi. Let's look into that possibility. Connections with known villains, especially those with records of violence and/or firearms possession. You know the sort of thing."

Suzanna paused, deep in thought. "But let's suppose Bryce didn't hire someone to murder Muir and didn't do it himself. Where does that leave us? We would have eliminated the only two planning officials in Muir's pocket."

"Agreed, ma'am," Tosh concurred. "I can't see any of the other four councillors killing, just because they could lose their place on the council."

Suzanna continued. "The three men we've arrested for drug dealing all have alibis, so that's them eliminated, as well." Her mind thought through the other possibilities as the others waited for her to continue.

"Mrs Allanach, the disgruntled landowner, remains a possibility, because she has no alibi, but we have no weapon, and the test of her clothing showed no sign of blood," Suzanna stated. "Though she could've disposed of them, I suppose. But my gut tells me it's not her. So, who?" She scanned the faces of her team, looking for flashes of inspiration.

Tosh was the first to speak. "I agree. I know she's still angry about being cheated out of money - so would I be - but she doesn't seem the type to have turned to murder. Cold-blooded, planned murder. And to be honest, she doesn't appear the sharpest-minded woman. Not sure she has it in her to plan and execute the murder."

Suzanna nodded. "Hmm!"

"By the way, ma'am," Mairi added, "evidence from forensics suggests the Brownlow's shotgun hasn't been fired in weeks. And the type of cartridges he had don't match with the shot pulled from the victim."

"Another dead end!" Suzanna said. "Any thoughts on where to look next, if it isn't Bryce?" No one offered any suggestions. "Okay. Let's focus on Bryce having hired a killer." A thought popped into her mind. "Tosh. Did you get that warrant to search Patterson's flat?"

"Aye. A team is going in this morning. Fingers crossed they'll find incriminating evidence, so we can do him for drug dealing as well."

Suzanna smiled and nodded in agreement. "Right, let's get to work."

Chapter Forty-Eight

The earlier rain had cleared and breaks in the cloud allowed the sun to shine through, brightening the mood of shoppers. Mist lifted from the warming pavement, and the tables outside the cafe now had dry surfaces. The seats had been wiped down by the cafe staff and several people supped teas, coffees and hot chocolates, and ate cake. Multiple conversations merged into a general chatter of voices. Smoke drifted across between tables, catching the throat of a fragile-looking elderly woman.

She coughed. "Would you mind not smoking?" the old woman requested. Her face was like a balloon that had lost air. Shrivelled and lined as if an entire flock of crows had walked across it. Her translucent skin clung to her skull. Her eyes had shrunk back into her head and lost their sparkle. But she'd taken the trouble to apply lipstick, and pearl earrings were clipped to both lobes.

"Poke off," the young smoker responded angrily. "It's a free country. I'll smoke where I want" The woman was dressed in stained jeans and a grubby green wax-jacket, her mousy hair tied back messily into a ponytail.

"There's no need to be offensive. I only asked you not to smoke."

"They're my lungs, not yours." Her ruddy complexion reddened further as anger contorted her face.

"But it's drifting across here. I'm having to breathe in your smoke. It smells disgusting and it makes me cough," she responded indignantly, then coughed again.

"Well, bugger off somewhere else for your coffee, you old hag. No one asked you to sit there," she growled, sneering at her, her eyebrows squashed together.

Most of the cafe conversations had paused, and heads swivelled towards the commotion.

"I was here before you, young lady," she replied in a draconian tone.

"Well, tough luck," she said aggressively, glaring at the other woman. "I'm allowed to smoke, and that's what I'm gonna do. Like it or lump it."

Passers-by turned their heads, curious why voices were raised.

"Can't you sit over there with the other smokers?" the elderly lady replied, her pitch rising. "There's no need to pollute the entire seating area. Non-smokers need somewhere to sit without having to choke on others' smoke."

A waiter scurried across to them. "Excuse me," he said to the young woman. "Would you be so kind as to move to another table? We have a spare one over there," he said, pointing across the paved area. "I'll carry your drink and the ashtray. No need to argue."

The elderly lady smiled at the young waiter, glad he had intervened.

The young woman noticed a Police Community Support Officer striding purposefully along the street towards the cafe, her focus directed towards the disturbance. "I didn't want to sit near the interfering old bat, anyway," she said vociferously. She got up and moved to the other table, taking her coffee with her. Like a moody teenager, she threw herself into the chair, which creaked its objections, then looked away from the cafe, the waiter, and the old woman. Her jaw clenched as she silently moaned about the interference with her liberty.

The waiter spoke quietly, looking into the eyes of the offended customer. "Sorry about that. I'll remove ashtrays from tables in this area. Hopefully, that will keep an area clear for you and other non-smokers."

"That's most kind. Thanks for your intervention," the woman said, smiling up at the young man as she straightened her skirt.

The PCSO arrived just after the waiter had removed the ashtrays and returned to the cafe. "Excuse me, ma'am. Is everything alright?"

"It is now, officer. Thank you for asking." She turned her head to look at the smoker, who had been rude to her. The PCSO's eyes followed the woman's stare.

"Was that woman offensive towards you?"

"Mildly. She told me to poke off when I asked her not to smoke near me. As you can see, she's moved now, so the problem has drifted away," she said with a smile, watching the woman's smoke blown by the breeze away from the cafe.

"Did she offer violence, or was it just a few cross words?"

"No. No overt threats, but her manner was rather hostile. I was a little worried she might attack me."

"Okay. I'll have a word with her." The PCSO wandered over to the woman.

"Excuse me. I'm PCSO Juliet Osbourne. Can I ask your name?"

"You just have asked. Why do you want my permission?" The woman was antagonistic, her face sneering at the questions. "Anyway, what's it to you?"

"I understand you were aggressive with that lady," she said, indicating with a glance who she meant. "And used offensive language. I'd like your name, please," she added with authority.

The woman glared at the troublemaker who had caused her to move tables and now to be questioned by this pretend police officer.

The older lady looked away to avoid the stare; she didn't understand why people had to be so nasty.

The smoker reluctantly answered. "Ainslie Reynolds. But I never swore at her. She's just an interfering old bag. Thinks she owns the public spaces. Told me I couldn't smoke. Where else could I smoke while having my coffee? I'm not allowed to smoke inside the cafe!"

"You need to respect other people. Your smoke was upsetting her."

The woman responded fiercely, "Well, she could have gone inside, couldn't she? It was her choice to sit outside. This country's becoming a police state, with everything you do controlled by the government. It's ridiculous." She jumped to her feet, upending the table, swearing. The remains of her drink spilled onto the PCSO's uniform.

All conversation ceased as the customers watched, open-mouthed, as the angry young woman strode away. The officer pressed her radio talk button and reported to the control centre what had just happened.

* * *

"Logan. How are you getting on with that trawl of the PNC?" Mairi asked.

"That was a long list you gave me. I didn't realise Bryce Haulage employed so many people. I'm about halfway through. No one has shown up on the system yet."

Mairi went back to her work, when just a minute later, Logan spoke. "Hang on, Here's one!"

Mairi joined Logan at his desk and leaned over his shoulder, curious to see what he had discovered. "What have you found?"

"This fella, Gregory Bell - one of the warehouse guys - has a history of violence. Assaults, actual bodily harm, and carrying a concealed weapon. He's done community service and two short stints in jail."

"Great. Keep looking, Logan. We'll pay him a visit." Mairi looked up and turned to Carl, having noticed him paying attention to the conversation. She exchanged a knowing glance with him before they both stood up simultaneously, grabbing their coats. They exited the room together, a purpose in their step.

It took just ten minutes to reach the haulage depot, and on showing their IDs were directed to a tall building in the corner, about the size of a small aircraft hangar.

The chirping of birds above grabbed Mairi's attention. Swallows flitted above their heads as they entered the open door. Mairi looked up and saw numerous nests clinging to the rafters.

A dour-faced man in his forties strode towards them, a challenging expression on his face. His black hair was greased back harshly over his head, glistening in the sun's light. "You can't come in here. This is a restricted area."

Carl showed his ID. "DC Penrose. This is my colleague, DC Gordon," he said. "We've been directed here by the lady in reception. She said this is where we'd find Mr Gregory Bell."

The man's face turned from officious to worried. "I'm Greg Bell. What do you want?"

Mairi spoke. "We just need a quiet chat, Mr Bell. Is there an office we could use, perhaps?"

"Aye. Follow me," he said gruffly. He led them to a small office in the back corner of the warehouse. Through the window, Mairi could see that it was a messy place.

Bell cleared some rubbish off his desk into the bin and stacked a load of forms into the desk's corner. They all sat in the rigid plastic chairs. "So what's this about, then?" Bell said.

Carl opened. "A simple question to get started. Where were you between 6 a.m. and 10 a.m. on the 25th of April?"

"Why on earth would you want to know that?" he responded, his eyebrows lifting.

"Just answer the question please, sir," Mairi said.

"I'm not sure. What day would that have been?" he looked at the calendar on his wall, his eyes scanning the dates. "Last Monday. I was at work that day. Usually start at eight."

Mairi pressed, watching his facial expressions for any sign he might not be telling the truth. "But did you actually start work at eight that day? Is there any record?"

"Aye. I will have clocked on as I passed through the gate. You can ask the HR girls."

"We will," Carl said, as he took notes. "And you live on Wallace Street; so, that would have taken you about five minutes to get here?"

"More like ten. I use me bike." They could see he was perplexed why they were asking, and they already knew where he lived.

Carl continued his questions. "So, you left home at 7:50 a.m.? Is there anyone who can confirm that?"

"Look, you still have'nae told me what this is about."

"We'll come to that in a minute, sir," Mairi interjected. "Please, just answer our questions."

"Me misses will be able to."

Carl enquired. "Where can we find your wife at this time of day?"

"She'll be on the tills at Morrisons. But the supervisor won't like you going in, taking her away from her work. And in any case, you'll start rumours running if you turn up there to question her," Bell warned.

"We can't work around everyone's convenience, Mr Bell," Carl stated. "We'd never get our work done."

"Are you going to tell me what this is about, or what?" Bell said, annoyance showing in his voice.

Mairi answered him. "Perhaps it would be best to leave it as 'or what' for the moment. If your alibi is confirmed, we won't need to trouble you again. No need to be worried if you've not been up to anything, Mr Bell."

Bell snapped back. "Stop mucking me about. Just tell me what this is about."

"Does the name Isla Muir mean anything to you, Mr Bell?" Carl responded.

"Isn't that the name of the woman who was found dead last week? Hang on!" Bell sat up in his chair and leaned towards the officers, challengingly. "You don't think I had anything to do with that?"

"Do you know Mrs Muir, or not?" Carl pushed.

"Never heard of her before she was in the papers."

Mairi asked, "How long have you worked here, Mr Bell?"

"Five years, or thereabouts." He frowned, obviously not under-standing why this was relevant.

"How did you hear about the opening and who made the decision to employ you?" Mairi continued.

Bell looked perplexed. "It was on the Job Centre board. I'd just got out of prison. I thought my record would go against me, but that Mr Bryce is a decent fella. He took pity on me and offered me the job, even though the HR manager recommended that he not take me on."

"Very compassionate of the man. So, you owe him, then?" Carl suggested.

"Well, I don't know if I'd have got a job if it weren't for him, but he's never asked for any favours, if that's what you're getting at." Bell paused, his mind correlating the facts.

Carl asked his next question before Bell had completed his analysis. "If not a favour, perhaps he's offered you some off-the-books employ-ment. Just one job for one payment? If we check your bank account, might we find a large payment going into it lately?"

Bell responded furiously. "You suggesting he paid me to kill that woman? I've been accused of many things in my time but being a contract killer takes the biscuit. You're barking up the wrong tree, copper." He stood abruptly. "If there's nothing else, I have work to do," he said gruffly, then opened the door and invited them to leave.

"Just one last thing," Mairi asked, "have you ever fired a shotgun?"

Bell ignored the question. His lips sealed. His hands in his pockets. Stern-faced. As he watched the officers leave the warehouse, he worried.

Chapter Forty-Nine

Carl parked his car in the Morrisons' car park, looking down at the damage inflicted on the car by Jack Reynolds' tractor a week ago. He'd not got it fixed yet. Mairi noticed Carl's attention was distracted. As he caught her looking at him, her eyes widened, asking a silent question. "I'll tell you about it later," Carl said as he walked towards the entrance doors. They found the check-out supervisor and asked to speak with Bell's wife.

"Cairstine Bell, you say. Just a minute," the supermarket supervisor said. "Aye. I thought so. She's on Till 5, but she's due her break. I'll get her for you. You can use my room to speak to her."

"That's very kind, Mrs Jackson. It would be better all round if we could speak with her in private. I trust you'll not tell anyone else about our chat. She's not done anything wrong. We just think she can help us with something," Mairi said.

"Aye. Sure. No problem. Cairstine's a good worker and kind-hearted. I wouldn't want people talking behind her back. I'll bring her here in a couple of minutes."

That had been much easier than Greg Bell had suggested. Carl and Mairi looked around the room, seeing rosters for the tills and shift patterns for the staff, in between company policy notices and a list of phone extension numbers. The furniture was sparse and utilitarian. The smell of polish and floor cleaners emanated from a corner cupboard.

"I hear you recently got engaged, Mairi," Carl mentioned.

"Yeah. Brodie popped the question in a posh restaurant. Down on his knee for all to see. Really traditional and romantic. Just as well I said yes, though. He'd have been hugely embarrassed if I'd said no." She grinned as she showed Carl the engagement ring.

"Very nice. He'd have needed a mortgage to buy that," Carl quipped.

Mairi admired the ring again. Carl was right. It must have cost him a fortune. She remembered her mam telling her that pop had never really proposed. Just said, 'shall we get engaged, then?' Like shall we tell folks we're going steady? She had agreed and they went to the jewellers together to choose the ring and he'd put it on her finger in a fish and chip shop.

"You're in a relationship as well, aren't you? Any plans to marry?"

"Yeah. Amy and I have been living together for the last two years but neither of us has broached the subject yet. Guess we might marry if Amy falls pregnant. I'd want the kids to have the stability of married parents. I know the divorce rate in the UK is ridiculously high, but many more relationships split up if the couples are not married. And I'd want them to have my name. Especially if we had a boy. Keep the family name going, you know!"

The door opened before Mairi could respond. Mrs Bell looked flustered and worried. "Mrs Cairstine Bell?" Mairi asked.

"Aye," she responded, sounding like a schoolgirl attending the headteacher's office. "You wanted to talk to me?"

"Yes, come in. Take a seat." They all sat. "It's nothing to worry about Cairstine," Mairi continued, using her first name to lower the formality of the situation. "We just need to know when Gregory left home on Monday morning."

Mrs Bell's hackles rose. "Why should you need to know that? He's kept his nose clean since he came out of prison. Not done anything wrong in five years now. He's stayed off the whisky."

"That's good to hear, Cairstine. But when did your husband leave home on the 25th of April?"

"How should I know?" Bell replied sharply. "I'm out the door by seven thirty when I'm on the morning shift? He leaves home after me."

Carl took over. "Were you on the morning shift on the 25th?"

She thought for a few seconds, then looked up at the rosters for confirmation. "Aye, I was. I'd worked the Sunday as well, but that's a later start, of course."

"Can you remember that day specifically?" Mairi asked. "Was he home when you left for work and had he been out at all?"

They waited while Cairstine thought back. "Aye. He was definitely at home until I left for work. I'd have been sure to notice if he weren't there."

"Does your husband cycle to work?"

"Aye. He's got one of those old drop-handlebar things. Gets a right speed from it. But regularly gets punctures on account of its thin tyres."

"Do you have a car?" Carl asked.

"A twenty-year-old rusting Corsa is sitting on the street outside our house, but it's not been driven for two months, since it failed its last MOT. It'll cost too much to have it repaired. But Greg hasn't got around to having it scrapped yet."

"Okay. Thanks for your help, Cairstine." Carl stood. "That's all we need for now. We'll let you get back to your work."

Cairstine's face relaxed, the stress abating, but Mairi was sure she'd be having a word with her husband later. She hoped it didn't cause them any difficulties. She didn't want to create undeserved collateral damage. Although a spouse's testimony could not be accepted on face value, both Greg and Cairstine's responses to their questions had seemed genuine.

"Just one thing." Carl said. "Get your husband to have that car removed. If it's on the street, it has to be taxed, insured and have a current MOT. You wouldn't want him to get into any trouble of over it, would you? I'll not say anything to the uniform guys for a few days."

Mrs Bell looked serious as she responded. "Thank you, officer. I'll have a word with him tonight. It'll be gone this week. I can assure you," she said, determined.

* * *

Suzanna had yet to hear from Mairi and Carl when she had Bryce brought up from the cells, where he had been held on charges of bribery and corruption, and suspicion of murder. He looked forlorn. His hair was uncombed, his complexion dry and cracked, and the start of a beard added to his scruffiness.

"Sit down, Mr Bryce," Suzanna ordered, her tone unwavering. He settled into the chair opposite her, his gaze fixed on the table, to avoid her accusing eyes. Bryce's solicitor, Craig Mitchell, took the seat next to him.

Suzanna spoke again. "We have conducted further investigations into the possibility that you murdered Isla Muir."

Bryce sat up straight, his eyes locking onto Suzanna's, his eagerness evident - perhaps wondering whether it would be good news or bad?

"We've uncovered new information," Suzanna continued, her gaze unyielding. "It appears Isla Muir had hired a private investigator to delve into your personal life." Anxiety surged across Bryce's face, overtaking his previous composure.

"It seems you harbour secrets you'd prefer to remain hidden, and Isla Muir was privy to these secrets." Even Bryce's solicitor appeared concerned, bracing for the impending revelations.

Suzanna continued. "I have a witness willing to testify that your company, under your direction, has been overloading trucks and falsifying Heavy Goods Vehicle safety tests."

"That's rubbish!" Bryce blasted back. "I know who your witness will be. An ex-employee. A madman who couldn't be trusted and was fired for gross misconduct. He'll no doubt be trying to get revenge for what he thought was unfair dismissal."

Craig Mitchell interjected, aligning with his client's defence. "I concur. Given the circumstances of his dismissal, this ex-employee's credibility as a witness would be highly questionable. No impartial jury would regard him as trustworthy."

Suzanna's gaze remained steady, her resolve unshaken. "I'm more than willing to test that in a court of law, Mr Bryce, once the independent Ministry of Transport inspectors conclude their surprise examination of your fleet."

Bryce stood, his face flushed with anger. "This is harassment! How dare you interfere? I'll have your Chief Super take you off this case."

Suzanna's eyebrows arched, her blue eyes widening in response. She stood and leaned in towards him, her voice a measured tone. "It sounds to me, Mr Bryce, like you are admitting to the planned bribery or blackmail of a senior police officer." She paused for effect. "Let me be clear. I was appointed to this case by Police Scotland, not by the said Chief Superintendent, so there's nothing you can do, anyway." She pulled back, her eyes still locked on his.

She sat again, Bryce following her lead.

Suzanna followed on. "This threat of exposure to unsafe practices may well be sufficient motive to murder Isla Muir. But this is not the only secret revelation made by the private eye. No, Mr Bryce, he also uncovered your ongoing affair with your accounts manager, Rosalind McCubbin."

Bryce didn't stir. Unable to deny the truth.

"Should your wife of thirty-two years be informed about this affair, it would undoubtedly lead to a messy divorce, resulting in the sale of your company and mansion to divide assets. Your life would be in ruins, and with the unsafe vehicle practices, you'd be banned from running any haulage company." Suzanna watched Bryce closely as she continued. "The threat of exposing either secret could provide a compelling motive for murder."

Bryce slumped in his chair, the fight having faded away. "But I couldn't have murdered Isla Muir. I was home at the time you said she'd been murdered. My wife can confirm that."

Suzanna's tone shifted, becoming more probing. "Are you a truck driver, Mr Bryce?"

"I used to be, but I pay other people to do that now." Bryce's face flickered with recognition of where the questioning was heading.

"Indeed, you do, Mr Bryce. You don't need to get your hands dirty anymore. Which leads me to my next point. Your association with a former convict, known for his violent tendencies. A man indebted to you for offering him employment."

Bryce evidently understood who the detective was suggesting could have carried out the murder for him. He spoke calmly. "Look. Just because I gave an ex-con a job doesn't mean he'd commit murder for me. Gregory Bell is a good man. He'd never murder anyone, let alone because I'd employed him just after his release. It's a ridiculous suggestion."

"Maybe not. But perhaps he would if you offered him a tidy *bonus*. We're looking at his bank accounts now and if we find a sizeable one-off payment, his extracurricular employment on your personal errand would be the obvious explanation."

Bryce sat back in his chair, satisfied that the police would get nowhere with this line of enquiry, because he hadn't paid Bell any 'bonus.'

The solicitor intervened. "Unless you have that evidence, and evidence that this Bell fellow murdered Mrs Muir, it's time this line of questioning stopped. My client will forthwith cease to answer further questions, instigating his Police and Criminal Evidence Act right to silence."

Suzanna had run out of roads to take. She had hoped evidence of Bell's involvement would have arrived by now. A knock came at the door and Carl popped his head around. Suzanna suspended the interview and left the room.

"Ma'am. Bell's wife has confirmed that he was at home when she left for work at 7:30 a.m. She says they don't have a serviceable car, and Bell clocked on for work at 7:57 a.m., having cycled to work. So, it would appear he couldn't have killed Isla Muir."

Suzanna considered Carl's statement before responding. "You said it would *appear* Greg Bell couldn't have killed Isla Muir but it's not impossible, is it?"

"I suppose not, ma'am. But our judgement," Carl replied, glancing at Mairi for concurrence, "is that both the Bells were telling the truth."

Mairi nodded agreement.

Suzanna knew Mairi well enough to trust her judgement. Another door closed. Where next?

Chapter Fifty

Logan was glad to be out of the office, released from the claustrophobic feeling it had created. Although he enjoyed being part of the murder investigation team, knowing he was contributing to the team's efforts to solve crimes, he disliked being stuck in the office every day.

PC Archie Gillespie was at the wheel of the police car as the two officers travelled along Brodie Avenue. Logan took in the surroundings. The flats along this road had all been built at the same time to the same design. Red brick doorways, the bricks extending upwards to a pair of narrow windows. The walls were pebble-dashed.

Both officers exited the car after Archie had parked on the street. Beside the part-glazed hardwood door, a bank of bell pushes invited callers to ring flats A to D. There was no point ringing any bells, though. Patterson was in a cell at the police station. And Logan had the keys that were confiscated from the suspect when he was arrested. He let himself into the entrance vestibule, climbed the stairs to flat D and opened the door.

"What a shit-heap!" Archie said. The place stank of garbage and smoke.

"Aye. I wouldn't keep a dog in here." As Logan finished speaking, a dog barked. The two PCs looked at each other, then to the door from which the sound had emanated. "You first, Archie."

The dog barked again, then growled. It sounded vicious. "Er! No thanks. You're the dog-lover. You'll deal with it."

Logan stepped forward and inched the door ajar. The Staffordshire Bull Terrier's snout rammed into the gap, its teeth bared, a throaty guttural sound warning Logan not to open the door further. He dragged it closed, making sure the dog could pull back and not get its mouth trapped. It barked again and didn't let up for the next few minutes as they searched the rest of the flat.

Logan called the station to request the assistance of the animal cruelty prevention charity. They'd take it in and look after it. They would have to wait for the dog to be removed before they could search that room. With gloved hands, the two constables lifted items, opened drawers, looked under and within the sofa and chairs, and emptied kitchen cupboards. Nothing!

"This guy's not married, and has no kids," Logan said. "How come the council provided him with a flat to live in? There must be loads of couples living with their parents who'd love to have their own place."

"Good point. He must know someone in high places."

Surprisingly, the animal rescue woman arrived just a few minutes later. They left her to get the dog out by herself, stepping onto the landing.

Logan knocked on the neighbour's door. He heard a shout from inside but couldn't hear the words spoken. As he waited patiently, Archie joined him. The door cracked open, and a wizened face peered through the gap.

"Hello. I'm PC Stevens," Logan said. "I'd like a word with you about your neighbour."

Having seen the police uniforms, the woman opened the door wide. She was a skinny, short woman, probably in her early eighties. Her grey hair was wrapped around multi-coloured curlers. Her buttercup yellow cardigan hung loosely over her off-white blouse that was tucked into her beige plaid skirt. On her feet were pink slippers held in place by wrap-over Velcro-fastened tabs.

"What is it you want to know, officer?"

"Well," Logan replied. "What can you tell me about Mr Patterson? What does he look like? Does he have any visitors? Does he stay in all day or go out to work? Anything, really."

"Aye. Well, I don't think he has a job, because he comes and goes at all times of the day. That blasted dog of his barks its head off for hours at a time. I've complained to the council. They said they'd warned him, but he's still there and his dog still barks. Useless lot!"

Archie knew it wasn't as simple as the woman expected for the council to deal with anti-social tenants, because his sister worked for the council and had mentioned it. "What about visitors?"

"I don't see them, on account of spending most of my day sat in my chair or on my bed. But I know he has many callers, often late at night, when I'm trying to sleep. They don't give a monkey's about other folks. I should have asked for one of those ASBO things. You know, anti-social behaviour orders. That's right, isn't it?"

"Aye. You'd have to get the council to apply for an ASBO. You canna do it yourself," Archie replied.

"Have you not seen any of his callers, Mrs...?"

"It's Mrs Kerr. Angela. Maybe I *will* ask the council to get an ASBO. As I said, I rarely see his visitors coming and going but I have seen one or two of them leave when I've been at the window. There's not one of them doesn't wear a cap and one of those hoodie things. Only people with something to hide would go around all day, with a cap on and a hood up. You mark my words."

Logan could understand why she'd think that, but he knew a lot of good kids who wore hoodies. It was just a fashion thing. An image to fit in with their peers. "Have you ever seen or heard anything that you thought might have been illegal?" he asked.

"Can't say I have. Sorry. Unless being noisy at ungodly hours is illegal?"

"If the noise is excessive and when most folks would be asleep, you can contact your Environmental Health team at the council," Archie said. "They can take action against the culprit."

"Aye. Well, I won't hold my breath on getting them to do anything." Mrs Kerr swayed on her feet. "I need to sit down, lads. Have you finished asking your questions?"

The two officers exchanged glances, Logan seeking confirmation from Archie that he could reveal Patterson's situation. Archie's eyebrows rose and he nodded.

Logan spoke. "I think you'll find your problem has gone away. Your neighbour is in custody and will undoubtedly be remanded, awaiting trial. The council will probably allocate the flat to someone else, as I reckon he'll be going to jail for more than a year."

"I hope you're right, officer. I hope you're right. Now, if you'll excuse me, I have an appointment with my chair." She stepped back and closed the door.

The officers tried the other neighbours in the block but discovered nothing of use. They stepped outside for a breath of fresh air and were about to return to their car when the block's entrance door opened, and the animal rescue lady emerged with Patterson's growling dog on the end of a rigid lead. She walked off toward her van. "The flat's all yours, officers."

"Thanks," Logan responded, respectfully saluting the heroic woman, then led the way back inside.

The one room they hadn't searched was Patterson's bedroom. Sheets were crumpled in the bed's centre. Pillows were strewn across the floor. One had been ripped to shreds. A cheap, pine, flat-pack wardrobe stood in the corner, the left door hanging off its hinges.

Logan foraged around inside the wardrobe but came up with nothing but dirty laundry. Hoodies, jogging bottoms, socks, and underpants.

He was glad to have gloves protecting his hands. Logan turned to Archie. "If this guy is a drug dealer, I'd like to know where he keeps his stash. There's nothing here!"

As the words left Logan's mouth, a thought occurred to him. He turned back to the wardrobe, then pulled it from the wall. Strapped to the back of the wardrobe was a clear polythene bag full of pills. "Eureka!"

* * *

Suzanna re-entered the interview room and took a seat opposite Bryce and his solicitor, Craig Mitchell. Both looked annoyed that they had been kept waiting for her return.

"Gentlemen, you will be glad to hear that Gregory Bell has an alibi for the time of Muir's murder," Suzanna stated.

Bryce's face relaxed with the relief.

Suzanna continued. "You will also be pleased to know that you will be released today."

Bryce turned to his solicitor and smiled, as if to say thanks. But his happiness soon subsided as Suzanna continued speaking. "But your release will be conditional, pending appearance in the Sheriff Court on the charges already put to you earlier."

The solicitor shrugged his shoulders, as if to say that was to be expected.

"I will, however, continue to investigate the possibility that Isla Muir was murdered by a person, as yet unknown, employed by you, Mr Bryce." Suzanna peered into his eyes as she continued. "You may not have had the opportunity, but you certainly have the means and motive to have been behind her murder." Her stare remained fixed on Bryce even after she finished speaking, emphasising that although he was being let out of the keep net, he was still in her pond. And she might reel him in again.

As Suzanna broke contact and stood, Bryce turned to his solicitor, his eyes seeking unspoken guidance. Mr Mitchell held out his hand, palm down, indicating his client should remain sitting as Suzanna left the interview room, leaving the formal release task to the constable on duty.

If Bell couldn't have murdered Isla Muir, she wondered, was there someone else that Bryce knew who could have done the job for him? So far, they'd not found another promising connection.

She ambled along the corridor as her mind revolved around the possibilities. The whole team was in the office when she entered, so she updated them on Bryce's release. Then she shared her thoughts with them about possible other connections.

"Ma'am," Logan piped up. "I've just returned from Patterson's flat, where I found a significant quantity of drugs."

"That's good to hear, Logan. What do you think that discovery has to do with Bryce? And with Muir's murder?"

"Well, I was thinking, Patterson is a violent man. He's involved in the drugs trade and Isla Muir is suspected of involvement in that same trade. Could someone have paid Patterson to kill Mrs Muir?"

"Okay. I see the drugs connection, but I don't see how Bryce fits into this scenario."

"I did background checks on Bryce's employees for criminal records and only found one, Greg Bell, who has now been discounted," Logan responded. "But we haven't looked wider than employees. Perhaps he has other connections; connections with the drugs trade?"

"Good thinking. We have masses of documents and his computer to scrutinise, to look for more evidence of bribery and corruption. We can check out his other contacts and see what turns up." Suzanna said. "As it was your idea, Logan, you get on to that... Mairi, you work with him, please."

"Sure. No problem," Mairi responded. "Come on Logan. Let's get to it."

"Hang on." Suzanna called as they turned and stepped away. "It's good that you're keen but we're not finished yet."

The two officers returned to the circle, Mairi apologising for being so hasty.

Suzanna went on. "Bryce is not the only one with a motive to kill Isla Muir, is he?" She waited for a response from the group, wanting their minds to churn, to uncover new lines of inquiry, her eyes flitting around the group inviting them to speak.

"We had been looking at Westwood for the murder," Mairi reminded them, "but he's just been cleared. He could have paid someone like Patterson to do his dirty work, though. Westwood is the top man in this area and Patterson must know him."

Tosh shared his thoughts. "I don't know why we didn't think of it before. He must be dealing with the low-life pushers every day. He'd know who had a natural bent for violence and was capable of murder. If it were Patterson, it would be more likely that Westwood was the paymaster, rather than Bryce."

Suzanna smiled, glad that they had reached this conclusion without heavy prodding. "Good thinking, guys. Okay. Let's stick with the original plan. Mairi and Logan look into Bryce's connections. Tosh. Carl. You two interview Patterson again and find out whether he had the opportunity to murder Muir. Then find out if Patterson's contact details are on Westwood's phone, before questioning him about his connection to Patterson - assuming there is one. I have a hospital visit to make."

Chapter Fifty-One

A strong whiff of artificial pine hit Suzanna's nostrils as she pushed through the heavy double doors into the ward reception area. She nearly tripped over a sign that warned of wet floors, it having been thoughtlessly placed. She could see the floor was no longer wet, so shifted the sign aside before approaching the reception. The nurse behind the counter frowned at her interference but said nothing.

Suzanna held up her police ID card. "DCI McLeod. I'm here to see Mrs Jones."

The nurse pursed her lips and glanced down at the ward plan before responding. "I'll take you to her. Come this way."

Suzanna followed the nurse along the corridor, passing side wards, emanating the echoey voices of busy nursing staff, then turned right into a bay containing four beds. Boyd Jones was sitting at his wife's bedside.

He stood, his face reddening. "What do you want?" he growled. "Haven't you done enough? It's your fault Laura got beaten up."

Skye Jones jumped to her feet and looked to her father. "Is this the policewoman who arrested you?"

"Aye. She's the one. The bastard who did this would have been in hospital now, instead of your mam, if she'd not interfered."

Suzanna stood still, her eyes flitting between the two Joneses, watching for any signs the situation might escalate.

"But, Dad, didn't she send the policemen to our house to protect us?"

The nurse looked as if she was about to interrupt when Boyd blurted his response, cutting her off. "Aye. But by then it was too late. They're all the same, coppers. They care more about sending people to jail than they do about real justice."

"I'm going to have to ask you to leave," the nurse broke in. "I can't have this disruption. The patients need rest, not conflict."

Suzanna acknowledged the need to maintain peace with a nod. She looked Boyd in the eye and spoke. "Mr Jones. I understand your anger. But your wife needs rest. Come with me. I need to talk with you." She turned and strode back along the corridor, not looking back.

Boyd and Skye exchanged glances. "Go on, Dad. I'll stay with Mam."

Boyd reluctantly followed the detective out of the ward. He caught up with her as she entered the hospital's foyer. By then, he had calmed down and, surrounded by large numbers of people, quietly waited for the DCI to speak.

She looked him in the eye. "Mr Jones. I can only apologise for what happened to your wife. Given your circumstances, I may have acted similarly. I just wish the custody sergeant had listened to you when you were booked into the station. We could have had officers to your home more quickly and saved your wife the beating she received." Suzanna paused, then continued softly. "How is she?"

Suzanna's face showed genuine concern and Boyd recognised this, speaking calmly as he replied. "She woke earlier. Even managed a smile. But she's in a lot of pain." His eyes welled up. "It will be several days before she can go home. And perhaps weeks before she'll be able to work again." A single tear escaped and rolled down Boyd's cheek; he quickly wiped it away.

"Look, would you like a coffee? I want to talk to you about getting justice for your wife."

"Okay. That'd be good. I'm parched." He followed Suzanna into the hospital cafe and she ordered him a white americano and herself a cappuccino. Her low expectations were met as the paper cups were placed on the counter, both having been made by an automated dispenser.

Suzanna handed Boyd his drink, then led the way to a seat in the cafe's corner. It was too busy to get out of earshot of everyone but at least they wouldn't be surrounded by ears.

She sipped her drink, then spoke in a friendly tone. "Look, Boyd. You were in the Paras. If you were in an Afghan village and saw an apparently innocent person being attacked, would you have intervened or just watched the person get a beating?"

He thought for a moment, his eyes roaming the room, before replying. "I see where you're coming from. You were doing your duty when you stopped me from hitting Patterson with that fire extinguisher."

"How many tours did you do in Afghanistan?"

"Two. Both in Helmand Province. It was like the wild west. Men waiting for our patrols to cross open spaces and take pot shots at us, or improvised bombs placed where they expected us to pass by. Two of my pals were killed on the last tour."

His eyes welled up again as he recalled the past. "And one ended up with no legs; just stumps protruding from his hips. It's an evil place." He wiped his eyes again and looked away from Suzanna, embarrassed to show his emotions.

"It must have been terrible. I can't imagine anyone returning from that place unaffected by what they'd seen or experienced." She paused. "When Patterson threatened your family, it was a soldier's reaction to counter the threat, as you'd been trained."

Boyd looked up again. "Precisely! Not that I'd have killed him. But I had to take out the threat to my wife and daughter. Then you got in the way..."

"Yeah. Sorry about that. But if you'd badly beaten Patterson in front of all those witnesses, you'd have been arrested and jailed for a long time... Then, while you were inside, he'd have taken his revenge on your family. Perhaps they would both have been beaten to death."

Boyd was quiet for a minute, absorbing what she'd said. He'd never thought about that consequence of his actions.

Suzanna gave him time to consider what she'd said before continuing. "What worries me now is what Patterson will do when he gets out of prison in a couple of years' time. He could go away for five or six years but he'd be out in half that time if he is well behaved."

"If necessary, I'll take the bastard out."

"You can't stand guard over your wife and daughter 24/7, Boyd. And you could end up with a long prison sentence if you did 'take him out'." Suzanna could see his mind churning, worry written across his face. She continued, "If you tell me what you know about Patterson's involvement in the drugs trade, he'll go away for double the time."

"Aye, but I'll go away as well," Boyd snapped back, sneering at the suggestion.

"Not if you turn Queen's Evidence! You agree to open up and give evidence against Patterson and anyone else you know who's engaged in the drugs trade with him. And we agree not to prosecute you for your involvement. That leaves you free and Patterson in jail for a long time."

Boyd looked interested. "But that would just delay him taking revenge."

"Let's be frank," Suzanna responded, her eyes fixed on his, "Patterson will always be a threat to you and your family. But if you help put him away on the drugs charges, he'll be incarcerated for much longer. Your daughter would have finished school and might have gone off to university by the time he's released. Maybe you could move away and settle somewhere else? If necessary, I could put you and your family forward for the witness protection scheme." She looked at him sympathetically. She could imagine the thought processes circulating in his mind.

"Perhaps you're right," Boyd responded. "Perhaps you're right..."

Chapter Fifty-Two

Tosh was in conversation with Logan when the DCI walked in and joined the two officers. "I've just had a result with Boyd Jones," she said. "He's agreed to cooperate and give evidence against Patterson on supplying drugs. I've said we'll not prosecute him on his role in moving the drugs around."

"Great," Tosh remarked.

"Jones has agreed to come in later to make a statement. Just don't let on about the evidence you already have, as he may clam up again if he thinks his evidence isn't needed. I'm hoping he can tie things together by telling us where he picked up the packages, from whom and where they were delivered to." Her eyes flicked between the two officers, ensuring they were both paying full attention. "If all goes well, we could take down the entire Dumfries drugs supply network. We'll invite in the organised crime boys as soon as he's made his statement."

* * *

Tosh withdrew Patterson's mobile phone from the evidence store and reviewed its contacts. Westwood's contact was listed but not Bryce's. It's what he expected. Although Bryce had a motive for Muir's murder, he doubted he'd have had connections with a low-life like Patterson. "Right. Time to drag him out of the cells."

Patterson looked belligerent, sat across the table from Tosh.

"Right then, Mr Patterson. You know full well you'll be going away for a long time for your attack on your colleague's family." Tosh paused. "Your flat has been searched-"

Patterson jumped in. "You canna go entering someone's home without them there."

"We certainly can, Mr Patterson," Tosh bounced back. "We had a warrant to search your premises on suspicion of drugs possession. And we weren't disappointed." His eyes locked on Patterson's. "You'll have to do better than taping a bag to the back of your wardrobe if you want to hide them from us."

Patterson slouched back into the chair, which creaked its objection, his lips curling into a sneer.

"We know your supplier was David Westwood. He's also in custody. So, I don't need you to tell me anything about that. We have sufficient evidence. But what I would like to know is where you were between 6 a.m. and 10 a.m. on Monday 25th April?"

The 'no comment' response didn't surprise Tosh. He calmly looked up from his notes and fixed the suspect with a piercing stare. "Look, Mr Patterson, if you have an alibi for that period, I'll not need to waste your time repeating the question."

Another no comment replay. "Okay, so you have no alibi for first-thing Monday the 25th. Great. You had an opportunity, then."

"An opportunity to do what?" Patterson asked.

"To commit murder, Mr Patterson."

"Murder!" He spat, as he rose from his slouch and leaned towards DS McIntosh. "Who do you think I murdered?"

"If you'll just tell us where you were at the time of the murder, we won't need to pursue this any further. Between six and ten last Monday morning?"

Tosh watched as Patterson considered whether to answer the question. "Look, I did'nae commit no murder last week or any week. Was in me flat Monday morning. I'm rarely up before nine any day."

"Was anyone with you that morning? A girlfriend, perhaps."

"I should be so lucky. Haven't had me end away since I screwed Megan MacDonald round back of the pub three weeks ago. My hand is my only companion most nights," he said, grinning. "At least I don't have to buy it drinks or seduce it!" He laughed at his own wit.

Tosh let the crudeness wash over him. "There's no one to corroborate your location at the time of the murder, then. Meaning you're still in the frame for it."

"Look, I told you. I never murdered no one. And I'll not answer any more questions."

"So you say..." Tosh thought it was pointless questioning the man further. They would need more evidence of his involvement before they could take it any further. Not having an alibi and knowing someone with a motive would not meet the threshold for a prosecution.

* * *

As Logan headed for the Evidence Room, two colleagues came running along the corridor, forcing him to step aside. "What's the rush, he shouted to their backs?"

"Domestic incident on Wallace Street," came the reply, as the officers exited through the doors.

'Wallace Street,' Logan repeated silently. 'Why is that name so familiar?' he pondered, as he arrived at his destination. But nothing came to him.

He booked out all the Bryce evidence and took it to a spare room, stacking the files onto the desk, along with his computer.

Mairi joined him and they got stuck in to scrutinising the files, trawling through them for any names and contact details, then logging them onto a database. Logan searched through Bryce's contacts list and downloaded a file that could be correlated with the list Mairi was building up. They were heads-down, working, not chatting, for the next two hours.

Logan fed Mairi with other contacts that emerged from his scrutiny of Bryce's electronic files and emails. Ones that had not made it into the contacts list. By the end of the day, they had a huge list that needed checking against the criminal database.

* * *

As the working day came to a close, they gathered in the incident room. "Okay, guys. One at a time. Updates, please," Suzanna said, standing square on to the group, with her feet firmly planted and her arms folded.

Tosh was the first to speak, sat on the corner of his desk. "Patterson has no alibi and it's possible he could have been paid by Westwood to murder Muir. But he couldn't organise a piss up in a-"

"Okay, Tosh. Understood. Although *unlikely*, could he have murdered her?"

"Unless he's got some hidden store or he's disposed of the shotgun, no. His car, an old Renault Clio, has not been seen passing any cameras, so he would have had to take a circuitous route to get to the crime scene. Again, probably beyond his capabilities. His bank account has little money in it and isn't used much, so if he had been paid, it would have been in cash. But we've not found any large sums on him or in his flat."

"I agree with the sarge," Carl stepped in, shifting his weight to his other foot. "Westwood has an equally dim view of Patterson. Said he wouldn't trust him with a job like that - even if he'd wanted her dead. I believe him."

"Okay. So, it's looking unlikely that Westwood had Isla Muir killed. What about the Bryce connections?" She turned to look at Mairi and Logan, who were standing side by side.

Mairi spoke. "We've extracted all the contacts we can from the electronic and hard-copy files, and I've entered them all into a database to enable correlation. We haven't yet had time to run the names against the PNC criminal database."

"Do you have a printout of this list?" Suzanna asked, curiosity in her eyes.

Logan reached behind him and picked up some papers from his desk, then handed them to the DCI. Suzanna scanned the lists, but nothing jumped out to connect Bryce's contacts with the other suspects. She handed the lists back to Logan. "A job for the morning, I think. Let's call it a day. Anyone fancy a drink?" Their faces lit up at the suggestion.

As the group broke up and they gathered their coats, Logan spoke to Carl. "Hey. Does Wallace Street ring any bells with you?"

"You are joking, right?" Carl responded. "Of course it rings bells. That's where Greg Bell and his missus live!"

"Ah! I thought it was familiar," Logan replied, putting the pieces into his virtual jigsaw. "Only there's been a call-out there for a domestic incident."

Mairi jumped into the conversation, frowning. "We had a word earlier with Cairstine Bell about encouraging her husband to get his broken-down car scrapped."

"Maybe she's taken the encouragement a step too far," Carl suggested.

Mairi's frown lifted. "Oh, well!" she concluded. "Nothing we can do about it. Let's get that beer."

They all nodded agreement and walked out of the station, chatting.

Chapter Fifty-Three

Wednesday 4th May

Suzanna hadn't stayed long at the pub the evening before, but it was good for them to have gathered socially, to talk about anything other than the case. Holidays, football and cars. No politics. A few whinges about the police HQ staff. But when the conversation drifted towards a particular sergeant within their station, Suzanna diverted them onto other topics.

She found out that Tosh and Carl liked her car, and aspired to own one similar, if they ever could afford it. But as both were in relationships, unless they made it to superintendent rank, that was unlikely. That was one advantage of being single, with no kids. Your money was your own. She greeted each member of the team as they arrived. Carl looked a bit shabby, but the rest looked like they hadn't drunk too much the night before.

"Did you get home alright, Carl?" Tosh asked, knowing that his colleague had to walk home, on account of exceeding the drink-drive limit.

"Yeah. No problem. The missus wasn't too happy, though. Said I shouldn't be drinking when I'm into work the next day. She shot off to work this morning without offering me a lift, so I had to walk to work."

Suzanna felt a little guilty at having led him astray, although how much people drink was an individual choice, of course.

"Logan. Mairi," Suzanna said, to catch their attention. "How long do you think it will take to finish the correlation work and check the PNC?"

Mairi looked up, making a quick calculation in her mind before responding. "A couple of hours, I reckon. There are a lot of contacts to check out."

"Tosh. Carl. Can you help?"

"Could do, ma'am. If you think that's a higher priority to writing up my report about the Westwood interview yesterday."

Suzanna responded after considered the priorities. "No. You and Carl get your reports completed. We'll review the progress later."

They all turned to their tasks, and Suzanna sat at her desk. She needed to rethink the investigation's direction.

They had investigated numerous lines of inquiry. Jones had given evidence against Patterson, and they'd passed that information to the regional organised crime squad to follow up. They had unearthed serious corruption within the local government. Criminal charges had been made against two of the councillors. But the murder inquiry was stuck.

All avenues seemed to have become cul-de-sacs. She stood and paced the room, stopping at the incident board numerous times. Pondering. She preferred real incident boards where she could see the most pertinent facts in one place and shift things around as she liked. She knew that most detective teams had gone away from such boards. Instead, they utilised virtual boards on computers. But she was convinced their electronic tools could never replicate the real thing. They didn't stimulate the mind like a physical board. She stared at her board.

As the patterns of pictures and words swirled in her mind, her thoughts cast aside the dead ends and looked for other possibilities.

What could they have missed? A thought popped into her head.

The team watched as she left the station, saying nothing. No idea where she was going or why.

* * *

Suzanna ambled up the grassy field, scanning the scene. It was devoid of animals now but in the adjacent pasture there were dozens of sheep and their offspring. Two lambs ran to their mother and bashed their heads into her udders to get the milk flowing. As they sucked the milk, their tails wagged rapidly, vibrating as if driven by a milk powered turbine.

She stopped at the place where, nine days before, Isla Muir and her dog - what was it called? Sunset - had lain, lifeless, having taken their last walk. Her mind wandered. At just gone seven in the morning on a walk that no one knew Isla Muir would be taking, she and her dog were blasted with a shotgun.

Suzanna re-imagined the scene on the day of the murder. Sheep and lambs nibbling at the grass. Organic, woolly lawnmowers. Clouds whipping across the sky, threatening rain. A woman ambles across the field, her dog off the leash (there was definitely no lead attached to the Labrador's collar when it was found). Sunset spots the sheep and charges across the field. They scatter in all directions, Sunset bounding after them, having fun. She doesn't want to hurt them, just chase them.

The dog hears a motorbike then sees someone in green and brown clothing dismounting and raising his shotgun. Sunset senses danger and runs to protect her owner. There's a bang as the first barrel fires. The dog falls to the ground, its life extinguished in a flash.

The woman is distraught. Her beautiful canine companion has been shot. It's golden fur, now red. She runs at the man waving her arms around, shouting. "You murderer." As she charges the farmer, the second barrel goes off. Isla Muir tumbles to the ground, fatally wounded. The killer is scared, mounts their bike and rides off.

What other explanation could there be? But *who* would have shot her? They had already checked out the neighbouring farm. The Mitchells' alibis were all sound. Could another farmer have been passing, seen the sheep worrying and taken action?

While Suzanna was pondering, the sound of a passing vehicle reached her. There must be a road or track nearby. She walked up the field towards the sound and saw a farm track running along the other side of the fence. As she walked alongside the fence, she noticed stretched wire, where someone must have stood on it, perhaps to climb over. There were welly boot prints by the fence and a fragment of fabric caught in the barbed wire.

Suzanna frowned. Why had no one reported this? She called in the CSI team.

* * *

The roar of a military jet tore through the air, capturing Suzanna's attention. It shattered the quiet of the summit, hurtling down the valley with a thunderous sound that reverberated in her chest. A sleek Typhoon jet painted a brief streak across the sky, vanishing toward the coastline before disappearing across the firth, heading towards the distant Cumbrian fells. As the jet's rumble faded into the distance, she found herself deep in thought. "I wonder," she murmured, her mind racing with possibilities. She withdrew her phone and placed a call.

Over an hour crawled by before the CSI team arrived. By then, she was impatient to move on. She had replayed the scene in her mind many times and kept coming back to the same conclusion. Someone other than Jack Reynolds had seen the sheep worrying whilst riding along that track. They had climbed the fence, shot the dog and the woman, then escaped the scene the same way. It wasn't the Mitchells or anyone from the other farms in the area. So who, then?

The CSI leader trudged up the field to where Suzanna stood, then introduced himself. "Pete Southergill, Head of Dumfries and Galloway CSI. You must be DCI McLeod." He held out his hand towards Suzanna.

She reluctantly took his hand, not feeling friendly towards the man, given his team's apparent failure to do their job thoroughly. "As I said on the phone, there is evidence, not in your report, of someone climbing that fence," she said, pointing to its location, "and heading in this direction."

Pete frowned, understanding why the DCI would be unhappy.

Suzanna led him to the fence, avoiding walking on the track taken by the suspect, and gestured towards her findings, a quiet intensity in her gaze.

The wellie boot imprints leading from where the fence had been climbed down towards the crime scene stood out. Pete examined the fence and nearby prints. "They could have been made after we'd finished our work. They look rather recent prints. If they had been here before, I'm sure we would have noticed them."

Suzanna hadn't considered that. Her annoyance waned; her face softened. "Accepted. But I'd like you to gather evidence anyway and let me know what you find. I assume forensics tests and analysis will inform us how long ago the prints will have been made?" Suzanna kept her eyes fixed on the CSI leader.

"Aye. Soil and weather analysis should give us a reasonable idea. We'll get our casts and soil samples completed as soon as practicable and ask forensics to prioritise their work."

"Thanks, Pete. I'll let you get on, then. I have other things to do." Suzanna strode off on a circuitous route back to her car.

Chapter Fifty-Four

Suzanna stopped her BMW on the track just before the Reynolds' house. She'd not been to the farm before, having left the locals to visit and interview its occupants. She wanted to see for herself where they lived. Although Jack had been released when the emerging evidence could no longer support his detention, she wasn't yet certain he had not been involved in the crime.

Not wanting the family to know she was looking around, Suzanna lifted the gate catch and opened it sufficiently to slip through quietly. She stood and took in the scene. The concreted track leading to the cow shed could hardly be seen under the mud and muck that coated it. The smell of cow manure overpowered her senses.

Atop its stand, a wind turbine whirred like a reverse aeroplane propeller. At a hundred yards, she could barely hear the generator rotating and the gears meshing as they drove it. Suzanna wondered why so many people were opposed to these clean electricity generators. Unlike power pylons, it wasn't an eyesore; instead, its long blades were elegant and its smooth, serene rotation calming. She imagined how, before long, with the drive towards a carbon-neutral economy, there would be multitudes of these turbines scattered or clustered around the whole UK landscape.

The farmhouse was stone faced, similar to most houses in the region and of its era, but the sides had been rendered. Small windows hinted of dingy rooms beyond. The front door hadn't seen a fresh coat of paint in twenty years and the lower part was marked by random horizontal stripes of dirt and boot rubber.

About thirty metres from the house stood a cowshed, and beyond that, a small equipment storage shed. Something caught her eye on the corner of the house, just below the eaves. She walked closer. It was a CCTV camera, pointing towards the cowshed. She smiled, turned, and walked up to the farmhouse front door.

After knocking and waiting, the door was opened by an unkempt woman, with ruddy cheeks and straggly, dark but greying hair, tied back into a ponytail. "You're not from that farm equipment sales lot are you, cause we've no need of anything right now?"

"Mrs Reynolds, I presume? I'm Detective Chief Inspector McLeod. Leading the murder investigation."

Margaret Reynolds backed into her house, her jaw clenched, and lips pursed, the door closing. "We've nothing to say to you. You've hassled my Jack enough already. Poor man. You can take yourself off back to that police station."

Suzanna leapt forward and blocked the door's travel with her boot, then pushed softly against it, gently overpowering the smaller woman. It was imperative that she gained her cooperation, and she couldn't do that from behind a hardwood door.

"I'm sorry to trouble you, Mrs Reynolds. Can I come in?" She pushed the door fully open and entered, not giving the woman time to respond, then closed it behind her.

Before Mrs Reynolds could rally herself and complain about Suzanna's unwelcome entry into her home, she spoke. "Look, the decision to charge your husband with murder was based on the evidence we had. If Jack had reported finding the bodies, instead of leaving them laying for someone else to find, I doubt he would have been charged."

Margaret had gone quiet, waiting for the detective to finish.

Suzanna continued, holding Margaret's attention with a steady stare. "You need to understand that Jack is not out of the frame for the murder just yet. Although the balance of evidence swayed in his favour, it could swing back. But I'm only interested in justice. I have no reason to wish an innocent man locked up. If we can find further evidence to support Jack's statement, we could eliminate him from the enquiry."

Margaret hesitated, then spoke. "Look, I know my husband. He's a good man and he'd never hurt any woman, let alone kill one. What is it you want? Let's not beat about the bush. What evidence might support Jack's statement?"

"I noticed you have a CCTV camera pointing out towards the cowshed and the store beyond. If the system has recorded Jack's movements, that would show precisely what time he left and returned. If you're confident of his innocence, it can only help his case if we see that."

"I take your point, Chief Inspector. My daughter, Ainslie, normally looks after the system. It was only recently installed, after the last quad bike theft, at the insistence of the insurers. She and Jack are out at the moment, so you won't be able to see any recordings until they're back."

"Your daughter, you say. Does she live with you?"

"Aye. Ainslie's a good girl. Not abandoned us for the big cities, like many of the youngsters around here," Margaret said proudly. "You canna run a farm with just two. Needs a team. Don't know what we'd do without her."

Suzanna wondered how her team could have missed this potential suspect. As Margaret Reynolds had said, it takes a team to run a farm, but no-one had thought to investigate who might have been helping the Reynolds manage theirs. Suzanna put her failure down to lack of familiarity with rural policing.

"If you could show me where the system is, that would be a start."

"Aye, it's through here, near the phone line," she said, leading the way into the rear lobby.

Suzanna recognised the make. In fact, following the theft of her cherished magnifying glass, she'd installed a similar device in her flat. "I'll need to take this with me for analysis. We can't afford to wait around for Ainslie to return," she said, unplugging it before Margaret had time to object. "I'll get it back to you as soon as possible."

Suzanna looked up at the locked cupboard across the room. "This will be your gun locker, I assume?"

"Aye, it is. I take it you'll want a look inside." She turned and went back into the kitchen, returning with a key. Unlocking the door, she stepped back and swung it wide for Suzanna to see into. There were two weapons clipped in place and a two empty slots.

"I take it one of the vacant slots will be the gun we have at the station but when was the fourth one last stored in here?"

"I couldn't tell you. As I told your sergeant, I have arthritis in my shoulder, so I never use them nowadays."

"So, what happened to the fourth shotgun?"

Margaret shrugged. "Ah dinnae ken. Jack will have likely sold it to someone else. Your licensing records ought to show who owns it now."

"Thanks for your help, Mrs Reynolds. I'll get this back to you as soon as I can. Given the number of thefts that have occurred, I assume you'll want to ensure your barns are covered."

"So true," Margaret responded. "In fact, while you hold on to that unit, we'll have no coverage, and our insurance will be invalidated!" She folded her arms and glared at Suzanna.

"I'll get it back to you as soon as possible," she reiterated as she left the house and squelched her way through the stinking sludge, back to her car.

Chapter Fifty-Five

The incident room was buzzing as Suzanna entered. Mairi, Tosh and Carl were conversing excitedly. She placed the CCTV hub on her desk and wandered over to the group. "What's got you lot stirred up?"

Mairi was the first to speak, a smile on her face. "We think we've identified another suspect."

Suzanna inclined her head, showing puzzlement and silently inviting Mairi to expand on her statement.

Mairi continued. "We finished correlating the Bryce and Westwood connections but found nothing. Then checked the PNC for known criminals. Still nothing. I decided to do routine checks on the Reynolds' household. The register of electors showed that the Reynolds' daughter is living at home, unless she's moved away and not changed her registration. So, I checked the driving licence records on the PNC and found her licence is also registered to the home address. And lastly, there's a motorbike registered to her... at the home address."

"Funny you should mention that," Suzanna responded. "I've just come from the Reynolds' farm and discovered that very fact. How come we didn't know this already?"

A set of blank faces stared back, then Tosh's broke. "My fault, ma'am. I was too focused on Mr Reynolds and neither of them mentioned a daughter."

"A lesson to be learned for the whole team. Ask more questions.

Beware tunnel vision. Don't allow the draw of the obvious to blind you to the obscure." They all nodded.

"But how did *you* find out about the daughter, ma'am?" Carl asked.

"I visited the farm and noticed a CCTV camera pointing towards the cowshed and barn, so asked Mrs Reynolds for a look. That's when she mentioned her daughter."

Suzanna was momentarily silent as she assimilated all the information. "Right." All eyes were on Suzanna as she issued her orders. "Carl, the CCTV hub is on my desk."

Carl glanced across at the white cube.

"Get that looked at ASAP. We need to see what movements there were around the farm on the morning of the murder." Carl immediately strode away.

"Mairi. Background checks on the daughter." Mairi turned to her desk and sat.

"Tosh. If you haven't already got the answer, we need to know what happened to the Reynolds' fourth shotgun."

"On it," Tosh responded as he walked away.

Palpable excitement filled the air. Suzanna returned to her desk just as the phone rang. "DCI McLeod," she answered. It was the Ministry of Defence.

"Hello, ma'am. Flight Lieutenant Mike Smith here. Photographic Intelligence at RAF Lossiemouth."

Suzanna noted the lack of a regional accent in his voice and smiled to herself. It was typical for an officer to be accent neutral, while in the ranks, regional accents were more prevalent.

"I've been asked to call you about your request. It *was* one of our jets that flew over you earlier today. And I can also confirm that a Typhoon passed over that same spot on the 25th of April, and within the time window you specified - it's on a track we fly regularly. *And* it had its cameras running."

Suzanna eagerly awaited his next statement.

"My guys have analysed the footage and have some stills they extracted from the brief video clip of that location."

"Marvellous. That's great news."

"I understand you are interested in any movement in that area. You might be pleased to hear that a motorbike shows up in the footage, travelling along a farm track."

Suzanna's face lit up as Mike continued.

"We slowed it down and analysed it frame by frame. We're talking about just one or two seconds of footage. I can post the hard copies to you but thought you might like to see what we've found before Postman Pat does his rounds of Dumfries."

"Yes, please, Mike. Can you send me the images?"

"The file size would be too large for email. What I can do is upload the files to a secure location, then send you a link and login details. Once you're logged in, you can download and print them. How does that sound?"

Suzanna replied with enthusiasm. "Wonderful."

"Right. I'll get that done. I just need your police email address."

Suzanna read out her contact details.

"By the way, I'm curious why you thought to ask for our help. I don't think anyone has ever been asked to look at fast-jet aerial reconnaissance imagery to help with a police investigation."

"My father was an RAF officer. I know from chats with my dad that ground attack variants normally have cameras. It was a long shot, really."

"Well, a long shot that paid off," Mike concluded. "I hope the images give you what you need." He hung up.

Suzanna spoke silently to herself. "And so do I. So do I..."

* * *

Twenty minutes later, Suzanna sat before her computer, the image files downloaded and cropped to focus on the motorbike and rider. With a quick tap, she sent the files to the printer, the soft whirring filling the room. As the prints slid out, Carl's voice broke through her concentration.

"Ma'am, I've had a look at the CCTV footage. And you're not going to like what I found." He paused for effect. "The period between 6:30 a.m. and 9:30 a.m. on the day of the murder has been wiped."

The hairs on Suzanna's arm stood up. They were definitely onto something. Deletion of the video was highly suspicious. "Right. Get the hub to the Digital Forensics department ASAP and have them recover the deleted the files, if they can. We need to know what the Reynolds were trying to cover up."

She turned towards Tosh, raising her voice. "Tosh, anything on the fourth shotgun?"

"Yes, ma'am. It's still registered to the Reynolds."

"Mairi. Background checks on the daughter?"

"She's never been charged with anything, although police had to be called to her school once because of threatening behaviour. And she was given a caution the other day for up-ending a cafe table and spilling coffee on a PCSO. Doesn't have much in the bank but isn't in debt either. However, Mr and Mrs Reynolds are in the red most months, and have large debts to feed companies and other suppliers, so barely keeping their heads above water. In fact, slowly sinking, I'd say. I guess that's why they put some of their land up for sale - to pay off their debts."

"Hmm!" Suzanna pondered. "The stress of her parent's financial situation could feed her anger problem, if she knew about the debt." Suzanna added. "We just need that CCTV footage."

With the freshly printed images in hand, Suzanna returned to her desk. Extracting her magnifying glass from its cloth bag, she leant over the first image, examining the rider and motorbike. She had digitally blown up the image as far as she could without losing definition but knew optical magnification would gain her detail that would otherwise be unseen. She was satisfied the image would stand up in court as evidence of the person's presence. They just needed to identify that person. But that was a job for tomorrow.

* * *

Suzanna was sitting on the sofa in her lodge, having eaten dinner, when her iPad jingled. It was James. A Skype video call. She picked up. "Hi James."

"Hi Gorgeous. How's it going?" James smiled, his eyes sparkling.

"Good, actually." Suzanna returned his smile. "Things have taken a turn in the right direction. We now have a strong lead about a new suspect."

"That's good. Do you think you'll be able to have the weekend off?" He said with a tinge of hope in his voice, after sipping from his coffee mug.

"If all goes well. I was thinking of going to Charlie's at the weekend. Would you like to join me in Cockermouth?"

"Aye. That would be great," James replied with enthusiasm. "Have you asked Charlotte yet?"

"We've already agreed to meet up soon but not specifically agreed to a stop-over. I'll check with her as soon as I know what's possible. Should I include you?"

"Most definitely. Perhaps we could fit in a fell walk and maybe go to her church on the Sunday?"

"Depends on the time we have. If I can get off on Friday evening, we should be able to spend all Saturday and Sunday with them. I could even stay through to Monday morning, given that Dumfries is just over the border. I guess you'd need to return to Edinburgh on Sunday evening, though?"

"Aye, you're right. I have a meeting with a client at nine on Monday." James drew a deep breath as he gathered his courage. "Look, Suzanna, I've been thinking."

The words caught Suzanna's attention, curious about what was to follow.

"I spend most nights in your apartment when you're here. I rarely sleep at home nowadays. It seems a waste to have the flat when I'm not using it. How about we make it official that we're a couple? That I live with you?"

Suzanna tilted her head to the side, her brow furrowing. "Is this a poor attempt at a proposal, James?"

James looked shocked. "No, no!" He exclaimed. But he didn't look horrified, just flummoxed at being misinterpreted. "I meant perhaps I should give up the flat. Rent it out. Not sell it." He paused. "Sorry, Suzanna. You caught me out with your challenge. I didn't mean to suggest that marrying you is the last thing on my mind. Far from it. I... I just hadn't reached a place where I thought you were ready to answer yes."

"When might you reach that place, James?" She teased.

James shifted uncomfortably and his two eyebrows kissed as he considered whether she was playing with him or testing his commitment. Was she inviting him to ask? Perhaps! He *had* thought about marriage. Was sure it would be good. Wanted to spend the rest of his life with this wonderful, beautiful, intelligent, sexy woman. So, what was holding him back? He hadn't bought a ring. It would be completely unromantic to pop the question now, over Skype. "Er! Maybe next week," he said hesitantly, trying to brush away his embarrassment with a cheeky smile.

Suzanna let him off the hook with a chuckle and a big grin. She changed the subject, avoiding further embarrassment and the need to respond to his proposal that he move in permanently. Although she loved James, Suzanna wasn't sure she was ready for that commitment. "I'd like to go to Charlie's church on Sunday, if we can," she said enthusiastically. "Perhaps we could all go out for a pub lunch afterwards?"

"Great idea. I'll need to say good night. Have to be up early tomorrow."

"Good night, sleep well, James. Speak tomorrow. Love you," she said before hitting the end call button.

She did love James. Perhaps making their relationship more permanent wouldn't be such a bad idea.

Chapter Fifty-Six

Thursday 5th May

The team gathered around the incident board for the morning briefing, but Carl was missing. Suzanna was about to ask Tosh where his DC was, when Carl burst into the room, holding up a USB stick, a smile on his face. "Got it. The undeleted CCTV video clips. It shows someone on a trail bike, leaving the farm at 6:30 a.m., with a shotgun over their shoulder and returning at 7:20. And it shows Jack Reynolds walking to the sheds and leaving on the quad bike around 6:45, then returning an hour later. Also carrying a shotgun."

"Great news, Carl. Okay. Time we brought Ainslie Reynolds in for a chat. And her clothes for testing. Maybe they will have human blood splatter? And find that fourth shotgun."

Carl, Tosh and Logan headed straight out to carry out Suzanna's orders, Carl tossing the USB stick to Mairi. She caught the stick, then looked to her boss for direction, accepting she would be missing out on the action.

"Mairi. Get the images downloaded from the stick and printed, please? I want to compare them with some other images I have."

"Sure, ma'am. Will do." She took the stick to her computer and plugged it in, then scanned the files for viruses before downloading them.

Suzanna pinned up the RAF's most useful image, then studied the board as she waited for the CCTV images.

Ten minutes later, Mairi strode over to Suzanna with a handful of images she'd just printed off. She compared them with the one her boss had just placed on the board. "Where on earth did that picture come from?"

"Not on earth, Mairi," Suzanna replied with a smile. "From the sky... An RAF Typhoon's forward-facing camera."

Mairi's eyes popped out of her head. She was about to ask her boss how she'd obtained that when Suzanna silenced her with, "I'll explain later."

Mairi turned her attention back to the images. The shape and colouring of the motorbike were the same in all images. As were the clothes and helmet worn by its rider. "I'd say that is the same bike and rider. Wouldn't you?"

"Yes, Mairi. I would..."

* * *

"Where have you been?" Margaret Reynolds asked her daughter as she walked into the kitchen and poured herself a mug of tea. "I haven't seen you since yesterday afternoon."

"I *do* have a life outside the farm, you know," Ainslie said belligerently.

"Don't you go taking that tone with me, young lady," her mother chided. "I needed to speak to you about the CCTV and you've not been around. And you didn't answer your phone. I was worried."

"I'm a grown woman, mother," Ainslie sneered. "With my own life. Not at your beck and call at every hour of the day. I have friends and interests."

Margaret ignored the rant. "There was a problem with the CCTV."

"Look, it's not that difficult to operate. You and Da need to drag yourselves into the 21st century. I'll not be around forever."

"I know, but the police have taken the CCTV hub."

Ainslie's jaw hit the floor, and her eyes widened. She hollered, "What! Why didn't you tell me before?"

"I tried to," Margaret snapped back. "But you made yourself unreachable. Too important to answer your mother's calls now."

Ainslie looked worried. "Why did they take the CCTV hub?"

"They wanted to check the footage of the morning that woman got shot, to confirm your Da's movements." As Margaret said the words, she wondered why they hadn't yet spoken to her daughter.

Ainslie relaxed a little. They wouldn't find anything incriminating. She'd made sure of that. As that thought crossed her mind, a flash of blue snatched her attention to the window. Another flash of blue. She stepped up to the window and saw a police car stop outside their gate; two uniformed officers emerged.

The flashing blue lights wouldn't have been used if they just wanted a chat. The police must have come for her. Ainslie ran. She had to escape. She rushed into the rear lobby and out the back of the farmhouse, heading towards the sheds.

As the police officers reached the front door, they heard a motorbike start up and race off, away from the farm. PC Logan Stevens raced back to the car as his colleague hammered on the farmhouse door. Another car arrived just as Logan exited the farmyard. It was Carl and Tosh. The passenger window whirred down and Logan took advantage to shout to Tosh that the suspect appeared to have ridden off on her motorbike. He indicated the track he planned to take in pursuit.

Carl immediately accelerated away, heading along the track where Logan thought the motorbike had gone. He fought with the steering wheel as the car sped down the farm track, its ruts jostling the car and embedded rocks bashing its underside.

The motorbike came into view. It was flying ahead of him, its rider standing on the footrests, her bottom hovering above the seat. He pressed down on the throttle, the engine racing as the car accelerated along the track.

The bike's rider glanced back over her shoulder, her head helmetless; long hair flowing in the airstream. Then she hit a rut, the bike becoming airborne. As the front wheel hit the ground, it twisted, the forks bending as it came to an abrupt halt. The rider flew over the handlebars, into a forward roll, then landed on her back. She was motionless as Carl skidded to a stop and leapt out of the car, followed by Tosh.

Carl ran to the woman, worried for her health. He'd had seen too many motorcycle accidents, and without a helmet on her head, the likelihood was she would fare worse than most.

The police response vehicle skidded to a halt behind Carl's car, and Logan jumped out. As Carl and Tosh went to the woman's side, Logan spoke into his shoulder radio mic to request an ambulance.

Carl knelt beside the young woman, extended his hand to her neck to feel for a pulse. As he touched her, Ainslie's eyes shot open. "Get ya hands off me!" she screamed.

She tried to sit up, but Tosh pinned her down and commanded her, "Stay down. You just had a serious accident. It's dangerous to move. We've called for an ambulance."

"Fuck that," she shouted back at him and struck his hand aside. "Get away from me." She rolled over and pushed herself onto her knees, then rose to her feet.

Carl could see she'd been lucky. Just winded by the fall. Nothing obviously broken. So, when she turned to run away, he grabbed an arm to restrain her. Ainslie spun around and swung a fist at Carl's face. He ducked the swing and grabbed her wrist. Tosh stepped in, grabbing her free wrist, and between them they turned her and took her back down to the ground as gently as they could, before cuffing her.

Ainslie continued to struggle and shout expletives. Once the cuffs were on, Carl glanced back at his car, noticing dents in the front bumper. He rolled his eyes. More damage to report!

* * *

The peace was broken by raised voices and scuffles. Suzanna opened the office door and watched as Carl and Logan man-handled a ranting woman along the corridor, Tosh following two paces behind.

The officers bundled her into the interview room, where she instantly kicked over the chairs and upended the table. Tosh entered the room. "Guys. This isn't going to work. Take her down to the cells to cool off. She can't do any harm there."

Carl and Logan dragged her back out of the room and away to the cells, their jaws clenched with the effort of restraining their prisoner.

Tosh returned to the office and responded to Suzanna's quizzical look. "She did a runner on her motorbike when we arrived. Had to pursue her down a farm track. Carl's car has suffered some minor damage to its bumper. I doubt we'd have caught her if she hadn't come off her bike."

Suzanna's eyes widened.

"Amazingly, she didn't suffer any major injuries in her fall. You should have seen the fight she put up when Carl tried to restrain her. She took a swing at him, so she's under arrest for the attempted assault of a police officer."

"Having had an accident, she should have gone to hospital," Suzanna said, with a concerned look.

Tosh responded with a shrug. "We called an ambulance, but she refused to go to the hospital, so we brought her in."

"Right. We'll let her stew for an hour but call for the duty doctor to attend. We need her checked out before we interview her."

"I've arranged for Miss Reynolds' clothing to be taken in for testing. But I can't see us getting the clothes she's wearing off her without a struggle."

"Okay. We'll play that sensitively. We need her to give them up voluntarily or there might be some more blood spilled on them. I take it forensics knows their testing is a pressing need?"

"Aye. They'll be onto the testing for blood as soon as they're in the lab. They said it wouldn't matter if they've been washed, as there will still be traces of blood in the fibre, although less than there would have been, of course."

Suzanna nodded, then returned to her desk to continue her work. She would lead the Ainslie Reynolds' interview.

Chapter Fifty-Seven

Two hours later, Ainslie Reynolds was brought out of the cells and into the interview room, having been cleared by the doctor as fit for interviewing. Apparently, she just had some bruising on her shoulder and back. This time, she didn't trash the room.

A female PC stood guard over Ainslie as Suzanna and Tosh entered and sat opposite her. After reading her rights, Suzanna addressed her in a gentle, sympathetic tone. "Hello Ainslie. I'm Detective Chief Inspector Suzanna McLeod. You've already met Detective Sergeant McIntosh," she said with the glint of a smile. "Sorry, we've had to bring you in for questioning. I'm wondering why you didn't wish to come in voluntarily?"

Ainslie sat looking down, picking at her nail cuticles.

"We just needed to ask you some questions and take some samples to eliminate you from our enquiries but now it seems we might have to charge you with assaulting a police officer."

Ainslie looked up, her eyes on fire. "Me assault that big bastard? It's him that assaulted me."

"I'm afraid there is evidence to the contrary," Suzanna countered. "Anyway, let's not worry about that for the moment. If you will cooperate with us, perhaps we will be able to release you to return home."

Ainslie's face brightened a little, but she returned to nail-picking, avoiding eye contact.

"You'll have heard about the murder of a woman and the killing of her dog on the 25th." Suzanna noticed Ainslie twitch at the mention of murder. "We know the murder occurred between 6 a.m. and 10 a.m. We also know that you left the farm on your motorbike at 6:30 a.m. and returned at 7:20, and that you were carrying a shotgun."

Ainslie looked surprised to hear the police knew about her movements. "How do you know so accurately what time I left and returned?"

"From the CCTV footage on the farm system. The one you look after for your parents." Ainslie looked like she was about to say something, perhaps, 'but I deleted that footage.' She thought better of it and zipped her mouth shut.

"So, Ainslie, I just need to know where you went that morning and what you shot - rabbits, perhaps?"

"Yes, rabbits," she said, clutching at the offered answer.

"And where exactly did these rabbits meet their death? On what part of the farm?"

Ainslie told them about the field she had been in that morning. One far away from where the woman had been shot.

"The only problem I have with that story, Ainslie, is that your father also went to that field and shot rabbits, around the same time as you, but he never mentioned you being there. And the only rabbits in the house were the two he had killed. Where did you go that morning, then? And if you shot rabbits, where are they?"

Ainslie was silent, evidently having no ready answer for the question. Another sign that she was hiding something.

"It must have been the day before I was in that field. It will have been Abbey Field that morning. I remember now. I didn't have any luck bagging rabbits. Missed with my first shot and they all scurried away."

"Now we come to the question of the shotgun you used that morning. Where is it?"

"It will be in the locker, of course."

"Well, Ainslie, when we visited the farm on the day of the murder, there were only three shotguns in the locker. One was missing. And only one of the three in the box that morning had been fired. The one your father had used. So, where was the shotgun you used and where is it now?"

"I always put it back in the locker. Don't know why it wasn't there that morning. Must have placed it down somewhere."

"If you always put it back, why wasn't it there the next time we looked and this morning? And if you always replace it in the box, why do both your parents think the gun was sold off sometime back, when your mother gave up shooting because of her arthritis?"

Ainslie didn't offer a response.

"Ainslie. If we are to conclude this situation speedily, we will need you to change out of the clothes you are wearing for them to be checked for blood traces. If there is no blood on your clothes linking you to the crime, we will have no reason to hold you. The PC," she indicated the uniformed female officer, "has some overalls for you to change into, until your clothes have been tested. If we leave the room, will you change for us, so we can get this wrapped up more quickly?"

Ainslie nodded acceptance, her face still down, avoiding contact.

* * *

It was mid-afternoon by the time Ainslie was led back to the interview room from her cell. Her face was red and firmly set as she dumped herself in the chair opposite Suzanna. She whinged like a teenage child. "You said it would be quicker if I changed out of my clothes. I've been waiting three hours in these horrid coveralls. And the food they brought me for lunch was shit."

"Sorry to hear the food wasn't to your liking, Ainslie," Suzanna responded, trying to keep a sarcastic tone from her voice. "We now have results back from the forensics laboratory. The good news is that the clothes you gave up when you changed into those overalls are clear of any blood traces."

Ainslie's face and body relaxed at the news.

"My officers have been busy while you were resting in the cells. We now have the shotgun you had been using. It was tucked away in the bike shed under a tarpaulin. Hidden, not locked away. The shotgun has been sent to forensics for checking. When they test it for prints, will they find your prints on that weapon, Ainslie?"

Ainslie nodded, so Suzanna commented she had for the recording. "We also have other evidence of importance. The clothes removed from your room and laundry basket have also been tested for blood and one set of clothes has been found to have blood sprayed across the front of the trousers and jacket. This blood has been sent for analysis. If it is found that this blood is of human origin, you can see what the obvious conclusion will be."

Ainslie just stared at the table.

"And when this blood is tested for DNA, if it's found to be a match to the murdered woman, then you will be charged with her murder. So, if you know the blood will match, why don't you save yourself some time and tell us what happened?"

"I want a solicitor."

"Okay," Suzanna concluded. "Interview suspended."

* * *

It was 6 p.m. before the duty solicitor could attend, and 6:30 before the interview recommenced.

346

"Right, Ainslie, let me tell you how I think things went on the morning of the 25th," Suzanna said, her eyes fixed on the young woman. "You took yourself off on your motorbike to shoot rabbits. For the sport, as much as controlling the numbers. As you rode along the track. Something caught your attention and you glanced into the field below to see a dog chasing your sheep. You know how damaging that is for the sheep, even if they're not bitten. Some die of shock, don't they, or miscarry if they're with lamb? When you saw this, you got angry. You dumped your bike, clambered over the fence and ran down the field, then shot the dog. But when the woman protested, you shot her as well."

"Pure speculation, inspector," the solicitor said.

"Detective Chief Inspector," Suzanna countered, looking to the stocky solicitor.

"I'm sure you'll be aware, Mrs Wood, if your client has told you the truth, that what I've just described is close to what happened. If not, I'd like to hear your client's version."

"You have yet to produce any evidence that my client committed this crime, so unless that is forthcoming, you must release her."

"There is just the matter of assaulting a police officer and inappropriate storage of a firearm."

"As I'm sure you're aware, Chief Inspector, not storing a weapon securely is not a criminal act. It's merely one of failing to abide by licensing requirements."

Suzanna slipped two images across the table for Ainslie and her solicitor to see. "As you can she, we have proof that you rode your bike along the track next to the field where the shooting took place, at a time that fits with the death of the woman and her dog."

Ainslie's mouth had involuntarily dropped open, clearly puzzled by how they had an aerial shot of her on the motorbike, as well as the farm security camera image.

"We also have your boots, Ainslie, to match against the indentations left near the fence and across the field to where the shooting took place. Additionally, we have fabric extracted from the barbed wire you climbed over that will undoubtedly match with your clothes. We can hold you until these checks have been completed. Why wait until the DNA test results come in, and the boot prints and fabric match? You know full well what they will confirm. If you admit the crime and plead guilty in court, your sentence will be lighter."

Ainslie looked at her solicitor, then responded, "No comment."

"Have it your way, Ainslie."

Just then the door opened, and Carl peered around the door. "Good news. The DNA results are in, ma'am," Carl smiled.

Ainslie's face dropped, and she murmured, "Okay, I'll tell you what happened."

* * *

After Ainslie's statement had been taken, Suzanna returned to the incident room. "Well done on the false good news, Carl. Your smile could have fooled anyone into thinking we had the evidence needed to put her away on a murder charge."

His face brightened at the praise. "Yeah. Happy days. It's brilliant that she's admitted manslaughter, even though the DNA evidence was inconclusive."

"I can't help feeling a twinge of sympathy for her, though," Suzanna said, her brow furrowing in thought.

Carl's eyebrows arched at the DCI's comment.

"If what she tells us is true and the dog was worrying the sheep, she may have been justified in shooting it. But because of her carelessness, she ended up shooting the woman as well. She should have applied the safety catch or broken the shotgun open as soon as she had shot the dog. But because she didn't, Isla Muir lost her life, and Ainslie will spend several years in jail."

"Your use of the word *may*, is correct, ma'am," Carl agreed. "From what I've heard over the years, when dogs have been shot, many of those shootings have not been seen as justified. The Act covers physical attack and chasing livestock when that behaviour may be expected to cause injury or suffering. That alone, though, doesn't give the farmer the right to shoot the dog."

"*Really?*" Suzanna said, not being fully conversant with the legislation. Having spent all her police career in cities, she'd not come across the situation before.

"It's a bit like an armed police officer shooting a criminal," Tosh chimed in. "It's only allowed as a last resort. If there are other options, they must be taken before discharging a firearm; the rule of minimal force."

"Yeah," Carl concurred. "The farmer should attempt to stop the worrying by other means, first."

The conversation dried up and the entire team stood looking at Suzanna, awaiting direction. "I know it's a Thursday," she said, "but I think we all deserve a drink. First round is on me. Just don't get in trouble at home afterwards," she added, looking at Carl.

With renewed energy, they all grabbed their coats and left the station, looking forward to unwinding over a drink or two.

Chapter Fifty-Eight

Friday 6th May

The next day, Suzanna and the team had the job of correlating the evidence and writing reports. They would all be allowed the weekend off. They certainly deserved it. But the job of wrapping everything up and getting it all together for the Procurator's office would extend into next week. She would let Mairi return home, though. The local team could handle the paperwork.

Suzanna looked up as a woman police officer walked into the room. She was about the same height and age as Suzanna. Dark pixie cut hair. Smart uniform, with chief superintendent pips on her shoulder.

She crossed the room, stood beside Suzanna and offered her hand. "Good morning, Suzanna."

It was the Dumfries and Galloway's chief superintendent, Gillian White. Suzanna had never met her, only spoken on the phone, but she'd seen her picture on boards and websites. She noted the shift to addressing her by her first name instead of her rank and surname. She stood and took the outstretched hand. It was firm, the shake both businesslike and friendly.

"I'd like to congratulate you on finding Muir's murderer."

"Thank you, ma'am, but she's being charged with manslaughter, not murder."

"The main thing is you've apprehended the killer of Mrs Muir and her dog. The press has been going mad about it. They seem more interested in seeking justice for the golden retriever than the woman!"

"We're an animal-loving country, ma'am. When a dog is killed, it's a bit like a child murder, because the victim is perceived as lovable and innocent."

The Chief Super continued. "You came to us on loan to lead the murder enquiry but in your short time here, as well as solving that, you've uncovered corruption and bribery in the county council, broken the drugs supply chain, with four dealers in custody, intervened in a serious assault, and identified cases of unlicensed possession of firearms." She smiled. "Outstanding work, Suzanna. I've never known one officer make such an impact in so little time." She paused. "Look, I know we didn't see eye-to-eye on the charging of Jack Reynolds, but I feel we could work together. I'd love to have you on my team permanently. If you're ever looking for a move, call me."

Not just the charging of Jack Reynolds, Suzanna thought. There was the chastisement for tackling Westwood and the interference with her investigation of Councillor Bryce. "Thank you, ma'am. I'll certainly consider your offer if the situation arises. You have some excellent detectives in your team, who I'd be happy to work with again," she said, her eyes scanning the office, settling on each one momentarily, and generating a smile on their faces.

"I'll let you get back to wrapping things up," White said. "I expect you'll want to get back to Edinburgh as soon as you can. But don't forget, we'd love to have you here." She turned to the others in the room. "Isn't that right, guys?"

Tosh replied enthusiastically. "Absolutely!" His face brightened at the prospect.

"Yes, ma'am!" Carl concurred with almost as much vigour.

Logan smiled and gave the thumbs up sign, but Mairi stayed silent and frowned.

It was late afternoon when Suzanna said cheerio to the team and headed out of Dumfries for the weekend. The sun was out. Blue skies and white cotton wool clouds drifted in the stratosphere. Aircraft vapour trails traced lines across the sky.

It was May, and spring had truly arrived. Daffodils lined the roads as she drove out of the town. The fields were spattered with sheep and their bouncy offspring. Suzanna had the roof down on her BMW, its six-cylinder engine throbbed as she accelerated out into the open countryside on her way to Cumbria to meet up with James and visit her sister.

She loved the feel of the air vortexing around the car's windscreen, ruffling her hair; the sun warming her skin. Suzanna felt more in touch with nature, her car, and the road than she ever could be in a standard saloon car. She overtook a slower moving vehicle, the engine roaring as the automatic gearbox changed down. Her car shot past, then her speed returned to legal cruising speed. She was in her happy place and heading to meet with loved ones in England's most beautiful county.

Epilogue

Monday 9th May

Suzanna was in a steady stream of cars heading along the A595 towards Carlisle at 50 mph. There was far too much traffic to consider overtaking, so she settled into cruise mode. Her weekend had been wonderful. She loved spending time with her sister and niece. And James, of course. The Saturday had been a time of catching up and having fun with Charlie, her husband, Pete, and their daughter, Athena.

They'd attended church with them on Sunday morning, leaving in high spirits. Then after a pub lunch, they'd squeezed in a walk up Sale Fell just outside Cockermouth. As expected, James left Sunday evening, but Suzanna had stayed on. He hadn't once had a dig at her about missing the Alpha course, and neither had Charlie. She did so hate being nagged at.

Today she'd have to inform Greg Lansdowne that she didn't want the counter-terrorism job, despite the certainty of a promotion. It was the MIT Head role she wanted. Her phone rang and she accepted it using her Bluetooth hands-free facility. "Hello."

"Good morning, Suzanna."

She easily recognised the voice of her boss, Superintendent Milne. "Good morning to you too, Alistair. How come you're calling me at eight on a Monday morning? You're not usually at work until eight thirty." As she said the words her hackles rose, goose bumps rising on her arms. What news might he have?

"Look. I wanted to catch you early because I've just heard that the date has been brought forward to break up your team. They're talking just two months now. And the new MIT head has been chosen."

Suzanna was impatient for him to finish his sentence. Concerned.

"Suzanna... It's not you!" Alistair stated, sounding as surprised as Suzanna now was.

Suzanna's heart rate accelerated. "What? They're stealing half my team and putting someone else in charge of them! Where does that leave me?"

"You've been assigned to head up the new counter-terrorism unit. The good news is it will mean promotion."

Suzanna silently swore. Greg Lansdowne must have influenced the decision. "I don't want the job, Alistair. I'd go mental. It would be a waste of my investigative skills."

"I understand. I know you wanted to stay in detective work. Oh! By the way, DC Usmani will be transferring to the CT unit as well. His racial background will be an asset to the unit, as well as his talents, courage and professionalism, of course."

"So, who will head up the new MIT?"

"It's a chap by the name of DCI Scott Aitkin. Haven't met him, myself. But I hear he's an excellent detective and team leader."

Suzanna thought she had heard the name before but couldn't think where. "Have they decided who will be moving to the MIT and who'll be staying on as the downgraded CID team?"

"Not yet. Apart from stealing Zahir and you, they're happy to let us decide who should go and who should stay."

"I'm glad to hear that. I'd already decided it would be Angus, Rab, Mairi and Zahir. But now Zahir's not available, it will have to be one of the comic duo. Murray, most likely as he lives out towards Tulliallan, whereas Owen lives in the city. There's not much to choose between them on competence as detectives."

A lay-by came into sight and Suzanna pulled into it, stopping the car and switching off the engine. She could feel adrenaline flowing in her veins, and her voice gave away the tension she felt. "Look, Alistair, I'm not moving to counter-terrorism. That's that. I've another call to make. I'll call you back."

She ended the call, her thoughts swishing around in her head. She would not let Greg Lansdowne have his way.

"Ah! Suzanna," Greg said, having answered her call. "I was expecting to hear from you. We'd like you to start next week."

"Well, you can take a running jump off the proverbial pier. I was going to call you today to tell you I didn't want the job but now you have underhandedly engineered my move, I'm even more determined. I could not work with people who manipulate others around them for their own means, irrespective of the other's wishes. If necessary, I'll resign from the force, rather than take that job."

"I'm really sorry to hear that, Suzanna. We had hoped you'd be persuaded to volunteer but it was evident that would not happen, so I was forced to intervene. Had to do what was right for the country, Suzanna. The people of the UK deserve the best we can get in roles that may prevent mass murder by terrorists. I couldn't let your personal desires over-ride this duty."

Suzanna was still angry, but she could see the sense in what he was saying. "Well, you should have worked harder on persuading me, instead of taking action that would drive me away. You obviously didn't do your homework well enough. It seems to me MI5 needs to replace you. To get the best person for your job because you're evidently are not up to it." She ended the call, still fuming.

Suzanna sat listening to the cars and trucks rushing past, staring blankly through the windscreen, her mind whirring. What now? With time, her heart rate settled and the colour of her face returned to normal. She started the engine and pulled out into a gap in the traffic, heading back to Dumfries but forward into an unknown future.

* * *

Reviews

Authors love reviews. We like to know what our readers think of our work. And it helps other readers decide whether to give the book a go. So, please leave a review, or at least a rating, on Amazon and Goodreads. Many thanks, Harry.

Acknowledgement

A massive thanks to my wife for putting up with my absence for hours/days/weeks at a time while I wrote and edited this novel, and for her feedback on the story. Special thanks to Jamie Salmon for his brilliant book cover, and my gratitude to the numerous alpha and beta readers who highlighted my mistakes and plot errors. I couldn't have done this without you all.

About the Author

Harry Navinski has always loved stories, reading by torchlight under his bed sheets when he should have been sleeping. He was first published in the Wyton Eye, the base magazine at Royal Air Force Wyton. Harry continued to write for magazines – in between maintaining, repairing and launching military aircraft – for many years.

It was the 1990s when he created and edited RAF Active, the RAF's magazine for sports and adventurous activities. Harry's articles, written from his involvement in numerous sports and challenging activities, included skiing, sailing, judo, and scuba diving, to name a few.

After his time in the RAF, Harry spent several years as a volunteer on anti-human trafficking work in West Bengal. Whilst in India, he blogged about his experience of life on Kolkata's streets, and he was encouraged to try his hand at writing fiction. After returning to the UK, Harry attended a creative writing course, and gained the motivation and inspiration to write his first novel, The Glass.

His novella, The Test, soon followed, along with his next novel, The

Duty. This second novel was inspired by his anti-human trafficking work, and he has vowed to donate all profits from its sale to the organisations he worked with in India, including Justice Ventures International, International Justice Mission and Joyya Trust.

His third novel, The Key to Murder, was published in August 2022, with the fourth novel, The Last Walk, eventually published in early 2024.

Harry loves to make his stories meaningful, as well as entertaining. His personal life journey influences his story lines, with plots often highlighting social issues, and raising awareness of hidden crimes. Snippets of interesting facts are scattered through his narratives, perhaps raising questions in reader's minds. And his involvement in sporting pursuits over many years brings realism to aspects of his writing.

You can connect with me at:

Harry's website: https://harrynavinski.com/

Twitter/X: https://twitter.com/HarryNavinski

Facebook: https://www.facebook.com/profile.php?id=100083231835540

Instagram: https://www.instagram.com/harry.navinski.crime.writer/

Subscribe to my newsletter:

✉ https://dl.bookfunnel.com/8cdmeo86no

Also by Harry Navinski

If this is the first DCI Suzanna McLeod book you've read, you have missed out on the three novels that come before it. The series starts with The Glass, is followed by The Duty, then The Key to Murder. There's also a novella, The Test, that provides some detail on Suzanna's backstory.

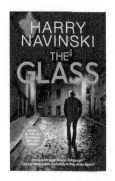

The Glass - A daring armed robbery, a meddling boss and a stolen heirloom.

Shots have been fired in Edinburgh's New Town. Criminals are on the run. Edinburgh's top female detective, DCI Suzanna McLeod, is under pressure to catch armed raiders before they strike again. But she must also recover her inherited magnifying glass, dealing with physical and mental challenges along the way and led by her gut right to the unexpected end.

DCI Suzanna McLeod is a fighting fit and highly intelligent crime fighter. Her Edinburgh-based team is legendary in Scotland for being one of the UK's best at locking up criminals. She has a reputation to live up to and a team to lead. But the Chief Superintendent is a by-the-book meddler and her team has personal problems that need her assistance.

When Suzanna's apartment is burgled, and a family heirloom goes missing, her focus is distracted. She just has to recover the antique magnifying glass. It was her inheritance from a distant relative whose actions had shaped her life. But she knows that catching the armed robbers must take priority. As the chase is underway, Suzanna takes on the most dangerous of the criminals. But even after the case appears to be drawing to a close, something is nagging at Suzanna's gut. What could they have missed?

5 Star Reviews for *The Glass*:

"*I could easily see it made into a TV series. The ending definitely left me hungry for more and I look forward to the next book in the series!*" Stacey W, England.

"*Loved the twists and turns of this fast-paced novel and look forward to reading more by this author.*" S Moore, Scotland.

"*An engaging book, with a new DCI on the block. Set in my home town of Edinburgh, it's atmospheric with twists and turns. I recommend it and I hope this is the first of many featuring DCI Suzanna McLeod"* Debbie Irvine, Scotland.

"Harry Navinski tells a tale that holds the reader's attention, with interest, drama and bonus pieces... In many ways, this book is more than a good fictional story. There are gems within." John, India.

"Clever and intriguing... Well written, easy read, left me wanting to read the next one to find out what happens next." Julie, UK Crime Book Club.

See more reviews on *GoodReads*.

Buy *The Glass* today, to uncover the twists and turns of this exciting mystery series.

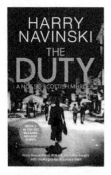

The Duty - A not-so-Scottish Murder

A nearly naked young woman's lifeless body is discovered on the riverbank in Queensferry. As the investigation unfolds, the identity of the victim and the perpetrator who callously dumped her in the water remain elusive. Meanwhile, a colleague of Edinburgh's top detective, DCI Suzanna McLeod, is brutally attacked with a knife, yet the suspect manages to slip away without a trace.

Now, DCI McLeod faces the daunting task of solving a murder and tracking down a dangerous assailant. From the picturesque River Forth to the far-reaching shores of the Ganges, she embarks on a relentless pursuit that uncovers a web of illegal immigration, slavery, and unspeakable brutality.

As Suzanna delves deeper into the case, she finds herself unexpectedly confronted with her own past, reuniting with old friends and colleagues and reliving the pivotal test that set her on the path to becoming a detective. However, her focus is put to the test as she grapples with a complex love life that reawakens the emotions of her youth.

The Duty is the thrilling second instalment in the DCI Suzanna McLeod crime-fighting series. If you crave a fast-paced narrative filled with intricate investigations, high-stakes confrontations with criminals, and captivating characters, dive into Harry Navinski's latest crime novel.

Much of this book is set in places far from Great Britain's shores, in countries where Harry has lived and worked, where memories, both good and bad, are powerful and fresh. As Harry wrote and edited this book, he shed many tears as memories returned, of innocence stolen, of suffering and pain, but also heroic determination. This book is not merely a piece of imagination. It is based on the realities and situations of the people who live out their lives in tropical Bengal. Although the names of the people, what they say, and what they do are fictional, the story truly represents the struggles of the people on which it is based.

Buy *The Duty* today to join in the excitement of the chase in tropical Bengal (All profits will go to the non-government organisations combatting sex trafficking and abuse of women, mentioned in the book).

5-star review – "Great Read. It drew me in from the beginning and didn't let go until the end and left me wanting more. A definite must read." Mrs C Newton

5 stars – A Great Read. "...it was a very interesting, informative and yet suspense-filled read, an eye opener to another world really, which left me desperate at the end of the book for the next one in the series." TallullahBelle

5 stars – "I thoroughly enjoyed Harry Navinski's second novel. It was an excellent crime thriller that plays out both in Scotland and India. DCI Suzanna McLeod and her team continue the battle to bring criminals to justice, and I love the way Harry has shown us more of her character in this book. Well worth a read." Graham Brewer

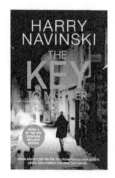

The Key to Murder

Winter arrives early for George White. He was already housebound and relied on carers, but no one expected the cheeky octogenarian to be murdered. What motive could there be? As Suzanna digs into his past, a darker side becomes evident, and a number of suspects emerge. The investigation uncovers a prostitution racket and sex trafficking. Suzanna's worry is that George's murder could be the first in a series. The chase is on to find the murderer before they strike again.

Reviews for The Key to Murder from Amazon and Goodreads

5 Stars – "A really good read. I enjoyed the other books in this series and I found this one even better. We hear some of the back story of the characters, which makes them more believable and likeable. The plot was good and very thought provoking. It is so good to read a book that is not littered with foul language." Kindle Customer

5 stars – "The story seems simple at first, but soon gets complicated. The characters are all well written and the solution is not obvious." Lillian13

4 stars – "I hadn't read any of the earlier books and this stands well as a story in its own right. Good, well developed characters and a strong story line, which will keep you guessing." C E Wake

4 stars – "I love the way Harry Navinski puts so much detail into describing locations and people because they are Crime novels, and you never know which bit of the detail will be relevant to the investigation and final conviction of the criminal(s)... I am hooked on finding out what happens to DCI Suzanna McLeod." Amazon Customer

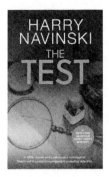

The Test - A 1920s murder and a failed police investigation. Time to call in London's incomparable investigator.

Victorian-era consulting detective, Silvester Locke-Croft, is called in to investigate the murder of a solicitor in 1920s London, uncovering hidden evidence and revealing the incompetence of Scotland Yard's detectives. His investigation concludes with dramatic exposure of the murderer, revealing corruption and collusion along the way.

The detective who wrote this short crime story bequeathed his estate to a relative who, on reaching the age of 18, passed a test he had set. In Harry Navinski's first novel, *The Glass*, his great-great-niece, now DCI Suzanna McLeod, passed the test to win herself the magnifying glass and the proceeds of his trust fund.

5-star reviews for The Test:

"One amazing, well written story! Brilliantly well crafted! A steady, well paced mystery! Intriguing, interesting plot! A fast read! Quick and easy! One fantastic, page turner! Hard to put down! So engaging! Suspenseful! Smart, likeable characters! One fantastic author! Read! Find out for yourself! Enjoy." Margaret.

You can get this novella **free** (as an e-book) by joining *Harry's VIP Club* to get occasional updates on new releases and offers.

Printed in Great Britain
by Amazon

38096730R00208